# Shadows
## *of* HOPE

Will the secrets and suspicions that circle Marissa's life
become the ultimate test of her faith?

# Shadows
## *of* HOPE

# GEORGIANA DANIELS

**SHILOH RUN** PRESS
An Imprint of Barbour Publishing, Inc.

Print ISBN 978-1-68322-545-4

eBook Editions:
Adobe Digital Edition (.epub) 978-1-68322-547-8
Kindle and MobiPocket Edition (.prc) 978-1-68322-546-1

Cover Design: Kirk DouPonce, DogEared Design

Published by Shiloh Run Press, an imprint of Barbour Publishing, Inc., 1810 Barbour Drive, Uhrichsville, Ohio 44683, www.shilohrunpress.com

*Our mission is to inspire the world with the life-changing message of the Bible.*

Member of the
Evangelical Christian
Publishers Association

Printed in the United States of America.

# DEDICATION

To my daughter Mallory, who knows what it means
to follow God in the darkest hour.

# ACKNOWLEDGMENTS

Many thanks to the team at Barbour for taking on a newbie and making this a great experience. I'm so happy to be part of the Barbour family!

To my super agent Tamela Hancock Murray, your loyalty and belief in me have made all the difference.

Becky Yauger, writing partner extraordinaire—thanks so much not only for helping me with this book in the early stages, but for cheering me on through the duration!

So much credit goes to my family, especially my husband, Troy, who walked with me through all the hard parts in order to get to the good stuff.

Last, but most importantly of all, I'm ever grateful to the Lord Jesus Christ for holding my hand and abiding with me daily.

# CHAPTER 1

*Marissa*

Seven dollars was a small price to pay for a latte and a little conversation. The rustling of newspapers, the quiet clack of computer keys, and the smooth jazz piped over the speakers were a daily ritual that soothed my anxiety.

"You okay, Marissa?" Tristan Hart dipped his head to meet my eye in a way that showed more concern than that of a typical business partner.

"Fine." The lie slid past my tongue. "It's still a little early."

"If we bought a coffeepot for the office—"

"We wouldn't have to meet at the crack of dawn." I finished his sentence, though it wasn't really the crack of dawn. This close to summer, the Arizona sky lit up well before our standing morning meeting at The Bean.

*Buy coffeepot*—my burgeoning mental checklist took another hit.

The aroma of beans and the gurgle of the espresso machine provided a backdrop to the soft chatter surrounding us. The foamy latte warmed my throat. Caffeinated fortification was exactly what I needed before powering through another day at the pregnancy resource center. The exponential expansion of our client list kept Tristan and me, along with our scant staff, busy.

As if reading my thoughts, Tristan pulled notes from his folio and checked off item one. "How are you coming along on hiring a receptionist?"

"The applications weren't impressive."

He removed his reading glasses—a new addition to his army of accessories since he turned forty. According to him, they gave him a look of gravitas that put clients at ease during their counseling sessions. Despite being a man—a fairly handsome one with thick brown hair and an inviting smile—he had the ability to make women in crisis spill their guts to him like he was their big brother or their best friend.

He'd had that effect on me for years.

Tristan set his glasses on the coffee-stained table. "You know, we're not looking for a rocket scientist. We need someone to answer the phones and update the files. Maybe you're getting a little picky." He pinched his fingers together to emphasize his point.

"We need a good fit." By good fit, I meant someone willing to work for a pittance. Those candidates were few and far between, especially if I added compassion as a qualification.

"Can you call the temp agency?"

"Done. Didn't you see the girl they sent yesterday?" I cringed.

His forehead wrinkled. "No."

"That's because I sent her away an hour into her shift." I took another swig to drown out the renewed irritation I felt at the temp worker sending a potential client to the women's clinic down the street just because I was out of the office for a few minutes.

"Can you continue to handle the workload without hiring another person?"

"That would be a resounding no." I added *Place ad online* to my mental checklist, right after *Buy coffeepot*.

Tristan offered his pen, but I waved him off. "If you'd write everything down like me, you'd get more done." How well he knew me, even more than my own husband.

Tightness gripped my stomach. I pushed the uneaten buttery croissant away, knowing I'd regret it in about an hour. *God's got this, God's got this, God's got this*. Repeating the phrase kept me sane. I forced a laugh that belied my anxiety. "You take enough notes for the both of us." Since college, in fact, when he was knee-deep in his PhD and I was a late-blooming undergrad. I'd been relying on Tristan, his trusty pen, and his open ear for a big chunk of my adult life.

Concern flickered in his amber eyes, but he let my glib comment stand without probing. More than likely he sensed I was ready to snap, and The Bean was not the proper place for a meltdown. Neither was our pregnancy resource center, New Heights, but at least there he trusted my professionalism to override my personal life.

Or what was left of it.

"Have you heard back on the grant proposal?" I glanced at my smartphone to make sure I hadn't missed an email. "The extra money would be handy. That way I can hire someone who will stick around and hopefully really appreciate what we do." There had been a summer influx of pregnant women in crisis that was straining our budget, but no one was ever turned away—except by the incompetent temp—from our center.

"Still waiting. Funds seem to be tight everywhere." He grimaced and rubbed his forehead. "But we'll rustle something up," he added with an extra dose of cheer that almost had me convinced. Then he pointed his pen straight at me. "In the meantime, you don't need to be shelling any more money out of your pocket."

*What about the coffeepot?* I wanted to ask but didn't. "Won't make that mistake again. Colin still hasn't forgiven me for my last round of spending." What I'd thought was a stealthy movement of money from my personal account turned out to be yet another point of contention with my husband, but the chance to pitch in to buy a quality used ultrasound machine was too good to pass up. I'd been so excited about the possibilities that I hadn't really considered the consequences. According to Colin, I tended to do that.

At the thought of my husband, I once again checked my phone, unsure whether I really wanted to see the email icon lit or not.

"Speaking of—"

"We'd better get to work." I scooped up my purse, purposely cutting Tristan off before he could talk about my husband. The last thing I needed were red-rimmed eyes to start the day. I had to be one hundred percent present and focused on the clients. They were the ones who mattered. My personal life could be sorted later.

Tristan closed his folio and capped his pen, then folded his napkin and rose to leave. "I'll meet you there."

Relief swelled inside me the moment he walked out the door. I hadn't realized I'd been holding my breath, anticipating the moment our conversation would turn from work to my home life. In all the years Tristan and I had been friends—only friends—I'd valued his input. Enjoyed mulling over situations from his perspective as a friend and as a psychologist. But not now. Definitely not now when I'd have to confess that he'd been right. Right about my decisions, right about my future.

Right about Colin.

I wrapped up the croissant and stuffed it inside my purse.

"Hey, Marissa, do you need a refill to go?" a familiar voice called to me from behind the counter.

"Yes, thanks, Kaitlyn." I handed my cup to my favorite barista, which she rinsed before adding plain coffee. "I didn't realize you were working."

"I got here late. Overslept." Her haphazard ponytail and unusual lack of makeup spoke for themselves. Though she offered a gracious smile, the usual lilt in her voice was absent. Kaitlyn had been happy—so very, *very* happy, in her words—all semester. Busy with college life, work, and a new boyfriend. Apparently one of the plates she'd been spinning had crashed.

"Late-night study session?"

"No, I'm just super tired," she said pensively. "Thankfully my boss let it slide."

A goateed man with an apron shot her a playful elbow. "This time. Next time you're out of here." He hiked his thumb over his shoulder.

Kaitlyn didn't return his spirited comment. She doused my coffee with cream and secured the lid before handing it over. "Here's some coffee to go with your cream."

I stuffed the tip jar and toasted her with the cup. "Just the way I like it. I'll see you tomorrow." Unless I remembered the coffeepot, which seemed like a bad trade considering how much I enjoyed coming to The Bean.

Kaitlyn offered a feeble goodbye then busied herself behind the counter, wiping at a stain that didn't seem to exist. "I'll be right back," she told her boss before stepping into the back room.

Man troubles—definitely man troubles. Poor girl. I didn't have the heart to warn her that it never really gets better.

The summer breeze kicked up my hair the moment I stepped outside.

Just as I reached my car, a buzz in my pocket signaled an incoming email. My stomach clamped. This was what I was waiting for, wasn't it?

I climbed into the car and set my coffee into the cup holder. Dropped my purse onto the passenger seat and turned on the ignition. Pulled out the phone.

Maybe it was nothing.

Or maybe it was everything.

My marriage was disintegrating long before I'd admitted it, and only in the last few months had I begun to acknowledge, even to myself, exactly how troubled it was. I never expected much, but after ten years of marriage I at least wanted some comfort and companionship. A little love and someone to snuggle. Someone to enjoy the late-night news with at the end of a long day.

A baby would be an unexpected bonus.

But reality had doused our fiery passion years ago. I'd tried it all, read the books, watched the television programs that promised that yes, even I could have a great relationship in just five easy steps. The problem was that nothing came easy. Nothing with Colin ever had.

The phone vibrated in my hand.

I wanted to know, right? Wasn't that why I'd gone to the trouble to ferret out the password for his university account and set it up to come to my phone? Tristan had expounded on the myriad of reasons why that was a bad idea. And yet I'd forged ahead, just like I had with the marriage even though I knew the reckless love Colin and I shared would only result in heartache.

Casting a furtive glance around the parking lot, I tapped on the mail icon. It wasn't like he'd know. Colin wasn't savvy when it came to electronics. And besides, experts recommended that couples know each other's passwords and have access to all online accounts. Never mind that it was supposed to be with the other partner's permission.

*Request a Meeting.*

If I read it quickly and then marked it unread, I could go about my day, at least until another message landed in his inbox ten minutes from now.

I leaned against the headrest and let the air-conditioning wash over my face. Why was I doing this? Tristan was right—I had a penchant for hurting myself. Nothing good could come of this, because even if *this* email was okay, and the next one and the next one, I'd always be waiting for one that screamed, "Infidelity!"

If only Colin didn't disappear for long periods of time and turn his back while texting, or if he hadn't lost his wedding ring that he never had time to replace. Maybe then I wouldn't be so suspicious, dissecting his body language and filling in the blanks because of all the things he didn't say.

Or maybe suspicion and paranoia were just my nature and I was fighting a losing battle.

I steadied my nerves and opened the email.

*I need to see you. Urgent. Thanks!*

What kind of meeting with a professor was urgent? The sender was PinkBunny91—odd, considering all the other messages he received came from accounts with real names. I reread, trying to parse out clues that clearly weren't there. *Urgent.* The word turned over in my head as I stared at the screen. A car honked, jolting me from my thoughts. Quickly, I marked the message unread.

Like so many things lately, this clue wasn't really a clue. Off, but not suspicious in and of itself. Guilt pressed over me. I'd violated my husband's trust. I wanted to uninstall his email account from my phone—I needed to, for my own sanity.

Yet I left it alone and braced myself for the next notification.

# CHAPTER 2

*Kaitlyn*

Getting knocked up was not on Kaitlyn Farrows's to-do list. Neither was getting a D in biology, but she had evidence of both stuffed at the bottom of her book bag in her work cubby.

Knocked up. Even the words made her dizzy.

*No—pregnant*, she reminded herself. Not knocked up. That phrase implied that the father wouldn't claim the baby and the woman was alone in the world. No one to turn to, no one to care. That wouldn't be her. Colin would find a legitimate way for them to be together.

She wiped down the front counter at The Bean for the umpteenth time, thankful the morning rush had ended. Although now that she thought about it, she needed the distraction.

The clandestine relationship she and Colin shared was understandable. His position at the university depended on their secrecy—something he'd sworn her to early on. And she never broke a promise.

But the secrecy would come to an end when she told him about the baby. They would be a real family. Everything would be all right.

It had to be.

"You're gonna scrub a hole in it." Jake nudged her and flashed an uncertain grin from underneath his unkempt goatee.

"Sorry, Jake." She stopped the vigorous circles and tossed the rag into a bin hidden under the counter.

"Something's got you bugged." He folded his arms across his skinny chest. "Spill it."

"I got a D in biology." Half true, at least. Jake didn't need to know the other half—that the professor most likely scored her low to avoid the appearance of favoritism. Giving her a C would've sufficed. In fact, it was probably a typo. Colin wouldn't do that to her. He knew how much she valued her education, despite the fact she'd spent more time mooning over him than learning the life cycle of a cell. But once he saw her "urgent" email—one she'd sent from the account she'd started as a teen rather than her university account that could potentially incriminate them both—he'd realize his mistake and fix it, just like he'd fix everything.

"That's a bummer."

"My parents are going to have my head."

"Only if you tell them." He nodded to a customer at the pastry counter then turned back to her. "I don't let mine see. It's definitely a don't ask, don't tell situation."

"Don't tell, for me, would mean I had to pay for it all myself." And if she could, she would, since at twenty-six she was an older sophomore who, by all accounts, should be taking full responsibility for her finances. Thankfully, her parents had been generous, if grudging, about paying for college. It never failed to surprise Kaitlyn just how many strings were attached to the tuition payments. "The Danishes are extra creamy today," she said, turning her attention to the customer who approached the counter. "Would you like to try one?"

The guy smiled in recognition—a fellow student in Colin's class. Her face grew hot, and she hoped he didn't notice. No wonder she'd stopped attending class regularly. She knew she couldn't count on herself not to give her feelings away. After she fulfilled the order, she started wiping down the espresso machine. The scent of the beans and the rhythm of her motions calmed her. Just stick to her routine, and life would be fine.

"I didn't realize your grades were that upsetting."

Kaitlyn jumped at the sight of Jake's face looming over her. "What?"

"Your grades. You're crying."

She touched her face, wet with tears she hadn't realized were falling. "Sorry. I know I shouldn't bring personal issues to work." She cast a furtive glance to see if the guy from class was watching.

"Don't apologize. You're the best worker I've got." Concern etched his forehead. "Do you need to go take care of it? Talk to your teacher or something?"

"I don't want to leave you shorthanded." She bit her lip. The only other girls on duty were scrambling to take care of an ever-increasing line at the drive-through window, which was always busier than the inside counter before lunch.

"Hey, I got this. Scram." Jake cocked his head toward the door.

She unwound her apron and mouthed a silent *Thank you* before leaving the floor. First, she checked her phone. Colin hadn't responded. If she hurried, she could catch him during office hours. The Mathematics and Science Department, with ever-present ears and eyes roaming the building, wasn't the ideal place to tell him about the baby, but going there under the pretense of dealing with her grade would at least get her an appointment.

Unease churned in her stomach. She'd feel better once she talked to Colin. He was so understanding, and she knew he'd do anything to help her. Telling him was the first step in righting the situation, and once that was over, together they could decide how to go forward. With him at her side, she could even handle talking to her parents. They were strict and religious, so they'd definitely be disappointed, but no more than she was in herself.

Cars filled the north campus parking lot. Kaitlyn cruised around, fingers crossed, waiting for someone to leave. She located a spot that seemed suspiciously close to a fire hydrant. It would have to do. Desperate times and whatnot.

By the time she'd hoofed it across the commons and woven her way between the Business and Social and Behavioral Colleges buildings, she was panting and her eyes were wet. Not crying—it couldn't be, because things were going to work out—but they were wet just the same.

"I need to see Dr. Kimball." She looked anywhere but in the eyes of the student worker who manned the office.

The girl blew a tiny bubble and let it pop before she answered. "His door's closed, so that means he's with someone."

Kaitlyn blushed to think what went on when he'd had the door closed with her—before she stopped coming to the office for so-called help. "I'll wait. I need to ask about my grade." She parked herself on a nearby chair and fidgeted with her phone.

What would she say? She wanted to be excited, but common sense dictated otherwise. Obviously their situation wasn't normal, yet. But once they acclimated to the idea of a baby—precious little bundle, a piece of them both—they'd be happy.

The door jolted open, causing her to jump.

"Thanks, Dr. K." A young blond bounced out of his office, her smile far too wide for talking to her professor.

Kaitlyn's stomach recoiled. Of course she wasn't the only coed who found Colin attractive. She'd seen a dozen girls get tongue-tied when he called on them during a lecture or when they asked a question. He'd patiently explained that until she came along, he'd never once had his head turned by a student. Young ladies came on to all the professors, and it was something they'd learned to ignore. What he had with her was different because she wasn't the typical college undergrad. She knew what she wanted and where she was going in life, had life experience and a maturity that set her apart—so he said.

She found herself smiling as she remembered the way his finger traced the line of her neck before twirling a strand of hair and pulling her close. The way he whispered in her ear had made her feel treasured and adored.

At the sound of footsteps, she glanced up and saw the ashen look on Colin's face when he caught sight of her outside his door. More than once he'd told her to stay away from him in public, but surely he'd understand. She rose on unsteady legs. "Can I talk to you? It's about my grade."

"Come on in."

She detected irritation in his voice, so she offered a smile to set him at ease. It was perfectly natural to see a professor about a grade. Anyone would do it, she thought, as she breezed into his office. "Glad I caught you before you left."

Colin cringed, though he seemed to catch himself and soften his features before he closed the door.

"Your office hours are posted," she whispered. "Sorry. I really need to talk." She attempted to infuse energy into her voice, but the concern on his face informed her she hadn't succeeded.

"The grade—I got your message." He made a wide berth around her then sat at his desk with his fingers steepled under his chin. "It was borderline." He studied her face with a gaze that caused her to blush as it had the first time they were alone.

"I understand. It's just that—"

"No special favors." He leaned slightly closer. "You said so yourself."

"Right. I did. A grade doesn't mean anything if it's not earned." She set her book bag on the floor. Should she keep talking about the grade or drop the bomb? Judging from the way he kept glancing at the door, her time was short. She lowered her voice for the benefit of the gum-popping student worker a dozen yards away in the outer office. "I have something else we need to talk about. Even more important than the grade."

"So you understand? I'm not trying to be unfair. In fact, I'm trying hard not to be unfair."

"You're right. I've been distracted all semester."

"Not entirely your fault." The chair groaned when he leaned over his desk. "You're disappointed." His green eyes searched her face, and she found that once again, unbidden tears were streaming.

She wiped her eyes. "Of course. I'm disappointed in myself. I should have my act together."

Briefly, his warm hand covered hers. "Me too." He drew back quickly, as if suddenly remembering where he was. He raked his hand through his chestnut hair, leaving it slightly tousled. "I wish you'd have waited for me to contact you."

"This couldn't wait." She folded her hands on her lap to hide the shaking. It was now or never.

"I can change the grade to a C."

"It's not just the grade. It's bigger than the grade." She breathed in deeply to scare up an extra dose of courage. This was harder than she thought it would be. A baby was supposed to be good news. She glanced over her shoulder to assure herself the door hadn't mysteriously opened. "Look, I know what your position here means to you."

"Changing your grade won't affect that. I'm happy to do it." His smile seemed stiff and frozen, so unlike the easygoing man she'd first fallen for. She really should've waited until he called. For the most part he was like her, afraid his feelings would be etched on his face. He'd said so a million times.

Kaitlyn bit her lip. "I'd appreciate that, but that's not why I came. We need to talk—really talk."

A whoosh of air escaped his soft lips. "I think we're on the same page."

"What do you mean?"

Colin scrubbed his face with his hands then pinched the bridge of his nose. A mixture of concern and sadness lit his eyes. "This." He motioned between the two of them.

"That's not the page I was on." She forced a chuckle. "I think you're misunderstanding. Or I am. Let me start over."

"Please, don't." He held up a hand. "It was a bad idea. I never meant for things to go this far."

"Colin, wait—" She bit her tongue. Calling him by his first name was a huge mistake in a room with cheap walls.

He winced, his jaw flexing. "This was never going to end well. You know that, right?"

"I can't believe you're saying this. Especially now."

"Would there ever be a good time?"

"You have to hear me out." She pleaded with him like a lovesick teen.

He gentled his tone. "You'll keep your promise, won't you?"

"You know you can trust me." A sick feeling swirled in her gut. She wanted to blurt out the truth—needed to blurt out the truth—but it was lodged somewhere between her throat and her better judgment.

Colin leaned closer. The scent of the aftershave she'd given him lingered between them. "I care for you more than you can imagine, but—"

"You care for your job more."

"I was going to say that it's just not a good idea. You have an amazing life ahead of you, and I. . .I'm not in a place where I can be part of that."

"You can. We can figure out a way." Thoughts jumbled in her head. Tell him or wait? Maybe if she caught him outside his office they could talk. Coming here tipped him over the edge. Made him think twice. Scared him off.

"No," he said softly in the same whisper he'd used when he told her she meant the world to him. So many, many times.

"What if I quit school? There wouldn't be a conflict."

His gaze hardened almost imperceptibly. "Listen to me, Kaitlyn. What we had is over."

A knock sounded on the door before it swung open. "Sorry to interrupt, but Dr. Crank said he wants to see you as soon as possible." The student worker seemed oblivious to what had just transpired, but nevertheless, Kaitlyn felt exposed.

She straightened and hoped her expression didn't give her away, even though those stupid tears started up again.

"I'm sorry, Kaitlyn." Colin rose from his desk and slid his arms into his suit coat. "Better luck next semester."

# CHAPTER 3

*Colin*

D r. Crank had a face that matched his name and an equally sour disposition. It was a combination that instilled both fear and determination in Colin Kimball, and the reason he shuffled Kaitlyn out of his office so quickly.

"Hold my calls," he said to the student worker—what was her name, Hayley? Hallie? they all sounded the same—as he straightened his suit coat. A request to see Crank was rarely a good thing, and Colin could only hope word about his extracurricular activities hadn't gotten out.

From the corner of his eye, he saw Kaitlyn quietly leave the reception area, shoulders stooped. The disbelief in her eyes when he'd said *it* was over—he didn't dare use the word *affair* because it sounded so lewd and tawdry—nearly undid him. He'd wanted to take it back, fold her into his arms, and smooth the worry lines from her features.

But he'd made his decision, and he needed to stick with it, for too many reasons to count.

Colin tapped on Dr. Crank's partially open door, his heart jackknifing in his chest. "You wanted to see me?"

"Come in." The older man attempted to right a stack of file folders. The stack avalanched back onto his desk, further exasperating the department chair. "Make yourself comfortable."

Colin scooped a pile of books off the seat and set them on the credenza that housed various bits of research and three wilting plants. Despite the clutter, he never underestimated the brilliant and widely published Dr. Herman Crank. It wasn't a question of who held all the cards but who owned the deck.

Dr. Crank peered over the rims of his reading glasses, drilling a hole with his gaze. "I suppose you know why I've called you in."

In fact, he didn't. Colin's knee bounced until he forced himself to sit still. Had someone caught a whiff of something amiss? He'd been so careful with Kaitlyn, never meeting in public and certainly not on campus. She'd even stopped attending class, for the most part. The fact she'd come in today had completely upended him, but out of everyone in the world, he trusted her. Trusted that she wouldn't expose their relationship. Trusted her not to say anything out of turn.

Trusted her not to tell his wife. Not that Kaitlyn knew about Marissa, as far as he could tell, but one could never be too careful.

Colin shifted in his seat. Wiped his palms on his pants. No matter what Crank said, Colin would come up with a reasonable explanation. He'd come too far in this department, in his career, to lose his position over a mistake.

*Mistake.* The word punched him in the gut.

He hated to think of what he had with Kaitlyn as a mistake, but he knew it was. Every cell inside him both clamored for more of her and at the same time derided him for even considering it. He wasn't an adulterous man, not really. Not in the ways that mattered.

He'd stay with his wife, and she'd never have to know what he'd done. To hurt Marissa like that was unthinkable, even though they'd spent the better part of the last five years carefully avoiding one another and any kind of intimacy that required letting down their guards. And there was still some part of him that wanted to take care of his emotionally wounded wife.

"Well?" Crank lifted a gray eyebrow, causing his forehead to pucker.

"No, sir. I'm not sure why you asked to see me." Sweat beaded at his hairline, and if he wasn't mistaken, he detected a gleam in Crank's eye. The old guy was actually enjoying watching him sweat it out. Colin straightened and met his boss's stare.

"It's come to my attention—"

Colin's heart stopped.

"—that you're on track to make tenure this year."

Relief whooshed through his veins. He steadied his breath before he spoke. "That's been my goal." He hid his hands as they continued to shake.

"The tenure committee will be meeting earlier than usual this year due to some restructuring going on, but we'd like to include you in the lineup. I assume you've been putting your tenure file together?"

"Absolutely. I've been working on it for a while."

"Good. Just a few housekeeping items, then." Crank grabbed the top folder from the failed stack and opened to a page littered with sticky notes. "We'll need to see some progress on your research. Another publishing credit would be good."

"I understand. A few months isn't much time."

Pursed lips signaled Crank wasn't finished speaking. "I assume you have projects and proposals under way. I believe we discussed a few of them at the start of last semester. I'm sure you'll have some type of update by then."

Colin drew a deep breath. If he hadn't spent so much time trying to be with Kaitlyn, he'd have made a lot more progress. Regret stabbed him, as it had so often over the last few months. He had to put that out of his mind now. Things with Kaitlyn were over, and he could move on with his career. With his life. With Marissa.

"There are a few end-of-year class evaluations turned in by your students, and I'd like you to take a serious look at the comments and see how you can apply them to your teaching. Of course, if you do make tenure, you'll have a full-time lecturer assigned to you. That will free up your time to get more research and publishing credits under your belt."

"That would be a welcome change." Slowly, his confidence returned.

"I'll give these to you." Dr. Crank handed over the evaluations, covered with his own notes in red ink. "Lastly, be aware that you'll be under scrutiny. During the summer, that weight is easier to bear by far, but you'll be under the microscope nonetheless."

"I'm ready for the challenge."

"Glad to hear it." The old professor folded his reading glasses. "I've been watching you for a long time. I'm sure you'll do fine. But a word of caution: I've seen many a man in your situation, and it doesn't take much to mess it up. I don't have to tell you that tenured positions are getting harder to come by."

"That's been my understanding. I really appreciate the opportunity to prove myself."

"Please understand that there are only so many resources to go around at a small institution like ours, and Dr. McAllister's name has come up more than once. There are several on the committee who feel she'd be a better fit. She's been around quite a bit longer and has an impressive body of work."

Colin rubbed his hands together. "I'll do my best."

"As far as I'm concerned, you're in the lead. Not too many people your age and with your practical experience have impressed me, but I think you're on a good track at this institution."

The compliment infused Colin with a burst of satisfaction. At thirty-five, Colin would be the youngest tenured professor in the department. Years of effort had gone into pursuing his PhD and his career as a biology professor. Marissa had put up with his being absent for much of their life together, but now it would all be worth it. He'd make it up to her once he got tenure and his position was secure.

"Get to it." Dr. Crank put his glasses back on, effectively dismissing Colin.

He closed the door with a soft click before allowing his shoulders to sag with relief. Lately, everything had felt like a close call, and he was done with that. From now on, he was walking the proverbial straight and narrow—at work and at home. If he put time and attention into Marissa, maybe they could have the kind of relationship they had in the beginning, before it got muddied up with her insecurities and her monthly schedule of disappointment.

"What on earth did you do to that poor girl?" Hayley—or Hallie— gave him a tsk-tsk when he rounded the corner to the main lobby.

"Who?" Colin strode past her desk, giving her a cursory glance.

The student worker cracked her gum. "The one who met with you. I don't think I've ever seen someone come out of your office crying before."

He'd been so focused on being called in to see Crank that he hadn't paid attention. He rubbed the back of his neck, frustrated. All the times he'd planned on what he'd say to break things off, he hadn't imagined her crying. That wasn't her style. She was, for the most part, confident and self-assured.

"She really wanted a better grade," he said before closing the door to his office. He packed up the files that Crank had given him to review. It would give him something to do this evening after baseball practice.

His heart lifted at the thought of coaching the kids. If he moved Tommy to second base and Jackson to the outfield, the team would have a better chance at this weekend's game. They had a lot of work to do, but this group of boys was particularly ambitious. He liked working with kids who took the sport seriously.

With office hours officially over, he closed the door and sat down. Loosened his tie. He looked forward to the day when he could shuck the tie in favor of a polo shirt like the rest of the faculty. For almost six years he'd been doing whatever it took to give himself an edge, which, unluckily for him, included a dress shirt and tie—and entirely too many hours on boring committees.

A smile of satisfaction spread across his face as he recalled Crank's confidence in him. Of course, there was a lot to be done, but this was the break he'd been waiting for. He wanted to share his news with someone. Kaitlyn's face, full of disappointment and confusion, flashed before him. For the last few months, he'd shared so much with her despite knowing he was wading in where he had no right to go. A knot formed in his throat. Maybe he should call Marissa. She'd be happy for him, if a little detached.

He wiggled the mouse on his desk and brought his ancient computer to life. The inbox was already filled with new messages, but only one stood out.

PinkBunny91. Kaitlyn.

For the second time today, she marked her message urgent. The arrow hovered over the email. Open or delete? It wasn't too late to tell her he didn't mean what he said earlier. That he was spooked when she showed up at the office. She'd forgive him, and he could slink off after baseball practice tonight and patch things up between them.

He rubbed his head to dull the pain.

Letting her go was hard. Doing the right thing from here on out would be even harder. And the truth was, there would never be an easier time to break it off than now.

Colin ground his teeth and hit DELETE.

# CHAPTER 4

*Marissa*

The buzz of my phone caused me to lurch. Normally I stashed it in my purse, never thinking about personal calls or emails or web surfing during the workday when my sole focus was serving our clients. But after the so-called urgent message this morning, I'd kept my phone close. I silenced it before the buzz could sound again.

"It's a boy." I digitally inserted an arrow to the pertinent appendage then framed the shot. A mixture of excitement and sadness pricked me every time I saw a new life on the ultrasound screen, especially those times the baby was near the same number of weeks as the one I'd lost so many years ago.

The young mother named Marjorie did little more than offer a feeble smile. "I had a feeling it was." Her eyes turned watery. "My husband would've been excited."

I handed her a tissue and waited for her to talk. Sometimes mothers in crisis just needed someone to listen. Marjorie seemed more private than most, but from previous conversations I gleaned that she'd lost her husband overseas, and her only blood relatives lived across the country. A tough fate for someone who hadn't even reached twenty-one.

She dabbed her eyes, already devoid of makeup. "I'm sure he's up there somewhere. I just wish he could see Li'l Jacob."

"You've already chosen a name?"

For the first time, a true smile lit Marjorie's face. "I'm naming him after my husband."

I set the transducer probe aside and squeezed Marjorie's hand before handing her a towel to wipe the goop off her stomach. "That's a great way to remember him. I'm sure he'd be proud." I clicked on the print icon and waited for the pictures. Once she had the gel cleaned off, I slowly pulled her upright and handed her the shots of Jacob.

"Thanks for everything." Marjorie pulled her shirt over her protruding belly. "I don't know what I'd have done without New Heights. It's been scary."

New Heights resided in a renovated, single-story home near downtown Elden Springs. The former living area served as a lobby, and the dining room was transformed into a boutique that stored a revolving stash of donated supplies for the mothers-to-be and babies. The bedrooms had become offices, one for me and one for Tristan, who also ran his private practice from a separate office with its own entrance out back.

"We're always glad when we can help." I opened the blinds to let in more light.

The ultrasound area was separated from my office by a privacy screen and was anything but clinical. Lacy tablecloths were draped across antique tables in front of large windows with matching coverings. The books on the nightstand and the vintage tray in front of the mirror on the table lent the room a bed-and-breakfast ambience—a peaceful quality that many young ladies desperately needed during such a high-anxiety time in their lives.

I'd done all of the decorating myself when Tristan and I opened New Heights shortly after I'd married Colin and decided I wasn't cut out for nursing despite my degree. Instead, I'd become an ultrasound tech because the thought of working with expectant mothers made me happy.

Of course, the opening of New Heights was completed before I realized that for me, conceiving a child would not come as easily as it did for the women we served. Out of habit, I glanced at the calendar and noted the date before returning my attention to my client. "Have you been to all your doctor appointments?"

Marjorie shook her head. "I went to the first one and got prenatal vitamins."

"Why didn't you go back?" Purposely, I kept my voice just above a whisper, trying to keep out any hint of judgment.

"They did a...test...and I can't go through that again. It felt so invasive." She wrinkled her freckled nose.

"Oh, honey. No, no. They don't do that every time. Just the first time, to make sure everything is okay. Unless you have other issues, you'll probably only need to give a urine sample and listen to the baby's heart-beat—that kind of thing."

"Can I do that here?"

Our town only had a handful of doctors to choose from, and one was already semi-retired. From the stories I'd been told, most of them herded the women through like cattle—especially ones they deemed less than savory, which, sadly, was how many of our clients were viewed.

I patted her arm, rigid with stress. "Unfortunately, we can't give you actual medical care. You need to see an OB or a midwife. In the end, you'll be glad you did."

She nodded without speaking.

We walked out to the lobby, and I handed her a pamphlet outlining the basics of what to expect at each month's doctor visit. "Come back next month and you can tell me all about your doctor and what they've said. By then we should have some more maternity clothes in stock for you to choose from."

"Hi, Marjorie." Christina, our seriously underpaid third staff member, motioned the young mother over to the boutique. "Boy or girl?"

"Boy."

"Great! We have some cute boy blankets that came in this week. Come see." Christina's contagious smile reeled Marjorie over to the bay window and they began to chat.

Noting the empty pitcher of water, I swept it off the table in the lobby and refilled it in the kitchen.

When I came out, two young mothers-to-be who'd had earlier appointments for referrals stood at the breakfast bar, slathering their toasted bagels with cream cheese. Other than their soft chatter, the house was quiet. No more clients on the books until after lunch. I slid the phone from my pocket and swiped the screen, then clicked on the email icon.

"What's happening?" Tristan's voice jolted me from behind.

Quickly, I stepped away from him and pocketed the phone. "Just finished with Marjorie. She's having a boy." I infused my comment with the same enthusiasm I'd normally feel.

"I meant the phone." He pointed to the bulge in my pocket.

"Just. . .stuff." My answer would never suffice, but it bought me time to think of something less ridiculous than the truth—trying to follow my husband's cyber trail.

Tristan's eyebrow crept higher. "Stuff, huh?"

"You don't need to know everything." I forced a smile and hoped he bought into it.

"Got any appointments?"

"Not until one."

"Walk with me." He opened the front door, and I reluctantly left the safety of New Heights, where he'd never engage me in a personal conversation.

The phone buzzed in my pocket again. If Tristan would just let me be, I could satisfy my curiosity and get on with the day. I took off at a brisk pace and stepped around the weeds springing up through the cracked sidewalk. "Needed to stretch your legs, eh?"

"Something like that." Tristan kept pace next to me, his presence comforting me like a porcupine.

I breathed in the fresh mountain air and pretended to enjoy the sunshine. Soon it would be too warm to take a midday jaunt. We passed a lawyer's office and a dentist's—both were also in renovated houses on our street. The faraway sound of children on a school playground permeated the air. Soon, we'd gone nearly a half mile without words cluttering the peace.

"What's going on?"

I snorted. "You lulled me into a false sense of security. Nice."

"I thought you said you knew all my tricks."

"Must've forgotten that one." I folded my arms against a sudden chill.

"Or you have a lot on your mind." He slowed his pace and caused me to match it.

"Don't use your psychologist's voice on me. It won't work." I'd already decided to stop dragging Tristan into my personal issues with Colin. Over the years, I'd told him far more than was right, until I realized that I was only reinforcing the concerns he'd had before Colin and I married. That was the last thing I wanted. Tristan's opinions meant far more to me than they should have. Plus, I was embarrassed that he was right.

"Did you forget who you're talking to?" He shoulder-bumped me, which always came out a little stronger than he probably intended, since he was a full head taller than me and stronger than he gave himself credit for. Like other fortysomething bachelors, he spent entirely too much of his free time at the gym. Between that, occasional dating, and writing a book he didn't think I knew about, he stayed pretty busy.

"I know, I know—you've known me longer than anyone else. Late-night pizza parties, scouring the courtyard fountains for coins, yada, yada." I bumped him back. "Some things are personal, that's all. It's not affecting my work, so can we leave it at that? Please?"

He stopped and gently grasped my shoulders, turning me to face him. "I'm not trying to butt in."

I narrowed my eyes.

"Maybe I am, but I can see that something's got you down."

"It's been a long week." I stepped away from his touch.

"You've been acting differently for months now."

"Then what took you so long to ask?" I challenged him before backing down. "Sorry. I really don't mean to be punchy. It's just not a good idea for me to spill my guts to you all the time. Know what I mean?"

"Isn't that what friends are for?"

Normally, yes. But after Colin accused me of considering Tristan as more than a friend, it was dangerous ground. Not that Colin's accusation had an ounce of truth to it. No attraction whatsoever existed between Tristan and me. On the other hand, what I had with Colin had burned through me like an inferno from the time I first saw him across the classroom laboratory minding his beakers.

If only that had lasted.

I resumed walking, not daring to look Tristan in the eye for fear he'd tease out everything in my head without me saying a word. He had a quality about him that elicited immediate trust, that made a person feel safe and understood.

It only took another eighth of a mile to cave. "I get the feeling Colin isn't being totally honest with me."

"Hmm." The single syllable held the barest trace of judgment. Or perhaps it was my imagination.

"I found a way to forward his email to my phone."

"I remember telling you that was a bad idea."

"I can't think of another way to. . .check on things."

"Have you asked him?"

An honest conversation with my husband? Not in this lifetime. Hadn't had one of those in years. But I refused to admit it out loud simply because it would make it real. Sometimes pretending was the only way to stem the loneliness.

"What's that? I didn't hear your answer." He held a hand to his ear.

"Funny." I inhaled the scent of bread from the bakery I frequented. "No, I haven't asked him. What am I supposed to say, 'Hey, got a hot date tonight?'"

"That might work."

"Maybe in your world. Let's face it, if someone isn't being honest, confronting them isn't going to suddenly make them see the light."

"It might."

We rounded the corner back onto our street. A breeze lifted my hair and gave me a momentary reprieve from my sulkiness. "You know how Colin is. He's not a talker." Anymore. Not like he used to be. We'd spent hours discussing books and movies and ideas, and more hours chatting aimlessly. We never ran out of things to say, until—

Not going there.

I shunned the sadness before it could take root.

"It's worth a shot. Better than sneaking around and reading his messages behind his back." Tristan bounded up the front steps. "One of you has to be honest," he said before disappearing inside.

I winced. Tristan had a way of pegging me and calling me to account. Never mind that I was only trying to save my marriage—and my sanity.

Once again, I pulled the phone from my pocket and stepped into the shade of an oak tree. Swiped the screen and held my breath. Sure enough, the screen was illuminated with the moniker PinkBunny91. Subject line: "Urgent, Please Read."

But when I pressed on the email, it had already been erased.

# CHAPTER 5

*Marissa*

Pot roast, baby potatoes, and salad with homemade dressing—Colin's favorite. The smell of dinner permeated the air, and I could only hope the meal stayed warm until we sat to eat. Every time the owl clock above the dining table ticked off another minute, my anxiety ratcheted up. I was like a nervous schoolgirl, peeping through the blinds at the sound of every car cruising by our house.

Waiting, hoping, praying.

When we first met back in college, I did roughly the same thing. Only back then I waited with excitement, knowing that he wanted to see me as much as I did him and that we had something special between us. A fire that couldn't be quenched.

Until it was.

Now I waited in anxiousness, fairly certain that he probably hadn't been where he said he was. No man spent that many hours at work and resisted every effort his wife ever made to drop by and see him. A stronger woman would follow him to find out. And yet, I didn't have proof other than the barely detectible scent of perfume on his collar when I dared to give him a hug, which could've just as easily been my overactive imagination. Or the furtive glances my way before he answered text messages on his carefully guarded phone. Of course, there was PinkBunny91.

But more than anything, it was the sense of unease when we were together and the way we ran out of things to say beyond polite conversation. The way our once passionate kisses had disintegrated into air kisses and our hugs had become friendly. Just, friendly—unless it was one of the days highlighted on the calendar, like today.

This evening, things were going to change, and it was starting with pot roast. I'd even taken Tristan's advice and deleted Colin's email account from my phone. I needed to trust him until his infidelity—emotional or otherwise—was proven. If he maintained that he was faithful, I needed to rely on that.

Love believeth all things, or so I'd heard.

The growl of an engine roared outside. It sounded nothing like Colin's Honda, but I couldn't resist the urge to look. I scanned the street and watched the muscle car from two doors down pull to a stop. Still no sign of Colin as the sun crept closer to the horizon.

This was silly. What I needed was something productive to keep my mind occupied. He'd be here anytime now since baseball practice ended at seven. He'd probably been held up by one of the parents, wanting to know why her son wasn't the star of the team or some such nonsense. And Colin, in his patient way, would appease her and highlight all the great ways her son could still contribute.

He'd make a great father, if he ever got the chance.

One day we'd have children and life would get better. *We* would get better. My heart squeezed at the thought of holding a baby, the desire that always hummed inside me and leapt to the forefront whenever the subject came up. Which, let's face it, happened fairly often in my line of work.

*God's got this*, I reminded myself for the umpteenth time.

I wandered to the mirror in the hall and checked my face and hair. Before I pulled the roast out of the oven, I'd given myself an updo the way Colin liked it.

Finally, Colin's car purred in the driveway. I hurried to the china hutch and grabbed the matches, lit the candles, and composed my nerves. Tonight would be the night we started to fix things and light the fire that brought us together. The embers still burned, somewhere.

The front door opened and closed with a soft click. Colin had yet to look across the cavernous living room to see the table set with the good china and stemware. Instead, he tossed his keys onto the side table and rubbed his forehead, eyes pinched.

"How was practice?" I shoved aside the possibility that he might have been somewhere else. My suspicions were my own. Unfounded and full of the doubts I had about myself. Slowly, I moved toward him.

He turned, taking in the candlelight and intimate place settings—next to one another instead of on opposite ends of the table—and the bottle of wine set out to breathe. Uncertainty flitted over his face as he glanced from me to the table. I could see his brain rapid-firing, trying to gauge what occasion he'd missed.

"It's not our anniversary." I infused my voice with playfulness, hoping to help him shed the weight of the day. "I just wanted to do something special for you."

Colin offered a reluctant smile. "It's a nice surprise."

I leaned against his chest and hugged him with more verve than our usual friendly gesture. It had been at least a month, maybe longer since a genuine embrace had passed between us. The scents of summertime wafted off him. He patted my shoulder before he stepped back to hang up his lightweight jacket.

"Practice was great. The boys are really coming together as a team." He brushed past me without placing his hand on the small of my back in that protective way he used to.

Naturally, those small gestures didn't last a lifetime for anyone. But I wanted more.

"Glad to hear it." I rubbed his shoulder as we made our way to the dining area. "Maybe I can come to your next game?" I held a hopeful breath. What did it say about our marriage that he'd never once invited me to a game or that I felt his office—maybe even the entirety of the small campus—was off-limits to me? I shook off the notion that it was anything but my own insecurities. I wanted him to have his own space and his own pursuits, to not feel smothered the way some men did.

He hesitated a beat too long. "Sure. That'd be great."

"Have a seat and relax. I'll get dinner on the table. It's your favorite." I hurried to the kitchen and took the salad from the fridge first. When I returned to the dining area, he was already seated, a distant look in his eyes. By the time I finished bringing in the roast and potatoes, he had already served himself and was eating.

"Thanks for dinner."

"I hope you enjoy." I scooped potatoes with a heavy dose of gravy onto my plate. Minutes passed in silence. Not exactly what I'd had in mind. "You seem a little distant tonight."

"Long day." He took a whopping bite, a mouthful to avoid conversation.

"We had a pretty full day at the center. Two new clients."

"That's nice," he said, making eye contact only with his beef.

"Hopefully we'll be able to expand and hire more staff soon. Real staff, I mean. We've run through so many temps lately."

"Hope it works out." He speared his meat.

"What's new at the college?"

"Not much." He chewed then took a drink.

"Winding down for the semester? Did you get all the grades turned in?"

"Yes."

"Maybe you can take some time off this summer, I mean, between sessions. Wouldn't it be nice to get away? Even if it's only for a few days, I think it would do us some. . .it would be fun."

He shook his head and looked up from his plate, as though really seeing me for the first time tonight. "I can't."

"Why not? We could head to the beach, do a little surfing. You haven't surfed in years. Remember when we went to—"

"Crank called me into his office today and—"

"Is everything okay?"

"Yeah, yeah." His tone softened. "Everything is fine—better than fine. In fact, he said I'm finally up for tenure."

A smile stretched my face. "Really? That's great." *Why didn't you call me?*

"I meant to call you," he said, as though reading my thoughts. It was uncanny how he did that. How he'd always been able to do that when he actually tried. "Things got busy at the last minute."

I reached out and covered his hand with mine. The feel of his skin made me want more. More of him, his touch, his life. I held his gaze.

"I'm so proud of you."

He nodded before withdrawing his hand and resuming his meal. "I couldn't have done it without you."

"You've worked so hard. This really does call for a celebration. What would you like to do?"

"Nothing yet. It's still a while before the tenure committee meets, and I have all kinds of work to do on my file before then."

"If you still have a while before they meet, then maybe we could—"

"Did you hear what I said? I have to hustle for the next few months to make sure I get tenure. I can't blow this."

"I guess we can take a vacation next year." I attempted to keep the disappointment from my voice but failed miserably. Colin seemed unfazed. I took a tasteless bite and set my fork aside. "You don't seem as happy as I thought you would."

He lifted his shoulder. "I still have a long road."

"I think we both do. We're in this together."

He looked up. Candlelight flickered in his eyes as he engaged me. "More than you know."

The next few months would be pretty harsh, but with the worry about whether he'd ever even make this step in his career over, he'd have more time for us. This could be the breakthrough I'd been praying for. Finally we'd have something new to talk about.

It wouldn't be the ultimate goal that we'd been hoping for, but there was still time for a baby. I wasn't yet forty and Colin was only thirty-five and eager to be a dad. He always had been from the time we met in college when he used to joke that we were meant to be a pair-bond—a random biology term that made my eyes roll.

The early days had been a happy time with Colin and his friend Adam, and soon after Adam's wife, Lani. An entire group formed around our cluster, which lasted a few years even after graduation and marriage when I started taking my faith more seriously and rethinking some of my choices. But all in all, they were good times, being young and in love.

Maybe we could get back to that place and start fresh.

I grasped his hands and tangled our fingers together. "If you're finished eating. . .the dishes can wait." I lifted my eyebrows suggestively.

His mouth moved but he closed it again. A moment passed before he gave my hand a final squeeze and pulled back. "I have some work to do."

# CHAPTER 6

*Colin*

Disappointing his wife was not what Colin had planned on when he came home.

He let out a long, slow breath the moment Marissa started clearing away the dishes. She'd said that she was fine, she understood he had a lot to do, and she wanted to support him until his tenure was secure.

What she hadn't said was how disappointed she was they weren't going to be together tonight, though he could see it reflected in her expression. He should've known when he walked through the door that she was up to something—from the way she'd swept up her hair and lit candles, to making his favorite meal and wearing the low-cut shirt—and he should've given in.

It wouldn't have killed him.

But he was exhausted from the years of trying and the subsequent disappointment every single month. From the hope and the failure for reasons they couldn't explain. From feeling like the entirety of their relationship came down to whether or not she found a plus sign in the window.

If he were completely honest, he'd have to admit he felt like a little less of a man every time it didn't happen. Yet he still wasn't ready to go for an adoption, and he'd told her so whenever she mentioned the young mothers at her work who were looking for that kind of situation. Who knew what kind of kid he'd end up with then? Having kids was too important to take any chances with the children of strangers, even though Marissa was relentless in telling him that wasn't something to be concerned about.

He pushed back from the table and grabbed the salad bowl and dressing. The least he could do was help clean up after her nice gesture, despite the fact he knew she had an ulterior motive.

The spray from the nozzle ran hard over the pan, and Marissa kept her back turned as she scrubbed.

"Let me get that." He took the sponge from her and edged her away from the sink.

"I can do it. You have work to do."

"This will only take a minute." He plunged his hands into the steamy water, despite her protests. Hadn't he, just this afternoon, vowed to work on his marriage? Supposedly, the small gestures counted as much as grander ones, but he knew he couldn't give her the one thing she wanted. Not tonight. Not after. . .

He pushed the images of Kaitlyn from his mind. Thinking of her now was wrong, just as it always had been. Only before, he'd been too caught up in what the younger woman could offer him and the escape he experienced every time they were together.

Colin squirted more dish soap into the sink and turned up the heat on the water full blast until he scalded his hands. Steam rose, and he focused on the sound of dishes and water until he was fully back in the present.

"You need these if you want it that hot." Marissa stood before him holding out yellow gloves. She turned off the water and tugged at his arm. "You're going to burn yourself."

He glanced down at his red hands, stunned he'd been so absorbed in his thoughts.

Marissa handed him a dish towel to dry off. "Truly, I can do these. You go on upstairs and get busy. You've got a lot on your plate tonight." She smiled, the corners of her eyes crinkling with pride. When she'd said she was proud, it wasn't an empty gesture.

And when he'd said he couldn't have done it without her, he was truthful. They'd walked a long road together. He didn't want it to end here.

Which made his decisions over the last few months all the more stupid.

"I appreciate it." He finished drying off and turned his back to her before his guilt mowed him over.

These things happened in life. He wasn't the first man to have an affair, and he wouldn't be the last. He and Marissa had grown apart, and Kaitlyn filled the void. Nicely. But now that he was done with that. . . situation. . .he needed to forget it and move on. Guilt wouldn't change the past, and it certainly wouldn't help him regain the love he once had for his wife.

Maybe telling her was what he needed to do to get them back on track. Or it could drive them apart for good. Marissa was always on the brink of what seemed like a pending breakdown, and loading her down with his indiscretions would only hurt her.

No, he needed to move forward without her knowing. Live with the guilt or get eaten alive by it, it didn't matter. What mattered was focusing on Marissa and trying to find some semblance of emotion for her, other than the nothingness he'd felt for so long.

It was what any decent man would do.

# CHAPTER 7

*Kaitlyn*

Morning sickness—right. If only it were confined to morning. But it seemed that every time Kaitlyn didn't eat, ate too much, smelled, or even saw food, she vomited. Not only that, but daily exhaustion washed over her like a tsunami until she thought she'd fall asleep standing. Making a whole new person was no joke.

"You look like crap." Sydney Donovan didn't mince words, and she rarely added honey to make them go down sweetly.

Kaitlyn ran a cool cloth over her face. Next time she hoped to have enough warning to at least shut the bathroom door, rather than subjecting her housemate to her issues. She rinsed the cloth and pressed it to her face to hide the tears she knew were coming.

"I haven't seen you this sick, well, ever." Sydney guided her to the edge of the tub and sat her down. "Should I take you to the urgent care clinic?"

Kaitlyn shook her head. Seeing a doctor was the last thing she wanted to do. It would make the situation far too real, even more than the pregnancy stick hiding in the drawer of her nightstand already had. Until she found a way to talk to Colin—which didn't appear to be anytime soon, since he wasn't returning her emails and calls—it was better to ignore the obvious.

Sydney squatted next to her on the bath mat. "You have to level with me, and don't give me a line about food poisoning. What's going on?"

If she concentrated on the coolness of the washcloth, maybe she could calm her stomach long enough to talk. She managed a shallow breath before peeling back the cloth. "I've got a problem, and I really don't know what to do."

"You're pregnant."

"Is it that obvious?" Shame coated her voice. She wasn't surprised her friend knew, but she hoped it wasn't that apparent to everyone.

Sydney pursed her lips. "Only to someone who steps into the same room as you."

Great. No one at The Bean had mentioned it, nor had they commented on her frequent trips to the restroom—yet another side effect of pregnancy that she hadn't known about. But that didn't mean she was hiding it as well as she thought she was. "Thanks for the honesty."

"Looks like you could use it." Sydney rose and helped Kaitlyn to her feet. "Let me make you some tea and you can tell me everything."

Before Kaitlyn could protest, Sydney was padding across the hardwood floor to the kitchen of the tiny A-frame house they rented on the outskirts of Elden Springs. She headed for the living room and curled up in the worn recliner that they both refused to part with. After sharing a house for the last two years, it was hard for her to tell which furniture and knickknacks belonged to her and what belonged to Sydney. It was much better than the roommates she'd had when she first tried to attend college and lived in the dorm. What a disaster. Now, being a slightly older, nontraditional student suited her—aside from screwing it all up by dating the professor.

"Oh, before I forget, your parents called and they want you to call them back tonight," Sydney said over her shoulder before igniting the burner under the kettle. "No excuses."

Kaitlyn leaned her head against the chair and closed her eyes. "I can't."

"You'd better. If you don't, they'll think I forgot to tell you. I don't want to get in bad with your parents. Know what I mean?" Sydney pulled out the tea bags and spoon. "Are you hiding anything else from them?" Her dark eyes drilled Kaitlyn.

"My grades," she sighed, weary. "But I'm not actually hiding that anymore."

"Oh boy. Did you tell them?"

"I sent them a copy."

Sydney folded her arms and shook her head. "Chicken."

"It's the first bad grade I've gotten since coming back to school. Not like before, when all my grades were terrible. But you know my mom and dad."

"At least you don't have to see them face-to-face," Sydney teased. "I would not want to be you."

"That makes two of us." She rocked in the recliner. Sydney's light-hearted mood was soothing. Moments passed and she woke with a start at the clatter of the teacup on the table. She sat up and rubbed her head. "Sorry. I'm wiped out."

"So I've noticed, and that wasn't even my first clue." Sydney settled on the love seat next to the picture window, her black hair spilling against the cushion. Outside, twilight faded to dark, making the pine trees appear as lonely silhouettes against the skyline. "Now, tell me what gives."

"I already told you."

"I mean the details. Who, where, when—I already know the what and the how."

Kaitlyn picked up her teacup and blew ripples across the hot liquid. Breathed in the scent of chamomile and spices. Relaxed against the headrest. Of all the people she knew, Sydney could keep a secret. On the other hand, Colin had trusted *her* to do so and she couldn't violate that.

"You're not saying much. Start with the who."

"I can't. I promised I wouldn't tell." Heat swirled in her cheeks.

"One-night stand?" Sydney winced.

"Nothing like that." She sipped and tried to calm her queasy stomach.

"What kind of fool relationship is it where you have to promise not to tell anyone? Is he married or something?"

"Of course not. It's his job. He's not supposed to be. . .involved with anyone." She sipped again.

"Don't tell me he's a priest, 'cuz you'll be in trouble with someone else"—Sydney pointed to the ceiling—"and not just your parents."

Kaitlyn widened her eyes. "He's not a priest, and I think God's going to be angry with me regardless of who the man is." She vaguely recalled the Sunday school lessons that taught on His love and forgiveness, but running to Him now just because she was in trouble seemed insincere.

"What other kind of job requires a man not to have a relationship? That's weird." Sydney's expression filled with disbelief. "So where did you meet this Mr. Wrong, and where is he now? And more importantly, why didn't you tell me you were this serious with someone?"

"I told you, he asked me not to say anything. It would put his job in jeopardy." She tucked her feet underneath her bottom and wished her friend would quit pressing. At the same time, it felt good to let it out, if only a little.

Sydney set her cup down with a clank and sat tall. "Oh my word. No, no, no. Did you. . .is he one of your professors? Is that why you aren't supposed to say anything?"

Kaitlyn felt her eyes go wide before she could moderate her expression.

"I'm right." Sydney shook her head and tsk-tsked. "This is not good. Do your parents know? Is that why they keep calling?"

"No one knows about him, and no one else even knows I'm pregnant." She choked on the last word.

"Not even *him*?"

"I didn't get a chance to tell him." *Before he kicked me to the curb*, she almost added. But speaking unkindly of him would only make her feel guilty once they were back together. The fact he hadn't returned her calls or messages over the last week didn't keep her from hoping that he'd eventually come to his senses.

"This isn't something you wait for the perfect moment to tell. The two of you have decisions to make." Sydney rifled through the magazines and take-out menus on the coffee table until she came up with her keys and held them aloft. "Tonight. Let's go. I'm driving."

"I can't."

"Don't give me any of that, just because the man's a teacher. You have every right to march right up to his door and talk to him. For crying out loud, you're carrying the man's child!" Sydney reached out and tried to coax Kaitlyn out of the chair.

Kaitlyn refused to budge. "You don't understand—I don't even know where he lives." She braced herself for Hurricane Sydney.

"What?" The shriek caused Kaitlyn to jolt. Sydney paced the living room, her dark eyes brooding. "Then where have you been meeting all this time?" She held up her hand. "Wait. I don't want to know. It's a good thing I'm going home for the summer so I don't have to think about it."

"It's not like that."

"How do you not even know where he lives? Obviously you two aren't as close as you thought you were."

No joke. It surprised Kaitlyn how far apart they actually were, considering how well their relationship had been going along. She shifted uneasily in the recliner. The motion made her queasy. "He never took me there because the dean of the college lives on the same road. He said it wouldn't be a good idea for us to be seen together."

"Then he shouldn't have been involved with you in the first place." Sydney scowled. "And you—you're too smart for this."

Tears pressed against the back of Kaitlyn's eyes. She lowered her head in shame. Of course Sydney was right. Her relationship with Colin was a bad idea from the start, but he'd won her over with those stupid, poorly delivered Shakespearean sonnets and abstract talks about the meaning of life. He'd seemed soulful and mature, the way guys her own age weren't. They had a connection that went far deeper than anything she'd known before, and she hadn't wanted to give up her chance to be with such an experienced, worldly man. In fact, she'd been more than a little surprised and flattered that he'd been so attracted to her in the first place.

Sydney crouched next to her. "Hey, I'm sorry. I didn't mean all that."

"You're right. About everything."

"I still think we ought to try to find him so you can talk. Can you call him?"

Kaitlyn fortified her shaky nerves before speaking. "He broke up with me, so he's not returning my calls."

"What a coincidence." The set of Sydney's mouth said she thought it was anything but.

"It really was."

"Have you looked him up? I'm sure his address is somewhere on the web."

"Already tried that." Kaitlyn sighed, not sure if she felt relief for telling someone about her situation or if she felt worse because it was all the more real.

The phone on the kitchen counter rang, and Sydney popped up to grab it. "It's your parents again."

Not for the first time, Kaitlyn wished they hadn't insisted on her having a landline. For safety, they'd said. In her mind, it was another way for them to control her from afar. Why was it that even though she was twenty-six, her parents had the power to make her feel like she was a naughty ten-year-old who just got caught stealing?

"Tell them I'm not here."

Sydney shook her head. "I will not lie for you. You have to talk to them sometime. . .about everything." She handed over the phone.

Kaitlyn closed her eyes and breathed deeply. She could handle this. She had to. Before she could change her mind, she pressed the button and started talking.

# CHAPTER 8

*Marissa*

"Still no coffeepot." The breeze ruffled Tristan's already floppy brown hair. The metal legs of the chair scraped against the concrete as he dragged it to the table outside The Bean.

I smiled sweetly. "I'll put it on my to-do list."

"I'm about to tattoo it on your forehead."

"I'd like to see you try," I challenged him with a smirk, which was infinitely better than confessing that no one talked to me until I arrived at The Bean, and I wasn't about to give up my morning conversations. Friends or not, I didn't really want to go there with Tristan. I tasted the latte, still too hot even with the lid off. "What I'm doing is keeping temptation away from our clients. We don't really want them OD-ing on caffeine while they're spending time with us, now do we?"

Tristan's eyes glinted. "Always thinking of the greater good."

More like survival—mine. Between Kaitlyn the barista and a few of the other regulars, I'd come to enjoy my routine.

While Tristan went inside to grab a cup, I fiddled around with the crossword that was left on the table by the customer before me. Some of the easiest clues had been left blank, and even though they weren't challenging, filling them in gave me a sense of satisfaction. I'd take the satisfaction where I could get it.

Tristan returned, ready to dive into his notes.

He opened his folio and poised his pen at the top of his checklist. "When does our new person start?"

"We still only have Christina, but we adjusted her schedule so we might be okay." I filled in a three-letter word for an Australian bird. Emu. "She'll be working two to three hours every afternoon."

"That doesn't seem like enough help."

"She's a student, so fifteen hours a week is perfect for her. Besides, it's all we can afford."

He held his finger aloft. "Not true. Our grant came in."

"What? That's great." I resisted the urge to jump up and hug him. "Wait. When did you find out?"

"Yesterday. I think you were with someone." His brow furrowed.

"And you forgot to tell me."

"Not sure how I could."

"Seems to be a lot of that going around lately." I stared languidly into my cup.

Tristan set down his pen. "What's that supposed to mean?"

I winced, annoyed with myself for not keeping my private life private. "Never mind—it's not you."

"Have you tried talking to him yet?" Tristan wasn't going to let it slide.

"I followed your advice to a tee." It hadn't worked, but I'd followed it. And since talking hadn't panned out, I regretted deleting Colin's email account from my phone. Had PinkBunny91 written again, or had he agreed to meet her regarding her "urgent" request? Maybe there was someone sending even more nefarious messages than PinkBunny. Without access to his email, I'd never know. But I didn't have the nerve to set up the account again.

"And he's not opening up?"

I waved him off. "No biggie. Hey, how'd your date go last night?"

"It was two nights ago, and you're changing the subject."

"Doesn't mean I don't want to hear about it." I flashed a grin over the rim of my cup.

Tristan drank his coffee before indulging me. "It was good. Sheryl is a nice lady."

"That's it?"

He offered a one-shoulder shrug. "Nothing else to tell. Do I think she's the one?" He glanced around, as though any one of the people on the patio could be reporting back to his newest lady. "Not likely, but she's good company. But nothing like you." He winked.

"Don't do that. It's creepy."

Tristan snorted and went back to his list. "So I think the grant will cover more than just fifteen hours a week. I'd love to see someone come in who can really get to know the clients and not just be there to answer the phones."

"I agree. You know what I see? I see New Heights becoming even more of a community. We need more birthing and parenting classes." Every time I saw the future of New Heights, something stirred inside me. We could actually make a difference in our town, caring for mothers and babies long after the birth.

But whenever I thought too hard about it, I always had to ignore the pang in my chest, wondering when it would be my turn. If Colin kept turning me down like last night, we'd never start a family.

For another ten minutes, Tristan and I focused on the business, talking about future funding and ideas for creating an environment that would encourage women not only to utilize our services, but also to give back when their lives were in a more secure position. We discussed adding parenting classes and a mentor program, and the logistics of each.

I glanced at my phone, once again wishing I'd left Colin's email where I could read it. What did PinkBunny91 look like, and why did I feel so threatened by her in particular? My obsession was bordering on ridiculous, and I wished the looping thoughts circling in my mind would quiet down.

"If you're not going to tell me what's really going on with you, then you might be more discreet." Tristan sat back and crossed his legs.

"What do you mean?"

"You—the phone. The whole forlorn gaze thing." He motioned in a circle with his pen as though cycling through the myriad things wrong with me.

"I hope you're a little gentler with our clients," I said to put him off. "And your private patients too, because they're your bread and butter."

He stared and said nothing, which had the uncomfortable effect of making me want to tell him everything. A bird chirped and a car honked, neither of which fazed him.

"Fine. I still don't think he's telling me the truth about everything." Air whooshed out of my lungs, a relief after holding the truth so close. "Last week he told me he's about to make tenure."

"That's a good thing, isn't it?"

"Then why is he so moody and distracted? I thought he'd be psyched. He's worked for this for so many years. It's all he's ever wanted, so I thought it would make his mood better, not worse." I finished the rest of my latte and fingered the cup. "It doesn't add up."

Tristan appeared thoughtful, studying me with intense eyes that seemed to see through me. Evaluating, as though trying to decide how much truth I could handle and how much he should hold back. Finally, he broke his gaze and spoke. "If it isn't a done deal, he probably has a lot on his plate. If he blows it now, his dream is gone."

"Is that what you really think?" My stomach knotted as I waited for his answer.

"I think. . ." He shifted in his seat and glanced at the people milling about. "I think you really ought to talk to him. You aren't going to be satisfied until you have a heart-to-heart."

"That's just it—he won't. I've tried everything." I lowered my voice to a whisper. "I've had enough, and I think I need to see for myself."

"What are you suggesting?"

"I want to follow him. See what he's up to." I could scarcely believe the words, and the shock on Tristan's face confirmed my craziness. Yet I refused to take back my comment. It was time for me to take action or Colin and I could never move forward.

"Why not just spend more time together? You know, take him to lunch. Surprise him and show up at baseball. That kind of thing. We can build it into the schedule if you need time off."

"You don't get it." I bit my lip, debating how much I wanted to reveal. At this point, I hadn't much to lose. I leaned closer to avoid broadcasting my troubles to the ladies at the table next to us. "I don't feel *welcome* to just show up. The college, the field—those are his places. It's kind of an unspoken agreement that they're off-limits."

"That's ridiculous."

"For most couples, yes. But for the last few months I get the feeling that we aren't most couples." Even saying it hurt. The times Colin practically ignored me stole my breath and my confidence, and caused me to prefer staying in bed to facing the world. I'd spent more than one Saturday hidden away with no one around to notice. If it wasn't for the days when I went to help my mother with shopping or appointments, I'd never leave or talk to anyone outside of work.

*God's got this.* Though I knew it in my head, I still needed to reassure my heart.

Tristan raised a quizzical brow. "Don't you think he'll notice you following him? You know, seeing as how he bought your car and all." He loved pointing out the obvious.

"For your information, my car is acting up again."

"Get to the point."

"The point is, I need your help." I matched his raised brows with my own.

"Oh no." He motioned his hands back and forth as though swatting away a bad idea. "Do not involve me in this."

"You don't have to actually be there." I kept my chin high despite Tristan's initial rejection.

He rubbed his face and crossed his arms over his broad chest. "This is not going to end well."

"Tell me about it."

"You can borrow my car. That's it."

"That's all I need." And to know that someone would be rooting for me when I finally mustered the courage to do it.

Tristan's phone rang. His expression lightened and a grin tinged his lips before he caught himself. "I need to take this." He rose and walked to the corner of the building. "Sheryl, I was just thinking about you."

I gave his new girlfriend a month. Tops. But I prayed that one day he'd find a keeper because he was a good guy. It was time for him to move forward, and if I could just figure out what my husband was up to, I could move forward too.

A woman could hope.

I turned my attention back to the crossword. A six-letter word for void of companionship. That one was easy.

Lonely.

# CHAPTER 9

*Kaitlyn*

Kaitlyn dragged herself to work and clocked in two minutes late. Not bad, considering she'd hardly been able to pull herself out of bed. At least Jake didn't seem to notice or mind—or ask questions about why her work habits had changed.

She tied the cheery baby blue apron around her waist and started helping the customers in the queue. The line snaked out the door, but no one seemed to mind, content to wait while listening to the light jazz and scanning the newspapers scattered throughout The Bean. A guy from her biology class tried to linger and flirt—and really, she gave him bonus points for effort—but she was not in the mood.

Breaking up with Colin—correction, being broken up with by Colin—sapped every ounce of her motivation. She'd had a few boyfriends in the past and gone through the string of breakups that most women had, but nothing like this. For months, Colin had lavished her with attention and made suggestions that led her to believe what they had together would last. He hadn't made promises, and therefore he'd broken none, but those would come in time. At least that's what she'd hoped.

None of that mattered now. She had more to worry about than a failed relationship, as the queasiness in her stomach attested.

If Colin only knew, he'd forget about breaking up, forget about protocol, and start helping. She couldn't even count the number of times he'd mentioned wanting to have children—definitely not a topic of conversation to have with someone he wasn't serious about. This would wake him up to see that his future happiness was with her.

And their baby.

He'd make a great father for their child. He coached Little League and occasionally, after a solid win, he'd let his guard down for her to see his playful side. The image of a baby in his arms made her wistful. If she didn't get ahold of him soon, he'd miss out on all the important milestones.

"Jake, I need to take a quick break," she said once the line finally dwindled.

"Sure thing. Check the bathrooms while you're back there."

She wrinkled her nose before heading toward the break room. She grabbed her phone from her book bag and checked for messages. Her heart sank a fraction when she saw there were none. Sure, she could go back to campus and force him to see her, but that would do nothing to win him back. It would only tick him off.

She pocketed her cell and opted instead for the wall-mounted phone obscured by an outdated vending machine. Before she could second-guess herself, she dialed the campus operator and asked to be connected to the Biology Department. Then she asked the student worker if she could speak to Dr. Kimball.

Her pulse jackhammered in her temples as she held her breath and waited. What would she say before he hung up? It had to be good to get his attention, but she couldn't blurt the truth about being pregnant. It wouldn't be right for him to find out that way. She had to see his face, note his expression, and figure out where they would go from there.

A full minute went by, and she willed the break room door to stay closed so her coworkers didn't hear her desperation.

This was it. He wasn't going to answer, and she'd have to leave a message with the student worker, which would anger Colin. Leave a message or hang up quietly?

She reached out her finger to disconnect, when the line went active again.

"Dr. Kimball." The sound of his voice sent shivers down her spine. The same understated tone that had wracked her mind for months. "Hello?"

"It's me." Her breathless words were so much less than she'd intended.

Silence bled over the line until he spoke. "Is there something I can help you with? The update to your grade should have been posted by now."

She closed her eyes. The grade—the only people *that* mattered to right now were her parents. She gripped the phone tighter. "I understand what you said—" She paused to choose her words with care, in case he wasn't alone in the room. "I understand what you said at our last meeting, but I need to talk to you again. It's really important."

"I offered to change your grade, and at this point that's all I can do for you."

"You don't understand—"

"Hold on a moment." His muffled words indicated that someone else was in the office. He said something to the effect that he'd chat later and to please close the door on the way out. A quiet response revealed a woman was in the room. A pang of jealousy shot through Kaitlyn and stole her breath. She steadied herself and waited until he uncovered the mouthpiece and spoke. "Now, as I said. . ." His words trailed, and she could imagine that he was scrubbing his hands through his hair, leaving it slightly mussed. How many times had she tried to smooth it down, only to see it come out at odd angles all over again?

"Just listen to me, please."

"I've already said everything I can on. . .the subject."

"I get it." She squeezed her eyes against the tide of emotion. "I'm not trying to say otherwise, but there are a few things that. . .need to be resolved."

"There's nothing more."

"Meet me. Please. Same spot, tonight after baseball practice."

Colin blew out a gusty breath. "Fine. But my mind is made up." He hung up without a goodbye, leaving Kaitlyn feeling uneasy and on edge, as though the slightest gesture would cause her to unravel.

This wasn't like him. This wasn't the Colin she'd been falling in love with. If only she knew what caused his change of heart. Or maybe his heart hadn't changed, but he was exhausted from keeping his work and his personal life strictly separate.

At least he'd agreed to see her. Now maybe they could work this out. To be together in their special spot would remind him what he was missing. She remembered how his gentle touch and soft breath had tickled her ears when he held her in the evenings as they watched the sun go down. He'd never given any indication, apart from his job concerns, that he wasn't falling as madly in love as she was. She knew she hadn't imagined it. What they had between them was not a one-sided affair.

How could he give that up?

She hung up the phone and returned to the floor. She went through a few more customers and fought the nausea rising in her stomach. If she could concentrate on something else rather than the strong smell of the beans in the grinder, she'd be able to hold it together.

"Are you okay?" Kaitlyn's favorite customer leaned against the counter.

"Marissa, hi." She tried breathing through her mouth to block out the thick aroma of coffee. "A lot on my mind. Sorry."

"You look pale." Marissa scrutinized her. "Maybe you should sit down for a minute."

Kaitlyn shook her head. "I'm fine." *As long as I don't smell the coffee.* She clutched her stomach.

Jake poured more beans into the grinder. The machine started to whir, sending out a pungent aroma that bullied past her nose, down her throat, and straight to her gut. The nausea burbled inside and acid stung her throat. Her feet responded before she could think, propelling her out the door to the side of the building.

Wave after wave, she vomited. Her eyes watered from the force, and her shoulders heaved while she struggled to catch her breath.

Fingers tugged at her hair, holding it back. "That's it. You'll feel better in a minute." Marissa handed her a napkin.

Kaitlyn wiped her mouth and tried to straighten. Embarrassment rushed over her when she realized the shrubs hadn't offered her as much privacy as she would've wished. "I can't believe I just did that."

"Those things happen. Here, I grabbed this for you." Marissa handed over a plastic courtesy cup filled with water. "Rinse."

Kaitlyn rinsed then took a sip to clear her palate. "I don't know what came over me. It must've been the smell of the coffee beans."

Marissa nodded, her gentle eyes taking in more than they revealed. "Glad I was here. I was just coming in for my refill before heading off to work."

"I'm afraid to go back. The smell is so strong inside." She took another sip to settle her stomach.

"Let's see. . . You don't strike me as the partying type, so I'm guessing you're not hungover."

Kaitlyn issued a mirthless chuckle. Here came the questions. "No, I'm not. And I don't have the flu or the norovirus or the—"

"And you've been exhausted." Marissa offered a genuine smile, which somehow made things seem not so bad.

"Just say it."

"You first."

Kaitlyn glanced around. The few people outside who had initially gawked had gone back to minding their own business. "I'm pregnant."

"That's what I thought. Congratulations." Marissa gave her a side hug.

"It's not like that." Kaitlyn studied the gravel, the shrubs. Anything but looking directly into the customer's eyes. She'd known Marissa from the time she'd started working at The Bean over a year ago, and though they weren't more than acquaintances, she still cared what the woman thought.

"It's always a little different than what you expect, especially the first time."

Kaitlyn looked up and met Marissa's gaze. "But I'm not married."

Marissa smiled warmly. "You're not the first unmarried person to have a child, and you won't be the last. What about family? Do you have a supportive family?"

Kaitlyn's throat knotted. The last time she'd talked to her parents was about her grade—she hadn't fessed up to anything else—and even that had spiraled downhill fast. What would they say about the way she'd sinned and ruined herself? She shifted and focused on the sound of gravel under her shoe. "Not really."

"Do they know?"

Kaitlyn shook her head. "I can't—I mean. . .I haven't told them yet. They're not going to take it well."

"They'll live. Trust me." Marissa gave her a firm hug then opened her handbag and pawed through it. "Listen, you come down and see me. I work at New Heights over on Burlin Avenue." She handed Kaitlyn a card.

New Heights Pregnancy Resource Center. Interesting. Kaitlyn put it in her apron pocket. "I hope you specialize in how to handle a crisis."

Marissa chuckled. "Things are not as bad as they seem. You'll see."

"Kaitlyn, are you out here?" Jake's voice sounded from around the corner at the front of The Bean.

"I need to go. Thanks for your help."

Marissa reached out and patted her back. "Really, please come and see me. Let us be your support system."

Kaitlyn swallowed the marble in her throat and offered a noncommittal nod.

"If not, you know I'm here for you. Okay?" Marissa's soft demeanor touched her heart. "I know it might not seem like it now, but you'll get through this." She squeezed her shoulder before stepping back. "I promise—babies are *always* a good thing."

# CHAPTER 10

*Colin*

Colin clapped his hands and called across the baseball field. "Bring it in, boys!"

The Tornados—all nine- and ten-year-old boys—sprinted toward home plate. They shouted and ribbed one another while they chattered on about this weekend's matchup against their crosstown rivals. Colin enjoyed seeing the kids excited to play the game that he'd loved as a boy. He shoved aside the desire to one day share the game with a son of his own, knowing that the likelihood diminished as the years went on. When he met Marissa, he hadn't thought marrying a woman four years older than him would be such a disadvantage. For now, he'd have to settle for borrowing the sons of his friends and neighbors on Tuesdays, Thursdays, and Saturdays.

"Who's going to bring down the house this weekend?"

"Tornados!" the boys shouted in unison.

"Who's going to show the Sharks who's boss?"

"Tornados!"

"That's right!" Colin, the boys, and the assistant coach, Adam, high-fived and whooped it up for a minute before Colin gave them final instructions to stay hydrated and get plenty of rest. One by one, the boys trickled out to the parking lot to meet their parents.

"Great practice. I think we have a chance this weekend." Adam packed up the extra balls while Colin dusted the makeshift bases.

Dirt and mud rubbed off on his sweats. Kaitlyn always wrinkled her nose when he showed up looking like he'd been rolling in the field, and he loved to tease her back by mussing up whatever outfit she'd chosen for their rendezvous. Of course, she didn't really mind but she always played along.

But ten minutes from now, it wouldn't be the same. Though it'd be so easy to slip into old habits, he had to be strong. His marriage and his career depended on it.

"You gonna keep ignoring me?" Adam chucked a glove at him and laughed.

The glove bounced off Colin, jolting him from his thoughts. "What?"

"Dude. You're acting weird. All evening you've been ignoring the kids whenever they said something and blowing off my suggestions. Something isn't right." Adam bent over, picked up the glove, and shoved it inside his duffel bag.

"I have?" Colin winced, afraid that what his closest buddy said was true. Anxiety hummed in his chest, the same way it always did when his private life came open for discussion. He set down the bases and rubbed the back of his neck. Grime and sweat dirtied his palm.

Adam stood in front of him, eyes narrow. "Are you and Marissa having problems again?"

"Again?" Colin snorted. "We never stopped." He hefted the bases and walked toward his vehicle.

"You don't have to talk about it, but you do need to know that people notice your weird behavior."

That couldn't be true. Colin had done a great job masking his private issues. No one at work had said anything, and Marissa—well, she always nagged. Nothing new there. He popped open the trunk. "You're the only one who's noticed."

"Hazard of having a longtime friend, bro."

He wouldn't be a friend for long if he knew, Colin thought. He grabbed the duffel from Adam and shoved that inside the trunk too. "We'll see you this weekend."

"Is there something I can do to help? What if we all get together this weekend after the game? Me and Lani, you and Marissa. We'll make an evening of it, all of us hanging out like the old days. I know Lani and Marissa aren't close like they used to be, but it'll be fun."

Colin slammed the trunk. The truth burned in his chest. There was no point in talking about it now—to Marissa, Adam, or anyone else.

Discovering the infidelity was how people got hurt, not the actual committing of it. Right? Cutting loose with the truth would only burden Adam.

"Dude, you're shaking." Adam clamped a steadying hand on his shoulder.

"I can't do it anymore."

"Do what?"

Colin shrugged Adam's hand away. "Never mind. I have to go." He casually waved to the last of the parents driving off.

"I know Marissa hates you being late, but you obviously have something on your mind. I'm sure she'll be okay." Adam kept his distance. "Just chill out for a minute."

"You don't get it." Colin closed his eyes and wished he was a better man. Wished he hadn't strayed. Wished he believed in God, like Adam and his wife. He'd given it a shot, but it just didn't square up for him. "I fooled everyone, even you."

"Fooled me?" Adam crossed his arms. "What's this about?"

"I'm not going home to Marissa—not until after I clear things up with. . .someone."

Adam's sharp breath indicated he knew exactly what Colin meant. "You're having an affair."

*Affair* was such an ugly word and hardly expressed the depth of emotions Kaitlyn had stirred up. Emotions he thought he no longer owned. It hadn't been cheap or tawdry, not a fling or a one-nighter. And if he were being completely honest with himself, he hated that he had to give it up.

But he hated lying to his wife even more.

He leaned against the car and faced his friend. Shame washed over him, and he couldn't look Adam in the eye. "It's not like you think."

"What—" Adam's mouth hung open. His hands fisted and he punched the air. "Tell me you're playing a sick joke. Tell me you aren't destroying the best thing that ever happened to you. Go ahead!"

"I'm not. It's done. I broke it off."

"Then why are you going to meet her tonight?" Adam stuck his finger right between Colin's eyes. "Answer!"

He shook his head and forced himself to speak. "I don't know."

"Unacceptable!"

"She said she needed to see me. All right? She said it's important. Now let it go!"

"What were you thinking?" Adam ran his hands through his hair. Disgust poured off him like sweat. "Does Marissa know?"

"No." Colin wheeled in a breath. "But she might suspect," he amended. The way she was always sneaking up on him and trying to peek at his phone. The extra calls she made to check on him when he was late. The way she always seemed like she had more to say but didn't.

"It'll kill her. She's already—" Adam stopped short of the truth.

It didn't matter. Everyone knew. It was no secret that Marissa was overly sensitive since they suspected they were unable to conceive again. She was devastated after the miscarriage several years ago—they both were—but worse, she refused to seek an answer. She was determined to conceive naturally. It was hard to stay in love as the months ticked by, and he wouldn't blame her if she felt the same.

Maybe he'd gone off and fallen for someone else before Marissa could. After all, she'd eventually want to leave him for a man who could give her the one thing she wanted most—a family. At this point, who was to say which one of them was at fault for not having kids? Without medical intervention they'd likely never know. But the way she'd acted over the last few years, she wanted a baby more than she wanted him. If she didn't get what she wanted, she'd probably start pushing the whole adoption thing.

Adam sat on the hood of his car, parked at the back of Colin's bumper. He clasped his hands between his knees. "I never thought it would happen with you and Marissa. Man, if it can happen to you guys, it can happen to anyone."

Colin snorted softly. He never thought he'd be the kind of man to cheat. Even the word sent sick aftershocks through his soul.

"You guys were like the power couple of our group back in the day. Madly in love. Going places."

"Things change. People change." He couldn't believe he'd hidden all his changes so well.

"Not that much." Adam's mouth tightened, and his eyes slanted against the evening sunlight. "Who is she?"

"Does it matter?" Colin slid his sunglasses on, thankful for something to hide behind.

"Not really. You're right—I don't want to know the details. Why didn't you tell me before? I mean, maybe I could've stopped you."

No one could've stopped him. The draw to Kaitlyn was too strong. Or he was too weak. She was the first thing he thought of in the morning and the last thing on his mind as he fell asleep with his wife stiffly at his side.

"Are you going to tell Marissa?" Colin asked meekly.

"No way. That's your job."

"Lani?"

"Man, Colin! You really put everyone in a bind. I don't like keeping secrets from my wife." Anger tinged Adam's words, but Colin didn't blame him. He used to feel the same way.

"Like you said, it would send Marissa over the edge."

Adam whistled low. "You mean to say you're not going to tell her?"

"What's the point? I cut it off. It's over. I'm staying with my wife, and that's all there is to it." Too bad the execution of his plan wasn't nearly as simple as it sounded. He popped a stick of gum into his mouth and checked the time on his cell phone.

"And yet you're on your way to meet. . .her." Adam's brow crimped with disapproval.

"She won't leave me alone. I need to make sure she doesn't get angry. When I broke it off, we didn't really get a chance to talk."

"So you're trying to keep her from going *Fatal Attraction* on you."

"No—she's not like that." Colin swatted the air. "C'mon, do you really think I'd be with someone like that?"

"I never thought you'd be with anyone but Marissa."

Silence wedged between them, ferreting out the guilt he'd tried so hard to keep buried. "Fine, whatever. My point is, she's hurt and upset, and if I don't step in she might talk. I can't let it get back to Dr. Crank. It'll blow my tenure."

"A student? You've got to be joking. You really are stupid."

"Fine!" Colin threw his arms open. "You can lay into me or you can help. Pick." He ground his teeth until his jaw ached.

"You're right. That won't do any good. But neither will seeing her. If you really want to end it, then let it go."

"But what if she talks?" A pang of regret hit him.

"So be it." Adam's expression sobered. "It's called consequences."

### Kaitlyn

Kaitlyn pulled her car to the edge of the cliff overlooking the pine-laden valley. The view was spectacular, if one wanted to force their car over the ruts and holes of the so-called road that led to the overlook. She rolled down the windows and switched off the ignition. Fresh air and the sound of birds in the distance filled her with peace that was scarce at school or at The Bean.

She pulled her cell phone from her book bag. No messages. Not that she'd been expecting one since Colin hadn't contacted her in nearly two weeks. This evening they'd finally have a chance to patch things up—that was her secret hope.

After five minutes, she climbed out of the car and walked toward a giant boulder that clung to the edge of the cliff. The sun hung over the horizon, coloring the clouds in brilliant reds and oranges. She loved the warmer evenings that summertime offered and had, more than once, imagined she and Colin would spend many such evenings together.

Of course, in her imagination Colin had already made her a part of his everyday life and they spent time together like any normal couple. Maybe it wasn't just a dream, it was a fantasy. Especially now that she knew he hadn't planned on going further with their relationship.

She paced the cliff. The breeze kicked up, tugging at her hair. She swept it off her face and behind her ear, then glanced back at the dirt road and willed Colin's car to appear. While this was a nice place to meet—and by far their most frequented spot—she'd been ready to move things up to the next level. A few times they'd gone to dinner and a movie in Mountainside, the neighboring town where both Sydney's family and her own lived. Colin felt less like he was under a microscope there, but it wasn't the same as having their love—or what she'd mistaken for love—out in the open.

Maybe he'd change his mind once he saw her tonight. He'd savor the same memories that were teasing her right now. Like the first time they'd discovered this spot. The hikes and picnics, and the way they cuddled until the sun went down. If she released the memories rather than stuffing them, she could almost feel his breath against her neck, and the smell that was uniquely Colin, a sultry mixture of musk and man.

Kaitlyn swallowed back the pain of his rejection.

Surely once he found out about the life growing inside her, he'd want to be part of that. What decent man wouldn't? She knew he was responsible and honorable, trustworthy and sincere. So many times he'd demonstrated those qualities, and even the fact he didn't want to jeopardize his job showed how seriously he took his career. Those were all good things, things that would persuade her parents that having a baby wasn't the end of the world and that she wasn't just a cheap and easy sinner, even though that's what she felt like most days.

She bit her lip. Marissa had said that babies were always a good thing. Right now, she desperately wanted to believe it. But as the sun sank below the distant mountains with no sign of Colin, she knew that having a baby right now was anything but good.

# CHAPTER 11

*Marissa*

The cinnamon-scented candles burned down to the nub on top of the fireplace mantel. The candles proved a good substitute for a romantic fire at the start of summer when the air was already stiff and warm. For the umpteenth time I checked the clock, and my hopes dwindled faster than the candles.

Where was Colin?

Practice had most likely ended at least an hour ago, and the field was less than fifteen minutes away. Calling would only irritate him, and I wanted him to come home in a good mood. I needed him in a good mood—not only so we could have a nice evening but because my ovulation kit said all systems were go.

Only I couldn't let him know that. If he found out, it would almost guarantee rejection.

Back in the days when we were both optimistic, we looked forward to these supposedly fertile days. After years of disappointment, we still tried, but the act itself was reduced to going through the motions. Void of passion.

Clinical.

Eventually we began to avoid one another, "forgetting" what time of the month it was. After all, if we weren't trying to conceive, then there was no one to blame for a lack of a plus sign in the window. Avoidance became the go-to way to fight through. Finally it became routine.

But it had to end. I wanted my husband. I wanted our life the way it was before we suspected it would always and forever be just the two of us. Before we fell asleep crying, tears on our pillows.

Lights swung into the driveway.

My heart picked up speed. I checked my hair and face in the hallway mirror. Tonight I left my hair down—didn't want to make my motives too obvious—and kept to my casual house clothes, velour sweatpants and a T-shirt we bought on our last trip to the beach. Not pretty but packed with memories.

The front door opened and closed with a soft click. Colin fumbled with both his gym bag and shoulder bag before stashing the latter on the table near the door, his back to me.

"Hi." I tried—and failed—to keep too much enthusiasm from my voice. "How was practice?"

Colin turned, his dark green eyes piercing me, causing my breath to hitch. The five o'clock shadow dusting his strong jaw and the firm set of his mouth still had the power to weaken me. He looked away and offered a shrug. "Good."

"You have a game this weekend?"

"Yeah. I think we're ready to win." His faint smile gave me a bit of relief.

"Come sit. Dinner is almost ready." I motioned him toward the living room, hesitant to touch him and bring him closer. These days it didn't take much to scare him off.

He adjusted the duffel bag on his shoulder, where I knew his work clothes lay crumpled. He always changed before heading to the baseball field. Handing me a bag of office-wear when he came home had become standard procedure. The first few times I'd been annoyed because of the extra laundry, but now, each time he came home to me I was so thankful, I didn't care how much laundry he produced.

He headed for the staircase. "No, thanks. I'm wiped out. Maybe I'll go take a shower."

I tamped down my disappointment. "Sounds. . .great. I'll serve dinner while you're in the shower."

"I'm really not hungry." Sadness tinged his eyes.

"Did something happen at work?" I moved closer, still without touching.

He shook his head and studied his shoes. "The usual."

Stress—that's what was in his expression, not sadness. I moved closer to my husband and drew him into a soft hug. "You must be exhausted. I know how much you want this promotion. You deserve it."

His rigid body finally formed to mine, and for the first time in over a month, he hugged me back. "I'm sorry," he said, his face buried in my neck.

"Don't apologize. You have a lot on your mind."

"I haven't been here for you." His words, so gentle, were muffled by my hair. The feel of his breath against my neck sent tingles down my back.

"You're not the only one. I haven't really been here for you either." A sole tear slid down my cheek. I was thankful he couldn't see it because my emotions were too raw.

"I promise to try harder." He paused, and I could feel him swallow. "I don't want to hurt you."

I pulled him tighter against me, both scared to hang on and scared to let go. "Don't put it all on yourself. Part of the problem is me. I know that, but we'll get back on track."

His embrace grew stronger, reminding me of the husband I used to know. Gradually his arms swept over my waist and my back as though relearning my body. He nuzzled my neck and his lips found mine.

The strength of his kisses left me weak and pliable, molded to his form. Moments later we were in our room, the way we used to be before lovemaking became baby-making. Before disappointment crowded out every other emotion.

Finally my husband was really home.

While I waited for Colin to come downstairs, I finished dinner and set the table, humming like a schoolgirl in love.

A ringtone sounded in the front hallway where Colin's phone lay on the table next to his shoulder bag and keys. I scurried across the living room and grabbed it before the tone ended. A text from Adam lit the screen.

*Why didn't you show up? I'm really disappointed. Was counting on you to be there for me.*

That did not sound like Adam, who tended to use the words *bro* and *dude* way too much for a man his age.

I checked the sender again to make sure it was Adam. Though the contact name said Adam, all the previous messages had been erased so it was hard to tell.

And what did he mean by that anyway? Had Colin not made it to practice? He'd talked about it when he got home. If Colin hadn't been at practice, where had he been? Texting Adam back might be the only way to figure out what was going on, but that might throw a kink into their friendship. Even though Adam was a friend to both of us, I didn't want to admit to him that I had suspicions.

Evidently the moments I'd just spent with Colin hadn't erased them.

My pulse hiccupped as I considered what to do. I could text Adam and ask, or I could try to pin down Colin, though the odds of getting a straight answer if he was trying to hide something were practically nil. Besides, I didn't really want to tick him off.

Text Adam. Ask Colin. I wavered between two bad options, beating myself up for not being able to make a decision.

So in the end I made the only decision I could. I set the phone back where it was and did nothing.

Happy or stressed? An emotional cocktail I wasn't entirely unfamiliar with.

I sat at my desk and mindlessly scrolled through my emails. Colin hadn't said much the rest of the night. He'd acted neither like a man in love, nor like a man who wanted to keep a safe distance from his wife. It seemed we were both conflicted.

Christina tapped lightly on my door. "Your next appointment should be here any minute."

"I have an appointment?" I looked at my nonexistent desk calendar and tried to decipher my schedule from a smattering of Post-its, a note on the back of a napkin, and an empty coffee cup.

"Her name is—" She peered at the appointment book in her hands. "Kaitlyn."

"Kaitlyn?" I perked up. Was it my favorite barista? She hadn't mentioned anything about an appointment this morning when I shuffled through her line. Then again, there were about six or seven people after me, and it wasn't likely she wanted to advertise it.

"She called just a few minutes ago and you had an empty slot." Christina's forehead wrinkled. "I hope that's okay."

"Absolutely. I'll go ahead and take care of the paperwork on this one." I attempted to tidy my desk and thought about Kaitlyn and the shadows under her eyes that weren't there yesterday. She needed someone to talk to and give her a little hope.

The electronic door chime sounded from the reception area, and Christina hurried out to say hello. I gathered my random notes and papers and slid them into the top desk drawer to sort later. Unfortunately, I'd done that yesterday too, and the pile was growing. I grabbed a client questionnaire and attached it to a clipboard with a dangling pen just as Kaitlyn tapped on the doorframe.

"Hi, Marissa." She paused and waited for me to motion her inside.

"Come on in. Close the door behind you."

She nudged the door shut and sat on the opposite side of my desk. Her eyes were red and slightly puffy. I offered her a box of tissue, which she refused. "I'm fine."

"Glad to hear it," I said tentatively. "I'm really happy you came in."

Her shoulders tightened and she shook her head so slightly I almost missed it. "I'm not sure why I did. Pregnant is pregnant, right?"

I smiled, hoping to put her at ease. "Once you get over the shock and start to make plans, you'll feel the excitement."

"I wish I could believe you." She looked skyward and blinked.

Again, I pushed the tissue box toward her, and this time she accepted. It seemed she wasn't entirely opposed to help, if one were persistent enough.

Judging by her jittery hands, she wasn't ready to fill out the client information sheet. In this moment it was too clinical for the young woman in front of me. Someone whom I'd almost come to think of as a friend.

Tears slipped down her cheeks, and she quickly brushed them away, as though embarrassed to be so completely and utterly human.

Was this what it had been like for my own mother? Always calm and in control, until she found out she was pregnant and the father—my father—suddenly decided to exit stage left.

Compassion for Kaitlyn stirred inside me. I rounded the desk and tipped up her chin, forcing her to look me in the eye. "Kaitlyn, I know things look bleak right now, but they'll get better. You'll get through this, and I'm going to do everything in my power to help you for as long as it takes."

She looked at me with hope. "You will?"

I squeezed her hand and willed her to believe me. "I promise."

# CHAPTER 12

*Kaitlyn*

The indignity of peeing in a cup—something Kaitlyn never anticipated when she started her day. The cup was labeled with her name,
though clearly there wasn't another client in the house. Or were they
called unwed mothers? Crisis pregnancy dropout failures? In her case, all
the monikers fit, or soon would.

Kaitlyn bit her lip and placed the cup inside the cupboard that
opened up into Marissa's office. The door on the other side of the box
squeaked, and she didn't even want to imagine what Marissa was doing
with the warm cup. Kaitlyn waited in the restroom for a few minutes so
she didn't have to watch what happened. She was already feeling sick
without adding to it.

She checked her face in the mirror. No makeup, swollen eyes, and
generally looking terrible. No wonder everyone at The Bean had tiptoed
around her. What she really needed was to get her act together, whether
or not Colin was going to be part of her future. Showing up to work late
and slogging through the day was no way to handle her mess.

Sensing enough time had passed, she took a deep breath, switched
off the light, and opened the door. Squared her shoulders before heading
into the hallway. Maybe her home pregnancy test was wrong. After all,
wouldn't that be why she'd have to take another test here? On the off
chance that the store-bought stick was somehow tainted?

Never mind that she'd missed her cycle and hadn't been able to eat
much more than a few saltines in the last few weeks. She steadied her
shaky hands and went back inside Marissa's office.

"Have a seat. Your results will be up in a minute." Marissa ushered
her inside and closed the door before settling behind the cluttered desk.
She folded her hands and smiled. "How are you feeling?"

"Honestly? A little nauseous. Sorry about what happened outside The Bean yesterday—it seems to be happening a lot lately."

"No, no—that's all right. I don't mean it that way. How are *you* doing?" She patted her chest as if referencing deep-seated emotions. Kaitlyn liked that about Marissa—always expressive, if a little corny. Trying to pretend like she hadn't just watched her having a breakdown.

"I'm still in shock." She studied her lap, and the way the skin flaked off around her fingernails. Since she'd gone back to school, she'd had to give up manis and pedis. "True confession: I was almost hoping that I'd come in here and the test would show that I'm not pregnant. That my results at home were wrong."

Marissa's face revealed no judgment. "That's a pretty common feeling. Do you think there might be a mistake?"

"No." The word solidified in her chest.

"I take it you have all the obvious signs?"

Kaitlyn nodded.

"Let's have a look at some dates here." She swiveled to face her computer screen. "When was the first day of your last cycle?"

"March twentieth. The only reason I know that is because I'm on the pill—" Kaitlyn bit her lip. "To control my acne," she quickly added. She didn't want Marissa to think she was easy, though the results spoke for themselves.

"You conceived on the pill?" A flicker of sadness tinged Marissa's expression.

"Yes, and I'm really good about taking it. Like I said, it's for my acne." She shrugged, realizing how dumb it sounded that she had acne at her age. "I don't know what happened."

"Life." Marissa held up her hands. "You know, sometimes taking certain meds like antibiotics can reduce the effectiveness of the pill, or if you'd just started taking the pill, it might not have been effective yet."

That would explain it. She hadn't really listened to the warnings about using backup contraceptives when the pharmacist dispensed the pills, because at that time she was only taking them to clear up her skin. But recently she'd had a bout of strep throat and had to take antibiotics.

She buried her face in her hands. "I can't believe I let this happen."

"You are way too hard on yourself, young lady," Marissa said softly.

Kaitlyn pulled her hands away and tried to figure out why Marissa was going so easy on her. "What do you mean?"

"If you're worried about what I think or don't think—or anyone here, for that matter—you can just let it go."

"I suppose you see a lot."

"It's not about that. We're here to help people get ready for the biggest joy of their lives. Whatever circumstances bring them in can't compare to the joy of the future." Marissa dipped her head to catch Kaitlyn's eye. "There *is* a future, and it's going to be good."

Kaitlyn managed a slight nod. "I almost didn't come here."

"Why not?" Marissa's head tilted.

"Because I figured this was a place for younger girls. I thought I'd feel out of place."

"We have all kinds of clients. Over time, you might even get to know some of them." She leaned back in her chair. "In addition to confidential pregnancy testing and counseling, we offer ongoing services too. In fact, our boutique—as I like to call it—is expanding daily. There are all kinds of maternity clothes, baby clothes, diapers—basically everything a new mom needs. We're really excited about it."

Kaitlyn took a deep breath—partly to settle her stomach and partly to steel her nerves. She glanced at the cup on the counter and willed it to come out negative. Though the services New Heights offered sounded great, more than anything she wished she could unwind the last few months and not even have need of them. Anxiety swirled in her chest and her heart started to race.

Marissa rose and crossed the office to an armoire that doubled as a counter. "Before we go any further, let's see what the test says."

Kaitlyn knew she was too old to cross her fingers and too far removed from God to pray, so all she could do was hold her breath and hope for the best. It was like sitting on a roller coaster and hoping all the nuts and bolts had been tightened because what you were about to experience was completely out of your control.

Marissa kept her back to Kaitlyn for a few moments until she was finished. Then she washed her hands and returned to the desk, a smile affixed to her face.

Kaitlyn's heart turned to dust. "Positive?"

"Congratulations—you're going to have a baby."

Tears formed in her eyes and fell fast and freely. It didn't matter that Kaitlyn already knew. Hearing it from a professional launched her situation into a whole new level of bad. She gripped the armrests of the chair and forced herself to calm down. Forced her heart to slow. Forced common sense to prevail.

She was a grown woman. She could handle this.

Marissa ripped tissues from the box, walked around the desk, and kneeled next to her. She placed a comforting arm around her, so unlike the reaction that came from Sydney—the only other person who knew. Kaitlyn squirmed but took the tissues. "I'm sorry. I don't mean to overreact."

"There's no such thing. Your body is going through so many changes right now, and you have a lot on your mind. What's happening is perfectly normal. It's okay to feel this way. It's okay to cry."

Kaitlyn pressed the tissues to her face and wept. Wept until her face tingled and her nose ran. Marissa waited patiently, hugging and murmuring reassurances that Kaitlyn found strangely comforting. Her breath hitched when she inhaled, reminding her of when she was a child and cried so hard over—what?—she couldn't even remember. Her mom had comforted her and held her tightly until the drama was over. . .and now she'd have a child of her own to do the same.

"This doesn't seem real." Kaitlyn sat up and squeezed the tissues.

"It'll take some time to sink in. Every day will get a little easier, until finally you realize a whole day has gone by without worrying, and instead you're making plans and preparing for your little bundle."

"That's just it—I can't make plans."

"You don't have to right now." Marissa paused while she resumed her position behind her desk. "You still have a few months."

Kaitlyn chuckled. "Really, I can't. I know this sounds awful, but the baby's father. . ." She stopped speaking before she revealed too much. Colin wouldn't want her to say anything, and if they got back together and he found out. . .

"What?" A question without judgment. "Is he in the picture?"

She never thought she'd be in this position, especially at her age. She wasn't a young teen who didn't know better, who came from a broken home where no one cared or had concern for her life. Quite the opposite. And things like this just weren't supposed to happen.

Kaitlyn pulled back and dabbed her nose. "He's not, at least not at the moment."

"I hope things work out for you." The sincerity in Marissa's eyes nearly extracted the truth from Kaitlyn—about everything. But logic prevailed.

"It's possible. We haven't been together very long, but it was going well." She worked the tissue between nervous fingers. "I know that kids do better with both parents in the home."

"Generally, yes."

"This wasn't the kind of situation I was hoping for. None of this is. I'm not. . .like this." She caught herself standing in judgment of the women who had come to New Heights before her then thought better of it. She glanced around the office that was decorated more like a nineteenth-century parlor with frilly lace curtains and delicate furniture. Like they should be having tea instead of discussing the fatherless future of her unborn child. She drew a fortifying breath. "What I mean is, I'd never. . ."

Understanding illuminated Marissa's eyes. "It still might work out."

"Only if I could get ahold of him to talk. He won't return my calls." The embarrassment stung, as did the realization that perhaps their relationship wasn't what she'd assumed. What if he really had used her? What if she was one of dozens of students he'd had a relationship with over the years and that's why it was so important to him to keep it quiet?

No. She couldn't go there. That wasn't who Colin was. He was a professor at the university, for crying out loud. Men in his position just didn't do things like that. When she finally saw him again face-to-face, he'd come to his senses.

Besides, once she had the conversation with her parents—if something so unsettling could even be called that—she was probably going to have to drop out of school. They'd already threatened to cut her off when her grades had slipped. Just like when she'd quit school the first time. Honestly, she was glad for it because their financial support had always made her uncomfortably obligated.

At this point it didn't matter. What mattered was appealing to Colin's responsible side—only that wasn't how she wanted to win him back. She wanted him to be with her because he wanted to be, not because he had to be. Knowing him, that was exactly how he'd feel. Then she'd never know if he was with her for their relationship or just for the baby.

Kaitlyn chided herself for allowing her thoughts to skip ahead. First, she just needed him to return her texts and get together.

"Are you saying he doesn't know he's going to be a father?" For the first time since Kaitlyn had entered the office, Marissa looked worried.

"No. I was going to tell him last night, but he never came."

"I'm sorry." Marissa's hand covered hers in a comforting gesture.

Kaitlyn smiled bravely. She wanted to think of Marissa as more of a friend than someone who had to coddle her. Besides, a woman like Marissa probably didn't know how hard it was to hold a relationship together. Every day she saw Marissa and her husband at The Bean, always looking perfectly happy. In fact, she was pretty sure she saw him working in the next room when she came in.

That must be what real love looked like.

And it forced her to realize that she'd given herself to a man who apparently didn't care for her at all.

Marissa walked back to her desk and glanced at her computer screen. Her face lit with excitement. "Look at this—according to the date you gave me, you're going to have a Christmas baby!"

# CHAPTER 13

*Marissa*

Over the next few weeks Colin was home more often, sometimes engaging with me and sometimes not. But he was always sullen and more than a little testy. Every time I spoke, he snapped at me then quickly apologized and tried to make up. It didn't matter that he was physically present and trying to behave like a husband, because his moodiness raised my suspicion infinitely more than his long absences and secretive texting.

I marched into Tristan's office and stuck out my hand. "Give me your keys."

He slid his reading glasses off his nose. "No please or thank you?"

I snapped my fingers and motioned for his keys. This was something I had to do before I lost my nerve.

Tristan's eyes slivered, and he raked me with his gaze. "If you need to go somewhere, I'd be happy to take you."

"Not likely."

"What's wrong with your car?"

"Besides the fact that it's barely chugging along, you know exactly what's wrong with it—Colin will recognize it. But I like your offer, so let's go." I loved that I didn't have to remind him what this was about. At least I was spared that indignity.

He remained motionless. The tick of the clock on the mantel more than measured the time—it measured the depth of our friendship. The way he scrutinized me revealed his conflict. Was he being a better friend by reeling me back from the cliff? Or was he being a better friend by driving off the cliff with me? I appreciated his thoughtfulness, but what I really wanted was his cooperation.

"Is there any way I can talk you out of it?" He shifted, causing his swivel chair to squeal.

I folded my arms. "Are you new here?" My bravado was a sham, but at this moment it was all I had. How far had I sunk that I had to resort to high school tactics to keep tabs on my husband?

Tristan stood, and not for the first time did I wish that my husband was as responsive as my best friend. "Wait for me in the lobby. I'll just be a minute."

I went out and fluffed the decorative pillows on the couch while I waited.

Christina stuffed her phone inside her school bag, shut off the computer, and closed the blinds. "Sorry I didn't get a chance to clean the boutique today."

"Busier than usual around here." I fanned the magazines on the coffee table.

"I know, right? We have new moms coming out our ears." Christina chuckled, her red curls bouncing. "Must be something in the water."

I stopped cold. Caught my breath.

Clearly I'd been drinking the wrong water.

"Is everything okay?" Christina paused, hand on the doorknob.

"Fine." I forced the lie. Usually I was so good at smiling through the disappointment, but today my cycle started again along with the predictable riptide of emotions. Hope and disappointment, the evil twins that haunted me monthly.

"Cool." She opened the door but paused. "By the way, is there any chance you'll be hiring again soon? We sort of need the help. I didn't really want to ask because I didn't want you to think I wasn't keeping up."

"No—you're doing great. Don't be afraid to come to me when you have concerns."

She brightened. "Thanks. So. . .will we be hiring? One of the clients was mentioning she needs a second job."

"Who's that?"

"Kaitlyn. She didn't ask for a job here, but I was just thinking she'd be a good fit, that is, if you're hiring."

Kaitlyn hadn't mentioned to me that she needed a second job, but it made sense that she wouldn't want me to think she was fishing around. I really admired that. "You're right, we do need help." I grabbed my purse and keys. "Tristan and I will talk it over."

"Did someone call my name?" Tristan emerged from his office just as Christina left the house.

"Let's go." I ushered him out the door.

"Where are we heading?" he asked after we situated ourselves in his nondescript beige car, which was perfect for my purposes.

"The baseball fields." I slid on my sunglasses.

"On second thought, take a walk with me." He climbed out of the car and waited for me on the sidewalk. I could see he wasn't going to make this easy, so I complied. "You know he'll still recognize you," Tristan said as we started on our usual route down the sidewalk.

"Funny."

"No, dead serious." He picked up the pace and forced me to keep up. "You do realize, don't you, that this will only make things worse."

"Only if he sees us."

"No guarantees that he won't."

I scoffed. "There are no guarantees about anything." Including marriage, children, and happily ever after.

"You seem a little upset." His tone left the door wide open for a lengthy explanation.

But despite the fact he was my oldest friend, offering more information on what was really bothering me would be oversharing.

"Look, a squirrel." I pointed.

He shot me a look of patient disbelief. "Let me get this straight. You've been a little tetchy all day and now you want me to help you spy on your husband, all because nothing is bothering you?"

I uttered a sound that neither confirmed nor denied his statement. I was good at that.

"If there's nothing wrong, then why would we go to the field to spy on your husband?"

"Because the sky is clear. It's a perfect day to see him. Please, it won't take long." I slowed down in front of the dentist's office and ignored the fact that if my best friend was a woman, we'd already be at the field. "Practice ends sometime between six and seven, then you can get home and do whatever it is you do at night." We turned the corner onto a street that afforded us more privacy.

"What exactly are you looking for?"

"I'm not sure. But I'll know it when I see it."

"Do you think some mysterious woman will suddenly wrap her arms around him right there in broad daylight?" He shoulder-bumped me.

"That sure would make it easier."

"Humor—your coping mechanism of choice."

"You should try it sometime. It works pretty well." I wrinkled my nose at him, both frustrated and comfortable that he knew me so well. "Look, I'm not sure how I'll know. When I see her—I'll feel it."

"It only happens that way in movies."

I stopped in front of the bakery just as they were closing shop. The concern that radiated from him nearly melted me. Why couldn't my own husband care for me like this? Tristan pulled me into a gentle embrace, full of strength and comfort.

"It'll be okay. One way or another—you'll work through this." His soothing tone crushed my barriers, and in that moment I felt way more for him than I ever should. Was that what happened to Colin? Did he have a close female confidant who got carried away? My heart stung at the thought.

Funny thing was, I knew Tristan felt too much and always had. Though our friendship never crossed the line—not even with a peck on the cheek—the way he thought highly of me and took care of me and tried to warn me off Colin in the first place all pointed to his true feelings. Even the fact he never settled down with anyone told me what I needed to know. The signs were there, but for years I'd ignored them. Just as I would now.

I wanted his friendship—needed it, actually—but without complications.

Slowly, I pulled away feeling suddenly colder than I had in his arms. But the summer breeze soon warmed me as we resumed our walk. I couldn't look Tristan in the eyes, knowing what it might cost me. Instead I focused on the sidewalk and the weeds springing through the cracks. "Thanks for talking me off the ledge."

"Does that mean you're not going to go?" He shoved his hands into his pockets and jangled his keys.

"My mind is made up. I'm tired of being a wimp. I want to take action, and this is the only way I know how." My shoulders drew tight as I tried to anticipate what would come next. "I'd still like it if you came with me."

"Do you really believe he's having an affair?"

"No." *Yes.* I grimaced. "I don't know. And before you bag on me for not just talking to him, let it be known that I've tried. More times than I can count."

"You asked him straight out if he's seeing someone." Tristan flashed me a knowing look.

I ignored the intensity of his gaze. "Of course not."

"Why?"

"Because I was afraid of his answer," I blurted before I could stop myself.

Several beats passed in silence. We rounded the corner and approached New Heights before he spoke. "If he is, won't it hurt just as badly to find out this way?"

"No," I said, searching my heart for truth. "Because I'd have you with me."

With sadness tingeing his eyes, Tristan shook his head, handed me his keys, and walked away.

It was just as well that Tristan didn't go with me because as much as I trusted him, I really didn't want him to see me at my worst. If my suspicions proved right, that was exactly how this mission would end.

I parked behind the boulders on the west side of the field. The blinding sun would hide me in the shadows if anyone should happen to look my direction, which was unlikely. The baseball fields were alive with kids and coaches, parents and pets.

Sunlight glinted off Colin's hair, the color of rick, dark chocolate. His sturdy shoulders and powerful muscles worked beneath his dress shirt. It appeared he hadn't had time to change after work. He loosened his tie, clearly aggravated at the way the last play went down, but his stern expression along with the whiskers dusting his face suited him.

With a pang in my chest I remembered the powerful attraction that first brought us together.

Even now I could watch him all day, the way he explained the proper stance to one of his players with his legs splayed and his bottom pressed against his slacks.

I scanned the faces of the women near the field. A cute redhead, a slightly overweight blond, and a curvaceous brunette wearing just enough to keep her from being arrested were the ones who seemed the most interested. They had to be mothers of the boys.

This seemed like a logical place for Colin to meet and interact with other women in our age group. Unease settled in the core of my stomach. It had never occurred to me when he signed up to coach that I'd need to look out for the mothers.

Maybe he was attracted to women he knew could conceive.

*Lord, help me to quit comparing. Help me know Your peace. I know You've got this.*

After watching Colin interact with the kids, an ache formed in my stomach. He reminded me of the old Colin, the man I fell in love with. The man who was surprisingly romantic, a scientist who recited sonnets and frolicked with me at the beach. But more than that it made me realize how long it had been since he'd been this way at home.

I was determined to change that, starting as soon as I knew he wasn't dallying with one of these women.

None of the mothers appeared overly suspicious during the rest of practice. Tristan was right—no one threw themselves at my husband in broad daylight. The brunette, however, made a point of tossing her hair and giggling loudly enough to catch everyone's attention from here to Phoenix. I searched Colin's face and posture for a reaction.

Oddly enough, he didn't have one.

Everyone started clearing off the field by six fifteen, more than an hour earlier than my husband ever appeared at home. My suspicions peaked. Where did he go after practice three times a week? Did he usually leave the field with someone? Did I really want to know?

The brunette was the last parent there, and as I could've predicted, she cornered my husband. But she didn't stop there—she moved on to Adam and continued to make animated conversation, hands gesticulating wildly.

Adam stonewalled her, and then she drifted back to Colin while her son kicked at the dirt, seemingly embarrassed by his flirtatious mother. Colin stood closer to her, mirroring a few of her gestures. She tossed her hair then laughed.

I leaned forward and swallowed hard. Would Colin be so bold as to leave with this woman and her son. . .in front of Adam? Surely not. Adam and his wife, Lani, were friends of ours, and there was no way he would keep that kind of secret from me.

I held my breath, scared to see what came next but too afraid to look away.

Suddenly, Adam glanced up and caught sight of me despite the glaring sunlight I'd hoped would keep me hidden. He froze, and his gaze bounced between me and Colin.

My heart slid down my spine. I put my finger to my lips, and Adam silently acknowledged me. I slid back into the shadows and debated my next move.

The last thing I needed was for Adam to out me. But he was Colin's best friend, and as honorable as he was, I knew where his loyalty lay. How would I explain to my husband why I was lurking in the forest above his practice? There was no reasonable explanation. Even in my desperate state, I knew that much.

I slunk back to Tristan's car and backed out of the cramped space. I prayed no one else saw me and that Adam would keep my secret.

As much as I wanted to see where Colin was going, I didn't have the fortitude to follow. Instead, I drove to Tristan's house and traded cars, and mercifully he didn't ask what happened.

At home, I puttered around the kitchen and heated up last night's lasagna, then tossed a salad and set the table. More than an hour passed with no word from Colin.

What if he left with the brunette? What if Adam told him I was there and he came home furious? Or worse, what if he came home and tiptoed around me as though nothing were wrong?

That would mean the worst thing of all—that I really was as fragile as everyone assumed.

# CHAPTER 14

*Colin*

It was almost eight o'clock before Colin realized how late he was for dinner. Work had gone from consuming to obsessive. He sped home, determined to make something of the evening. Only, when he walked through the door, the disappointment on Marissa's face nearly broke him. She smiled with a seemingly painful effort.

He'd once heard a pastor say you could tell if a woman knew she was loved by the look on her face. At the time he'd dismissed the pastor's ridiculous words since he didn't put much stock in preachers, but it all came crashing back on him now as Marissa's lips quivered. He didn't need to see the worry lines around her eyes to know he was a miserable failure.

"Have a seat. I'll fix your plate." She eased away from him before he could kiss her. He'd waited too long.

He caught Marissa by the arm and spun her back to face him. He leaned forward and brushed her lips. They seemed foreign, cold. Not the mouth of the same woman who'd set fire to his heart so many years ago. He willed the feelings to come back but knew it would take more than a kiss, a dinner, a year's worth of loving to resurrect the feelings that were as dead as his latest experiment back at the lab.

"Sorry I'm late." His keys rattled when he tossed them onto the table in the hall. "Time got away from me. I went back to work after practice." He was quick to explain, sounding guilty even to his own ears. Why did the guilt slay him now, when he'd actually stopped violating his vows?

Adam—it was because Adam talked to him again at the field after Tommy's mom had finally left. The way his friend pleaded with him to come clean with Marissa had only stabbed him in all the raw places he'd conveniently closed off over the last two months. He never should have told Adam. He'd had to explain all over again why it was a bad idea to tell his wife about—

Colin choked as unbidden images of Kaitlyn shot to the forefront of his thoughts. Kaitlyn in all her innocence and acceptance, loving him simply for who he was. Never asking, never assuming, never demanding more than he could give. Making him feel more like a man than he had in years.

Marissa's eyes searched him, probing as though she wanted to believe. "You must be under a lot of pressure."

He nodded. "Dr. Crank and the members of the tenure committee are watching everything I do. But I'm making progress." Never mind that his experiment was a bust, which set his research back to square one.

"Maybe one of these days I can stop by and take you to lunch." The hope on her face crushed him.

He didn't want to say no, but he hated the thought of having her on campus. That was his sanctuary, the place he went to feel like he mattered and was making a contribution. He pushed back the fear that Marissa would hear a suspicious remark having to do with Kaitlyn.

He'd done a good job keeping his relationship a secret. There were a few raised eyebrows when Kaitlyn came during his office hours in the early days, but she'd been quick to learn that he needed to keep his private life completely separate from his work life. He was more comfortable that way. And the same applied to Marissa.

Colin cleared his throat. "How about if I stop by New Heights and take you to lunch? It would do me some good to get off campus." The suggestion burned his tongue. The last time he walked into New Heights, Tristan was all chummy with his wife. He'd wanted to set Marissa's so-called friend in place, but he kept his trap shut. He always sucked it up when it came to Tristan because he didn't like friction.

"That'll be nice. We could try the new deli around the corner." Marissa nodded, her reaction void of joy or relief, or anything else he wanted to see.

Maybe she was more perceptive than he'd given her credit for. Had she noticed something amiss in his behavior? He'd covered all his tracks, even going so far as to label Kaitlyn's cell phone number with Adam's name, just in case Marissa ever saw a call come through. He shrugged off the thought. Guilt was playing with his mind, plain and simple. There was no reason to feel bad now that he'd come to his senses.

Adam was wrong on all levels. Telling Marissa would only dredge up what was best left buried. He may have strayed, but he came back. Kaitlyn was only a brief interlude in his life, and even if he and Marissa never relit the fire they had in the beginning, he would keep his vows and protect his fragile wife from his indiscretions.

Since Kaitlyn was out of his life, there was no need to send Marissa over the cliff. Not when she'd been fighting so hard just to cling to the ledge.

# CHAPTER 15

*Marissa*

It took more than a week for Colin to fulfill his promise of lunch, and even then it was sandwiches and sodas, the blandness of which perfectly matched our marriage.

"The clinic looks good." Colin craned his neck, noticing the paint on the eaves for the first time.

"It's a house, not a clinic."

"Right. Sorry." He pulled back like a turtle into its shell. Only then did I realize I'd snipped when I hadn't meant to. He was only trying to make conversation on an otherwise silent walk back to New Heights.

Maybe he wasn't having an affair and the problems really came down to me. My issues. I no longer thought of our infertility as *our* issue, not since Colin had given up trying. If only he realized I was doing it for him. Always for him. The only thing he'd talked about since we married was starting a family. The grief over the miscarriage had never really ended, even though I knew my baby was in God's loving hands. But the disappointment over not being able to conceive since was still crushing.

I hesitated before touching the hem of his sleeve. "I didn't mean to be grumpy." Or morose or dull or any number of things I'd been during lunch. I searched his moss-colored eyes. Sometimes I could still see the man I married reflected in those eyes. Sometimes I could still see myself.

Colin's smile was strained. "I understand."

In that moment, I believed he did, and though I wanted to melt into his arms and be the couple we used to be, I didn't dare. Instead, I inched closer. "I'm really glad you came by. Would you like to come inside? We've made a ton of improvements since you were here."

He hesitated long enough that I knew no matter what he said, he wanted to leave. To be anywhere but in the same building as Tristan.

Before Colin could answer, I let him off the hook. "You're probably busy."

"Incredibly." The light returned to his eyes. A breeze tousled his hair, and more than anything I wanted to reach out and smooth it into place. He offered a genuine smile. "Hey, soon I can take long lunches, just like the big boys."

"I'm really proud of you. It's been a long time coming." I edged toward the front door, the awkward exchange reminding me more of a dating couple, unsure where they stood with each other and how far to take the moment—except without the hope that the other person might really want them. I only had the hope that my husband wasn't actually planning to leave me for someone else. Someone younger.

Someone fertile.

Dutifully, Colin leaned over and pecked my cheek. "I'll see you at home."

"I'll be waiting," I said, then immediately wished I hadn't. The desperation hung between us, separating us like an invisible wedge. I wanted to ask him to call if he was going to be late until I realized I didn't even know what late was. For the last few months, late was normal, just like him not answering his cell phone was normal and avoiding eye contact when he walked through the door was normal. And him not touching me in the night unless I forced the issue was sadly, perfectly normal.

Sweet relief filled my lungs when I walked inside New Heights. It wasn't just a refuge for mothers in crisis. It was a refuge for me. A place where I could throw myself into other people's lives and work with them until their fear turned to joy. It satisfied so many longings inside me, yet now it pained me on the same level.

"Christina, I'll be in my office. If anyone calls, can you take a message? I'll need a few minutes alone." I breezed past her and prayed she didn't notice my glassy eyes or the tightness in my voice.

Behind the closed door, I released a deep breath. Relief and pain. Relief and pain. There was only one way to move forward, a way that I'd been avoiding for years. This was a last resort, and the possibility of it not working crushed me like an anvil. It would really mean that

I'd tried everything and failed.

Before I could second-guess myself, I dialed the number. A number I knew by heart. A number I'd dialed a hundred times before hanging up after the first ring. I bit my lip, waiting. One ring. Two. Three.

"Highland Fertility Clinic, may I help you?"

When I finally emerged from my office, Kaitlyn was waiting for me in the lobby. "Oh, hi. It's nice to see you."

She seemed puzzled. "Did I come at the wrong time?"

I glanced at the clock on the far wall and a tiny memory jolted inside me. "Goodness, I forgot. I don't know what's gotten into me. Come on in." I ushered her into my office for the interview we'd set up yesterday during my morning coffee run. "I hope I didn't keep you waiting long."

"Did I catch you at a bad time? I can come back." She motioned to the closed door, her tone unassuming.

"Of course not." I sighed, shoulders slumped, as I took a seat behind my desk. "It's been a bit chaotic."

"I know how that goes." Her book bag dropped to the floor with a thud as she situated herself.

My promise to help her in every way I could came rushing back. I issued a practiced smile. "But that's no reason for us to postpone. I hear you're looking for another part-time job."

"Not too many hours, but I could sure use the extra income."

"Did they reduce your hours at The Bean?" So many businesses were barely skimping by, making cuts to stay afloat. I'd heard it multiple times from the young mothers who came in and needed referrals to social services.

"No. In fact, they're bumping me up, thankfully."

"Are you sure you can handle an extra job, along with school and The Bean?" I hoped concern translated in my question, not judgment. "I think you'd be a perfect fit here, but I am concerned about your health foremost."

She nodded stiffly. "I don't have much of a choice right now." She hesitated as if debating how much to share. I liked that about her. She never spilled her guts or threw a pity party, but instead looked for ways to help herself and forge ahead.

How could the father of her baby leave her to fend for herself? What kind of idiot man would do that?

Kaitlyn cleared her throat and fussed with the hem of her tank top. "My roommate moved home to Mountainside for the summer, and my parents aren't picking up the extra expenses this year because of my grades. But I never expected them to," she added quickly. "It's something they always offered. It's totally fine, though." She looked away. "I can handle it."

"Of course you can. And if it gets to be too much, you can always cut down." I leaned back, hoping to put her at ease. "Are you getting over your fatigue and morning sickness?"

Her nose wrinkled. "Not really. I feel like sleeping all the time." She held up her hand. "But I won't let that interfere with work."

"I'm not asking as a boss. I'm asking as a friend." Oddly enough, that's what I was starting to think of her as—a friend. Never before in my career had I crossed the line. Professional relations only, without the personal involvement. Mostly. But there was something about Kaitlyn that was different, an emotional maturity that I wanted in a friend. And there was the small fact that, aside from my mother, I was without female friends altogether.

Her face relaxed a fraction at a time. "I'm exhausted."

"Fatigue is pretty normal in the first trimester. It's not easy making a whole new person." I winked to lighten the moment. "Have you been taking care of yourself? Taking your prenatal vitamins?" I could tell by the way she rolled her lip under her teeth that she hadn't been. Not entirely uncommon for mothers without a support system at home. "Do you have an OB or midwife picked out yet? I think I gave you a referral last time." Unlike me, she probably hadn't had a midwife in mind for several years ahead of time, just in case.

"I've looked at a few, but I haven't made the call." Her sheepish expression told me she likely hadn't done much investigating whatsoever.

But we had that in common and my heart was soft toward her. How long had I waited to make an appointment at the fertility clinic? And I wasn't proud to admit that I made the appointment two months out—which gave me plenty of time to reconsider.

But Kaitlyn didn't have that luxury. I tried to keep my tone strong but gentle. "You need to see a doctor. It's for your benefit, and the benefit of your baby. I'm sure a lot of things seem overwhelming right now, but the baby will be here before you know it."

Kaitlyn rubbed her forehead and squeezed her eyes. "You're right. My to-do list grows longer every day. But to be honest, the number one thing I need to take care of is getting another job." She studied her hands in her lap. "I had to drop out of school, and I really need to cobble together full-time hours." The sad undercurrent in her voice was haunting. It was obvious she was disappointed in herself.

"Oh, Kaitlyn. I'm sorry." Briefly I considered asking Colin what kind of help was available for students like Kaitlyn, but he was so busy lately I didn't dare add to his workload, even with a simple question. Who else did I know who could help? I pulled out the stash of business cards I'd accumulated from various networking events and Chamber of Commerce meetings over the years. "Maybe you can still enroll for the fall. It'll be cutting it close with your due date, but it's been done before."

She seemed to weigh my words. "No matter what, I will go back for spring semester. I'm not giving up."

"Excellent. I have some great childcare providers I can recommend." My fingers sifted through the cards. "What are you majoring in?"

"Accounting."

That was the last thing I expected to hear, considering she was much more of a people person than other accountant-types I knew.

The tension around her eyes eased as she talked about academics. "My family was surprised too, but you know what I like? I like that numbers are predictable. I like that one plus one always equals two." She issued a deep sigh. "I guess that makes my recent choices even stranger."

I reached out and covered her hand with mine. "Give yourself some grace. We all do things we later wish we'd done differently. But good things really will come from this." I swallowed hard, praying she would begin to experience the joy of the tiny life growing inside her.

She nodded absently. "I'll have to take your word for it."

"I've seen it a hundred times." I sat straight and slid back into work mode. We hadn't discussed duties, hours, or pay, but somehow it didn't matter. What mattered was that Kaitlyn was a good fit and a conscientious person. What mattered was my promise to do everything I could to help her. "So, how soon can you start?"

# CHAPTER 16

*Kaitlyn*

Kaitlyn wasn't sure if she was more excited or scared about having a new job—correction, a second job. In fact, the only thing she was certain about was that she'd graduated to a new level of confusion.

She pasted on a cheerful smile and entered New Heights—this time as an employee, not a client. Hiring her had to be some kind of breach of protocol, so she was determined not to let Marissa down.

"I'm here," she announced.

"Thank goodness! I need backup. Let me show you around." Christina chattered away and urged Kaitlyn into the kitchen, which was decorated much like the rest of the house with vintage knickknacks and doilies. "We use the kitchen as a break room so we can keep our purses and whatnot out of the way. Usually we leave snacks and tea out for the clients, but you can also have whatever's in here."

There was something about New Heights that made pregnancy seem. . .not so scary. Well, it was still terrifying to think of being responsible for a tiny baby, especially if Colin didn't come around soon. But the overwhelming peace at New Heights at least made her feel less alone, like she had a chance of having a baby and not completely messing it up.

Christina leaned against the counter. "You look nervous."

"Is it that obvious?" She set her book bag on the table, reluctant to give up the one thing that hid her growing belly. Of course she wasn't really showing yet, but she still felt the need to wear baggier clothes to hide her sins.

"You'll be fine. Marissa thinks you'll be a great fit here or she wouldn't have hired you."

"I guess so." She paused, wondering how many of her private fears were safe to reveal to a virtual stranger. And yet, the warmth in

Christina's eyes showed a maturity and understanding beyond her obvious early twentysomething years. "What if I don't know what to say to the mothers or don't know how to help them? I mean, I don't even know how to help myself."

Christina gave a sweet chuckle. "First of all, relax. Most of your interaction with the moms will be in the boutique—that's what Marissa is calling the donation corner. For the most part you'll be helping the girls pick out items they can use for their babies, or maternity clothes—that type of thing. C'mon, I'll show you."

Together, they left the kitchen and went into what must've been a separate dining room when the house had been lived in, judging from the chandelier sparkling overhead in the late morning sunlight. The east-facing window let in a lot of warmth—something Kaitlyn was becoming all too sensitive toward lately. She shed her lightweight cardigan, though it did little to diffuse the heat wave.

"Let me get the shade pulled," Christina said, as though reading her thoughts. "Sometimes I forget how hot it feels when you're pregnant."

"You mean, you have a baby?" That would explain a lot, like the way Christina had always seemed so relaxed.

A slow smile spread across the younger woman's face and her eyes turned teary. "I did. Last year I gave birth to a baby girl. Seven pounds, two ounces, and the most perfect head of soft, fuzzy hair I ever saw." She cast a glance out the window as she slowly let down the shade. "But as much as I wanted to, I couldn't keep her. I knew I was making the right decision."

"I'm sorry." Kaitlyn wished she had something to fiddle with to keep her stupid nerves in check.

"Don't be." Christina's face brightened. "Sometimes giving a baby up for adoption is the most loving thing a mother can do. I was only seventeen at the time, and I knew I couldn't care for a baby, no matter how much support I had. The father didn't want to have anything to do with us, and I needed to finish high school. I wish I'd known about New Heights back then, but I probably still would've made the same decision."

Christina was even younger than she appeared. Kaitlyn palmed her shoulder. "It looks like you're doing a great job helping people who're having a hard time."

"I'm still new, but it really feels like I'm doing something that matters, even though I mostly answer phones and set appointments."

"Honestly, you made me comfortable the first time I came in. That means a lot—you know, first impressions and all."

"Good to hear." The teen's grin widened. "Anyhoo, I think you're supposed to start by sorting all the stuff in here." She motioned around the piles of clothing, diapers, baby trinkets, blankets, and other assorted contraptions that Kaitlyn couldn't begin to identify. "Last week one of the department stores donated a bunch of racks and plastic hangers, so now we'll have more room to hang clothes."

"So I need to hang and sort?"

"I think so. I'll let Marissa explain when she's finished with her client. She'll have a better idea what she wants done." The phone in the living room rang. "I'll leave you to it. Let me know if you have any questions."

Kaitlyn perused the stacks. Evidently someone had attempted to sort and organize the piles of donations, but the mountain of clothing remained. She picked up a pair of enormous faded denim overalls with stretchy elastic at the sides. Was this what she'd be wearing in a few months? She'd never been overly particular about fashion, but wow, this wasn't what she'd expected at all. She grabbed a plastic hanger and hung the item on a rack in the corner.

Next she picked up a tiny hat and booties set and marveled at the size. Could a human be that small at birth? It was hard to imagine. As an only child, she had zero experience with babies or kids of any size. She placed the set to the side until she could figure out what to do since those obviously wouldn't go on a rack.

While she worked, Christina's story buzzed through her head. Adoption. Maybe that was the solution to her problem—though she hesitated to think of the tiny life inside her as a problem, per se. Since Colin hadn't returned her calls or texts, and she hadn't bothered to try again in the last week, the hope she had in him was fading. Fast.

But somehow she had to confront him. He at least deserved to know what he was really giving up. It wasn't just about her, and it wasn't just about him. It was about the tiny life nestled inside her that they had made together.

Kaitlyn steadied her nerves as she stepped out of her car and popped a few coins into the metered parking. Her mission wouldn't take but a few minutes. The quicker she got it over with, the quicker she could start making decisions for the future. If Colin wanted to be part of it, fine. If not. . .well, she could handle it, especially now that she had help from Marissa and the people at New Heights.

The campus was eerily quiet with only the occasional summer student strolling by, nose to smartphone, and a few hotshot guys tossing a football on the grassy square, swearing and carrying on like kings of the world.

No wonder she'd been attracted to an older man. He'd been a welcome relief from the usual crowd—selfish and immature, eyes on the weekend instead of planning a life. She and Colin had never gotten that far, but they would have if he hadn't gotten cold feet because of his stupid job.

She worked the rim of her silver keychain—a gift from Colin—between nervous fingers as she stood in the shadow of the brick building. Angry bees swarmed inside her gut and made her second-guess having shared enchiladas with Marissa at lunch. She placed her hand on her stomach and willed it to settle.

Everything would be better in a few minutes.

She'd tell Colin and he'd come to his senses—or not—and life would carry on.

A sharp intake of air propelled her through the front doors. So what if she was there? She had every right to be since she was a student, or at least she would be when she reenrolled after she had the baby and got back into life.

The air-conditioning sputtered overhead inside the building that smelled like musty old pages from a stack of books. The smell of education, as she'd come to think of it. She turned to her left and climbed the red-tiled stairs that curved toward the biology department, each step stronger than the last.

A doddering, sweater-vested man ambled down, barely giving her a passing glance. She recognized him as another biology professor, aka Colin's coworker. Colin would be livid if he saw them anywhere near the same vicinity.

She bit her lip and forged ahead, hand gripping the wooden banister. It was Colin's own fault for not calling her back. If they were still officially together, she'd be more careful, but he didn't have the right to tell her where she should and shouldn't be.

At the top of the landing, she caught her breath. The glass double doors separated her from the office area. It was her last chance to bail.

Colin poked his head out of his office and her nerves buzzed. She stood, frozen, as he said something to the student worker manning the desk. He glanced her direction and his face turned to stone.

Anger muscled over fear inside her. Kaitlyn raised her eyebrow in a challenge and remained in place. Let him come to her.

Colin's cheeks reddened. His gaze skipped over her as he resumed talking to the student worker. Just as hope deflated in Kaitlyn's chest, Colin hustled toward the door and silently motioned for her to step back.

She angled out of view and backed down the staircase just enough to stay out of the student worker's line of sight.

Colin closed the door and joined her. "What are you doing here?" he demanded, his tone husky and raw. He peered around the curve of the staircase to ensure their privacy. "I told you before—"

"If you had returned my calls, I wouldn't have come." She ground her teeth and met his threatening gaze.

"There's no reason for us to talk." His hand sliced through the air for emphasis.

"You have no idea." She swallowed. Tears bit her eyes but she refused to let them fall. She didn't want to soften his heart with tears, which in her mind equaled manipulation. She wanted him to feel the same rush of emotions for her that she felt for him. It had to be buried inside him …somewhere. "Can we talk?" She searched the depth of his eyes for the old Colin. The one who lavished attention on her and told her she meant the world to him. The one who made up silly sonnets that made her both laugh and cry. "Please."

He looked away, his eyes darting between her, the staircase, and the office behind him. The lines around his eyes lost their hard edge, and he rubbed the bridge of his nose as though stalling until he could figure out what to say. His conflicted expression filled her with courage.

"I'm not a student anymore," she blurted. It was easier than saying the rest of the truth, and maybe it gave her a shot with him. After all, that's why he said they couldn't be together. Maybe now they could have a relationship out in the open, and she could win him back without resorting to telling him about the baby first. If that was the only reason he came back to her, she'd never know if he really had feelings for her— or if he was only there because of his sense of duty.

Surprise darkened his features, but he said nothing.

"That's good news, right?" Her voice sounded feeble, even to her. She stopped before she said anything that would come across as begging.

"I trust you made a choice that's in *your* best interest. I don't understand it, but I—good luck." His neck bobbed with a hard swallow.

"Maybe you can reconsider, you know. . ."

He shook his head. "I told you where I stand."

The truth smacked her. "Does that mean that everything you said was a lie?" His words came rushing back to her. The sweet words of encouragement and consideration that made her feel like more than just an undergrad, more than just another face in the crowd. He really saw her and made her feel like a competent woman who could literally do anything. Those few brief months had changed her entire image of herself, and now it was disintegrating like the last moments of a remembered dream.

The tightness around his eyes returned. "I can't talk about this here—"

"Then let's go somewhere—"

He held up a hand to silence her. "I can't talk anywhere." He threw a glance over his shoulder at the office and lowered his voice. "My feelings were real, but it's over. Over. I won't change my mind." He backed up the staircase. "But I wish you the best. Really. You have a great life ahead, and one day you'll forget all about me."

"Dr. Kimball." An older man leaned out of the office doors and scanned the stairway. Kaitlyn had been so preoccupied she hadn't noticed him coming, but immediately she knew her conversation with Colin was over—along with whatever chance she thought she had.

"Be right there." The tips of Colin's ears turned red, and his eyes skipped between her and the older man. "Hope things turn out okay for you," he stuttered in her general direction. He turned his back and jogged up the rest of the stairs before Kaitlyn could respond.

A single tear trekked down her cheek as she whispered a solemn goodbye.

### Colin

*"Hope things turn out okay for you."* Was that the best he could do?

Colin was grateful for Dr. Crank's interruption. Hopefully the department chair hadn't overheard Kaitlyn, as it would doom him to failure. He'd been so foolish to get involved, and now all this sneaking around was the price he had to pay.

"Did you get my memo?" Dr. Crank's jowls shook the faster he walked. He ushered Colin into his office and shut the door with a decisive thud.

"I'm sorry. Did I miss a meeting?" Colin tried to control the tremble in his voice, but the adrenaline from the encounter with Kaitlyn still thrummed through his veins.

Dr. Crank tilted his head, eyebrows drawn. "No." He paused, his hand still on the doorknob. "Is something wrong?"

"With me? No—she was just concerned about her final grade."

"Who?"

Colin's stomach cratered. One slipup would ruin him. "The

girl—never mind. What did you want to see me about?"

Dr. Crank studied Colin's face for seconds that seemed more like hours before turning away and taking a seat behind his desk. He motioned for Colin to follow suit. "I wanted to congratulate you, but it seems you have a lot more going on than I thought."

"I don't understand." Colin shot up a silent prayer to whatever god might be listening. How much did his boss know? If he'd overheard even a smidgen of the conversation with Kaitlyn, Colin would be ruined. He'd been so careful to keep watch while they were talking. He drew a fortifying breath and sat tall.

Dr. Crank offered an almost imperceptible shake of his head. "This," he said, holding a phone message aloft, "is the reason I called you in."

Colin leaned closer to inspect the tiny writing. "What is it?"

"I got a message from the editor of the *Life Cycle Journal*. He's a friend of mine."

"I had no idea." Colin rummaged through his thoughts to pair the name with the many submissions he'd made over the last six months.

"You weren't supposed to. What good would a publishing credit be if I'd just handed it to you through one of my connections?" A slow smile creased Dr. Crank's face.

"You mean. . ."

"That's precisely what I mean. Dr. Edmund McCallister said your analysis on the protein experiment you conducted is"—Dr. Crank slid on his bifocals and peered at the note—"masterful."

"Masterful?"

"That's the word he used. In fact, he said it's the most insightful piece he's read in a long time."

A flash of joy shot through Colin, and his heart started to race for a whole different reason than before. "That's great." He swiped his palms on his slacks. "That's the best news I've heard all day." If only he could work out the bugs in his current research.

"I don't have to tell you what an acceptance of this magnitude means for your chance at tenure." He eyed Colin over the rims of his glasses, his voice taking a serious turn.

"I understand."

Dr. Crank set down the message and folded his hands on his desk. "About the other thing." He cleared his throat.

"Other thing?" Moisture beaded at Colin's hairline.

"The girl." Dr. Crank's knowing eyes penetrated Colin's defenses. "Be careful. You never know what some of these coeds are thinking. One misstep, one rumor, can destroy a career."

"I—I understand."

"Some of these kids are so eager for a grade or to get one-up on the teacher, you never know what they'll do or say. Do you get my meaning?"

Colin nodded. "Absolutely."

"We want everyone in our department squeaky clean. And since I'm the one who's pulling for you, I need you to be nothing but a Boy Scout."

Boy Scout, indeed.

If that's what Dr. Crank wanted, that's what he'd get. Now that Kaitlyn was out of the picture, it was smooth sailing from here on out. He might have been dishonorable in the past, but he refused to let it affect his future—both at work and at home. Relief swept over Colin as he realized how close he'd come to losing it all for something so foolish.

Thank goodness it was over.

# CHAPTER 17

*Marissa*

Lord, have mercy." My mother, Alina Moreau, patted her chest and issued an exaggerated sigh.

"It's not that bad, Mom." I wondered what the penalty was for lying in front of a church. Judging by the anxiety roiling in my stomach day and night, my marriage was, in fact, that bad. Mentioning our troubles had been a terrible idea.

Mom's puffy white hair ruffled in the breeze. She waved to a group of elderly women who helped one another up the front steps of the church. "Let's go for coffee when the service is over, and then we can talk more. What's the name of that little shop?"

The last place I wanted to go was The Bean, not with Kaitlyn working. So far I'd managed not to spew my troubles on her when she herself was in desperate circumstances, and I didn't want her to overhear my life story now. My personal garbage needed to stay personal. That way New Heights would continue to be a safe refuge for me during the day—the knowing looks of Tristan excluded.

"I need to get home early today." I silently devised a way to tie up the bits of information I'd unraveled in the car. Mom didn't need my troubles added to her worry-laden life.

"You know, if Colin started coming with you on Sundays it would help your marriage."

Come to church with me? Getting him home for dinner was hard enough. Church was out of the question. I almost wished I'd told Mom that I needed to stay home because for once Colin was actually there, relaxing and listening to the Sunday talk shows.

Mom leaned closer. "A rough patch or two—perfectly normal for married couples."

Over half ended in divorce, but there was no use bringing that up when she was trying to make me feel better. I stalled, desperate to end the conversation before we entered the house of God.

Mom's wizened eyes raked over me. "Hard times are to be expected. And don't think that what happened to your father and I will happen to you. Our relationship was nothing like yours."

She was right. Each relationship is unhappy in its own special way.

"Let's not talk about it. I'll be okay," I said, as much to convince myself as my mother.

"Have you talked to Colin about how you feel?"

I couldn't lie twice. Instead, I studied the cobblestone steps and the scuff on the tip of my shoe. "Not really. I mean, I think he knows."

"Nothing is ever resolved by ignoring it." Somehow Mom had become Tristan's echo.

Though I'd already learned the hard way that pushing Colin would do more harm than good, I forced a smile of agreement. "He's been really busy. He's up for tenure."

She leaned close, the smell of coffee coloring her breath. "It isn't another woman, is it?"

I offered a slight shrug. What was I thinking, blabbing to Mom? Though she wasn't argumentative, she was still tenacious and would wheedle me until I gave up all my secrets. How could I confess that I suspected his heart lay elsewhere, even when he was by my side every night?

I hadn't peeked at his email again for any further signs of Pink-Bunny, and I hadn't checked for texts, but I still noticed the flicker of fear in his eyes every time his cell phone chimed. I noticed the hard edge in his voice whenever I asked a question. I knew him—had always deeply known him—and his behavior wasn't normal.

Only we were too far apart for me to come right out and say so.

"You need to confront the issue head-on—whatever it is." Mom nodded her head, agreeing with herself.

"Like I said in the car, something is just. . .off." I glanced at the doors of the church, opening and closing. The old-fashioned bell gonged from the steeple. "Can we not talk about this?"

She fisted her hand and pumped it with vigor. "Just lay it on the line. There's nothing wrong with taking charge every now and then."

The same way she did? I cringed, remembering Colin's reactions whenever she pressed an issue or took a firm stand. Needless to say, they weren't the best of friends. I ushered her up the steps, taking care that she didn't lose her balance. "Let's get inside before the service starts."

"Fine. But the longer you take, the longer it'll be before I have grandbabies to snuggle with."

And there it was—both the reason for her extreme interest and the root cause of my unending anxiety. The wall that would always stand between me and true happiness.

Mom approached the doors slowly and lowered her voice. "You're no spring chicken."

"Thanks for the reminder."

"I'm being serious. You and Colin need to get a move on. I'm the only one of my friends who doesn't have grandchildren. Do you know what that's like?" She squared her shoulders. "No pictures to show, no plays to attend, no awful coloring pages stuck to my refrigerator."

"I'm sure there are worse things in life." Though I couldn't imagine what. I placed my finger to my lips. "Shhh."

She drew her chin up and whispered rather loudly, "All I'm saying is that you're a good-looking couple. Once you have babies, my pictures will put that Marva Beecham to shame."

"I'll do the best I can." I turned my cell phone to silent mode.

"Whatever's going on with you and Colin, work it out." She patted my arm. "Then you can get busy, if you know what I mean."

"I know, I know, I know." As usual, her pushing had made me rigid and cranky. And it really wasn't a wonder that I refused to be pushy and confrontational with Colin.

The late afternoon sun badgered the boutique at New Heights. I pulled the sheer curtains across the window, though they did little to disperse the heat. Kaitlyn fanned herself, her face flushed.

I angled the small fan toward her. "Sorry about the heat. It gets pretty bad in here during the summer. We'll have to get new blinds." There was little chance of that happening, despite the influx of grant money. Those funds were directed toward more practical purposes, like staffing.

Kaitlyn's mouth puckered with worry.

"Do you want to talk? Is everything okay?"

"As okay as it can be. I'll be fine. I just need to keep busy with my work." She was entirely too young for the wrinkles spidering across her forehead. She stopped fanning herself and hung a maternity dress on the rack.

"You've seriously done wonders in here." The clothing that had previously been heaped into less-than-tidy piles was now neatly hung on racks, and baby goods had been cleaned and separated onto shelving units against the wall. "I'm impressed. I don't know where you get the energy."

"Some days I don't know either. Guess you learn to do what needs to be done. I have a feeling I'll be getting better at doing that." She flashed a brave grin, a thin veneer to mask her worry.

I reeled her into a quick side hug. "You are going to make a great mom."

The expression on her face froze. She bit her lower lip until it turned white. "I. . .I haven't decided what I want to do. I mean—Christina was talking about adoption, and I just got to thinking. . ." Her voice trailed again, and she offered a slight shrug.

A weighty sigh filled my lungs. How had I become attached to Kaitlyn and her baby so fast? Though I took an interest in all our clients, this was different. She was different. Maybe it was because I'd been struggling against infertility for so long and my time was running out. In Kaitlyn I saw so many things that I wanted for myself.

I turned the fan full blast. "It's a perfectly viable choice. I guess I hadn't realized you were considering it."

"I'm just thinking through my options." She studied the flimsy curtains with a distant longing in her eyes. "It's so hard to know what's right, or what I will or won't regret in the future. What if I make the wrong choice and screw everything up? I always thought I was ready for life and the real world, but this is big."

"It is, but this is where you're at right now. It's good that you're taking time to think clearly and get ready for the future. And believe me, you're not someone who's going to screw everything up." Quietly I prayed for the wisdom to offer helpful words without overstepping her personal boundaries. "Have you talked to your family yet?"

"No."

I leaned on a clothing rack. "Is there anyone close to you that you can confide in?"

"I'm pretty close to my roommate, but she moved to Mountainside for the summer. That's where my family is too." She grabbed a few items off the rack and sorted by color. "At this point, I'm closer to you and Christina than anyone else. I know that sounds ridiculous since I barely started working here, but I feel like I've known you forever."

"Well, I have been going to The Bean for ages."

A sly grin illuminated her face. "You really get to know a person by their coffee order."

"Mine probably says I don't sleep nearly enough."

"Among other things."

"Such as?"

She laughed. "It's a trade secret."

For a few minutes we worked companionably, unloading the last box of donations that had come in during the night. I'd already had one appointment this morning and two booked for late afternoon, but New Heights was quiet for the moment. It was hard to know whether to be thankful for the reprieve or disquieted because my thoughts always pummeled me most when I wasn't distracted with other people.

After my conversation with Mom, failure had hollowed out a niche in my chest and lodged itself tightly. Why I'd ever opened up to her I couldn't figure, other than I needed to know someone had my back. Someone besides Tristan, who'd started to look at me differently over the past few months since he discovered Colin and I had issues. Perhaps his sidelong glances were my imagination drumming up interest from a man—any man—since my husband was clearly uninterested. I chalked up Tristan's unusual closeness to that, because to dwell on the possibilities was dangerous.

"To answer your question, I haven't told anyone yet." Kaitlyn's confession sliced through my thoughts, bringing me back to the present. She continued to sort through the box, separating the baby toys from the blankets, never lifting her gaze.

"Why?" Though I understood her situation was different, as every mother's was, I couldn't fathom keeping such news to myself.

Kaitlyn paused her work and stared at nothing. "I could say that the baby's father wouldn't give me the chance, or I could say that my parents won't understand, but that would be dishonest." She looked at me with confusion and sadness.

I raised an eyebrow, hoping she'd continue without my having to probe.

Her shoulders lifted with a deep, weighted breath. "The truth is, I'm scared."

"Of?"

"Rejection."

"You said that you've already broken it off with the baby's father." I didn't mention that it was clearly the other way around. There was no use pointing it out. I grabbed a pile of baby clothes to sort.

"It's hard to explain." Her brow wrinkled as she considered her words, how much she wanted to reveal. "It's like. . .I keep hoping he'll come to his senses without me telling him. That way I'll always know he came back for me." Her neck bobbed with a thick swallow. "If I come right out and tell him, it's like my last hope. If he doesn't come back knowing that I'm pregnant, he never will. But as long as I haven't told him, I can still hope."

My heart deflated. Who could reject such a sweet young woman, the perfect blend of potential, innocence, and kindness? Anger quickly replaced sadness. I set the pile of clothing aside. "If that's the kind of person he is, you're really better off without him. I know it probably doesn't feel like it right now, but you can do this—whatever you decide. You're not the first single mother and you won't be the last, but you are one of the strongest I've met. You have a strong work ethic and a good head on your shoulders." I strengthened my tone and forced her to look me in the eye. "You can do this."

She breathed slowly and nodded, as if to convince herself. "I can." Her meek voice betrayed her beliefs.

"You're about ten weeks along now, aren't you?"

"Exactly."

"Follow me. There's something I want you to hear."

# CHAPTER 18

*Kaitlyn*

The gel was warm on her belly, but Kaitlyn still shivered. She steadied her breathing as she watched Marissa pull a contraption from a drawer next to the examination table.

"It might be a little early, but it's possible we'll hear the baby's heartbeat." Though Marissa's smile was genuine, sadness tinged her hazel eyes. The same sadness had been there before, but outright asking about it seemed like a bad idea no matter how much Kaitlyn wanted to know. Hopefully there would be a right time and she could repay the kindness that had been her strength over the last few weeks.

Kaitlyn adjusted the towel tucked into the waistband of her capris and squirmed to get comfortable.

"Lie still and we'll see what we find." Marissa turned on the small machine. "This is called a Doppler, and I'm going to use the wand to detect sound."

The pressure of the wand made Kaitlyn wish she'd used the restroom—a room she frequented all too often nowadays. Static pulsed from the box. "Is everything okay? I don't hear a heartbeat." Except her own, pounding in her ears. Until this moment, she hadn't realized how much she wanted everything to be okay with the baby. As hard as it was to adjust to the idea of being an unwed mother, the thought of losing the baby suddenly seemed more frightening.

"Wait for it." Marissa cocked her head and listened intently. "There it is."

"I don't hear anything."

Marissa adjusted the volume. "It doesn't quite sound like you'd expect."

A rapid *whoosh-whoosh* pulsed through the box, sounding more like an out-of-control washing machine than a tiny baby. "It sounds fast. I haven't been drinking caffeine—promise."

A warm smile spread across Marissa's face. "I can't give you medical advice, but your baby's heart sounds about as strong and normal as I've heard at this stage."

Kaitlyn relaxed and listened as a tear slid down her face. What had only been a "problem" and a constant source of anxiety was now a little life that needed protection and love. A baby, tiny and full of potential.

Marissa handed her a tissue. "Isn't it wonderful?"

Her throat constricted, and a nod was all Kaitlyn could manage. She swiped her cheek with the tissue and took a deep breath that infused her with resolve. "Thank you. I needed this."

"I know." Marissa smiled warmly and turned off the box. "Amazing, isn't it?"

"True confession," Kaitlyn said as she wiped the goo from her stomach. "I still haven't been to the doctor. I have an appointment, but I can't even tell you how many times I almost canceled."

Marissa looked away. "I know the feeling."

Unease crept over Kaitlyn. She wanted to ask Marissa about her family, or if she and Tristan even had one. Neither one seemed to have pictures of kids at New Heights, but come to think of it, they weren't really affectionate either, other than an occasional hug or shoulder pat. Kaitlyn always assumed they were just a private couple.

What if Marissa had lost a baby? That would explain why there was sadness in her eyes, but the likelihood of someone staying in this line of work under those circumstances seemed pretty small.

Kaitlyn sat up and adjusted her shirt and waistband. "What should I do with the towel?"

"The hamper is in the corner. Every few days I take it home and wash everything." Marissa busied herself at her desk. Silent moments passed. "If you'd like, I can come with you to your appointment." She looked up with such a grace-filled expression that Kaitlyn wanted to weep. "It's your choice. I just wanted you to know the option is there for you."

"I appreciate that—more than you know." Obviously the baby's father went to the first appointment with most new moms, but the chance that Colin would come around grew dimmer with each day that passed.

Which was totally unfair to the tiny life growing inside her.

"Do you mind if I make a phone call?" She scooted off the bed.

"It's pretty slow right now. Go ahead. Do you need to use my phone?" Marissa stepped out of the way. "I'll leave you to it."

With the door closed, Kaitlyn mustered enough courage to lift the receiver. If she called from a different number like the day she'd called from The Bean, Colin might actually answer. She dialed, formulating what she'd say. She'd have to come right out with it before he hung up—nothing fancy, nothing perfect. Definitely not the way she ever would have planned, but it was her only choice.

Her heart hammered harder with each ring. This was it. No excuses. Even if he rejected her, she at least would have done her duty. It was up to Colin whether or not he wanted to do his.

After several seconds, it clicked over to voice mail.

Kaitlyn stiffened as adrenaline continued to pump through her veins.

Leave a message or hang up? She set the receiver in the cradle, realizing she had no idea what to say to a machine. She'd come so close to getting it over with and forcing him to face the issue.

She marched out of the office and into the kitchen to get her cell phone from her purse. Quickly, she punched in a text message before she could talk herself out of it.

One way or another, Colin was finding out today.

# CHAPTER 19

*Colin*

I'M PREGNANT. THE BABY IS YOURS.

Colin stared at his phone in stunned silence. Why would Kaitlyn send this text to him? Did she really think she could win him back this way?

Laughable.

If it wasn't so outrageous.

He turned the ringer off his phone and shoved it into his desk drawer. No way would he respond to her ridiculous ploy. Answering her would only play into whatever it was she was trying to accomplish. It wasn't unheard of for a young woman to be a little clingy to the person she called her first love—he'd grown squeamish when she'd told him—but saying she was pregnant bordered on delusional.

Colin wiggled the mouse on his desk and focused on all the emails he needed to shoot off before the end of the day. More meetings, another request for documentation pertaining to tenure, correspondence with the editor of the journal. Each email blurred into the next until he was no longer typing but clicking his pen between his restless fingers.

"Knock, knock." The student worker appeared in his doorway, eyes shining. "Did you return Dr. McFee's call?"

Quickly, he scanned his desk for the message. "I— No." He sifted through paperwork.

"Sorry, but I didn't write it down. I told you when you came in. Also, a student phoned but she didn't leave a message."

He wiped his hands on his khakis, leaving a faint damp trail.

The girl lingered until he looked up. "Are you all right?"

Colin swallowed and waited a beat. "Why do you ask?"

She motioned to her forehead. "You're— I mean, maybe it's just hot in here. Do we need to put a call into maintenance about your air-conditioning?"

He swiped his brow, taken aback by the moisture, and he began to note the erratic rhythm of his heart. Air—he needed air. He rose and opened the window, keeping his back to her. "That'd be great."

"I'll get right on it, Dr. Kimball."

He trained his eyes on the grassy quadrangle. "Can you close the door on your way out?"

The door clicked. Colin released his breath in a long whoosh. He spun and opened his desk drawer and pulled out his phone. Maybe she'd left a follow-up message, an "oops" with an apology. She'd realized she texted the wrong guy. And anyway, if she really was pregnant—an impossibility, as far as he was concerned—she wouldn't send a text.

No new messages.

He closed his eyes and tried to count how many times she'd tried to talk to him, even saying it was urgent. But the situation didn't add up.

First, judging by the issues he had with Marissa, he probably wasn't even capable of fathering a child. Second, she'd said she was on the pill for other medical reasons, though she hadn't offered further explanation. And then there was the fact they'd only been together a few times before guilt had taken a bite out of his conscience.

But it didn't necessarily take more than once—as a biology professor, he knew better than anyone.

Colin slumped into his chair and rubbed his forehead. The odds of there being a baby and that baby being his were miniscule. It was just the type of thing a desperate young coed would invent to try to save a relationship. He'd heard it a thousand times around campus. He just didn't think Kaitlyn would be one of them.

Quickly, he deleted her previous text. Even with Adam's name still attached to that phone number, Marissa would know it wasn't really Adam if she happened to read it. He tossed his cell back into the drawer and tried to refocus on the pile of work in front of him.

The phone rang in the lobby.

Colin's heart stuttered. What if that was Kaitlyn? Even if she was lying in order to trap him, she could do real damage to his career. Though she'd promised not to tell anyone, she'd obviously reached a new level of desperation. Now he had no choice but to confront her. Maybe he'd go see her tomorrow after he had a chance to calm down.

His hands curled into tight knots. He was going to have to tell her the truth, that he was married and he needed to stay with his wife. End of story.

With a plan in mind, Colin set back to work. He'd go find her at her job, though he couldn't remember which coffee shop she worked at. In a town the size of Elden Springs, it might take a while, but he was determined to hunt her down.

Eventually.

# CHAPTER 20

*Marissa*

Honesty has always been my mother's best quality, unless she's being honest about me.

"You don't look so good." Mom's eyes raked me over before I slammed the car door and went around to the driver's side.

Deep breath, I could do this. The fact I didn't look well wasn't a surprise. I had a mirror; I could see. That my own mother pointed it out so bluntly caught me off guard.

Distract and redirect—I was getting good at this. "Which doctor are we going to today?" Slowly, I backed out of her driveway and around the newspaper I'd already run over on my way in.

"Heart specialist. And before you ask, it's just a checkup." She opened her enormous purse and pulled out a bottle of lotion, then proceeded to slather it on her hands and forearms. The car suddenly smelled like a spring meadow and White Shoulders all at once. "Why haven't you been sleeping? You look like you got punched."

"Mom!"

"Right in the eyes."

"Enough."

"I know a lady, she has this cream—"

"I don't need cream!"

She held up her hands in mock surrender. "Well, you're a little cranky too."

One day I'd be old enough to say whatever I wanted without a filter, just like my mother, but that day was not today. I sighed and slid my sunglasses on to deter further scrutiny. "Why didn't you tell me you had an appointment?"

"Clearly I did tell you. That's why you picked me up." She was using her faux patient voice, the one that made me feel like I was a kindergarten dropout.

"I meant sooner, Mom. I need to know ahead of time because of my work schedule."

"You said you're always happy to take me, but I guess I can find someone else. Marva's daughter always takes her—maybe she can take me too."

"Mom." My groan ricocheted through the car. "I can take you, but I have a job. Marva's daughter stays home, remember? I want to help—"

"Because Marva just calls her up," Mom mumbled and I tuned her out. I highly doubted Marva's daughter was on call to taxi her mother around town, but I wasn't about to argue the point.

"Never mind," I said, giving up the battle. Mom was relentless, and I was no match for her. In fact, I was the opposite, passive but peaceable. Better to hold something inside to the point of bursting than to drive everyone away with a barrage of words.

"Did I tell you Marva's daughter is having a baby?"

No, but it put the cherry on top of my day. Bittersweet news, as pregnancies always were. I stepped on the gas a little too hard. "That's great. When is she due?"

"October. But if you saw her, you'd know she has to be due sooner than that." Mom folded her arms over her purse. "Of course they keep telling me, 'You're next, you're next.'"

"To have a baby?" I felt my nose wrinkle when I glanced at her.

Her hand wheeled in a slow circle as though I needed to catch up or get a move on. "No, silly. To have a *grand* baby. Not that I'm trying to rush you."

I held back everything I wanted to say, the reasons and excuses, hopes and fears, and most of all the sense of failure that hovered over me like an ominous cloud. At this point, all I wanted was to get Mom to the heart specialist emotionally unscathed.

Mom gazed out the passenger window, muttering about the neighbor's azaleas before bringing the conversation back around. "I always wanted to have more kids, you know. At least three or four more. That was always my dream."

"No, I didn't know." Briefly, I wondered what life would've been like with a father and a passel of siblings. How different birthdays and Christmases and family get-togethers would've been. It had always been just Mom and me, which was why I'd never changed my last name. I didn't want her to be the only one left. Sorrow nestled inside me, right next to the failure. "Why didn't you?"

She snorted and whipped around to lance me with one of her infamous mom gazes. "That's pretty obvious."

I turned down Grove Avenue, away from the heavy current of traffic. "I always assumed you didn't want a husband or more kids." In fact, she seemed to let me know with audible sighs and constant fatigue that I was taxing enough.

"Do you really not know me that well?"

I hated to admit that I didn't. I only knew what she let me see, enough for me to realize how much I lacked without a father. But I had shared her dream for a larger family, particularly a father who would be there to tuck me in and go to the daddy-daughter dances. I wanted a dad who would go to career day at school. A day each year when I was left sitting at a table alone while the other girls ate lunch with their doctor, firefighter, and executive fathers. Mom couldn't come—she had to scrap for every hour of work she could get for us to still be poor.

She shrugged. "I learned the hard way that you're supposed to find love before you have a kid. It's pretty hard for a single mom in the dating pool."

I recoiled. The words felt like a slap, and once again I was the little kid who knew she was out of place and in the way.

"I don't mean it like that," Mom said as though reading my thoughts. "I mean, you can't bring home just anyone when you have a child. And let's face it, there aren't a lot of good men in the dating pool to begin with. Not everyone finds true love like you."

A highly debatable point, but I wasn't going to say so. The simper on her lips told me she was needling me for information in a not-so-subtle way. I hated when she did that, especially since I'd started doing it too.

"Bottom line, I never found the right man." She shrugged again, but I could actually feel her longing, probably because it was so like my own. I remembered the nights I'd prayed for a father, as days bled into years without an answer. While my mom did everything she could, working early, working late, cooking and cleaning, and trying to make a life for us, I couldn't deny the gaping hole I'd felt without a dad.

At the stoplight, I paused to really look at my mother—a woman who had to work too hard for too little in order to care for a kid who didn't appreciate her sacrifices nearly enough. I reached over and squeezed her hand. "I'm sorry it didn't happen like you dreamed, but I know that God is with us, even in our disappointment. I have to believe that."

Her lips tightened and her neck bobbed with a swallow before she infused her voice with a lilt that was too bright to be real. "Well, you can make it up to me with grandchildren."

Back at New Heights, I closed the door to my office and counted down the days until my appointment with the fertility specialist. What if I went through the treatments and still couldn't get pregnant? Would Colin finally be amenable to adoption? The thought of talking about it made me cringe. As closed off as he'd been, our fertility problem was the last subject I wanted to bring up despite knowing he was as desperate as I was for a child. The brief moments I'd watched him at the baseball field confirmed what a patient and generous father he'd be, and I knew that if I could only give him a child, we'd be okay.

A knock sounded on the door, startling me from my reverie. "Come in."

Kaitlyn poked her head inside, a blond rope of hair dangling over her shoulder. "I finished sorting the donation bags. You should see some of the cute maternity clothes."

I managed to muster a smile. "Make sure to take some home with you."

"Are you sure? I mean, I'm not really showing yet." She stepped fully inside my office and motioned to her midsection where a tiny baby bump would soon form.

"Definitely. In fact, it wouldn't hurt for you to stock up on things as you see them come in—diapers, baby clothes—really, whatever you think you'll need. In fact, I have a list for new mothers—"

"But I haven't decided yet." Her voice quavered.

"Right, sorry." I hung my head, realizing I'd overstepped. How a mother could consider giving up her child was beyond me, and that was dangerous for my line of work. Adoption was a solid option that I'd helped set up in dozens of previous situations, and had even asked Colin to consider numerous times, but as my own problems continued, I understood it less and less. Finally I looked up to meet her gaze. "I hope you know I don't mean to be. . .pushy. Sometimes I get overly excited."

"Actually, I appreciate that. I need someone in my corner." She hesitated then started to back out of the room.

"Wait. . .do you want to talk?" I gestured to the chair across from me.

She glanced over her shoulder before slipping back inside my office and shutting the door. "There's not much to tell, and you've probably heard sob stories like mine a thousand times." She issued a nervous chuckle.

"Not true." I held up a finger. "Every sob story is different in a thousand little ways."

She laughed for real this time. "It seems almost ridiculous, the position I've put myself in." The chair squeaked as she sat. "I can't believe I ever let myself get caught up with someone who would do this to me."

"Do what?" I closed my appointment book and the glaring date with the fertility doctor. "I take it you told the father?"

Kaitlyn's shoulders slumped. "You're not going to believe this—I can hardly believe it myself—but I texted him."

"That's a new one to me—see, your story *is* different." I offered a sidelong smile and hoped she'd continue to talk.

Her eyes widened. "There was no other way. I tried to see him in person and I tried to talk to him on the phone, but he's avoiding me completely." She released a disgusted sigh.

"Did he text you back?"

"No. Nothing. At first I thought maybe he just needed to let it sink in, you know, like I did. But it's been a few days." At this, her voice cracked. "So I guess that's my answer. I'm in it alone."

"Not alone—and don't ever feel like you are." I reached out and covered her shaky hand. "As for him. . .some men you are better off without. Truly."

Her bottom lip quivered. "I don't know what I'd have done without you. Being here has made all the difference for me."

I glanced skyward to acknowledge providence. "It looks like we met up at just the right time."

She pushed out of the chair. "I guess I'll see you tomorrow morning, if you come in for coffee."

"You can count on me. And make sure to pick out some cute maternity clothes before you leave today." I smiled as she thanked me and closed the door.

That night, I dug deep inside myself and prayed and wept. So many needs, so little left inside me to even offer them up to God.

But He knew; He always knew.

I prayed for my marriage, and I prayed for my fertility appointment. I prayed for my sanity and for hope. I prayed for Kaitlyn and that the father of her baby would come to his senses and step up like a man.

It haunted me to think of another child growing up without a dad and ending up like me.

# CHAPTER 21

*Colin*

Home or work? Was one place worse than the other to confront Kaitlyn with the text message she'd sent?

Colin saw the stupid message every time he closed his eyes, every time he looked in the mirror to shave, every time he stopped working long enough to think about anything at all. Still, it hadn't prompted him to immediate action; in fact, he'd sat on the information for days. Before he did anything, he had to figure out if it was even true.

He spent the morning in the lab, noting observations that would help with the revisions of his paper, plus it kept his mind occupied. Assuming Kaitlyn was telling the truth—and really, it was a fifty-fifty shot—her news would keep. Besides, considering all he'd been through with Marissa, the odds of him fathering a child were pretty small.

But so were the odds of Kaitlyn lying.

Maybe the baby wasn't his. She was a college coed, and even the most seemingly innocent ones were doing things that would make their mothers blush. Kaitlyn wasn't immune to that type of behavior—after all, she'd been with him. Who was to say she hadn't also been with someone else?

The thought made him apprehensive in unexpected ways. Jealousy, shame, remorse—a veritable hodgepodge of emotions. He'd been so stupid. Sure, he'd done what any other red-blooded man with opportunity would've done in his shoes, but he should've been smarter. Now he'd have to find an out-of-town clinic and get checked.

Colin muttered a curse that hadn't poisoned his lips in years. He set down the test tube and removed his goggles. Completely pulled out of his experiment, his thoughts spun out of control as adrenaline slammed through his veins. He drew a deep breath and recalculated the odds in order to comfort himself, but still his heart rate kicked up a few notches.

As a biologist he knew that life found a way not only to sustain itself, but also to reproduce.

There was no way around it. He had to confront her and make her admit the truth so he could get on with his day. Get on with his life.

Get on with fighting his way back to where he always should have been—loving Marissa.

Colin had better things to do with his time than loiter outside The Bean, waiting for Kaitlyn to get off work. After leaving his office, he'd driven to all the coffee shops he could think of, looking for her car. Better to confront her in semi-public where there was no chance of losing his resolve to let her go.

Hidden behind the pine trees in the corner of the parking lot, he still felt conspicuous. Despite the heat, he kept his windows rolled up. The tint would be enough to keep anyone from noticing him, and even if they did, there was nothing criminal about being at a coffee shop. He noted the position of her car in relation to the drive-through line. If he caught her just at the driver's side and kept his back to the front entrance, he'd be fine.

Minutes ticked by, giving his heart time to ramp up as he imagined every possible scenario and outcome. Either she was lying and she'd fess up once confronted, or she was telling the truth and his life would be wrecked. His own fault, but wrecked nonetheless.

At eleven o'clock, the back door opened and Kaitlyn exited alongside a skinny young punk. Colin fisted his hands. Logically, there was no reason to be jealous, especially since he'd been the one to end the relationship. But he still couldn't stop looking.

The man—correction, kid—leaned over and gave Kaitlyn a hug that lasted a little too long. She smiled up at him, her silky hair fluttering in the breeze. Clearly the unkempt guy was crazy about her. Who wouldn't be? It sure hadn't taken her long to turn her attentions elsewhere. In a way, it gave Colin a smidgen of peace. Maybe that was why she hadn't tried getting ahold of him again. In fact, maybe the baby belonged to this kid.

Briefly, he considered driving away. If he left now, she'd never be the wiser. He would go back to work—back to Marissa—and try to jump-start his marriage. There had to be some remnant of their love inside him, unless what they'd had together had never been actual love.

Which would explain a lot.

When he and Marissa had first met, he had been smitten. There was no other word for it. An exotic older woman whom he considered a catch. It made him feel superior to lure her stormy affections away from the other seemingly sophisticated and successful men in her life. But exotic eventually turned into dull, and stormy affections turned into constant need to the point where he simply wasn't up to the challenge. She drained him in more ways than one.

Colin rubbed his temples and stuck his keys back into the ignition. The engine purred, causing Kaitlyn to turn her head. Eyes wide, she left the man she was talking to and beelined for Colin's car.

He climbed out before she could hop inside. As she approached, he angled away from the entrance to the coffee shop, keeping his backside to the main road. If no one saw his face, he could deny being there.

"What are you doing here?" The edge in her voice caught him off guard.

Colin fixed his eyes on her, noting the rigidity of her posture and the firm set of her mouth. There was a different air about her that he couldn't quite place. A quiet resolve and a lack of playfulness that wasn't like the Kaitlyn he knew.

Suddenly it hit him—she was telling the truth. She was pregnant. The realization sent a new wave of adrenaline crashing through his veins. The only question was, whose baby was it? He leaned away from her and made an effort to keep his tone neutral. "I have a better question. Who's the guy?"

Her mouth tightened as she crossed her arms, highlighting her curves. "Why do you care? Really, after ignoring my calls and texts and emails, kicking me out of your office. . .why?"

"I think it's pretty obvious." He lasered her with his gaze, hoping she'd be flustered enough to tell the truth.

"Does it matter?" She unfolded her arms and fiddled with the strap of her purse, which she quickly used to shield her stomach. "Why are you here?"

"Who's the guy?" His voice softened with desperation that he didn't want to feel.

Kaitlyn slouched and her face relaxed. "He's my boss."

"Your boss?" he scoffed. "You bounced back pretty quickly." He tore his gaze away from her, unsettled by his conflicting emotions.

The warm breeze lifted her hair until she wrangled the errant strands back into place. "It's not what you're thinking, and you should know better." She glanced at her stomach. "The hug—he was just being a friend. I told him I've been having a hard time, but I didn't tell him about the baby. Not yet."

*Baby*—the word made him flinch. He choked down the gravelly lump in his throat. "So you were serious about. . ." He motioned to her waist, which somehow seemed thicker, though she couldn't possibly be that far along.

Her expression, incredulous and hurt, pierced him. She clutched the charm on her necklace and raced it back and forth across the chain he'd given her. "You really thought I made it up? Why, to trap you into being with me? I'm not some desperate young student out to get a man. I guess we don't know each other as well as I thought."

"I didn't mean—"

"I don't care what you meant. You're showing a really ugly side of yourself, and if that's who you are then I don't want to be with you." She turned from him and strode away with finality in every step.

After a moment of indecision, Colin scrambled after her before she could climb inside her car. He caught her by the arm. "Wait, please."

Kaitlyn stopped but refused to look at him. "I can't believe you came here to see if I was telling the truth. Then what, you were hoping to be off the hook? Guess what, there is no hook. I only told you because it was the right thing to do, but you don't have to feel obligated to help. I can do this by myself. I have new friends, a new job—"

"You took a second job?" His stomach soured as he realized that not only had she taken on a second job, but her pregnancy was the reason she'd quit school. Remorse assaulted him. He scrubbed his face with his hands, wishing he could walk back the clock and undo the unthinkable.

"Yes. I have to find a way to support the baby." Her voice strengthened with each word.

Colin floundered. "I. . .don't know what to say. This is overwhelming."

She grimaced. "Welcome to my life."

"You don't understand." He plumbed his thoughts for a way to express his feelings without crossing the invisible line that would reel them back together. "I want to be there for you—I want to be with you. But I can't."

Kaitlyn's head tilted back, and she released an exasperated sigh. "You've given me every excuse in the book, starting with your job. But as I see it, you're a grown man and you can do what you want with your life. The way you had us running around in secret, it's almost like you're. . ." Her eyes saucered.

Time stopped.

The cars in the drive-through, the man at the back door still staring at them, the fact that Colin's heart rate tripled—none of it mattered.

"That's right, Kaitlyn," he said as he wheeled in a breath to fortify his nerves, realizing his life was about to change forever. "I'm married."

# CHAPTER 22

*Marissa*

Every year we vowed not to go through another summer without air-conditioning, and every summer there were a thousand reasons we had to. At least according to Tristan.

"Even with the grant, we just can't afford it." His chair squealed as he leaned back, hands clasped behind his head. His dark eyes studied me until I looked away.

I soaked in the atmosphere of his office, sparsely decorated but filled with peace. Books and plants, cheap imprints of famous works—nothing to hint at his personal life or interests but designed to completely put one at ease. "Our clients are hot. That's what happens when you're pregnant."

"We could reduce hours and I can pick up the slack. We don't really need two workers."

"No," I cut in before he could entertain the idea. "Things are working out really well with Kaitlyn and Christina. I feel like we finally have a real staff—people who can relate to our clients. They're only part time so they can't be costing us that much."

"But air-conditioning *would* cost us that much." He leveled his gaze at me until I finally relented.

"Fine. I just hate seeing everyone leave my office sweating. It makes me nervous." I wrinkled my nose.

Tristan chuckled, lightening my mood. I loved him for that.

"How's your book coming?" I shot a glance at his laptop.

"Wait—how did you know? I haven't told anyone."

"I didn't. Just took a wild guess. I figured there was a reason you're locked in here pecking away at the keys between clients." I leaned over his desk and tried to peek at the screen.

Tristan quickly angled it out of my line of sight. "I figured it couldn't hurt to look for a supplementary source of income, that's all. My private practice is okay, but you know how it goes."

"It's not like you haven't talked about writing a book before." It had been several years, but how well I remembered his dreams. I admired that he dared to dream them. If anyone could pull it off, it was Tristan. "And I agree, we probably both need an additional income stream for the days ahead."

His lips thinned. "Don't tell me you're going to be one of those desperate people who tries to save a marriage by having a baby."

"Of course not." I watched a butterfly dance outside the window instead of really thinking about his words. Besides, my chances now were slimmer than ever since I'd once again postponed my appointment with the fertility doctor. If I failed with medical intervention, then that was it. I wasn't ready to face a dead end, especially since Colin didn't think adoption was a good answer. "Just. . .I know how hard the grants to fund this place are to come by. That's what I meant."

Tristan pinched the bridge of his nose and once again leaned back in his chair. His brow furrowed. I didn't like it when his brow furrowed—it meant he was about to start probing, and that was the last thing I needed.

"I'd better get going. I have a client coming in soon—if you consider an hour from now soon." I forced a laugh.

"Your favorite defense mechanism is showing again." He offered a feeble smile.

I gestured toward him and feigned annoyance. "Quit trying to analyze me."

"I wouldn't do that—it wouldn't be ethical."

"You do it every day."

"I love when you call me out on things, but we're talking about you."

"Well, let's not."

Moments passed before he spoke. "I know you don't want to get personal, but it's too late. I already know you *that* well."

I scoffed. Folded my arms. Glared.

"Before you dismiss me, listen." He turned on his therapist voice.

"It's okay to need help sometimes, and if you don't want to talk to me—as a friend—I can refer you to someone. I think Dr. Graves would be perfect."

"Why would I spill my guts to a stranger?"

"You don't have to spill your guts. But maybe she can help you balance out—get rid of the high-highs and the low-lows."

"I don't have high-highs and low-lows." Lately, they were all lows. "And don't you dare suggest medicating me."

"I said no such thing."

"You were about to."

"You're not a mind reader."

"You wish." I smiled, pleased I'd changed the subject.

Success was fleeting. "Have you talked to Colin?"

"About what?" My throat tightened.

He smirked, shifting into friend mode instead of let-me-refer-you-for-help mode. "The weather—what do you think?"

I relaxed a fraction. "No. I don't think I need to anymore, and besides that, he's busy now with the whole tenure situation."

"So everything you've been suspecting—all gone?"

"Don't sound so incredulous. I mean, yes, all gone." With my fingers I started ticking off the ways I knew my husband was faithful. "He comes home almost on time, he's not disappearing at odd times, and it feels like he's almost trying."

"Almost trying."

"That's what I said. Look, it's not perfect, he's not perfect, but my gut feeling over the last few weeks tells me that everything is fine."

"Fine."

"Quit repeating me."

"Repeating you is the only way I can get you to hear your own words." He shrugged as though his reasonableness should win me over.

And it did. Thoughts that I'd cataloged and tucked away surfaced before I could squash them. "The obvious things—texting and whatnot—those have stopped, as far as I know." I drew a deep breath to steady myself. "But he is acting strangely, even for him."

Tristan's eyebrow quirked. "Such as. . ."

"I know he's under stress at work, but his moodiness—especially over the last few days—I haven't ever seen him like this. It's almost like he's skittish and sad and. . ."

"Hmmm." Tristan's sigh was noncommittal. "As a friend, I still think you need to talk to him. Get everything out in the open."

Like that would help. Negative anticipation surged inside me as I considered the possibilities. "Maybe."

"In Marissa-speak, that means no."

I met his gaze head-on. "Don't sound so sure of yourself."

"You like that about me."

"Does your new girlfriend like that about you?" I grinned as a flush crept up his neck and settled in his face.

"Probably." Not even a hint of a smile touched his mouth. "But she doesn't know me like you do."

I looked away. "I really should get busy. Kaitlyn will be here soon, and there are a ton of donation boxes to sort."

As if on cue, the chime on the front door pinged and Kaitlyn walked in. "Hello?" she called out. She was punctual and quiet, calm and efficient. Maybe that was what I liked so much about her. Though we were opposites, she had a steadying effect on me. Maybe that's why when she was around, I wasn't vacillating between high-highs and low-lows. I was there to support her, and my behavior, as far as I could tell, was normal.

"Back here." I rose from my seat and shot a glance at Tristan. "Have fun with your book."

# CHAPTER 23

*Kaitlyn*

**M**arried.

The word made her want to barf, but to be fair, everything made her want to barf. She felt even more dirty and used than she had before, and that was saying a lot. So much for Colin changing his mind and being involved in the baby's life. Now her fate, and the baby's, was certain.

She curled up in her comfy chair and switched on the television. Mindless viewing seemed to be about all she could manage after working two jobs.

Kaitlyn had slogged through the days since Colin's surprise visit to The Bean with a smile planted on her face that she knew wasn't genuine. The only person who really seemed to notice was Marissa, but she never pried. Kaitlyn liked that about her boss—no, *friend*.

With Sydney gone, Kaitlyn had come to rely on Marissa. They filled the space between clients with friendly chatter, and even the silences weren't uncomfortable like they were with some people. There was nothing boss-like about the older woman, no unreasonable demands or cross looks on the rare occasions that Kaitlyn flew into New Heights late, no feeling of being watched. At New Heights, she was free to be herself, complete with the ups and downs she was coming to associate with a rush of hormones and a big change in her life.

A day-old piece of coffee cake stared at her from the counter—a nice perk for employees of The Bean. It never had been good for her waistline, but that didn't matter now. She meandered to the kitchen and plopped onto a barstool. She stared out at the night sky and nibbled on the cake. It didn't really taste the same as it used to, but she needed to eat something. Mom's pot roast sounded good, with tiny potatoes and gravy, but considering she was still hiding her secret, dinner with her parents was unlikely.

She sighed and slid the plate away, unsatisfied.

The doorbell rang, rattling her thoughts and jump-starting her pulse. Colin—it had to be. He'd only come here once in passing, but maybe now he was coming to make things right.

Only he couldn't. He was married.

The doorbell rang again. She climbed off the barstool and checked her face in the tiny mirror on the wall next to the phone. Matted hair and no makeup. Great. Not that it mattered.

She dusted the crumbs off her shirt as she hustled across the hardwood floor in slippery socks. She pressed her eye to the peephole and her hopes sank, then lifted.

Marissa.

"Come on in." She closed the door after Marissa entered. "What brings you by? How did you even know where I live?"

"I looked it up on your application. I know that's probably violating all kinds of laws, so. . .sue me." Marissa grinned and held out a brown sack. "I had some extra dinner and thought you might like some."

Kaitlyn took the bag and peered inside. She pulled out the wrapped sandwich. "Thank you. What kind is it?"

"Roast beef. Hopefully it's not too heavy for your stomach."

Kaitlyn startled. It was almost as if God had answered an unspoken prayer, though the likelihood of that in her sinful state was nil. "It's perfect. Come in and sit with me." She led Marissa to the counter and offered her the empty barstool while she cleared her old school books off the other. "It's been a while since I've had company. You'll have to excuse the mess."

"Looks fine to me. You've been pretty busy." Marissa hung her purse on the back of the chair and leaned on the counter. "Eat up. I have a feeling you're not gaining nearly as much weight as you should."

"Is that your professional opinion?" Kaitlyn took a hesitant bite and absorbed the flavors. Juicy roast, mayo, and a hint of horseradish. It worked surprisingly well. She launched into another bite.

"The usual disclaimer, I'm not a doctor and blah, blah. But yes, I thought it would be good to make sure you're eating enough—enough of the right foods." Marissa eyed the coffee cake. "What does your doctor say?"

Kaitlyn groaned and motioned to her full mouth. No way did she want to admit she hadn't gone yet, not after how much concern her friend/boss had shown over the past month. It was embarrassing to admit how often she—a grown woman—had chickened out. She swallowed. "This is a great sandwich. Thanks so much for bringing it by. I guess I haven't been eating well."

Marissa took a seat and shot a glance at the refrigerator, presumably wondering if there was enough food in the house. Shame nibbled at Kaitlyn, knowing that people would assume that as a single mother she couldn't take care of herself. Hadn't she had many of the same preconceived ideas before she became one herself? Not that it was entirely untrue, but she certainly had enough money for food and rent.

Quiet buffered the room, and Marissa shifted in the swivel chair before speaking. "I didn't want to bring this up at work, and if I'm being too nosy you can tell me. It won't hurt my feelings."

Kaitlyn's stomach turned. She set down the sandwich. There were about a thousand things she didn't want to talk about, even with Marissa. The fact that the father of her child admitted he was married topped the list. "What's on your mind?" she asked tentatively.

"Tell me how you really are." Marissa held up her hand as if to ward off objections. "I know you say you're fine, but. . .I know."

Panic lit inside Kaitlyn. How much did Marissa know? How much was she willing to admit? Colin was right—this town was too small to get away with anything. She closed her eyes. "I don't know what to say."

"I *know* this kind of life change can't be easy."

The panic subsided, and Kaitlyn opened her eyes. "Right, of course. It's not, but now that I have a job at New Heights and school is on the back burner, I suspect everything will smooth out." She tamped down the shame of Colin's revelation and what it meant for her and the baby. "Eventually."

"I'm glad that having a second job is working out for you, but that's not what I meant."

That's what she was afraid of. Kaitlyn pasted on a phony smile. "You caught me. I haven't called the doctor."

"And your parents?" Marissa's expression remained neutral but firm.

Kaitlyn lowered her eyes and shook her head. "I know it shouldn't be this hard, but I haven't. I just don't know how."

"Well, for goodness' sake, don't put it in a text."

"Why would I do that?"

Marissa's eyes widened. "Isn't that how you told your baby's father?"

"I guess I did do that." Kaitlyn winced then glanced at her stomach. It pooched out, just a fraction, but noticeable to her. "I can't hide it forever, but there's just no good way to talk to them."

Marissa laid her hand on Kaitlyn's arm and leaned close. "Really, what's the worst that could happen? You are a smart, well-adjusted woman, and you have a good head on your shoulders. In my book, that means your parents can't be all bad."

"They're not." Kaitlyn was quick to jump in.

"Then why won't you talk to them? Sure, they might be upset at first, but they'll get over it and come to realize they have a grandchild on the way." Her eyes sparkled with hope and assurance that Kaitlyn wished she could tap into.

"You're right, sort of. I mean. . ." She paused, searching for a way to account for her lack of confidence. "I'm a grown woman. It's not like I'm in high school, right?"

Marissa nodded but said nothing.

"It's just that I'm afraid they'll judge me."

"Is that the type of relationship you have with them?"

"Yes and no." Kaitlyn tried to think of a way to put their relationship into words. "I love them, and I know they love me, even if we don't always get along. Sometimes their love for me feels harsh, but it's always there. I can always count on it, from both of my parents. Sometimes when one is angry I can go to the other, and vice versa." She rubbed her stomach—an annoying habit she'd caught herself doing a lot lately. "That's one thing that makes me sad for my baby—if I decide to keep it—that they'll only have me. No father." She choked down the ever-present lump in her throat. "I'm afraid I won't be enough."

"Are you still considering adoption? It's a viable choice." Marissa's words held no judgment, thankfully.

Kaitlyn sloughed it off as though the decision hadn't kept her up late into the night, every night. "I'm still considering it. A baby should have both parents whenever possible—at least I think so. I can't imagine what my life would've been like without my dad. I can't see how life without a dad would turn out well."

"I turned out okay." Marissa's smile vanished as quickly as it came, like she wasn't at all convinced. "Whatever you decide, you have my support. I bet your parents will end up being more supportive than you think too."

Kaitlyn motioned to her belly. "But this wasn't how I was raised, and I know they'll be disappointed."

Seconds ticked by before Marissa spoke. "They'll be more disappointed the longer you wait."

The truth hit her square in the conscience. She nodded while pretending anxiety wasn't swarming her gut. "I guess I'll need to go to Mountainside soon. Maybe I can hang out with my friend Sydney while I'm there, so that'll be something to look forward to."

Marissa swung around behind her and grabbed the cordless phone off the wall. She smiled broadly. "No time like the present to make plans."

Kaitlyn scrubbed her eyes while silently counting the cost. She took the phone and dialed. Waited for it to ring once, twice, three times, as her heart quick-stepped inside her chest. Really, that couldn't be good for the baby.

"Hello?" Mom's voice nearly brought Kaitlyn to tears.

"Hi, it's me." Flashes of the last time they spoke caused a swell of apprehension. Her grades—they'd fought over grades. How mundane that seemed right now. Kaitlyn fumbled through the not-so-pleasant pleasantries and finally mustered the courage to say she was coming home next Sunday. They needed to talk. Her somber tone must've said plenty since Mom agreed and kept the conversation short.

Marissa smiled too brightly for the occasion. "That wasn't so bad now, was it?" She hung the phone back on the wall.

"That wasn't the hard part."

"Baby steps." Marissa offered a reassuring smile.

It was just like her newfound friend to push her further than she wanted to go, but in a necessary direction. And with humor—Kaitlyn liked that about Marissa. She was like a boss, a friend, and a big sister all rolled into one.

But there was still no way she could tell Marissa that she'd been dumb enough to fall for a married man.

# CHAPTER 24

*Colin*

Throwing himself into his work and baseball practice was the only way Colin knew to run from the truth.

Or was it the truth?

Relief trickled through him every time he allowed himself to think that Kaitlyn was mistaken. That the baby wasn't his. But then he'd remember the sincerity in her eyes and the steadiness of her gaze when they spoke in the parking lot at that rinky-dink coffee shop she worked at.

After a taxing day at the university, Colin was excited to hit the field with the boys. Fresh air, sunshine, rowdy kids—exactly what he needed. Only it ended up as just another distraction in a line of useless distractions.

Was the child Kaitlyn carried a boy? He'd always wanted a son. Then they'd be out here on the field together, along with football and camping and hiking. It was how he'd always imagined his life. . .except he had to consider Marissa. Like it or not, he was still married, and he wasn't giving up.

Somehow he was going to have to tell her, unless Kaitlyn decided to give up the baby, in which case his life could go back to normal. Was she even considering the possibility? If she wasn't, she was going to need his help. A wave of resentment swelled inside him but quickly ebbed.

It was his fault too. Kaitlyn hadn't done it to herself.

What if. . .what if Kaitlyn went to Marissa's office? The idea sat like a cannonball on his chest. No—the odds were small. Marissa helped teens who were pregnant and in trouble, not people like Kaitlyn, adults who had their lives together.

A ball whizzed past his head, jolting him from his thoughts. "I think that's enough for today." He brought the boys into the huddle and halfheartedly led the team cheer.

"Great practice, Coach." Tommy's mom sidled up to him, reeking of hair spray and desperation.

"Thanks." He kept his head down, eyes on the equipment he was packing. He should've always kept his head down—then he wouldn't be in this mess. "Make sure Tommy stays hydrated before the game this weekend." He turned his back, effectively ending the conversation. He was relieved when she walked away.

"That's a little harsh, man," Adam said once they were alone.

Colin dropped the bases, creating a plume of dust when they hit the ground. "The last thing I need is Tommy's mom hanging around. I have enough problems." He met Adam's stare head-on. "As I'm sure you well know."

Adam threw his hands up. "You haven't heard any judgment from me."

And that was the problem—his best friend's silence condemned him with the same intensity as any words spoken aloud. Colin wiped sweat from his forehead as the sun beat down harder now than when practice began.

"I take it you haven't told Marissa."

"All things considered, that's kind of a dumb question," Colin snapped.

"Dude, just checking." A flash of annoyance lit across Adam's face then dissipated just as quickly. "Lani's been wanting to get together with you guys, and I have to say, there's no way I can face Marissa with what I know."

Colin resumed packing equipment. "Sorry."

"I'm not the one you should be apologizing to."

"I can't apologize for something she doesn't know about." Colin popped open his trunk.

"So you're never going to say anything? It's really over with the other woman?"

The words *other woman* rang loudly in Colin's head. He'd actually become *that* man, the one everyone hated, the one who couldn't keep his pants zipped. The one who actually went for it the moment the opportunity presented itself.

He stopped. Scrubbed his eyes with the heels of his hands. "You want the truth? Because it's ugly, and our friendship is as good as over if I tell you."

Adam paused, his neck bobbing in a hard swallow. "Hit me with it."

"Yes, it's over with her but I wish it wasn't. No, I haven't told Marissa and wasn't planning to—but now I don't have a choice." Adrenaline slammed through his veins as he glanced around to ensure their privacy. Once he told Adam, there was no going back. No pretending it wasn't real, and no more putting off telling his wife.

"Go on. I already knew all that."

"It's worse."

"What could be worse than—" Adam's eyes took on a hard glint.

"She's pregnant, and yes, it's mine."

Adam's face went slack. Moments ticked by before he spoke. "I don't even know what to say."

Colin looked away and focused on rearranging the gear in his trunk. "Join the club."

"Not a club I want any part of. I mean—I'm still here for you, but you have to come clean with Marissa."

"You're not telling me anything I don't already know." Colin swiped a grimy hand through his hair. The secret that weighed so heavily on him was finally out—at least to one person. But the relief he'd been hoping for didn't materialize. If anything, he felt exposed.

"Dude, I'm here to be your friend and help you any way I can, but you have to man up and do the right thing."

Colin agreed, except at this point he had no idea what the right thing was.

# CHAPTER 25

*Marissa*

Catastrophize—a fancy word for my tendency to float the worst-case scenario as the most logical outcome.

"I'm telling you, you have to quit doing that." Tristan slowed his pace, trying to force me to match his stride on our daily walk. But the last thing I wanted to do was stop and look into his eyes and see pity.

I hated pity. The problem was, I needed to stop being pitiful in order to stop receiving it. I added *Stop being pitiful* to my mental checklist.

"I'm not catastrophizing. I really think it is that bad." I quickened my steps but he didn't match me. Now that we were no longer talking about the change in weather and our influx of new clients, I was ready to get back to New Heights.

Tristan stopped and spun me to face him, his warm hands firm on my bare shoulders. The chilly breeze ruffled his hair and carried along the scent of freshly baked bread from the bakery a few doors down. "You're killing yourself with worry. This obsession you have with what Colin may or may not be doing isn't healthy. And yet. . ." His dark eyes crinkled at the corners and his mouth tightened. "You refuse to come right out and ask. It's hard to watch you self-destruct like this. Tell me why you won't confront your husband."

"Because I'm afraid, all right? I'm afraid of being right." I stepped out of his grip and rubbed the speckles of rain from my bare arms. "There, I said it."

"Now we're getting somewhere." He resumed our walk, tossing a casual wave at the elderly man who'd been faithfully baking bread longer than I'd been alive.

I added my greeting before catching up to Tristan. "Don't try to psychoanalyze me. You have your own issues, like why you can't keep a girlfriend and commit."

"Hmm. . .classic deflection."

Having a psychologist for a best friend definitely had its downside.

Tristan stepped around a caterpillar inching its way toward a crack in the sidewalk. Dark clouds hung low, and thunder rumbled in the distance. "What's the worst thing that could happen?"

"He could be having an affair."

"And. . ."

I hated his leading tone, but I still played along. "And he could want to leave me for her because she's better than me, and prettier and younger."

"And. . ."

"Then I'd be alone."

"And. . ."

My voice rose an octave. "And I'd grow old, eating cat food and watching soap operas on a lumpy couch!"

Tristan sat on a low stone fence that bordered the animal clinic. A simper played on his lips. "See? It's not so bad."

"I just said I'd be eating cat food." I drilled him with a glare.

A wide grin creased his face as he ignored the fat raindrops that began to fall around us. "I guess since I'm a commitment-phobe, I'll be sitting next to you, on said lumpy couch. Except. . ." His eyes softened, drawing me into their chocolatey goodness. "I'll be eating takeout."

I whacked his shoulder. He caught my hand and gave it a playful squeeze before locking me into his reassuring gaze. "Trust me, even if the worst turns out to be true—and it rarely does—the actual event isn't nearly as bad as the idea of it."

A surprise awaited us when we arrived back at New Heights.

The tiny mewl of a newborn baby was like music—and a buzz saw—to my heart. But I couldn't help myself. I crossed the lobby swiftly and reached out for the tiny bundle. "Marjorie—I had no idea you'd delivered."

The young mother placed the burrito-wrapped infant into my arms. "Two days ago, and it was way harder than I thought. I wish I'd taken a birthing class or something."

Her words reminded me to look into scheduling a birthing class as I cooed. "You're just a handsome little fellow."

"You're the first person I wanted to see my son. This is Jacob."

Tristan gave a cursory nod to Marjorie and her newborn before heading to his office for his afternoon appointments.

A blue knit hat covered Jacob's tiny head, and his eyes remained closed with wispy lashes feathering his skin. His rosebud lips puckered and loosened, as though he was dreaming of warm milk. I held back tears as I whispered to him. "You are so beautiful, little man. I bet your mama is the proudest mother ever."

Kaitlyn peered over my shoulder. "Look at his cheeks. So adorable."

The feel of this tiny life pressed against my body stirred a longing so deep inside me that I began to ache. Still, I didn't hand him back—I couldn't. Instead, I closed my eyes and breathed in the newborn smell that offered both peace and pain.

Marjorie sat in the rocking chair across from the reception desk. A weary, mother-of-a-newborn smile spread across her face. "If it wasn't for you, I never could've gotten through my pregnancy."

Warmth seeped into my heart and soothed the raw places. "I'm really glad we could help you, but don't discount your own strength."

"Trust me," Marjorie said to Kaitlyn, "you're in good hands with Marissa. She'll get you set up with everything you need to be a good mom."

Kaitlyn drew back, not meeting anyone's gaze. "I haven't actually decided yet, you know, whether or not I'm keeping it. It's all so scary."

Marjorie flashed me a knowing look. Silently, I moved to Kaitlyn and handed her little Jacob.

"No. . .I. . . ," she protested.

"Shh. You'll wake him." With a gentle hand, I completed the transfer. Jacob settled into the crook of Kaitlyn's arm. Her eyes glistened with unshed tears in what I could only call a Baby Magic Moment. Soon her rigidity softened into a natural cradle.

"No matter what you decide, it won't be long before your little one is here." I palmed her arm, hoping she'd realize how crucial it was to start making preparations, one way or another.

Marjorie smiled mirthlessly. "Boy, ain't that the truth. It might seem like a long time off, but it comes around quicker than you think."

A pained expression flashed across Kaitlyn's delicate face. "That's what I'm afraid of."

It seemed fear was making a visit to all of us, without discretion. I offered what I hoped was a comforting hug. "We're here to back you up. Have confidence that you'll make the right decision." I had to remember to pray more diligently for her and trust that God would answer. Trust that He had this.

"I can't put it off anymore." Kaitlyn's shoulders heaved. "I'm going to talk to my parents. Waiting for the weekend is the same as chickening out."

We gave her a round of "atta girls" and continued to coo at Jacob until my cell phone buzzed in my pocket. I excused myself and closed the door to my office before pulling the phone out. Tentatively, I answered the unknown caller.

"This is Kelly from Dr. Lopez's office. We had a last-minute cancellation for this afternoon, and you're at the top of the wait list. Would you be available to come in at four o'clock?"

My heart rapid-fired. I clutched the cross dangling around my neck and considered the implications of finally seeing the fertility specialist. Once I started the process, there was no looking back. And if it didn't work out and there was nothing they could do for me, then I was at the end of the road. I cleared my throat to steady my voice. "Yes, I'll be there."

# CHAPTER 26

*Kaitlyn*

Alone. There was no other way to describe the hollowed-out, empty space in Kaitlyn's heart that her parents' love used to occupy.

She climbed inside her car and pressed her fist to her mouth, determined to keep a neutral expression. What a letdown. After talking with Marissa and Marjorie, she'd been so sure that her conversation with her parents would turn out fine, or at least not bad. She straightened her back and swallowed her tears. No way was she going to have a breakdown in their driveway, not with her mom peeking out from the blinds and reporting back to her dad.

*Dad.*

The word took on a new meaning after today. She'd expected the disappointment and even a smidgen of judgment. What she hadn't expected was the raised voice and purpling face, then being told to leave and not come back while her mother stood silently by.

Now Kaitlyn was at odds with the man who'd loved and protected her, who'd raised her to think for herself and be true to that person. Evidently he didn't love that person as much as he thought.

Kaitlyn refused to look back. She eased out of the driveway and headed home, desolate. She cranked the music in an effort to stop herself from replaying the ugly scene over and over, each time ending up the same—with her on the road. . .and on her own. Rain began to splatter against the windshield, blurring the view. She changed the radio station, searching for something upbeat and cheerful, but she ended up settling for boring talk radio. It helped steady her nerves as she drove through the storm back to Elden Springs.

Without her parents' involvement, she was going to have to rely on Marissa and New Heights more than she'd ever planned. She'd been watching the young women who came through the doors, each one with a different life story, most of them painful. Several were planning to give their babies up for adoption, and an equal number were ready to take on the challenge of single parenting. A few couples came in, teens who were young and unprepared for the realities facing them, but they seemed to have the most bravado, as though by being young and in love they could conquer anything.

Emotion welled inside her as she considered for the thousandth time what would be best for her baby. Would she be enough for a child to rely on? Sure, she was resourceful, but she'd always believed that a child needed both parents. Why should she cheat the kid out of the joy of having a mother and a father? Although, judging by what happened to her tonight, that didn't always work out either. Life offered no guarantees. Just look at Marjorie who had lost her husband overseas, yet she was facing parenting with courage and hope.

Courage and hope. It would take a heavy dose of both, but it wasn't impossible. She was reasonably competent and hardworking, and she had a lot of love to give.

At that moment, it became clear to Kaitlyn what she had to do: she had to keep the baby.

This life growing in her belly was hers to love. Hers to cherish. Hers to protect.

She paused to give thanks to God—whether or not He was actually listening. A whisper of joy stirred inside her, sustaining her until she arrived home.

She hadn't even kicked off her flip-flops and set down her soaking wet purse when the doorbell rang. Unusual since it was almost dark, and she rarely had visitors.

Had her parents followed her, wanting to make amends? She stiffened as her pulse kicked up a notch. All these adrenaline rushes lately couldn't possibly be good for the baby. She straightened her back and forced herself to breathe deeply several times.

She could handle this.

They'd hug. They'd cry. And then they'd work through this together, just as they always had.

The bell rang again.

With a final breath, she swung open the door.

"Colin." Her voice hitched in her throat at the sight of her former lover—she realized now why he'd never referred to her as a girlfriend—rocking on his heels, hands stuffed deep inside his pockets as he hunched over to avoid the rain dripping from the roof. Hair disheveled and circles under his eyes, he looked sheepish, unlike the hardened version of himself that she'd encountered at the university and at The Bean.

He threw a glance over his shoulder—another of his habits that suddenly made sense. "Can I come in?"

Kaitlyn stepped aside and allowed him to enter, quietly breathing in the scent of aftershave and academia that was uniquely Colin. "What are you doing here?"

Hands still inside his pockets, he looked from her to the love seat as though asking permission to be in her space. "I think it's fair to say we need to talk."

"I'm glad you think so." Hesitantly, she closed the door and moved into the living room, situating herself on the recliner that sat opposite the love seat. She motioned for him to make himself comfortable.

Acid seeped into her stomach as she waited for him to say something that would magically fix this situation. But the longer they sat in uncomfortable silence, the more the heartburn ate her from the inside out.

Colin's eyes locked onto her. "I'm sorry for the way I acted. It was wrong."

She nodded, unsure what to say. Unsure where she even wanted this conversation to lead. Clearly she didn't want another woman's husband, and yet that's what she had sitting in front of her. The father of her baby. At least she hadn't told her parents that part. There had been no need once the initial news was delivered. If they didn't want to be involved, then it really made no difference.

Except to her—and whomever Colin was married to.

She swallowed hard and hoped the heartburn would subside. "I understand that it must've been a shock."

"Understatement." Colin leaned forward and rested his elbows on his denim-clad knees. "I really don't know what to say except that it's a mess. I should've been straight up with you from the beginning about..." His unsaid words thickened the air.

"Your wife?" she prompted.

"Yes, my wife." His words sounded feeble, like those of a man who wasn't sure where his marriage was even headed. Or maybe it was her wishful thinking. If he wasn't married, would he want her? She didn't want to be the reason a man left his wife, but if he did... would they be together?

She sickened at the thought of what she'd become—a woman who was desperate in an ugly and complicated way. The acid burbled inside her, leaking up her throat, and her salivary glands tingled. She clutched her chest and rose abruptly. "Sorry, I need to—"

Kaitlyn scurried down the hall and burst into the bathroom, threw open the toilet lid, and leaned over. Her eyes watered as she released. Why now? Humiliation swept over her as she finished and flushed away her dinner that had turned sour not long after talking to her parents. She swiped her eyes with the back of her hand.

"Let me help." Colin entered the room and grabbed the hand towel, then turned on the faucet and dampened the cloth. He tugged at her shoulder and helped her stand before pressing the cool towel to her face.

Kaitlyn leaned against the counter and took the cloth from Colin. Her stupid body couldn't have waited until he was gone to heave?

Suddenly she felt strong arms encircle her, pulling her into a rock-solid chest. She breathed deeply, remembering when she freely enjoyed burrowing into Colin—no guilt, no second thoughts.

She drew back and dared to meet his weighty gaze. Wasn't this what she'd been hoping for since she'd seen the plus sign in the little window on the pregnancy test? More than anything, she wanted a father for her child and for that man to hold her and tell her they would have a happy ending.

But not at someone else's expense. She wasn't that desperate or cruel—at least she didn't want to believe she was.

"Feeling better?" He smoothed the hair back from her face, his touch both tender and searing, and then he cupped her cheek and searched her eyes.

She nodded without pulling away.

Colin's brow flexed. "Does this happen often?"

Unable to meet his gaze any longer, she studied the tiles on the floor and her chipped-polish toenails. "More than I thought it would, but supposedly once I'm past the first trimester it'll get better."

"How far along are you?" The concern in his low, sonorous voice reminded her why she'd been so drawn to him. One of many reasons which she was trying daily to forget.

"About twelve weeks, give or take."

"Does your roommate—what's her name?—help you?"

Kaitlyn eased away from his touch, her face hot. "Sydney—she's gone for the summer."

Colin leaned against the counter next to her, their arms brushing. "I'm really sorry you've had to deal with this alone. I admit I was a jerk."

Her mouth puckered as she bit back accusing words. Now that she knew his situation, what good would a guilt trip do? They had nowhere to go from here. Had he also apologized to his wife for having an affair? Did she even know? As much as Kaitlyn wondered—had been wondering for days—she wasn't going to ask. Even more guilt would pile on her if she started to think of his wife as a woman with feelings, a woman whose life she'd damaged.

"Come." Colin grazed her hand, tugging just hard enough to guide her out of the bathroom before he let go. He hovered over her until she was situated on the love seat then disappeared into the kitchen. Cabinet doors opened and closed, then the faucet ran. He reappeared at her side with a cup. "You probably need to hydrate."

Funny that he had the nerve to tell her what she should do, but she didn't refuse the offering. She drank deeply to cleanse the sourness in her mouth.

"Slow sips," he whispered as he crouched next to her and watched.

She pulled the cup away and frowned. "I'm fine now, really."

Colin held up his hands and backed away, then sat in the recliner and continued to scrutinize her every motion. He rubbed his hands together, started to speak, and then stopped.

"Just spit it out," she said before setting the cup down with a clatter. "I know you didn't come here to watch me get sick, so why are you here?" She hated the sharpness of her tone, but she couldn't help it, not now, with all the anguish of the past few months simmering at the surface. "Are you here to make sure I stay quiet? To make sure I don't cause trouble for you at work?" Her hands fisted. "Or with your wife?"

Colin blanched. Myriad emotions flickered across his face before he spoke. "I came here to try to do the right thing."

"Which is what, exactly? I hope you have a good answer, because I'd really like to know what the right thing is now that I know you're married." The last word clogged her throat. Hearing it out loud, it sounded even worse than it did in her head.

He pushed out of the recliner and sent it rocking. "I don't know." He paced the room, seeming to fill the small space with ragged concern and angst. "For the life of me, I wish I knew. I wish I could go back—" He cut himself off.

"Just say it," she murmured. "You wish you hadn't been with me."

"That's not—" He ran his hand through his hair.

"Can't bring yourself to keep lying to me?" The softness of her voice belied the venom in her veins. To think how he'd deceived her every time they were together made her sick.

Colin spun to face her. His jaw ticked. "I never led you to believe we had a future."

"No one said you did, but I certainly didn't think you were married." She hugged her knees to her chest.

"Really?" He paced in front of her, his shoes squawking every time he spun and turned. He lowered his voice and leveled his gaze at her. "Can you honestly say you had no idea?"

"Of course not. You don't even have a wedding ring—you know, the universal symbol for marriage." She stabbed the air toward his empty finger.

"So what? I lost it." His mouth tightened before he spoke again. "Think about it. Think about our whole so-called relationship and tell me you didn't know."

The bluntness of his comments caught her off guard. So many times since finding out the truth, she'd asked herself if there were clues she had missed. The clandestine meetings away from campus, never being invited to his home, and the stretches of time she didn't hear from him all pointed to his needing secrecy to protect his job. But in hindsight, they meant so much more.

She sighed, defeated. "I guess I saw what I wanted to see."

In two steps he was at her side, lowered to one knee. "I did too, and I'm sorry for getting so angry. I just don't know where to go with this."

"What are we going to do? What happens now?" The answers, whatever they were, terrified her.

Colin eased onto the seat next to her as the clock in the kitchen ticked loudly to mark the moments. She hated that having him here was a comfort, especially because she knew it wouldn't last. Already she had to anticipate the moment he'd walk out the door, leaving her to guess whether or not he'd be back. The difference from just a month ago, when she felt so confident in his feelings for her, was startling. Scary how life could change so fast, and the changes were only beginning.

Finally he spoke. "I don't know what the right thing is now, but I know that I can't leave you alone in this." No declarations of his feelings for her, only a sense of duty. Matter of fact. Clinical. He was a scientist, after all.

"How involved can you be?" She faced him and searched his eyes for answers. When he didn't offer any, she continued. "Does your wife know?"

He shook his head, his chin no longer high.

"Then how much can you really do? I don't want to sneak around, and I obviously can't hide." She motioned to her stomach. "Not for long."

"Assuming my. . .wife. . .isn't a factor, I want to be as involved as possible." His shoulders heaved as he sought her gaze. "I want this baby."

# CHAPTER 27

*Marissa*

Monsoon season was late in making its thunderous appearance, but the first storm was a doozy. Lightning fractured the sky and rain pummeled the city with a vengeance.

After my appointment at the fertility clinic, I came back to New Heights to finish some paperwork and put out more feelers on other classes I wanted to hold for the mothers. There was no need to hurry home—Colin never did—but tonight was different because I was eager to tell him all about the appointment. Waiting to talk to him was sweet torture.

Shortly before dark, I scurried out of New Heights, dodging puddles all the way to my car where I slid inside, dripping wet. Rain and makeup ran down my cheeks, causing me to look like a ruined watercolor.

I added *Umbrella* to my mental checklist.

By the time I got home, I was shivering and opted to climb straight into my pajamas and then make tea before starting dinner. I had to cook something to make the evening special. Literally everything sounded delicious as though I'd been starving for a decade. When I finally made a decision—lemon garlic pasta and an enormous salad with all the fixings—the chopping, stirring, and sautéing helped me dial down my excitement. Once that was done I pulled out a loaf of sourdough bread and buttered it generously.

Nothing says joy like carbs.

With dinner staying warm on the stove, I pulled a festive tablecloth out of the linen cupboard and set the table with china and real silverware. Two place settings for now, but one day it could be three.

Nervousness spun inside my stomach as I fiddled with the stemware. What if the treatments didn't work? The more I hoped, the more I'd have to lose. Remaining infertile would be a crushing blow, one that I wasn't entirely sure I could weather.

But I wouldn't be in it alone. Colin would see it through with me. No matter how my arms ached to hold a child, my husband wanted it even more. He always had, since the moment we'd said "I do." He'd covered up his disappointment over the years since the miscarriage better than I had, but I knew.

I *knew*.

Colin was meant to be a father. Infertility had strained our relationship over the recent months—or years, depending on how one looked at it. The back-and-forth between hope and disappointment had become a vicious cycle, but now, with prayer and modern science, we could be parents.

I could be a *mother*.

The clock in the hallway chimed. Eight thirty. Colin would be here soon, and I still needed the perfect way to tell him. I couldn't get too carried away or he might think I was already pregnant. Of course, considering our marital track record, that would be silly. Maybe I could sit him down to dinner and when we were situated at the table—

When had talking to my husband become so ridiculously hard? Forget it, I was going to be casual and just let it out.

The key jangled in the lock of the front door, sending my heart into a staccato rhythm.

I smoothed the front of my pajamas—why hadn't I thought to change?—and held my breath. Now it was too late to think of some clever way to tell him our lives were about to change. I would just tell him right away. His eyes would light up like they had the first—and only—time I was pregnant before. Only this time it would work out.

It had to.

Seconds passed before he walked inside. His hair was soaked, and dark half-moons hung under his eyes, which seemed tight with fatigue and worry. Even his clothing was rumpled and in need of a good cleaning. How had I been so absorbed in my own internal drama and suspicions that I hadn't noticed my husband's haggard appearance?

All that was about to change. Colin worked hard and had struggled with me for so long that he deserved a fresh start—we both did.

I brightened and willed him to look at me, to notice me the way he used to. Instead, he set his leather satchel down and leaned against the table in the foyer, his back to me. His muscles moved beneath the fabric of his shirt as though he were trying to turn himself around but couldn't stand to face me.

Anxiety nibbled me from the inside, but I quashed it. Nothing would spoil this night, not when I'd worked so hard to set aside my fears and go to the appointment. I cleared my throat, but still he refused to turn. His shoulders began to pump up and down, and I could hear his deep breaths from across the room.

"Colin, what is it?" Concern laced my voice. I hadn't even considered the possibility he'd had a rough day at work, or worse, didn't make tenure. I steeled myself for the worst as I shuffled across the floor in my slippers. Tentatively I approached him from behind, unsure whether to reach out or let him be.

He glanced over his shoulder and managed to avoid eye contact. "We need to talk."

The words no one wants to hear, especially on a night of celebration. Without his tenure and the money that would surely come with it, we'd be hard-pressed to pay for the treatments, but we'd be hard-pressed regardless. Somehow we'd make it work like we'd always made everything work, from money to marriage. We'd become masters of making do.

"Come in and you can tell me all about it." My stomach clenched as I silently prayed for the patience to hear him out, and for a good response from him when it was my turn to talk. Surely my news would change his mood.

Colin spun to face me. Darkness camped in his gaze as he began to weigh and assess me in an unnerving way. "You need to sit down."

"What happened?" I backed into the living room, never taking my eyes off him as he rubbed the scruff on his face and followed me. The leather couch squeaked when I sat and patted the space next to me.

But instead of sitting with me, Colin perched on the edge of the recliner at a comfortable distance and rested his elbows on his jittery knees. "I really don't know how to tell you this."

"Is it about the promotion?" I scooted closer and tried to offer comfort. "It's going to be okay. There will be other opportunities in the future, and you're brilliant—everyone thinks so." I paused and tried to come up with something else to say to alleviate his angst. "And I have some good news that might cheer you up."

His knee stopped bouncing, and he finally stared at me head-on. "This isn't about my job."

My mouth opened but I had nothing to say. What else would distress him like this? Worry pooled in my stomach as possibilities began to take shape. My worst fears gelled into the palpable tension that now hung between me and my husband.

Sadness tinged Colin's eyes and his breath became ragged. "I messed up."

"Whatever it is can't be that bad," I said, more to myself than to him.

"It is." His jaw ticked and his face turned red. "And there's nothing I can do to fix it."

I refused to weave him a safety net of comforting words, but instead waited for him to give voice to the fears that had been building inside me for months. It wasn't just me. It wasn't just my imagination.

I wasn't crazy.

"I've been having an affair."

His confession lanced me with unimaginable pain. A jagged breath lodged inside my chest as I fought to compose myself. Colin would not have the satisfaction of seeing me cry even though tears stabbed the back of my eyes. Fire licked my throat and kept me from speaking, which was fine because for the first time since I could remember, I had absolutely nothing to say.

Colin studied the floor for a moment before burying his face in his hands and mumbling, "I'm sorry. So sorry."

Was he? Who really knew?

I sat in stunned silence, unable to move as the realization assaulted me. My husband had shared himself with another woman. Anxiety squeezed my lungs. I clutched my chest and panted to catch air, but I still began to feel light-headed and tingly. I shut my eyes and willed my heart to slow.

It had been years since I'd had a real panic attack, and I didn't need one now. Not with Colin watching and triumphing over me because he found someone new and better.

"Marissa, did you hear me?"

When I opened my eyes, Colin was by my side. "Of course I heard you." I tasted the bitterness in my words. He deserved nothing less.

"My apology—I meant it. I'm sorry." His voice faltered.

I rose on shaky legs and pushed past him. I needed to get away, to be alone and have my breakdown in private.

"Wait."

I stopped, knowing there was nothing he could say to make it better or go away or turn back time. Nothing.

Nothing.

"What?" I asked without turning around, afraid the slightest movement would send me to the ground.

"There's more, and you need to hear it now." He spoke from behind, and I could tell he was getting close. Too close. "Look at me, please. I have to know you're okay."

"I'm not okay. There's nothing about this that's okay." The mockery in my tone was the only mask I had for the hurt. I froze in place and prayed I could escape before my entire body went numb the way it had during my last panic attack. Slow, deep breaths did nothing to calm me, and I feared falling with only Colin to catch me, if he even would.

He walked around me and reached for my shoulders.

"Don't touch me," I said between breaths.

Colin drew his hands back to his sides. "You might as well know everything. Do you want to sit again?"

"Don't bother asking me what I want. It's too late." My pulse throbbed from my temples to my toes.

"I know this is hard to hear." He shook me slightly.

I yanked away. "You should've thought of that before. . ." I couldn't bring myself to finish.

"I know that—do you think I don't know how badly I screwed up?" He squeezed his eyes. "Trust me, I know."

"Trust is the last thing I have for you." Light-headed, I could hardly speak. I almost wished I'd let him steady my shoulders, but the thought of his touch—a touch he'd willingly given to someone else—sickened me.

Sorrow tinged his voice. "I never meant for this to happen." After thoroughly destroying me, all Colin had to offer was a cliché.

"An affair isn't something you accidentally do." I turned to leave but he walled off the staircase with his body.

"Just listen, please. I have to get this out." His urgency scared me.

What more could there be? My worst fears had already been proven. Nothing else could hurt me, and I didn't really want the details. I didn't want to know who she was or what she looked like or how I compared.

It was obvious I compared poorly or we wouldn't be having this conversation.

"I need to be alone." My lips and face began to tingle and my arms were numb. "Whatever it is, just say it."

Colin's shoulders heaved. His jaw ground furiously again, as though he somehow cared. Was he going to ask me to forgive him and stay together? Or was he going to ask for a divorce?

*Divorce.*

The word spilled new dread into my heart. I guess there really was something worse than hearing my husband had slept with another woman. He wanted to be with her forever, that had to be it. Maybe they were already making plans, and of course I was the last to know.

How could I convince him to stay? God hates divorce, and there was no way I could be part of that. Somehow we'd have to get through this.

"There's no easy way to say this."

"Should've thought of that before." Now the top of my head was tingling. I needed to leave. I could feel my limbs weakening, and I didn't want a panic attack to add to my humiliation. I needed to escape this nightmare with at least a smidgen of dignity.

Colin lowered his eyes and pinched the bridge of his nose. "The woman," he said, shame coating his voice. "She's pregnant."

*She's pregnant.*

Those were the last words I heard before I blacked out.

# CHAPTER 28

*Marissa*

Tristan's theory about a negative event not being nearly as bad as the anticipation of it was crap. Pure crap.

I lay in bed for two days, calling in sick and wishing I had the energy to get up and face life. Before Colin's confession I'd pictured my reaction to such news in detail. I'd hold my chin up, wish him well, and walk away to start a new life with self-respect.

Instead I hid under the covers without changing outfits or showering, and my hair smelled bad even to me. Then there was the humiliation of having the man who destroyed me be the one to see to my daily needs. Not the picture of grace and self-respect I'd previously imagined, and the funny thing was, I didn't care.

I didn't care about the calls I wasn't returning, I didn't care about eating or drinking, and I didn't care whether or not Colin saw me for who I really was—a weak, codependent, infertile woman.

On the third morning Colin came into the bedroom—which was now officially mine, according to the sleeping arrangements of the past few days—and opened the blinds. I squinted against the bright light and rolled over to face the wall.

"You need to get up. This isn't healthy." The bed sank behind me when he sat. He nudged my back, and I could feel him lean closer until he was hovering over my shoulder. "You have to talk to me. I gave you time."

I jerked away, silently willing him to touch me again and at the same time loathing myself for wanting it. "I don't have to do anything."

"Fine." His clipped tone punctured me. The bed rose when he stood, and my body was cold in his absence. "There's some pancakes for you in the kitchen. I have to go, but you can call me when you're ready to talk."

Well, that was a first.

I kept my eyes closed until he left. I teared up, and once again I was crying. Not the gut-wrenching sobs that strangled me the first day but the soft cry of the desperate. What was I going to do? What was *he* going to do? I couldn't begin to know his mind when I hardly knew my own. If only I had the strength to walk away, but I didn't see that happening. More than likely I would hang on to him until the bitter end—and he would be the one to decide when that was.

Maybe he already had.

The thought of facing the future alone terrified me, but at least I knew I wasn't crazy. I hadn't imagined all the signs that pointed toward his unfaithfulness, though that was of little comfort.

It didn't take long for the bedroom to heat up with the blinds open. I threw off the covers and swung my feet to the floor, willing myself to get up, if for no other reason than to make the room dark again. But once I was up and mobile, the thought of pancakes drew me downstairs.

Why had he gone to such trouble? He hadn't made breakfast for me in years, and frankly, I was surprised he could even find his way around the kitchen. Either he was feeling terrible or he was ready to talk divorce, and I wasn't making any bets.

My legs ached from days of inactivity, but I made it down the stairs just as the doorbell rang. It was entirely too early for visitors, and I was in no condition to see a magazine salesman or a meat-truck man, and I especially didn't want anyone telling me how much God loved me. Not right now when I was too raw to hear it.

The doorbell rang again, three times in succession, keeping me from my pancakes. Perhaps Colin had forgotten his keys, and that was okay. He could stay outside and sweat out the summer heat.

The doorbell was replaced with incessant knocking and a booming voice. "I know you're in there. Open up."

Tristan.

There had to be some little lie I could conjure up in the next ten seconds that would send him away without him digging into my personal life. Or telling me to get help, aka get medicated.

I moderated my expression before I opened the door. "What brings you by?"

Tristan held up a coffee cup and motioned for me to step aside. "You can't possibly miss our morning meeting for the third day in a row and think I'm not coming to check on you."

"I thought I texted you that I wasn't coming in today."

"That must've been your imagination." He quirked an eyebrow and handed me the cup.

The blessed scent of strong coffee made me rethink getting rid of my friend, and I was almost grateful for Tristan's intrusion.

He closed the door and walked inside, then proceeded to make himself comfortable. Would he have done that if Colin had been home? I scoffed.

"What's that for?" he asked, peering over the rim of his cup.

"I just can't believe you're here. Did you see Colin leave?" I padded over to the recliner and sat, allowing the warmth of the cup to seep into my hands. Familiar comfort.

"As a matter of fact, I waved to him when he turned the corner." Tristan smirked, as close an acknowledgment as I'd ever get that he sensed the unspoken tension between them.

Of course, there was no reason for Colin to be territorial over me when he had someone else in his arms. Apparently that had been wishful thinking on my part.

"Clearly you're not sick." He crossed his leg over his knee and scrutinized me. "But you could use a shower. What gives?"

"Why are you here, really?"

"Besides the fact that we've had to reschedule ten clients—three new ones—there's the small fact that your mom asked me to come look for you."

"My mom? Why?" I sucked in a large breath the moment I remembered my mother. "I forgot all about her doctor appointment. I need to go." I stood abruptly.

"No, it's okay." Tristan motioned for me to sit back down.

"I dropped her off just now and promised I'd come check on you. Because forgetting your mom is flaky. . .even for you." His humor disarmed me.

For the first time in days, the urge to cry was a little less insistent. "Thank you for helping her. I guess I should call her later."

"Not only that—you should talk to me."

I trained my attention on my coffee cup rather than meet his scrutiny. "There's nothing to say. If I don't feel well, I don't feel well."

"Ah, but there's the rub. Not feeling well can mean so many things, especially coming from you." Tristan sipped his coffee, apparently ready to wait me out the way he always did to get me to say things I didn't even want to admit to myself.

I leaned against the recliner and rocked, taking in the sweet aroma of coffee made just the way I liked it. "How's Kaitlyn?"

"Sick, but at least *she's* still coming to work," he said with a hint of displeasure in his voice.

"I'm sorry, but I just can't. Not today."

Tristan leaned forward, close enough that I could feel his gaze raking over me. "That's fine, but can you at least tell me why? It's not like you to shut me out."

The weight of his concern was too much to bear. Why couldn't my own husband care for me as much as the man who'd become my best friend? If a man as amazing, thoughtful, and successful as Tristan cared about me, then maybe I wasn't the problem.

Yet shame still scorched me. Colin's cheating slashed my heart in ways I hadn't imagined. Telling someone else would only make it more real, and I could never un-tell the secret. And Tristan of all people. . .I didn't want to lose the esteem I apparently had in his eyes.

He laid a soft hand on my leg and stopped me from rocking. "Whatever it is, it can't be that bad. And even if it is, we can work through it together."

I swallowed hard to steady my voice. "Remember when you said that the bad thing I was dreading wouldn't be as bad as the dread itself?"

"Vaguely."

"Do you remember what we were talking about then?" I prodded him to come up with the answer so I didn't have to say it out loud.

Light dawned in his eyes. He sat back and let out a long, slow breath while shaking his head. "How'd you find out?"

"He told me a few days ago." How many had it been? I couldn't tell for certain since pain had a timeline of its own. I curled my legs to my chest and began rocking again, the soft squeak of the recliner offering a bit of comfort.

"I'm so, so sorry." The timbre of his voice held the sorrow he claimed. "I had no idea he'd really do that to you."

I could feel my lips purse. "Come on now, you can't have believed he was squeaky clean. I know he's not your favorite person."

"Probably not for the reasons you think."

The only tidbits Tristan could know about Colin were the things I'd told him, which admittedly were more than I should have. "What do you mean by that?"

"Nothing." His gaze flitted away. "So. . .you've been holed up in here ever since?"

"Not very big of me, I admit." I shrugged, apathetic. So what if the world went on around me? I was no longer part of it, at least not in the eyes of the one person I'd worked so hard to matter to. Of course, there was my mother who needed care and attention, and I fully planned to give her just that—as soon as I could pull myself together well enough to fake it in front of her.

"Hey," he said as he laid his hand on the arm of the recliner, bringing my attention back to him. "There isn't a wrong way to respond, as long as you're not harming yourself."

"Who said anything like that?" The alarm in my voice startled me.

"I mean 'you' in general. People. Everyone."

My muscles relaxed, and I resumed gazing out the front window, wishing Colin hadn't opened the blinds there either. The light hurt.

"Have you eaten?" he asked hesitantly.

"I was just about to heat up the pancakes Colin left. Do you want some?" I took another sip of coffee.

"No thanks. I ate at The Bean." Tristan mirrored me and took a drink. "By the way, Kaitlyn is really missing you. And Christina. We all are."

I smiled. At least I mattered to some really great people. "I guess I can come in today." The thought of slogging through a day of meeting with expectant mothers and showing them their babies sent a chill through me. Normally I could rejoice with others, but not today. Maybe not ever again. I stood, determined to hide my real feelings from my friend. "But first I need to eat something."

"And shower. Definitely shower." Tristan wrinkled his nose before he smiled, lightening the air around me.

"Thanks, I'll take that into consideration." Even as I returned his smile, tears pressed against the back of my eyes. I stood and hustled toward the kitchen before he could see, but in usual Tristan fashion, he followed.

"So. . .what are you going to do?" Tristan leaned against the counter while I unwrapped the plate of pancakes.

"What do you mean?" I pulled butter from the fridge. Today I'd need a lot.

"Well, I don't want to pry, but what are you going to do about Colin?" It was so unlike him to ask a direct question that it caught me off guard. Usually he led me to ask the questions myself.

I met his gaze. "What can I do?"

A flash of unease swept across his face. "Are you going to stay with him? Walk away? Get help? You have decisions to make."

My mouth opened and closed at the possibilities. I'd thought about what I would do if it ever came to this, but without believing I would ever take action. To take a stand wasn't in my nature, especially when it came to men.

Speechless, I peeled the lid off the butter while refusing to look at Tristan.

It had to be because of my father—or more specifically, my lack of one.

From my earliest memories, I'd always attached myself to the man of the moment—uncles, teachers, and, as I grew, boyfriends. Always wanting to earn their approval, I sacrificed myself in order to be noticed and loved.

The realization seemed both poignant and cheesy. Psychology 101. Something Tristan probably pegged about me from the start.

And in his own special way, he did it to me again. Sweet Tristan, whose favor I never had to earn and who always stood with me, even when I took a long and twisted path.

"You have a say in what happens to you." Tristan's soft expression melted my defenses, what few I had left.

"I know that." I angled away from him so he couldn't read my face.

"Do you? You need to believe you have equal say in your relationship. You deserve to find joy in life." Tristan approached me slowly. "Now, tell me the things you haven't said yet."

I shook my head, unwilling to let him into my vulnerable places. Why would I fess up about my shortcomings? Shortcomings that were now highlighted by another woman's accidental success.

Or maybe it hadn't been a mistake on her part. Maybe she'd wanted to lure Colin out of our marriage. I'd heard that story more than once at the center from women desperate enough to make that gamble. Colin was handsome, an up-and-coming bigwig in his field. Any woman in her right mind would love a shot with him.

"Pancakes—nothing soothes the ego like carbs. Right?" Finally I faced him, my vision hazy with tears.

He palmed my shoulders. "No more deflecting, no more defenses." His neck bobbed, and he momentarily glanced away. "It's okay to be hurt and angry. It's okay to feel whatever it is you're feeling."

My breath shuddered until I held it to compose myself. Before I could think twice, I blurted my most painful secret. "I'm infertile."

He startled but didn't pull away. "I'm sorry. I had no idea." He released my shoulders but held his close position. "Do you think that's why Colin. . ."

"That's not it." I shook my head vehemently. "It's just that. . .she's pregnant." The sobs came on strong. "The woman he's with is going to have his baby."

Tristan drew me into a tight embrace, where I released days' worth of betrayal and years' worth of bitterness.

# CHAPTER 29

*Colin*

"Congratulations, for the second year in a row—city champs!"
The group of boys cheered loudly enough to startle the rest of the customers in the pizza joint. Colin looked over the group with pride. These kids were like a second family. He would do anything for each one of them, and they all knew it. After a few more encouraging words, the pizza arrived at the tables and the hungry boys dug in.

"Good job, bro." Adam offered a firm handshake and a wide grin. "Time to celebrate."

"Kind of sad to see the season end." Colin sank into a booth and slung his arm over the back of the seat.

"It is, but Lani is going to be glad to have me home more." Adam slid a slice of meaty pizza from the metal tray onto a paper plate and shoved it in front of Colin. Then he served himself. "How about Marissa?"

Colin scoffed. He hadn't meant to, but after days of trying to coax Marissa out of her funk, he'd given up. This time she was going to have to pull herself out.

"Dude, what's happening now?" Adam leaned close and spoke in low tones covered by the whirrs and beeps of the video games nearby. "She's not excited to have you around more? Have you told her?"

Colin glanced over his shoulder. The kids all busied themselves with cheese and pepperoni, and the parents were huddled in their usual clusters, talking about the game-winning home run—as he should be. Putting on a game face during an actual game was one thing, but schmoozing parents after the fact when he was so broken inside was another. He leaned over the table. "Yeah, I told her. Things went from bad to worse."

"What you told me was about as bad as it could get." Disapproval lurked in his eyes. "Does she want to leave you?"

Colin grabbed a straw and tapped it until it tore through the paper. "She hasn't said so. But then, she hasn't said anything."

"Nothing?"

"She stayed in bed the last three days. She may have gone to work yesterday, but I'm not sure." He picked up his cup and twirled the ice with his straw.

"You don't even know if your wife has been out of bed?" Fire lit Adam's eyes and his hands balled into fists. "Then what are you doing here?"

Colin slammed his cup onto the table, harder than he'd meant to. A few parents looked his way but quickly resumed their own conversations. "I had to coach the game. I'm not going to let these kids down."

"But you'll let your wife down?"

Colin hated the judgment in his friend's expression. Too bad he'd told his secret—he'd known at the time it was a bad move. "You have no idea what it's like to be with Marissa when she goes into one of her moods."

"Do you even *hear* yourself?" Adam's eyes pinched at the corners.

Colin looked away and focused on the lights and buzzing of the games, the laughter of happy children, the smell of cheap pizza—anything but his life. After taking a swig of soda, he forged ahead. "I hear myself, and I know it's bad."

"Did you or did you not cut it off with the other woman?" Adam demanded answers that he had no right to, but Colin was in no position to argue.

"I did, but Marissa's still freezing me out."

Adam leaned closer and spoke in a loud whisper. "You made sure Marissa knew you ended the affair?"

"Not exactly."

"What do you mean, not exactly?" Adam swiped his hand over his reddened face. "If she thinks you'll leave her, then of course she's inconsolable. Maybe I should have Lani give her a call. She could probably use a friend right about now."

"That's just it—I'm not certain we're going to make it."

Adam shook his head. "Don't tell me you're considering leaving Marissa instead of staying and working on it like a man."

Taking a jab at his manhood wasn't going to send Colin scampering back home to a woman who seemed to enjoy sulking. Maybe if she'd talked to him right away he wouldn't even be considering divorce. Except...

The baby.

Would Kaitlyn accept him if he ended his marriage? She was hardly in a position to turn him away, at least not if she wanted to finish school and give their baby a good life. On the other hand, she certainly had her own mind about things. That was one of the qualities he'd fallen in love with.

But was he in love? It seemed like such an arbitrary word that really had no value. Not when it came to making the nitty-gritty decisions in life.

He resumed stirring his drink with the straw. "I don't know what I want to do."

"What about what she wants?"

Colin shot his friend a pointed glare. "She won't tell me what she wants. She shut me out."

"Can you blame her?" Adam's tone softened, causing Colin to consider Marissa when it was simply easier not to.

Colin flashed a thumbs-up to the kids a few tables over who were trying to get his attention. He hated the shame he felt creeping over him, but it was deserved even if he didn't want to admit it. One thing he knew for certain, once the news came out, he could lose his team and probably his shot at tenure. He was about to become the town pariah, and there was nothing he could do about it. He sighed with resignation. "It would be a lot easier if she would just talk about it, but it's like she's given up. I feel bad enough. It was a stupid mistake."

"Of course it was." Adam lasered him with a sharp look. "The question is, what are you going to do about it?"

# CHAPTER 30

*Marissa*

The days following Colin's revelation bled into months that ate me from the inside out. Time blurred, and eventually my survival instinct kicked in to the point where I could eat, barely. Sleep made a few rare and stingy visits, leaving me exhausted and looking like I'd been sucker-punched in the eyes. Still, I kept up the facade, or so I thought.

After the last client of the day walked out the door, Christina pinned me with sympathetic eyes. "You look blue."

I stiffened, caught. If there was one thing I prided myself on during this abysmal season, it was the ability to scratch out a smile at New Heights. Pouring myself into others was a good thing, even though doing so was an ever-fresh reminder of everything I didn't have. I could no longer skirt over my infertility the way I once had back when I too had hope.

"Yeah, you aren't yourself today." Kaitlyn eyed me over the copy of the pregnancy book she was perusing.

"Tired, mostly." I bit back anything resembling a lie. No matter how big my phony smile was, it wasn't big enough to hide behind. I prayed they wouldn't make further comments and force me to say anything untrue, but the last thing I wanted—or could even imagine tolerating—was to bring the ugliness of my life to New Heights. It was the only place where I could escape, even though the escape was less satisfying than it had been before I canceled my next appointment with the fertility clinic.

There would be no baby in my future.

A shudder rumbled through my body. Quickly, I focused my attention on the diaper covers that had come in this morning. "How many clients are we up this month? We'll need to get those numbers to Tristan. It's important for the grants he's looking into."

"I just did the tally yesterday." Kaitlyn set the book on the floor next to her, jumped up, and dusted her bottom. Briefly I envied her youth, but she wouldn't be jumping for long. At almost five months, her baby bump was developing quite nicely. She crossed into the main room and opened a desk drawer. "Twenty-two this month, and fifteen last month. That makes a grand total of fifty-eight people we're serving, including *moi*."

I pulled the rest of the diaper covers out and threw the plastic bag away. "No wonder I'm worn out." Ultrasounds, referrals, keeping up with the donations—it was enough to keep the three of us plus Tristan busy full-time. But with Tristan building his private practice, I was left shouldering the majority of the work.

Christina sat on the opposite end of the boutique and shook a baby rattle like a maraca before placing it in a basket of toys. "Are you sure that's all that's wrong?"

Kaitlyn parked herself back on the floor next to me. "I was wondering the same thing. You've been unusually quiet."

"Are you saying I'm usually noisy?" I quirked my brow and slid into a practiced smile. "Why don't you ladies tell me what you really think?"

"I'm being serious." Kaitlyn's bright green eyes widened.

"So am I." I picked up the next bag and pulled out a soiled onesie. Gross. I peeked at the rest of the items, which were all in a similar condition, before setting aside the entire bag. The mothers who came to New Heights were already having a hard enough time without having to contend with clothes where a diaper bomb had exploded.

"C'mon now," Christina said as she tidied the box of toys. "You're always helping everyone else—including us—but you won't let us do the same for you."

My arms deflated against the plastic bag as I considered her words. What she said was true. But as much as I cared for them, I wasn't willing to let them into my personal life. Not like that. Having Tristan flash me discreet pitiful looks was bad enough, but at least he hadn't brought it up again, and neither had I. It wasn't like there was anything he could say that would fortify my crumbling life.

Besides that, I'd been spending more time on my knees than ever before, and I was determined to let God pull me up this time. I wanted to be strong and full of courage. I wasn't there yet, but I was taking baby steps the same way I'd always advised our clients.

Kaitlyn scooted closer and spoke softly. "You don't have to say anything—I know there are things I don't want anyone to know either, so I get that—but you should know that you can talk to us too. It goes both ways."

I hugged her. "Thank you. I really do appreciate it, and maybe one day I'll be ready to talk about what's happening, just not now."

"In any case," Kaitlyn said, resuming her perusal of the baby book, "you need to take care of yourself and make your health a priority. It'll make whatever you're going through a little easier."

I studied the changes in my young friend that I'd been too caught up in my own issues to notice. The circles under her eyes had lightened, and she was developing the pregnancy glow. Her entire countenance had shifted from defeated and stressed to strong and maternal. After she'd let me off the hook on my issues, I didn't dare ask what had happened to lift her up but could only assume the father of her baby was somehow coming around. She'd tell me when she was ready.

"It looks like you've been taking your own advice," I offered, hoping to deflect her attention.

"I have." She sat taller and set the book onto the pile of knit blankets she'd been working on before she started reading about the fourth month of pregnancy. "I took the doctor's advice and started exercising."

"And eating right?" I remembered her house and the sense I had of her bare cupboards. Since then I'd tried to make sure we had a cornucopia of healthy snacks here, available whenever she or the other mothers needed one.

"Trying." She winced. "But mostly exercise. It really does make a difference in how I feel. Maybe you should come with me."

"Go on a walk? I do that." Sometimes, or at least I used to.

"I have something a little more exciting in mind." She waggled her eyebrows. "We'll start this weekend."

# CHAPTER 31

*Colin*

Colin stood at the door and hesitated. His heart ricocheted in his chest in a way it never had the whole time he was cheating. Why was visiting Kaitlyn with honorable intentions more guilt-inducing than the affair? Apparently he wasn't the smooth operator he'd thought he was.

Rain splattered on the porch around him, mucking up the hem of his slacks. Still, he waited. It was his duty to go in and check on the mother of his baby. If he didn't help her out, she could end up at New Heights. What a disaster that would be. Except she wasn't like the other people Marissa worked with—druggies and homeless women, battered women who needed help through their pregnancies. He could safely set that worry aside, especially if he stepped up and made sure Kaitlyn didn't feel desperate and alone.

He knocked, eager to get inside, check on Kaitlyn, and then get home to his wife where he belonged. Maybe she'd finally be ready to talk. Or maybe she'd still sulk and freeze him out. There was just no telling with her nowadays.

The door cracked open and Kaitlyn peered out. "What are you doing here?"

"You should check the peephole before you open the door." Consternation niggled inside him. It could have been anyone at the door—a salesman, a missionary, or an intruder. Then what would she do?

"That doesn't answer my question." She still didn't open the door all the way, even though the rain was falling harder and the back of his shirt was getting soaked.

"I came to check on you." He shoved his hands inside his pockets. "Can I come in?"

"Just for a minute. I—" She paused and glanced away. "I have things to do." She wore her discomfort on her face, the way her brow puckered and her mouth tightened in ways he hadn't seen when they were together. Slowly she backed up and let him inside.

The room was hot and muggy, and Kaitlyn was dressed in shorts and a tank top that revealed a small, firm mound. Her hair was in a high knot on top of her head, and her face glistened.

"No air-conditioning?" Colin glanced at the worn love seat and the recliner with patches of torn leather. The decor was sparse and none of it new, that he could tell. Maybe she was in a worse financial situation than he'd surmised from her age and maturity level.

"Please don't judge. I'm really not in the mood." Her tone held a sharp edge that made him recoil. She planted herself in the recliner without offering him a drink or a seat. "So. . .you're checking on me. After not seeing you for the last month, I thought you'd changed your mind about being part of the baby's life."

Colin sank into the love seat and crossed his ankle over his knee while he considered his words. How could he know what to say when he didn't even know how he felt or what his role should be? He shifted, the leather squeaking beneath him. "I will not change my mind about wanting this baby."

"That's good to hear, I guess." Kaitlyn rubbed her stomach as she met his gaze. "Does your wife know you're here?"

"I told you, don't talk about her." The defensiveness in his voice surprised him. It had been a long time since he'd defended Marissa—something he'd done for years when his family started to question what kind of woman she really was. It was a role he was too familiar with. A role he'd abandoned the first time he kissed Kaitlyn and found admiration in her eyes, unlike the dependency and disappointment he'd come to expect from his wife. A role he never wanted to fill again.

"You do realize that you're going to have to talk to me about her someday. It's not like we won't all be in each other's lives."

Unless he left Marissa—an option he'd only briefly considered. Then he'd be free to be a father, unhindered. Maybe he and Kaitlyn would eventually ride out the bumps and make a real family. That was the only thing he'd ever wanted but hadn't yet found.

No. He wasn't going there. It would be wrong to drop Marissa, drop their marriage, when she had been true and faithful, despite their issues. He wasn't a quitter.

Colin fastened his eyes on Kaitlyn. "Let me handle my wife and my marriage. I'm only here right now to check on you and make sure everything is going well." He hated the coldness in his voice, but to let his guard down for an instant would wreak havoc on his decision to patch up his marriage—if only Marissa would talk.

"Like it or not, our paths are going to cross." Kaitlyn's frankness rankled. Though she was more confrontational than Marissa, she still wasn't generally this forward.

He had to stop comparing the two women. Even thinking about them at the same time felt like a betrayal—though he wasn't altogether sure to which one. His heart was split, and it ticked him off that he'd chucked his morals for an affair. Maybe some sick part of him wanted Marissa to know, to inject some kind of emotion other than perpetual disappointment into their marriage. Or maybe he'd subconsciously been looking for a surefire way out.

"You're awfully quiet for someone who showed up on my doorstep." Kaitlyn challenged him with a fiery expression.

"Look, I know this isn't easy for you, but it isn't easy for me either." His excuses sounded flimsy even to him, so he charged ahead where he hadn't wanted to go. "I thought you were on birth control."

Kaitlyn's lips pursed. "It takes two, obviously. You could've taken steps too since nothing is foolproof."

The irony of trying for a baby with Marissa year after year, month after month, cycle after crazy, whacked-out cycle, and then impregnating Kaitlyn after being together less than a handful of times, chafed. He relaxed his shoulders and forced meekness into his voice. "Sorry, you're right. I'm still adjusting to all this." He pushed out of the love seat and stood in front of the picture window, absorbing the view of the cloud-covered mountain until he calmed down. He spun to face her. "You're looking a lot better than the last time I saw you."

"Thanks—I think." She padded to the kitchen just a few steps away and opened the refrigerator. Aside from a half gallon of milk, a carton of eggs, and various condiments, it looked empty.

Not good. A pregnant woman needed food. He didn't want to risk the health of his child. Or Kaitlyn.

He hated that he still cared about her. That he could sense the worry under her bravado. Sure, the circles under her eyes had faded and she wasn't clinging to the toilet bowl, but she still wasn't the perfect combination of focused yet carefree that she was when they met. What would it take to restore her?

Kaitlyn poured herself a glass of milk and glanced over at him. "You want some? It's all I have."

He shook his head. "I'm good."

Rain pattered against the window and smudged the view, but the sound of it soothed him. Kaitlyn ambled over to the window and stood within reach. The urge to hug her nearly overpowered him, but he folded his arms across his chest. He wanted to hold her and tell her that everything would turn out okay and life would be good, but even he didn't know that to be true.

"When is your due date?" he asked casually.

"You mean our due date." She glanced over her shoulder and flashed a challenging smile before turning away again. Traces of her strawberry shampoo lingered in the air. She was so close he could reach out and twine his fingers in her hair the way he used to when they snuggled in the car at the scenic overlook. When it was just the two of them and nothing else in the world—his job, his wife, his own life—mattered as much as being with a woman who admired him the way Kaitlyn did.

"Our due date." He repeated the phrase in his head, allowing reality to soak in. He was going to be a father—technically already was. "All right, when are we due?"

Kaitlyn chugged the milk and set the empty glass on the end table before she faced him and smiled. "Christmas."

Colin flinched. Much sooner than he'd anticipated. His gaze drifted to her belly. "That's. . .wow."

She scoffed before easing into a thin smile and rubbing her stomach. "I guess that was my initial reaction too."

"We need to start making plans." He sounded way more confident than he felt.

"That's kind of hard when you're married. Three's a crowd and what-not." She folded her arms and turned her gaze back to the mountain.

"Are you saying that if I wasn't married we would be together?"

Kaitlyn whipped around, horror etched on her delicate face. "*You* are the one who broke it off with me, who wouldn't let me come by your office, who refused my calls, ignored my texts. Or have you already for-gotten? Just because I'm pregnant doesn't mean that changes anything between us."

"But if I hadn't—"

"You did and nothing can change that." She stepped around him and paced the worn rug. "And had I known you were married, I'd *never* have been with you. Our relationship actually meant something to me—I thought it was real. Instead I find out you were just keeping me on the side."

Colin stormed to the kitchen and leaned his fists on the counter. "No—I didn't think of you that way. That was the problem—I fell too hard and did all the wrong things. I didn't want to give you up. I wasn't just 'keeping you on the side.'"

"But that's how you treated me, and I let you! If that's not bad enough, what about your poor wife?"

"I told you to keep her out of it." Instantly he regretted his venomous tone, but he was desperate, so very desperate to keep his two crumbling worlds apart as long as possible.

"You're the one who wanted to talk," Kaitlyn countered, "and she's an important part of what's happening. You might want to start with telling me her name."

"Don't go there. I'm handling it. I told her about the baby, end of story." At least as far as Kaitlyn needed to be concerned. "You need to understand that some things have to stay private. Besides, I'm up for tenure, and I could lose my job if anyone finds out. Trust me, you don't want that to happen."

She rubbed her temples, clearly exasperated. "Forget your job for a minute. Whether you realize it or not, how involved you are in our child's life is in your wife's hands."

The truth landed like a hard slap. He'd always been in charge and made the decisions, but when he really stopped to consider, Marissa always had a way of controlling him behind the scenes. Subtle manipulation. Wasn't that what his family had been telling him all along? For years her shifting moods had trumped everything.

What if she didn't want him to be part of his child's life? It would be inconsistent, considering the job she devoted herself to. She loved babies, and in the back of his mind it hadn't occurred to him that she'd throw up a roadblock.

Finally he ceded the point. "My wife and I are still working through it, but I stand by what I said before—I want this baby. I plan to be involved as much as you'll let me."

For the moment, Kaitlyn seemed content to let it go. She rubbed her belly again.

"Can you feel it move?"

Her nose wrinkled. "Don't call our baby 'it.'"

"Don't tell me you've already picked out a name."

"Not yet, but. . ." She glanced down, her cheeks reddening. "I've been calling the baby Little Nugget."

"Little Nugget?"

She giggled, a glimpse of the Kaitlyn he adored. "Don't make fun of me. Back when the baby was the size of a nugget, it stuck in my head."

Colin drank in the sight of the young woman carrying his child. "Little Nugget it is. Can you feel Little Nugget move?"

"Not really. A few flutters, but I'm not sure if that's Little Nugget or indigestion." She smiled, her green eyes lit with the affection she'd had for him. "This month I get to find out if we're having a boy or a girl."

"That's really exciting." More than anything, Colin wanted to go with her to the appointment, to be present for every stage of development. This was what he'd been waiting for. But even though he was sure he'd figure out a way to deal with Marissa, Dr. Crank and the others didn't know about it at work. Their decision would be coming down anytime now. If it came out that he'd had an affair with a student, there was no way he'd get tenure, even if she wasn't enrolled anymore. He still had to keep it quiet, at least until he could figure out how to juggle all the balls. There would be no doctor visits for him.

He edged closer and willed Kaitlyn not to move away. "So tell me about work. Have you cut back on hours?"

"No. In fact, I picked up more at my other part-time job."

"Is that a good idea? Where are you working?"

Kaitlyn took a step backward. "We're not together anymore, so if you want me to stay out of your business, you need to stay out of mine."

### Kaitlyn

At first it felt like tiny air bubbles popping inside her abdomen, but when the bubbles became fluttery butterfly wings, Kaitlyn knew—it was Little Nugget. She'd been enjoying the private moment until Colin showed up.

Now he was here, and he wanted her.

Or did he? The hungry glint in his eyes since he walked in, rain-soaked and uneasy, was in total contradiction to the words he wasn't saying. Maybe he was just as confused as she was, especially since he had a wife at home to consider. Were they going to stay together? If she were in his wife's shoes, she wouldn't dream of staying with him, not in this lifetime. But all she could glean from the conversation so far was that his wife knew and he'd deal with her. No clues about what his wife was thinking or whether they were staying together.

But it didn't matter anymore, not to Kaitlyn. She didn't want a man who cheated on his wife—of that she was certain. The only capacity in which it mattered to her was how involved Colin could be with their child, which depended entirely on his wife.

Kaitlyn resumed her place in front of the picture window and felt her stomach, smiling at the flutter that was so soft it might just as well be her imagination.

"I want to help." Colin's breath feathered the back of her neck.

She stiffened. "There's not much you can do, at least not yet. I suppose at some point I'll need to start buying stuff for the baby."

"What about food?"

Kaitlyn moved away from him. She sat on a barstool at the kitchen counter, a safe distance from Colin. Fire still burned inside her gut every time she considered the way he'd lied and used her, allowing her to believe that what they had was the first hint of love. But if she wasn't careful, if she didn't stay completely guarded, then his confident stride and beckoning eyes would undo her resolve.

She just wasn't that strong.

Colin swaggered into the kitchen and started opening and closing the mostly empty cabinets, causing Kaitlyn to cringe. When they were together Colin had made her feel beautiful and strong, full of life and capable of accomplishing anything. The last thing she wanted now was for him to think she couldn't take care of herself.

"I eat at work," she said, rushing up behind him and closing the cupboard, barely missing his fingers.

He jerked his hand back and cocked an easy grin. "Is that so?" His eyes grazed her stomach then moved slowly up to gauge her expression. He stood close, too close, with one arm against the cupboard and the other on his waist. "That's my baby too, and I need to make sure Little Nugget is getting enough nutrition."

His words, a reminder of their intimate time together, sent a shiver down her spine. The idea of having a tiny piece of Colin inside her was beautiful and horrible at the same time. She pulled her gaze away before she weakened. "Of course I eat at work. It saves time." She moved around him and replanted herself in front of the window. Mountains—focus on the mountains and the way the sunlight peeked through the clouds and cast rays across the forest.

"I can give you money."

She flinched.

"I didn't mean it that way." The sound of his shoes on the floor warned of his nearness. "I want to help. I want to do all the things that expectant dads do."

Kaitlyn whipped around to face him. "Really? Like paint the nursery and come to all my doctor appointments?"

"What if I said yes?" He didn't look so sure of himself.

"Then I'd say I already have someone who wants to come with me." She folded her arms in defiance.

"Are you trying to tell me there's someone else?" His challenging expression shrank.

Let Colin hang from the noose of his own making. "Does it matter?" She refused to admit that her boss—and these days closest friend—had offered to come with her anytime she wanted.

"It does." His back went rigid. "For the same reason you said my wife matters."

"Well, not to worry—I'll handle it."

Colin looked away, his mouth firm. "Touché."

Kaitlyn leaned her head against the cool window and closed her eyes. She rubbed her stomach and tried to focus on the baby's movements. Was it wrong to feel a smidgen of gladness over Colin's jealousy? After pouring her heart into him, and the agony she'd felt at his rejection, she had to admit she was pleased that he didn't want her with another man.

And what did that say about her? Maybe her parents were right—she didn't have a moral bone left in her body. She'd traded it all out for Colin's demented version of a relationship. To his credit, he'd never actually used the word *love*, even though that was what she craved. What she'd craved from the beginning.

Suddenly she felt his breath on the back of her neck. His hand slipped beneath hers to caress her stomach. The wall of his chest grazed her back without pressing closer.

"What are you doing?" Her voice trembled.

Colin's hand whispered over her belly. "Little Nugget is my baby too."

# CHAPTER 32

*Marissa*

Zumba.

Of all the places I didn't belong, this one topped the list.

"I was running behind and was worried I'd missed you." Kaitlyn's eyes brightened when I moseyed inside the room with wall-to-wall mirrors, not to mention wall-to-wall women with top-of-the-line workout gear.

I glanced down at my baggy sweatpants and T-shirt that said "Everything's Better with Butter." Slowly I eased into the room and shifted my gym bag to hide the picture of the giant cow that adorned my front side. "I'm not really sure I can—"

"Of course you can." Kaitlyn grabbed my hand and pulled me to the corner of the room where I set my bag next to a set of old hand weights. "You're going to love it."

Feeling naked without my oversized bag, I heartily disagreed. I'd almost turned around and left when I purchased the visitor pass and saw what class my young friend had roped me into. But my car was in the shop and I'd relied on Tristan to drop me off. Now I was stuck. "So this is your favorite workout?"

"Sure is!" she said as the music came on. "I found out the other day that my parents forgot to put a stop on the auto-payments to the gym, so I figured I might as well get some use out of the membership."

Sweet Kaitlyn. She was quite the study in contradiction. Grown up in so many ways but still relying on her parents for a gym membership. Responsible enough to work two jobs but irresponsible enough to be in the position to need to in the first place. I prayed life wouldn't hit her too hard as it did so many single mothers.

Like my own mom. Would she have been a little less demanding of me had she not needed to work so hard? More understanding, less anxious? What would her life have been like? What would my life have been like?

Maybe I wouldn't have had insecurity and its ugly sister jealousy hounding me growing up. Maybe I'd be more ambitious and ready to tackle whatever life threw at me with confidence. But I'd never know.

I rubbed my arms against a sudden chill. "I still don't know if this is a good idea." The music began to thump louder and vibrate throughout the room.

"You'll thank me later," she said as she dragged me right to the middle.

"Can't we stay in the back?" I cringed at the possibility of someone watching all my missteps and foibles.

"You can see better from here."

I glanced around nervously at all the women—and a few men—in the room who were perfectly comfortable revealing more of themselves than I did even when I went to bed by myself. There was no way my body could compete with any other woman in the room.

And that was the rub. Without my realizing it, I'd started to think of myself in competition with other women. How could I not? Back when I hadn't been paying attention, someone had stolen my husband right out from under me. What kind of person could do something so low and horrible?

I shoved those thoughts and images aside when the instructor appeared at the front of the room and started marching in place for a few beats before diving into pelvic swings that utilized muscles I hadn't been in touch with for years. Pretty soon I was busy enough trying to follow the moves and keep in time to the Latin beat that I forgot all about my pity party.

A few times I caught Kaitlyn smiling in my general direction whenever I mastered a particularly sassy move. Even she looked happy and relieved in a way I hadn't seen since before her pregnancy when I only knew her from The Bean, and that made me smile even more. Maybe there was something to this exercise thing—something I'd always avoided at any cost in favor of curling up by the fire with a good book.

The hour wore on as I wore out. I was careful to keep my eyes from veering toward my reflection lest I be discouraged. It didn't take a mirror to know I was a sweaty mess and not the most coordinated woman in the room.

But I felt good.

Being a drippy mess was much better than holing up at home by myself, brooding and filled with angst, wondering where Colin really was when he was supposed to be at the college writing about his boring proteins. I was finally doing something for myself, and it helped to know that in some small way I was making progress. Toward what, I hadn't a clue.

When the music stopped and all the people in the class started to clap and high-five one another, my lungs burned and my arms felt like noodles. Worse, my torso was shredded from all the swivels and thrusting required by the cardio dance class.

"Tell me you don't feel good," Kaitlyn challenged me with a raised brow, peeking over the lip of her water bottle.

"Fine, you were right." I flipped up the straw on my bottle and took a long pull. "It's definitely not my usual speed, but I liked it."

She waved goodbye to a few other women her age before speaking again. "You look happier than I've seen you in a long time."

"Funny, I was thinking the same thing about you."

Kaitlyn's eyes slivered. "You're changing the subject."

"Tristan tells me I'm a master at it." I winked.

"I can only imagine what he'd say if he saw you just now. I'm sure he'd be impressed." She elbowed me and wiggled her eyebrows.

"I'm sure he'd laugh." Not that I particularly cared what Tristan thought about my exercise. I started out the door along with the stream of people who somehow looked fantastic for having just finished a one-hour power workout. "In any case, exercise can only help, right?"

"That's what my doctor tells me." Kaitlyn hiked her gym bag higher on her shoulder and steered me toward a long counter, complete with barstools. We situated ourselves and chatted while the springy-stepped girl working the counter finished with her last customer. Kaitlyn proceeded to order some kind of green grassy drinks and then handed one to me.

The first whiff exuded hay and soot, a far cry from the specialty coffee I was used to receiving from my friend. "What *is* this?"

"If I tell you, you won't drink it." She raised the kiddie-sized glass. "To our health."

I wrinkled my nose, raised my glass, and slammed the drink before I could talk myself out of it. My mouth puckered as a shudder worked the length of my body.

"What do you think?" Kaitlyn's hopeful expression goaded me.

"It's every bit as bad as it looks." I set the glass on the counter along with enough money to cover both so-called drinks. "Next time I'll leave the grazing to you."

"Trust me, you exercise and drink this regularly and you'll be zipping right along."

"I'll stick with the exercise." My body still hummed with energy—I refused to believe it was from the muck—and for the first time, I considered starting a normal routine. "How often do you come?"

"Last year I came at least four or five times a week." She glanced down and sighed, her countenance deflating. "But then I got...sidetracked."

"But now that you're back on track, are you ready to start a routine again?" I mentally ran through my already burgeoning schedule to see where I could make adjustments. If only I'd written everything down like Tristan had been hounding me for months, I could sign up for a gym membership today. I had to make sure I had time to spare before making the investment.

Oh, who was I kidding? With my marriage disintegrating and Colin spending more time away, not less, I had all the time in the world. He'd never notice I was gone. Funny thing was, with adrenaline zinging through my veins, I didn't care—at least not the way I did even a week ago. Maybe it was time to do something for myself instead of obsessing over my husband.

In some ways, doing things for myself seemed selfish. I'd always been taught to put God first, then others, then myself—if there was time. But considering I hadn't been doing such a great job of putting God first over the last few years, my priorities were already questionable. Now that I thought about it, Colin had overthrown God's position, and that was a recipe for failure.

"Now that I'm in my second trimester, I think I'm ready to get back into this. Not too tired to function and not too big for a good cardio workout." Kaitlyn slid off the barstool and patted her perky stomach.

At the mention of her pregnancy, I looked away and fished around in my bag for my phone. I pulled up Tristan's number and started texting. "I need to let Tristan know I'm ready."

"Did I say something wrong?" Kaitlyn's tone lost its enthusiasm.

"No, not at all." My mouth tightened with the lie. How could I explain about my loss? How could I explain about my failure to move forward? How could I tell her that I was jealous of her and every woman who walked through the doors of New Heights, every woman who wandered the streets with a coveted baby bump? I followed Kaitlyn to the lobby and considered my words. "It's just. . ."

"Personal? Believe me, I understand," she offered without judgment as sadness crept over her delicate face. "Lately my whole life is deciding what to tell to who. Sometimes it's easier to just hold it in. Know what I mean?"

"I do, but I also know it's not healthy to hold everything in." I braced myself for her to throw my words back in my face.

"It's not, but sometimes it's nice to be with people who don't have to know everything to still care about me." She locked eyes with me, and in that moment we understood one another, a call to a silent truce on digging for details in one another's lives.

Secrets were safest when they remained between me and God. Where she stood in her faith, I couldn't be sure, but I knew my young friend needed space to just be. Without comment, without question, without judgment. I knew because I wanted the same thing.

I shoulder-bumped her. "I'm right there with you. But believe me, if I ever decide to talk to someone besides Tristan—good grief, he always knows everything anyway—I'll come to you."

We pushed through the front door and a warm breeze rushed over us. The sun was finally out again and beat down on my face, continuing the rejuvenation that had started inside the sweaty gym. Maybe it wasn't selfish to do a few things for me. Maybe with God's help I could work my way out of the funk I'd been drowning in. Maybe it wasn't too late for a new beginning after all.

"Look, Tristan's here." Kaitlyn pointed at his freshly washed car pulling into the lot, gravel crunching under the tires.

He honked and waved when he spotted us.

I turned to Kaitlyn and felt awash with relief. "Thanks, I really needed this. I'll see you Monday?"

"Bright and early at The Bean." She gave me a thumbs-up. "I have a new drink for you to try."

"As long as it's not grass." I wrinkled my nose, knowing there were probably myriad new things I needed to try in order to be healthy. Finally I was starting to feel ready, confident that I could make some decisions about my marriage and my future. No matter what had happened, Colin and I could work through it together, and based on the fact he hadn't said otherwise, I was pretty sure he was willing to give it a shot.

After waving goodbye to Kaitlyn, I decided to get home and hunt down my husband. It was time we talked.

# CHAPTER 33

*Colin*

Fire licked through Colin's veins when he drove around the corner. There was his wife, climbing out of Tristan's car with a stupid grin on her face. What had they been talking about? What was the jerk even doing at *his* house? It wasn't like she didn't get enough time with her *business partner* during the week. Colin pounded the steering wheel.

It was his own fault for heading out to work and leaving Marissa without a car, but it was Saturday and she hadn't gone anywhere but work in weeks. Still, he should've waited around and offered to take her wherever she needed to go.

Tristan's car rolled out of the driveway and headed toward Colin. He pretended not to see the man's cool wave as he passed by.

Colin wasn't stupid. He saw the way Tristan looked at Marissa—a look that had deepened over the years the more time they spent together. When he'd first been introduced to Tristan when they were all finishing school, it seemed like any other study-buddy relationship. Add to that the fact Tristan came off a little geeky in college with his lanky frame and wire-rimmed glasses, and Colin had nothing to worry about back then.

But somewhere along the line, Clark Kent had evolved into Superman.

Colin pulled into the space vacated by Tristan's stupid car, slammed the gear into PARK, and snapped off the ignition. He clamped his mouth shut and forced himself to calm down. There was nothing to get worked up about. He was a man of science and reason. Logically, seeing Marissa climbing out of another man's car did not automatically equal infidelity. But he was also a professor of biology and knew that some instincts were too powerful to control.

Unless he was just making excuses for his own behavior.

Colin climbed out of the car and slammed the door. At least he and Marissa were home at the same time. Maybe she'd finally be ready to talk. As much as he hated to admit it, Kaitlyn was right—his future relationship with his child depended entirely on Marissa's good graces. Without her support it would be impossible to spend time with his son or daughter without feeling like he was sneaking around. And he was done with living a lie.

"You're home early." Marissa eyed him suspiciously when he walked inside, ratcheting up his already high-strung nerves.

"I saw you with Tristan, so I guess you really weren't expecting me." He moved closer and took in her casual—make that downright hideous—outfit. At least she wasn't dressing to impress.

"What's that supposed to mean?" She wiped a bead of sweat off her forehead.

"Nothing." His jaw clamped, and he tore his gaze away, moved into the living room, and took a seat while his wife watched him with something resembling concern. He immediately bounced back up. Pacing was more comfortable. "We have to talk."

"Boy, I'll say we do." The hint of sarcasm in her tone grated what was left of his nerves.

If only he hadn't actually seen Tristan. It wasn't as if he didn't know his wife spent time with that man, but now on Saturdays too? He forced himself to dial it down a few notches and think logically like the scientist he was. They had a slew of things to discuss, and none of it had to do with *him*.

"Are you actually mad that I got a ride from Tristan?" Her eyes widened, incredulous.

"Of course not." His denial came too quickly.

"That's right. You, mad at me for being with someone else. That wouldn't happen."

His fists clenched in anticipation of one of her moods, but instead she laughed, one of the chiming, steeple-bell laughs that first drew him to her. But this afternoon, with the sunlight streaking through the window highlighting Marissa's slightly dampened hair, her derisive laugh cheapened his feelings.

"I would've given you a ride," he contended. "If that's all you were looking for."

"Of course that's all—what kind of crazy talk is this?" She folded her arms and matched his stance. "Oh, I get it now. You think because of what you're doing that everyone else is a cheater too."

Arguing wasn't going to accomplish anything. Colin relaxed his stance and hoped Marissa would follow. This might be their only chance to talk, and he intended to make the most of it. "I'm sorry. I have no right to be. . .jealous." He nearly choked on the confession, but at this point he had nothing to lose by being honest, and he hoped for the same from her. He moved closer and gauged her reaction. "For what it's worth, she and I aren't even together anymore."

Marissa shot him a questioning look.

He raised his hands defensively. "I broke it off a long time ago." Going to check on the mother of his unborn child wasn't cheating. The quiet moment they'd shared, the intimacy of caressing her newly rounded belly, did not count. Not in the ways that anyone would care about.

"I guess that's a starting point." Marissa's shoulders unbunched. She sat in the rocking recliner and tucked her feet underneath her bottom.

Colin took the seat closest to her and forced himself to sit. With any luck they'd be there a while to hash out what the rest of their lives was going to look like.

"I never knew you were that jealous of Tristan." Her voice tripped with a hint of optimism.

"You spend a lot of time together."

"You knew that when you married me." She closed her eyes and shook her head. "But that doesn't really matter right now."

"You're right. We have other things to discuss." Colin tried to organize his thoughts. How best to bring up the baby without freaking her out and sending her into another bout of depression? He eased back against the couch and tried to appear casual. "So. . .we need to talk about my baby."

*Marissa*

Colin's words gutted me. Moments ago I'd been elated to finally hear him admit he was jealous. Petty of me? Maybe. But after weeks of despondency and hopelessness that left me hollowed out, I deserved it.

It lasted ten glorious seconds before he detonated an emotional bomb that wiped me out.

*"My baby."*

I crossed my arms and masked myself with indifference. "I thought you were going to say you're ready for a divorce."

Colin's face screwed tight and he swiped his hand through his already-tousled hair. "Of course not. I don't want to throw away a decade of marriage for a mistake."

I was relieved, but I wasn't going to say so. Our relationship, so fiery in the beginning, had flamed out long ago, yet there was still so much shared history. Our climb from living in a shack with carpet that looked like it had a bad comb-over, to living in an upper-middle-class neighborhood. Our journey from students—me, slightly older and nontraditional, and Colin, younger and optimistic—to a working professional and a professor on the brink of a promotion. Our marriage was rife with struggles, but I couldn't imagine sharing life with anyone else.

Still, I wasn't ready to release my heartbreak and let him off the hook. Knowing myself, I might never be. My breath came more rapidly. "Well, what about *your* baby?" My heart ached all over again, like I was hearing about his baby for the first time. The pain of being childless was now a pain I'd have to suffer alone.

He glanced away, appropriately shamed. "I'm sorry. There really isn't a good way to bring this up. I just need to get it in the open."

My so-called husband, ever the pragmatist. I cocked my head. "Go for it," I said, as if he hadn't already.

I chided myself for my dark thoughts. For a split second I closed my eyes and willed myself twenty minutes into the past, when I was ready to face new challenges with hope. Then four minutes into the past when Colin admitted jealousy. I locked those feelings into place before speaking again.

"Tell me what you're wondering about," I said, holding myself together.

Colin released a weighty breath, signaling he was on the verge of either exasperation or a deep revelation. His dark eyes warred between angst and hope. "I just need to know you'll support me having a relationship with my child."

I wanted to be a big enough person to say yes without hesitation, offering my blessing to him for the benefit of a child who had no part in his or her parents' sins. I'd dedicated my whole life to the unborn and babies in crisis, never imagining myself mixed up in a situation just as heartbreaking. I'd championed for babies just like Colin's—babies who needed their fathers. Babies like I had once been. What kind of child advocate would I be if I kept him from his son or daughter? I'd be a fraud and a hypocrite.

And yet. . .by conceding, I would now be committing to sharing my husband with another family for the rest of my life.

The clock ticked in the hallway and dust motes floated freely in the afternoon sun. Despite the yearning on his face, I couldn't force an answer.

*Lord, have mercy.* A prayer I'd heard my mother utter thousands of times. So appropriate now as I needed God's unfiltered mercy more than ever. Mercy on our lives. Mercy to see me through the coming years. Mercy on my unforgiving soul.

I swallowed the cotton in my throat and willed myself to meet his eye. "You can't bring the baby here," I pronounced, despite the fact he'd be visiting his child without my watchful overseeing. But really, it made no difference now. Either he'd cheat again or he wouldn't—I had no power one way or the other.

"I wouldn't ask you to let me." He sounded just north of caring.

I flicked my hand dismissively. "I won't stand in your way."

Colin sagged, apparently relieved. "You don't know how much this means."

Oh, but I did.

"I've been thinking," he said lightly, as though we'd only been engaged in small talk over tea and scones. "Maybe we could try counseling."

I pushed out of my seat, not believing what I'd just heard. Water, I needed water. I fished inside my gym bag I'd dropped next to the chair and came up with an empty bottle.

"What do you think?" he asked as I headed for the kitchen where he couldn't see my face.

"I guess—if you think it'll help." I couldn't bring myself to feel joy like I would have a month ago. Not because he sounded insincere, but because his baby was now his focus and our marriage was simply an afterthought.

# CHAPTER 34

*Kaitlyn*

Guilt plagued Kaitlyn for days after Colin's visit. They hadn't done anything wrong, per se, but the closeness they'd shared, his strong hands on her stomach, was more than his wife would appreciate. It was more than *she* appreciated now that she knew what kind of man he really was.

"Aren't you about out of here?" Jake glanced at his giant watch, snapping her out of her thoughts.

Quickly she resumed arranging the display of mugs and bags of coffee beans rather than allowing her mind to wander now that the morning rush had slowed. "I guess I wasn't keeping track. The morning went by so fast."

Jake leaned against the chrome counter and crossed his ankles. "You seem to be doing a lot better than you were a month ago."

She lowered her eyes as she set the last mug in place. "In what way?" Hopefully he didn't bring up anything she wasn't ready to share. But if not now, when? Her bulky blue apron wouldn't hide her bulge much longer.

Jake scanned the nearly empty shop. "It's just that I was getting worried about you there for a while. Not to be mean, but you were kind of sick—"

"Wow, thanks."

"And pale—"

"I get it." She grabbed the towel from her apron and snapped it at him.

"And tired, like you were dead on your feet." He shook his head, his brown curls flopping into his eyes. "If I didn't know better, I'd think you were knocked up."

Kaitlyn inhaled the aroma of dark roast coffee beans as she weighed the consequences of telling the truth. Now that her parents knew, who did she really have to hide it from? Towel in hand, she placed her fist on her hip and stared him down. "That's a tacky way to put it, but if you must know. . ."

Jake did a double-take then went slack-jawed. "Dude, no way."

Kaitlyn shrugged. "Babies happen."

He offered a sloppy grin. "Who's the culprit—I mean, lucky guy?"

"That," she said with a sassy toss of her ponytail, "is none of your business."

"Ha! Now I know the old Kaitlyn is back." Jake moved closer and shot her a playful elbow. "Get out of here now—your shift's over."

Kaitlyn laughed at his goofiness. It was good to finally tell Jake and gain back the old camaraderie. At least one thing was normal. Someday it would be nice to talk openly about her plans for the baby and show everyone the fun stuff her pregnancy tracker app told her each day. Too bad she'd promised Colin she'd keep her mouth shut. As her father taught her, a person was only as good as their word.

She clocked out from work and tried to ignore the pang in her chest over losing her father's love. No, that wasn't quite right. It was his respect she'd lost, and there was no getting it back.

As she drove to New Heights, her thoughts turned to what kind of relationship Colin would have with their child. Suddenly, something occurred to her—did he have other children? He'd hidden his wife from her, so it was reasonable to assume there could be children, and he'd left no trace of himself on social media—the go-to way to check on someone without them knowing.

Remorse and regret brewed inside her. What if she'd wrecked not only a marriage but an entire family? No wonder he was being completely tight-lipped about his situation. He was probably trying to protect his kids as long as he could.

After a short drive through town, she pulled her car to a stop in front of New Heights and rested her head on the steering wheel. Now it was even more critical that she keep quiet—if not for Colin, then for his innocent family.

The afternoon dragged on much more slowly than the morning. She missed coffee—a lot. Even though her doctor said she could have some in moderation, she didn't want to take any chances. Several clients came and went for appointments, referrals, counseling, and myriad other details that she needed to coordinate. The satisfaction that came from helping other women like herself couldn't be measured by a paycheck, but that didn't make the day go any faster.

The clock on the mantel in the lobby inched toward five when Marissa opened the door to her office. "Is Tristan finished with his client?"

Kaitlyn scanned the appointment book and compared times. "No. She came in late so he might be a while. It was Isabelle, and she usually"—she lowered her voice—"has a lot to talk about."

Marissa smiled just before her eyes narrowed as if she'd just thought of something important. "Are you taking off right away?"

"I don't have to, why?"

"I have an idea." Marissa motioned for her to come into the office then closed the door with a soft click once she was inside.

Hopefully whatever idea Marissa had involved working a few more hours a week so she could buy groceries before Colin came around again. The humiliation of her empty cupboards still haunted her, but until recently she hadn't even been hungry. Morning sickness had been one big appetite killer.

"Have a seat over here." Marissa gestured to the table before she unrolled a long sheet of fresh exam-table paper.

"Is this what I think it is?" she asked hesitantly as she situated herself. Though she knew Marissa would have said yes to an ultrasound anytime, she hated asking for things because it always made her feel even more broke than she already was.

"If you're due at Christmastime, that makes you about twenty weeks. If the baby cooperates, we might see what you're having—unless you don't want to know."

"Of course I want to know." Unexpected joy filled Kaitlyn as she thought about Little Nugget. The paper crinkled beneath her as she lay back and pulled up her gauzy top to reveal her baby bump. "My stomach looks so much larger without a shirt covering it."

"It's adorable." A wistful expression flashed across Marissa's face before she turned around and began to rummage through the drawer near the ultrasound machine. She pulled out a towel and handed it over. "Tuck this into your shorts to keep the gel off. It might be a little cold since I already turned off the warmer."

"I don't mind—anything to see Little Nugget." Kaitlyn secured the towel and then placed her hands behind her head, tilting enough to have a clear view of the screen.

Marissa rolled her chair next to the table and pulled on a pair of gloves. "Little Nugget? I haven't heard you say that before. Cute!"

"I'm not sure Nugget's father thought so." At least judging by his funny expression. But to be fair, he'd gone along with it.

Marissa's eyebrows peaked as she smeared the gel. Apparently she was curious but respected the silent boundaries they'd somehow negotiated, and for that Kaitlyn was thankful. Marissa pressed the tip of the wand against her belly and shifted it around, stopping every few seconds to take a measurement and click a photograph. It all looked like static and fuzz to Kaitlyn.

"Do you see anything yet?"

"I'm seeing all kinds of good stuff," Marissa said, never pulling her gaze from the screen. "From what I can tell—and remember I'm not a doctor, yada, yada—your Little Nugget is looking healthy. See the heart beating?" She pointed with her left hand at the flutter on the screen.

Tears sprang to Kaitlyn's eyes and her breath hitched. "I can't believe it." She swiped away the moisture so she could see. "It's like a tiny miracle."

"It really is." Marissa's eyes misted too, and her lower lip quivered.

Kaitlyn smiled, thankful to have a friend who shared her joy so fully. A friendship without complications. "Thank you for taking the time to do this."

"Of course." Marissa's expression brightened. "I'm sorry I didn't think of it sooner. I guess we've been a little busy around here."

"That's an understatement." Kaitlyn's tired eyes and sore back were a testament to that. "Just curious," she said, hoping her question didn't violate their unspoken agreement, "why did you choose this over working for an OB or another doctor? I'm sure you'd probably make more money—not that I've been eavesdropping on you and Tristan's conversations."

Marissa laughed, releasing the strong scent of peppermint gum that made Kaitlyn a little nauseous. "If you didn't catch some of those conversations, it would mean you weren't paying attention."

"You're qualified to do ultrasounds anywhere, aren't you?"

"The only thing I'm really allowed to do here is show women images of their babies without making any diagnoses, but I was a registered nurse before I became a licensed sonographer. So long story short, I can do this anywhere." Marissa set down the wand, her shoulders sagging. "I really thought this was what I wanted to do for the rest of my life."

"Please don't tell me you're leaving." Kaitlyn propped herself up on her elbows. "This place wouldn't be New Heights without you."

Energy seemed to leak out of Marissa before she answered. "I don't plan to leave anytime soon, but honestly. . ."

"What?" At this point, Kaitlyn didn't care if she was overstepping since her boss almost seemed ready to share. "I mean, this is important work you're doing here. I can't imagine where I'd be right now if not for you and Tristan, Christina, and even the clients. It's like a family here. So many women in my situation need that."

Marissa offered a feeble smile. "And *that* is precisely why I do what I do." Her shoulders heaved with a deep breath. "Maybe someday I'll branch out. You never know what's in store, right? I mean, after all, you got me to try Zumba."

Kaitlyn giggled. "Trying a new workout is a lot different than trying a new career."

"Touché." Marissa picked up the wand and resumed her inside look of Little Nugget. Her eyes turned misty again, and this time it didn't seem like it was out of joy for Kaitlyn. What could have Marissa this upset? She and Tristan seemed to be getting along fine, at least as far as they let on in public. Of course, one never knew what went on behind closed doors.

It was better not to press the issue. If Marissa wanted to open up to her, she would. Kaitlyn settled back again and tried not to look into her friend's eyes and see the angst. Finally, she couldn't stand not knowing. "Is something wrong? I mean, I don't want to pry, but you seem a little upset."

Marissa set down the wand and stared blankly at the wall for several seconds before speaking. "I'll tell you, but you can't repeat it. Please."

"You have my word."

"At this point, I can't seem to get pregnant." The tight expression revealed how much it cost Marissa to admit what was obviously painful.

The paper bunched underneath Kaitlyn as she sat up all the way. She clutched her chest. "Oh no. I. . .can't imagine."

"I'll bet."

Kaitlyn detected an artificial happiness in Marissa's voice and immediately caught her breath. "I'm sorry. . .that was the wrong thing to say. I guess I don't know what to say. It must be so hard for you to be here, doing what you do, in your situation."

Marissa's mouth turned down. "I didn't know I had a problem until years after we opened New Heights. I have to admit, doing the job has gotten more painful, but—" She shook her head. "That's not for you to feel sorry for me about. Just like you don't want anyone feeling sorry for you. Deal?"

"Of course." Kaitlyn pulled her shirt down, unwilling to put Marissa through anything more. Her aunt had dealt with infertility for years, and Kaitlyn remembered the grief that always seemed to be present at family gatherings when there were small children and babies.

"Hold on, we're not done." Marissa motioned for her to lie back again and lift her shirt. "We haven't gotten to the best part."

"Are you sure?"

Marissa placed her hand on Kaitlyn's forearm and locked onto her gaze. "Yes. Remember when I promised you I'd do everything I could to help?"

Kaitlyn nodded. That had been the first time she'd felt any measure of hope since she'd seen the plus sign in the window of the home pregnancy kit. It was the moment she'd actually believed she could do this, with or without Colin.

"I meant what I said. My personal issues are just that, and I'm not going to let them keep me from doing my job—or sharing the joy with my friend." This time Marissa's eyes brightened when she smiled.

"If you insist." Kaitlyn lay back, crinkling the paper beneath her. The wand pressed firmly on her stomach, and she watched the screen, still not entirely sure what she was seeing, except she noted a head every few moments before it disappeared.

"And here's the money shot." Marissa clicked the mouse to capture the photo. "Do you see it?"

"See *it*?" There was only one *it* she could think of, and the screen wasn't clear enough for her to identify it herself. "Does that mean it's a boy?"

"No, silly. Look closer at this part that looks like a little sandwich." Marissa beamed. "You're having a baby girl!"

# CHAPTER 35

*Colin*

The counseling session was a bust.

The leather couch squawked as Colin shifted closer to Marissa. He noted the therapist's scrutinizing gaze assessing his every move. It wasn't like he was trying to fool her with his body language by inching nearer to his wife to look like a supportive husband, but he needed an edge. Having a female counselor—a Christian one, at that—already put him at a disadvantage, or at least it felt like it so far.

"The early years were wonderful." Marissa's wistful recounting of how they met unearthed fond memories.

Colin smiled at her and reached for her hand. She stiffened under his touch, and he saw Dr. Graves notice, even though the older woman's face betrayed nothing. Given the number of diplomas on the wall, she supposedly knew what she was doing, yet Colin still felt uneasy.

"How do you remember your first years of marriage, Colin?" The doctor examined him and scratched a note on her pad.

He cleared his throat and slung his arm over the couch. "The same."

"What do you feel brought and held you together?" Dr. Graves tilted her head.

*Hormones and a hot wife*, he thought but didn't dare say. Colin rubbed the scruff on his chin as he dug around for a more meaningful answer, but he couldn't do better than the truth. That's what had brought them together—plain old chemistry and instant attraction that neither one had a reason to deny. That was back before she took the whole God thing seriously. It was fine when they were first together and church was for Christmas and Easter, but then she took it too far. Just like she took everything too far. But to be fair, neither one of them was the same person they were when they'd met, not by a long shot.

"Colin?" Dr. Graves prodded.

He pulled his arm off the back of the couch—Marissa wasn't leaning toward him anyway—and clasped his hands at his knees. "Like my wife said, we met in college and were instantly drawn together. We spent every minute we could with each other and never got tired of it."

"Are you saying you're tired of it now?" Marissa's tone turned combative. She ran her fingers through her long, tangly hair. Hair that he used to love running his own fingers through. "What am I saying? Of course you are. That's why you found someone else." The disgust in her voice burned.

Dr. Graves held up her hand, her rings glinting in the afternoon sunlight that fell through the office window. "We'll go there in a minute. But before we do, I want to hear about the foundation of your relationship, your common beliefs and interests. I'd like to get an understanding of the two of you as a couple."

Marissa settled back in her seat before launching into all the memories of the good and idyllic. Funny how he didn't remember them the same way, but the last thing he wanted to do was contradict his wife. He needed to repair their relationship so they could move forward and come to a compromise about the baby, one they could both peaceably live with.

It only took minutes for her to get to the miscarriage and how it affected everything from the way they communicated to their intimate times. His face grew warm at the recounting, and he hated the way Dr. Graves's gaze flicked between him and her notepad. What was she writing? He'd give his eyetooth to have a look.

Focus—he needed to pay attention to what Marissa was saying. Somehow the topic of the miscarriage always upset him nearly as much as it did her, only he didn't have the luxury to cry. Out of habit, he searched for a box of tissues and handed it to Marissa. The vulnerability etched on her face undid him every time. Made him feel like less of a man because he couldn't protect her from her raw emotions, nor could he provide the one thing she really wanted.

Only now they both knew it wasn't him.

Colin didn't know if that made him feel better or worse. Was it wrong to be elated because he finally had a child on the way? Probably. But he couldn't change his feelings, just like he couldn't change his feelings back when he met Marissa and went wild for her.

Just like he couldn't change his feelings and force himself to love her now.

He cringed at the unbidden realization.

Dr. Graves noticed. "Did you have something to add?"

"No. Sorry." He edged away from Marissa and crossed his legs, trying to appear more casual than he felt. He directed his gaze at the leafy tree swaying in the breeze outside the window. "It's an upsetting subject."

"That's understandable." Dr. Graves referenced her notepad before glancing at Marissa. "Please, continue."

Marissa sniffled and began speaking with a wobbly voice that Colin had to steel himself against. The age-old desire to protect her crept over him, even though he knew she'd reject him if he reached out. So he stayed still and let her talk.

Did he really not love her anymore? The new thought nagged him and refused to let go. It just didn't seem possible, not after all these years. Sure, he'd screwed up, but he felt bad for it and was trying his best to set things right again. It was *his* suggestion to come to counseling in the first place, though he wouldn't have chosen a Christian therapist. But he'd given in and let Marissa have her way. Didn't that count for something?

Love.

Was there any between them after all these years? He certainly couldn't picture his life without her, but at the same time an endless future together seemed painful. That wasn't anyone's definition of love.

The fact that he wanted to stick it out had to mean something. He just didn't know what. Colin glanced at the clock on the mantel and willed it to move faster.

"Would you agree?" Dr. Graves looked straight at him, blinking rapidly.

Colin shifted, trying to recall what Marissa had said and coming up blank. He scratched his chin and studied the pattern in the carpet.

"What do you think held you together all these years?" Dr. Graves prompted.

Marissa scrutinized him from the side, working the tissue between her fingers.

He drew a deep breath and told the truth as best as he understood it. "Here's the thing: we've gone through a lot of good times and bad times together, and that really affected how we felt about each other. When I was down, she was strong. When she was down, I tried to be strong." He glanced between the two women. "The lucky thing was, we never fell out of love at the same time."

Marissa turned to face him, eyes wide. Her lips parted like she wanted to speak but nothing came out.

"Would you agree with that, Marissa?"

"No, not at all." She shook her head, her lower lip trembling. "Because I never fell out of love."

*Marissa*

Myriad emotions jammed in my throat at Colin's revelation, and suddenly our relationship made a whole lot more sense than it had ten minutes ago.

He'd been falling in and out of love ever since the miscarriage, or maybe sooner.

I clenched the tissue in my hand and braced myself against the tears that pressed on the back of my eyes. Crying would only make me appear weak and even more undesirable than I apparently already was. I hated that I felt that way with him.

"I'm sorry. I didn't mean that the way it sounded." Colin's foot twitched as he expelled the nervous energy he'd been trying to deal with since the moment we walked into Dr. Graves's office. This whole thing had been his idea, but here he sat, barely following along in the conversation and looking everywhere but at me or the therapist. Did he only suggest counseling so he'd have a safe place to drop emotional bombs? So that if I happened to fall apart there would be a professional to clean up the wreckage?

My mouth hung open and I wanted to speak, wanted to say something profound that would make him realize that he loved me more than his job, more than his sports. More than his lover. But I had nothing more to add after having sliced open my gaping wounds for the majority of our first session.

"Honesty is a good place to begin," Dr. Graves offered before capping her pen. "The question is, where do the two of you want to go from here?"

I smirked—the only defense mechanism I had left. Where, indeed?

The old-fashioned church bells pealed as Mom and I stepped out of the stone building. Clouds hovered over the city, on the verge of spewing rain. The low rumble of thunder soothed me, even as the prayers had soothed me moments ago.

Ever since the counseling session, I'd been focusing on finding peace somewhere—anywhere—besides home. I stayed longer at work, started attending Bible study, and took two cardio classes instead of one. I was about to ask Mom to go out for lunch, just to avoid Colin's gazes that vacillated between coldness and pity.

If I'd learned one thing about myself, it was that I didn't want him to stay with me because he felt sorry for me. That was no way to win his love. I wanted to be the woman he desired and thought about, the woman to occupy his mind and his heart.

But there had been an uncomfortable shift inside me since our appointment. Instead of being desperate for his attention, I was mad.

Mad at him, mad at her, mad at life. I was trying hard not to be mad at God. I'd been down that road after the miscarriage and never wanted to walk that thin line again.

"Why don't we go get Colin and come to my house for lunch?" Mom clutched my arm as we said goodbye to our friends and made our way down the steps.

I smiled and played it cool. "How about we go out to lunch, my treat? We haven't done that in a while."

"Sunday is a family day. You need to see your husband sometime."

"I see him every day." *Mostly.*

"If your schedule is as busy as you've said, then you're not doing any more than waving hello and goodbye. That's not good for a relationship." Mom clucked her tongue. "I can make pasta; you can toss a salad. I have fresh sourdough bread too. Doesn't that sound good?"

Truthfully, nothing did, but I wasn't going to say so.

I opened the car door for Mom and eased her inside. With a prayer on my lips, I went to the driver's side and prepared to tell her everything—she was going to find out sooner or later. There wasn't much chance a baby would stay hidden forever.

So I blurted out the truth, ashamed and spent, as though the confession were my own.

"Lord, have mercy." Mom fanned herself with the Sunday bulletin. "I knew things weren't good—I mean, you didn't exactly keep your troubles a secret—but an affair? A baby?"

Since there was no good answer, I shrugged. "Well, at least now you know." I switched on talk radio and hoped it would discourage her from diving into the gritty details. But I was wrong, so wrong.

"What's her name?"

"I don't know." I waved to the pastor as he walked by, and prayed for divine intervention. For God to nudge him toward our car so we could somehow change the subject. But he smiled and waved and walked on as though he hadn't a care in the world. Wasn't he hearing from God today?

"What's she look like?"

"How on earth would I know that?" My fists closed around the steering wheel.

"Knowing you, I figured you'd find out."

I thought back to the day I spied on him at the baseball field, the day Adam saw me but apparently didn't rat me out. Thank goodness for small favors. Back then I'd convinced myself I wanted to know, no matter how bad the truth was.

But it was different now. The truth had slapped me cold and hard, and the last thing I wanted was to know all about Colin's lover. My face pinched at the naked truth that barreled over me in a fresh way every time I thought about it, which was all day, every day. Now I felt the need to protect myself from the perfect woman—perfect hair, perfect teeth, perfect ovaries—who had lured him away, because the more I knew about her the less I'd like myself. And I wanted to like myself—I really did.

Mom laid a gentle hand on my forearm. "Don't drive yet. You're too upset."

"No, I'm not." I looked down and found my white-knuckled fingers trembling, and I was breathing in small sips of air. I closed my eyes and attempted to reorient myself.

*Breathe in through the nose, out through the mouth.*

The last thing I needed was a panic attack in the church parking lot. Though tongues would wag eventually, I wanted to fend them off as long as possible. My mini-meltdown wasn't helping.

"Sorry about that." My eyes remained closed as I shut out everything but the present moment. I was here, Mom was here, everything was okay for now. "I don't know what came over me." The panic dissipated as quickly as it had come on, and for that I was grateful. The coping techniques that Tristan had been trying to teach me for years were finally working.

"It's good to get it all out." She handed me a bottle of water and insisted I drink. "You should have come to me sooner. I don't know why you always think you have to do things on your own."

Probably because I didn't need her pushing me until I knew my own mind on the subject, but I didn't want to hurt her feelings by saying so.

"Now you know everything." I capped the water and handed it back.

"What are you going to do?" She scrutinized me in that special Mom way that always forced out the truth no matter how hard I was trying to hold it back. Only this time, I had no answers.

"What is there to do? Colin cheated and a baby is on the way." I forced my gaze directly ahead and focused on the cross atop the church. Where was the help in my present time of trouble? I swallowed the self-pity that floundered in my chest.

"With some hard work, you two can fix things up. At least you're not talking about divorce." Mom crossed her arms over her purse.

"No, we're not. No one has mentioned that." A small dose of relief swept through me.

"You know God hates divorce."

"I know." My clipped tone startled me. "Don't worry about that, okay?"

She fastened her seat belt. "Have you forgiven him?"

"I...I guess so." I sat motionless as I really tried to think through her question. Had I forgiven him? My heart bled raw every day, and I was in survival mode. Forgiveness was not on my radar. "Maybe not."

" 'Forgive us our debts, as we also have forgiven our debtors.' " She quoted the familiar prayer. "Don't you want to be forgiven also?"

"Yes, of course."

She tucked her finger under my chin and forced me to face her. "Then you have an obligation to forgive your husband." Her words pierced my conscience, opening a new set of wounds.

True forgiveness seemed elusive. It was one thing to ponder but another thing to practice. Even now he could be in the arms of his child's mother. He could relapse at any time. He was creating a whole new life with someone else.

How could I ever truly forgive Colin when he had the power to hurt me again?

# CHAPTER 36

*Colin*

Colin hid behind the newspaper when Marissa's newly repaired car pulled into the driveway.

Coward—that's what he was.

He couldn't hide forever, but he was still at a loss when it came to conversation with his own wife. She'd opened up at counseling but quickly shut down on him when they got home, and she'd been keeping to herself ever since. How long could he go on prompting and prodding and trying to make her open up? Maybe after a morning in church she'd be more amenable to working things out like Christians were supposed to.

Voices outside caused him to peer over the paper where he saw the fluffy white hair of his mother-in-law pass in front of the window. His jaw clenched, and he snapped the newspaper shut with the creases in all the wrong places.

Great. It was hard enough to fight for normalcy, but to fake happiness in front of Alina was going to be impossible. He could always say he was on his way to work, because that's where he should've been anyway. With the latest setback in his research and the committee ready to make a decision on tenure, it wouldn't hurt to log in a few more hours.

He tucked the newspaper under his arm and stood, eking out a smile when the women walked into the house. "How was church?"

"It was so good," Alina said as she set her giant purse on the table in the entryway. "You should come with us next week. There's room in the pew right beside us."

Colin felt his face twitch, but he still managed a smile. His marriage had been going well until his mother-in-law persuaded Marissa to start getting serious about church. But what good was all that church stuff if she was still depressed? What good was it if she wouldn't even forgive him?

"We stopped in to see if you wanted to come to lunch with us." Marissa's tone almost dared him to accept. Might serve her right if he did, but he'd be the one being punished. He needed to talk to his wife alone—no therapist and certainly no mother-in-law.

"I can't. I've got a lot of work to catch up on." He looked away, scooped the coffee cup off the end table, and headed for the kitchen.

"Suit yourself," Marissa called out behind him.

"Hold on now." Alina's firm tone caused him to stop and turn around. She motioned for everyone to settle down, and then she challenged him with a firm look. "I think we can all go to lunch and enjoy the day together. We're all adults here."

Colin's shoulders sagged, and the newspaper wafted to the ground. "You told her, didn't you?"

"She was bound to find out. It's not exactly the type of news you can hide," Marissa said matter-of-factly. "I didn't realize it was a secret. I figured as long as I knew, who's left to hide it from?"

"You don't get it." He met Marissa's eyes over his mother-in-law's head. "What do you think will happen to me, to my chance at tenure, if word gets out?"

Marissa rolled her eyes and flashed some strange version of jazz hands. "Oh, so sorry. We wouldn't want to wreck your reputation. That *is* the most important thing, after all."

"Come on, you know what I mean. It's not like I have tenure yet." He gestured wildly, ignoring Alina's wide-open stare. "I might be up for it, but they can still fire me for any reason. Do you know what that would do to us financially?"

Marissa shrank back. "Fine. You're right. But this is my mother, and one way or another she was going to find out. If it makes you feel any better, I haven't been going around telling random people. It's not like I enjoy everyone knowing I can't keep my husband happy at home." Her mouth quirked. "By the way, when do you plan on telling *your* family?"

Colin's ears burned, and anger surged inside his chest as his gaze shot between his wife and his gaping mother-in-law. "This isn't really the time to be discussing this. We can talk about it later."

"Let's go to lunch. Everyone will feel better with a full stomach." Alina stood between them with hands raised like a crossing guard. "After you take me home, then you can have a deeper conversation, but for now let's all calm down."

Colin set his coffee cup back on the end table and took long strides to get around the two women who were determined to gang up on him. He didn't need this kind of ambush on his one day off. He grabbed his keys and his cell phone. "I have to go," he said just before slamming the door.

Fire boiled inside him like a cauldron when he backed out of the driveway and jetted down the street. He pointed his car toward campus. The distraction that his work provided would soothe his nerves and keep him out of the house until Alina left.

In truth, he hadn't really thought much about telling his family. Throughout his life, they always had his back, and up until Marissa's snide remark, he had no reason to assume they wouldn't do the same now. Mom might be a little upset, but no one had wanted a grandchild more than she did. Eventually she'd get over the shock of the situation and enjoy having a baby to dote on.

It was the university faculty he worried about. Even if Kaitlyn was no longer a student, they still had standards they were bound to uphold. They could easily pass him over for tenure without explicitly stating the reason. If Kaitlyn's parents raised a stink, he might even be fired.

His stomach soured. How much did her parents know? This was the kind of loose thread he couldn't let dangle, and he was ticked at himself for not asking about it before.

Instead of heading to his lab, he changed direction and pointed his car toward Kaitlyn's house. The last time he'd seen her went well.

She was warming up to him, and their relationship would work out as long as he didn't put himself in a compromising situation. The stomach thing—he couldn't slip up and try to touch her that way again. It made him want so much more.

Nerves batted around inside his chest as he stood on the porch and waited for her to answer the door. If he'd been thinking clearly, he'd have brought a load of groceries to make sure she was eating well, despite her pride.

"You're here." The surprise on her face didn't bode well. It hadn't been that long since he'd been by, had it?

"I told you I'd be back."

"But I never know when." The challenge in her voice erased what little confidence he had. Wariness flickered in her eyes before she stepped aside and allowed him to come in. "Sorry, I'm a mess. It's not a good time."

"Is it anything I can help with?" He palmed her shoulder and studied her face. Fatigue lined her eyes, and her mouth was clamped.

Kaitlyn attempted to run her fingers through her messy bun, which only drew down more blond hair to feather around her chin. She shut the door and took her usual spot on the recliner. "No. I just heard from my roommate, Sydney. She's not coming back to school, and I don't know how I'm going to afford this place without her. I mean, it was fine over the summer because I knew it would only be a few months, but I can't afford the rent by myself forever. Never mind." She pressed the heels of her hands to her eyes.

Colin knelt by her chair and lifted her chin to force eye contact. "Hey, I want to help. It's okay to talk to me about your life, your needs. It all affects our baby, and if I can ease some of the pressure, then I'd like to help."

"There's not much you can do about my roommate situation." She sighed and looked away. Maybe she was just as afraid of connecting with him again as he was with her.

He covered her small hand with his and squeezed. "You're not going through this alone."

"That's what everyone says, but sometimes it sure feels like it." Kaitlyn thrust her chin higher and smiled. "That's life, and I can deal with it."

While he loved her attitude—a complete one-eighty from Marissa's neediness—Kaitlyn's expression was phony. He wanted her to be real with him. They had a child to raise together and they needed to be honest with one another, even if that wasn't how they started out.

Colin backed off and headed for the kitchen. He opened the refrigerator, and the contents appeared to be in the same sorry state they were the last time he was here. Nothing but condiments. "You still haven't been to the grocery store?"

"I eat at work. I already told you that," she called from the adjoining room.

He opened the first cupboard. "Noodles, crackers, and mushroom soup? Not sure where you were going with this."

Kaitlyn stood there with fire in her eyes. "What gives you the right to come over and check out my kitchen?"

Colin rolled his neck to ease the tension. How many women were mad at him today? "Look, I just need to make sure you're taken care of."

She fisted her hand on her waist, which had substantially thickened since he'd last seen her. "You have a *wife* to take care of. Don't you think that's enough? Do you really think you can come to my rescue too? That might be a lot more than you bargained for."

He softened his voice. "Are you in that bad of shape?"

"If I was, could you do anything about it?"

Not likely. His paycheck was already stretched so thin it was see-through, but the responsibility was weighing on him, and it actually made him feel good, like he was needed in a positive way. "The baby is as much my responsibility as yours."

Kaitlyn shook her head and walked away. She opened the back door and let in a warm breeze. "You say the words, but I'm not feeling them."

Colin followed her to a small redwood deck that overlooked the forest and joined her at the railing. He watched a family of squirrels scamper up and down a tree. "What would you like me to do? Just say it, and I'll do whatever you ask."

"That's the problem." She met his gaze with an intensity that made him draw back. "There's nothing you can do, not with the situation as it is. This isn't ideal for anyone, least of all your family."

"This child is going to be my family too."

Her lips firmed, and she hesitated before she spoke. "Let's just drop it, okay? You've done your welfare check, now you can go home."

The wind kicked up, further loosening her hair and blowing it into her eyes. Colin tucked an errant strand behind her ear. "Is that what you really want?"

Seconds ticked by while her eyes probed him. "I don't know what I really want."

"I know the feeling." Colin pulled his eyes away and turned his focus back onto the squirrels. "It seems like there aren't any right answers."

"That's exactly how I feel." She leaned over the railing, her arm brushing his. "It's like I want to be happy because there's a baby on the way. A baby is supposed to be a happy occasion, but the circumstances suck."

"They do," he admitted, glad to find common ground. "How are things working out with your parents?"

"The same. I haven't heard from them since the day I told them. They're probably still in shock."

"They'll come around eventually, won't they?" He couldn't imagine abandoning his son or daughter when they needed him most, but so many people took their children—even their adult children—for granted.

"It's hard to say. I hope so."

Colin worked up the courage to continue, and at the same time he tried to sound casual. "Do you think they'll call the university?"

Kaitlyn's eyes closed, and a vein in her temple pulsed. "Is that all you care about? Your precious job?"

"It'll be kind of hard for me to be a responsible parent without it," he shot back, more sharply than he should have.

She softened and turned away. "Good point. No, they haven't called the university because I never told them you work there. We never got that far in our conversation. Once I told them I was pregnant, it went downhill really fast. Honestly, you'd think I was fifteen with the way they reacted."

"Maybe they just need to get used to the idea." Like Marissa, and even her mother. Even he'd had to get used to it, though now that he had, he wanted everyone else to catch up. It was time to move forward and make plans rather than pointing fingers and making accusations, deserved or not.

She faced him again, her expression so open and free it reminded him why he fell for her in the first place. "Who knows if they'll ever get used to it? This is happening whether they want it to or not. What matters right now is us figuring out what to do."

"I'm glad we're starting to see things the same way."

"I need to know how our baby is going to fit into your life." Her pleading expression nearly undid him, but he didn't have solid answers for her. Not yet. The counseling he and Marissa were going through just didn't work that fast.

"I told you I'd figure that out. Please don't ask any more about my situation. I just can't go there."

"I mean, I know nothing about you. Do you have kids?"

Her question gutted him. Colin swallowed hard. "Kids—no."

"Just one child, then?"

Old wounds revisited. He hated the question because there was no good way to answer. He was supposed to have a child, but to say he didn't felt like a betrayal, that because it didn't make it to full term it hadn't existed at all. He breathed in the pine-scented air and looked away. "I can't talk about my family. Just. . .don't go there. Please."

"That's fine. I get it—I don't really want to get personal either. Which means you stay out of my cupboards." Kaitlyn's light tone showed just how in tune she was with him. He liked that about her.

"Deal." He reached out and clasped her hand in a way that was more than businesslike, less than familiar.

"By the way," she said as she rubbed her stomach. "We're having a girl."

# CHAPTER 37

*Kaitlyn*

Kaitlyn pressed her hand over her swelling stomach. "I feel the baby." Christina closed the filing cabinet and beamed. "It's about time. Aren't you almost six months along?"

"Twenty-two weeks. I've felt her before but not this strong." Kaitlyn leaned back and allowed her belly to protrude while she closed her eyes and concentrated on the sensation. *Move again, Little Nugget.* "I love feeling her wiggle."

"I'm so jealous." Christina's wistful tone caused Kaitlyn to smile. Her friend plopped onto the empty sofa across from the desk. Only a few clients had come in for afternoon appointments, leaving the girls plenty of time to visit. "I can't wait until I find the right man and get married. The first thing I'm going to do is have a baby. I actually miss being pregnant."

"You miss being hot all the time, hungry, sleepy? Hemorrhoids?" Kaitlyn emphasized the last word for effect. "There are some things no one warns you about."

Christina offered a faint laugh, and her eyes took on a faraway look. "That's about the time I started the pregnancy waddle. But yeah, I miss it. I miss my baby so much I ache inside, but I know I did the right thing."

"I thought you had an open adoption. Can't you see him?"

"It's complicated."

Kaitlyn wished she hadn't asked. The more she asked of someone else's private life, the more likely they were to ask about hers. Until Colin was ready to go public, as he'd eventually need to, she had to keep quiet. The secrecy was slowly killing her, but she'd made a promise.

She sat in the swivel chair and jiggled the mouse to wake up the computer. "I totally understand complicated—say no more."

*Complicated* didn't begin to describe what she was going through, especially with Sydney not coming back for school. Her mom and grandmother needed her help at home, thirty minutes away in Mountainside.

Then there were Colin's stupid visits that muddled her up more than she wanted to admit. The way he touched her hair and spoke gently to her, the way he made himself at home by looking into her cupboards— he was the old Colin. The one who loved spending time with her and made her feel beautiful and cared for. But the way he left money in the refrigerator where she'd find it later made her feel cheap, reminding her that he belonged to someone else who apparently didn't want to let him go. Someone he didn't want to let go of. Not that she wanted to be with him even if he did.

Now they'd be in each other's lives forever—or at least for the next eighteen years. Of course, since coming to work at New Heights, she'd heard stories of fathers who were one hundred percent involved up until the baby was born and actually needed feeding, care, and someone to provide for basic needs. That seemed to be a good time for a father not bound by marriage to conveniently disappear. She'd even heard stories of married couples and fathers who split shortly after the birth when late-night feedings replaced late-night parties, when a mother's attention shifted to her little baby instead of her big one. Thankfully New Heights was here for all of them.

"Christina, you wouldn't happen to be looking for a roommate, would you?" Kaitlyn doubted it, but she had to try.

"No. What happened to yours?"

"She's not coming back to school. Some kind of family issues." The sound of her roommate's voice when she'd called saddened her. She'd been looking forward to her friend's return, and not just for the rent money. As much as she hated to admit it, she needed the emotional support.

"That stinks. I know how hard it is to find a good roommate in this town. It took me months, plus I went through a few fuddy-duds. But I'll keep my ears open."

Marissa and Tristan bustled inside the front door, laughing and joking. She held up a bag and motioned for the girls to join them in the kitchen. "I picked up fresh bread and treats from the bakery. Come get some."

Kaitlyn smiled, eager to share her baby's movement, but she caught herself just in time. There was no need to bring up something that would be hurtful to Marissa, now that she knew about her friend's private struggles. She pushed away from the desk and followed Marissa and Tristan into the kitchen. "Smells delicious. I love sourdough."

Christina joined them and peeked inside the bag. "Muffins too? You spoil us."

"It's our pleasure." Tristan opened the refrigerator and pulled out the butter. "Plus we like to eat too." He nudged Marissa.

"I eat plenty." Her eyes widened as if to silently shush him.

Kaitlyn's heart yearned for someone she could care for openly the way Marissa and Tristan did. Maybe someday. There had to be a man out there whom she could love, who would in turn love her and her daughter, despite her messy situation.

She washed her hands before grabbing a slice from the steaming loaf. "Let's dig in. I'm starving."

"Guess what?" Christina said, mouth full of bread. "Kaitlyn felt the baby move."

Kaitlyn paused her bite and gauged Marissa's reaction.

Marissa eased into a smile and her eyes twinkled. "That's great news. Pretty soon we'll be able to feel the baby move too. Then you'll have to watch out for all of us reaching out to pat your tummy."

Kaitlyn savored the warm buttered bread and swallowed. She loved the way Marissa was happy for her, despite her own pain. Despite the pain she endured every day as woman after woman came through New Heights struggling to deal with the one thing Marissa couldn't have. Kaitlyn shook her head, awed. "As long as it's just you guys touching my stomach and not random strangers."

"You'll probably get plenty of those too." Tristan winked before strolling out of the kitchen with a muffin in hand.

"Are you coming to Zumba tonight?" Kaitlyn asked after polishing off another bite.

"You know," Marissa said as she sat at the table, "that class is strangely addicting. I didn't think I'd like it, but it's kind of fun, and I feel great when it's over."

Kaitlyn pointed her hunk of bread toward Marissa while speaking to Christina. "You should see her. This woman has some moves."

Christina perked up. "I should come check it out too."

"You should. I could give you a guest pass for the first class." Kaitlyn swallowed her buttery bite. "We'd have fun together."

Marissa offered a crumb-filled grin. "We would! And when it's over you feel like you could conquer the world—or at least make it through tomorrow."

Joy bloomed inside Kaitlyn. For all that Marissa had done for her, she was grateful to have found a way to pick up her friend's spirits too. Despite the difference in their ages, they'd formed a solid friendship, and Kaitlyn had confidence that one day they'd get past the secrecy and have a deeper bond.

As she watched her two new friends, and even considered Tristan in the next room, she realized she wasn't alone. Just because her parents had shut her out, her closest friend had moved, and Colin couldn't be a daily part of her life, she still had people who cared.

Perhaps God wasn't so angry with her after all.

### Colin

The chipper student worker leaned inside the open door. "Dr. Crank wants to see you in his office."

Anticipation churned inside Colin's gut. This was it. The moment he'd been waiting for during his entire professional career. The college had been buzzing about the coming announcements all morning. He wiped his hands on his slacks and pushed back from the desk. "I'll be right there."

The girl nodded and retreated to the outer office.

Colin grabbed his sport coat off the rack and steeled himself for the good news. This had to be it. School was about to start, so the timeline would be cutting it close. Though Colin had already told his teaching assistant that he'd soon take on additional duties, they'd need an official meeting to transfer more of the load so Colin could make more time for his research.

His brain churned with myriad to-do lists vying for his attention. It would take time away from Marissa, but she would understand. This would benefit them in the long run, not to mention his daughter.

*Daughter.* The word rang in his mind, eliciting a sense of awe and responsibility. He'd do whatever it took to provide a good life for her—the best education, dance classes, pretty clothes. This promotion was the first step toward security for everyone in his life.

Colin knuckle-tapped Dr. Crank's open door. "You asked to see me?"

"Right, yes. Have a seat." The older man scratched the tuft of white hair on top of his head.

Colin closed the door and moved a stack of science journals from the chair to the overburdened credenza. He forced himself to sit still and look Dr. Crank in the eye.

"I'll come right to the point."

*It's about time.* Colin nodded and remained silent.

Dr. Crank rubbed the bridge of his bulbous nose. "Things didn't quite go as I'd hoped. When I put forward your name to the committee, there was a favorable response, but as you know there are several qualified people on our staff. That's fortunate for us and our students, but not such good timing for you."

"Wait a second. Are you saying that I'm not getting *tenure*?" The words tasted like poison, and he could only hope he was hearing wrong. That there was an addendum to the story that gave him a happy ending.

"That's precisely what I'm saying." Dr. Crank met Colin's gaze with a strange mixture of sternness and empathy.

Cotton filled Colin's mouth as he tried to formulate his words, words that would cause Dr. Crank to go back and fight for his position.

"What about my research? I'm so close to a breakthrough, and I really needed the extra time in the lab that tenure would've made possible."

"I'm sorry, but the committee decided to go a different direction." Dr. Crank slid his glasses on and peered down at his notes. "You'll be receiving a formal letter, but I wanted you to hear it from me first. I only regret that we didn't get the decision announced sooner so that everyone could adjust their plans accordingly, but you know how these things go."

Actually, he didn't. But now wasn't the time for details. He didn't know exactly what it was a time for, considering that he'd banked everything on making tenure. He'd poured his life into his research and this institution, and still come up short. It didn't add up.

"I. . .I don't know what to say." Colin's throat constricted in a way it hadn't since he was a child being reprimanded with his nose stuck in the corner. Which was exactly what losing his shot at tenure felt like now.

"You don't have to say anything. Just know that I appreciate the work you do here, and I want you to continue with it. You still have all your classes to teach, and once you finish your research and get a few more publishing credits, I'm sure your elevation in this institution can be revisited. In the meantime, keep up the good work." Dr. Crank turned to his computer and began to type, effectively dismissing Colin.

He rose on legs still shaky with adrenaline and left the office, dejected. It was one thing to feel the sting of rejection and entirely another to realize how much his failure was going to cost his baby.

The question was, what could he do about it now?

# CHAPTER 38

*Marissa*

Fat drops of rain splattered against the kitchen window as I sipped my tea and watched the sunset through the clouds. So many changes in our lives, so much uncertainty. Strangely enough, I was starting to make peace with the unknown. At least a little.

My gut clenched when I heard the car door slam. Colin and I had been carefully coexisting, both desperate to hear from one another while at the same time preferring the comfort of silence. At least I hoped he wanted to connect with me since he was the one who offhandedly suggested counseling. The first few sessions hadn't gone well, but I was determined to go back. Determined to fix our lives.

I went to the living room to greet Colin, who grunted in my general direction without making eye contact. He slung his shoulder bag on the table in the entry and faced away from me. His dress shirt was soaked, revealing the muscles across the expanse of his back. Had he been working out more? Or just taking better care of himself since he'd found someone new?

"How was your day?" I twined my fingers like a nervous schoolgirl, waiting for him to acknowledge me with even the smallest look.

"Fine." His standard answer when his day was anything but. Finally, he gave up and turned around and brushed past me.

"We have a few more clients at New Heights, so I call that a good day." My words were more to jump-start a conversation than to tell him what happened with me. I already knew he wasn't the least bit interested in New Heights.

"Mmm." Colin bounded up the stairs two at a time, avoiding me like one of the toxins he occasionally droned on about.

Thunder rumbled outside, and the hair on my arms prickled.

What was causing his agitation? Even in our darkest moments, he rarely ignored me completely. The new behavior stirred up the anxiety I worked so hard every day to snuff out.

I followed him up the stairs to our room where he was changing in the closet. He hadn't yet moved his clothes out even though we no longer slept together, but the fact that he hid himself was another sign of how our relationship had changed.

"You're awfully quiet." I stood in the doorway with my arms folded. There was no way I was letting him leave the room without some kind of response.

He leaned out of the closet, his eyes hard and icy. "Usually that means that someone doesn't want to talk."

I held up my hands. "So sorry that I'm trying to have a conversation with my husband when he comes home from work. . .unless that's not where you've been."

Colin's cheeks reddened until he looked ready to combust. His mouth puckered, a white ring forming around his lips. "I don't appreciate your insinuation."

Yet he didn't deny its truth.

I ground my teeth to hold back regrettable words. There was nothing truthful I could say that wouldn't ignite an emotional brush fire.

He pulled a gray shirt over his head, tousling his hair. "Are you *trying* to get me to give up on our marriage?"

"Haven't you already?"

Colin picked a hairbrush up from the dresser and hurled it against the wall.

I jumped back, though the brush wasn't anywhere close to me. My stoic, methodical husband was finally angry, showing a rare display of emotion. Inexplicably, it soothed me. I uncrossed my arms. "I'm sorry. That wasn't fair."

Colin deflated onto the bed and scrubbed his face. Protracted moments passed before he looked up at me, eyes swollen with fatigue and a hint of regret, and spoke. "I *know* this is all my fault. I *know* I brought this all on myself. But do you have any idea what I'm going through? How hard this is for *me*?"

His words branded my conscience. In truth, I hadn't considered his feelings, believing that whatever repercussions he suffered were his just punishment. But his sorrowful expression softened me, taking me back to a time when he was in grad school and lost the coveted TA position to a kid who had stage fright in front of the class but was somehow still believed to be God's gift to teaching.

The bed depressed when I sat next to him, hands folded in my lap. I missed being beside my husband in bed, and I missed having someone at least pretend to connect with me at the end of the day. Most of all I missed the comfort of knowing that no matter how life was smacking me around, I wasn't in it alone.

"I'm trying my best." His body trembled next to mine. "You have no idea how hard I am working to put things back together."

"I am too."

"Are you?" Colin faced me, his eyes searching mine for truth. "Because it sure doesn't feel like it. You're determined to make this as hard on me as possible. You don't speak to me for days and then you pour your guts out to a stranger—"

"She's our therapist."

"We wouldn't need one if you would just talk to me and work it out."

Ire simmered inside me. That he had the gall to lay any blame at my feet was unconscionable. "Well, we're talking now." The sarcasm burned my tongue, and regret soon followed. How would our marriage ever get back to anything resembling normal if I continued to shut him out? And yet, shutting him out was the only way I could remain sane, since resentment mushroomed inside me every time we spoke. No matter how hard I prayed or what I did, I couldn't get past the anger.

Colin stood abruptly and paced. "It looks to me like you don't want our marriage, like you're ready to toss it out. You're just waiting for me to pull the trigger." He leaned close, until our noses were almost touching. "But I'm not going to, so you might as well start trying to get along."

"What, exactly, is keeping you here?" The tremor in my voice ticked me off. I'd already spent too many years playing the weakling wife, and

I regretted every wasted moment and every ounce of pity he'd spent on me. Was that the only thing keeping him here now, when he clearly preferred to start a new life with someone else?

"Because I don't quit. I may get sidetracked, I may get knocked down, but that doesn't stop me. No matter how hard things get or how low I sink, I don't give up."

"Great." I threw my hands in the air. "Does that make me your charity project?"

"You're my wife, and I wish you'd start acting like it."

"Oh, so now I'm the one not playing the part?" I rose and stationed myself by the window, focusing on the raindrops smearing the view. "*I've never forgotten who I was and what that meant.*"

"You might not have done *that*, but you sure checked out of life more than a few times."

"That was not my fault." I ground my teeth again, pressing back the hurt and anger, the aching loss that blanketed me whenever I thought of the child we should have had. "Clearly you didn't care as much as I did, and that's not my fault either."

"Don't you dare tell me how I felt." His voice rose, causing the hair on my neck to stand. "I was there with you every step of the way, only you were too self-absorbed to see it!"

"I'm done! I won't listen to this anymore." I hardened my expression and forced the tears not to fall. I would never be weak enough to let him defeat me again. Not when I was, apparently, required to share him with another family.

"Remember how I said that sometimes I fell out of love with you?" He paused, his nostrils flaring. "This is one of those times."

# CHAPTER 39

*Marissa*

Colin's words seeped into my soul like poison, leaching out every iota of confidence I'd recently gained. Stunned, I had nowhere to turn. Not even the comfort usually found in scripture could ease the ache in my chest.

I tiptoed down the stairs and past his office, grabbed my keys and purse, and left. Not that I had anywhere to go or a listening ear that wouldn't make me more confused than I already was. Mom would launch into another diatribe about how God hates divorce, which I already knew. Briefly I considered visiting Kaitlyn, not to talk about my problems—goodness knew she had enough of her own—but to simply be with a friend.

I sighed and drove the opposite way. No matter how good my intentions were in visiting her, she was starting to be able to read me, and she didn't need the weight of my own sorry issues in addition to her own.

But the burden of loneliness pressed against me, compelling me to find someone to talk to, which was how I found myself at Tristan's house.

"You look terrible."

"That really wasn't what I wanted to hear." I scooted around him and stopped in the living room, startled by the presence of another woman, who seemed equally surprised to see me. "I'm sorry." My gaze bounced between them. "I didn't mean to interrupt. I should go."

"Don't bother." The leggy brunette snatched her handbag and cast a look of disdain at me. "I was just leaving."

I didn't remember seeing another car outside, but I hadn't been paying attention to anything but finding the comfort of a familiar face. "Really, I can go."

"It's fine." Tristan's clipped tone made me think it was anything but.

He turned toward the woman whose eyes flashed with fire. "I'll see you out." He disappeared around the wall that separated the living area from the foyer and spoke in a hushed tone. "It doesn't have to end this way."

"Clearly it does. What just happened is proof of that." The woman's glass-shattering pitch ended the conversation.

I shrank myself to try to blend in. What had just happened? If only I'd gone to Kaitlyn's instead, Tristan would be working things out with…whoever his most recent lady-friend was. I never could keep them straight, and since none of the relationships lasted too long or seemed too serious, I rarely tried.

The soft click of the door ended their interaction. I heard Tristan release a heavy breath before he came back around and met me on the sofa.

"To what do I owe the pleasure?" He casually took up a cup and sipped his tea—a nightly ritual of his since college.

"Sorry for interrupting. I had no idea you had company." I fidgeted, unwilling to set down my purse in case Tristan confessed to wanting to be alone.

"Her name is Sheryl."

I was momentarily surprised that he was still with the same woman, but I tried not to let on. "I had no idea Sheryl was here."

His eyebrow tented. "You didn't see her car in the driveway?"

It was a question I'd already asked myself and didn't have an answer for. "I guess I wasn't paying attention. I really feel bad. Maybe you should go after her. A woman wants to be chased when she leaves. Trust me, I know."

"So you left and Colin didn't follow?"

I eased back against the plush sofa and relaxed. "Has he ever followed me? Actually, he didn't know I left." This time. That didn't account for all the other times he never came for me. I'd spent our entire marriage chasing after him, being the one who loved more. Who loved at all.

Tristan took a final sip and stood. "As long as you're here, you can help me with the dinner dishes."

"Does that mean you're not going after her—Sheryl?" I followed him into the kitchen where a Bach cantata played in the background and an explosion of pots and pans and casserole dishes littered the counter. I wrinkled my nose. "What on earth happened in here? No wonder she left."

"Funny." He shot me a pointed look. "You must be masking something."

I grabbed a dish towel and whipped it at him. "Quit trying to read me."

Tristan leaned against the counter and searched my eyes for a breathless moment. "I don't have to try."

Quickly I turned away, anxious to dry dishes that weren't yet washed.

"And no, I'm not going after Sheryl. This one was never going to work out. We're on two totally different paths." He plugged the sink, turned on the hot water, and squirted in blobs of soap. "That happens sometimes," he said, not meeting my eye.

"No offense, but it seems to happen to you a lot." I scraped the pasta off the first dish and placed it in the sink, then started the next. The man needed a dishwasher, but for years he'd refused to budge, saying they didn't get the dishes as clean.

He grimaced. "There's no point in sticking it out with someone who isn't right for me."

"But you need a good woman—you deserve one." I piled several more dishes into the sink, the sudsy water sloshing over the lip.

He started scrubbing furiously. "Do any of us really deserve those things? I'd hate to think God would give me what I really deserve."

"Don't go philosophical on me." I moved to the other side of Tristan and started to rinse the dishes he'd washed.

"Speaking the truth, that's all."

"So do you care to tell me what happened tonight? Maybe I can help. I have a lot of experience in trying to patch things up."

Tristan laughed, rightly so. "I'm good with letting this one go. I wasn't just saying that to make you feel better for showing up unannounced on my doorstep."

Despite his words, I knew he wanted me there. He, too, was comforted by the familiar, and I didn't need Tristan to put on his psychologist's hat to tell me so. We'd been through so many ups and downs that standing next to one another at the end of a down seemed natural. Except lately, he'd been doing more of the giving, and frankly, I was tired of being on the receiving end. I wanted to be the strong one.

Yet Colin's words burned through me like acid, stealing my resolve to get a backbone.

The casserole dish in Tristan's hands seemed to have taken on an enormous job this evening, with some kind of tomato-based sauce splattered everywhere. I pointed with the dish towel. "You sure went to an awful lot of trouble tonight for someone you're just as happy to let go."

Tristan stopped and let the dish slide under the soapy water, then turned to face me. "If you must know, I like her well enough, but she seems to be a little jealous. . .of you."

I looked away. "Oh, that again?" It wasn't the first time he'd given up a romantic relationship in order to sustain our friendship. Funny how any woman would be jealous of me, all things considered. Tristan needed someone strong and secure, someone who worked as hard as he did but knew how to get him to lighten up and play. Someone full of compassion who also had a good sense of humor. He deserved that, and I reminded myself to keep looking for the perfect woman for him because that's what good friends did.

He shrugged and resumed scrubbing. After a minute, he handed me the dish and started the next. "I told her to meet you before getting upset, but she didn't seem to want to. She has a lot of old insecurities."

"You keep going for that type." I sprayed the suds off the casserole dish. "What does that say about you?"

Once again he stopped and locked eyes with me. An unspoken current passed between us, one I chose to ignore. I don't know what he wanted to say or what was on his mind, but I could guess. Thankfully he was too much of a gentleman to go there.

But he wasn't too much of a gentleman to not pry into my marriage. "So what happened tonight? Do I need to worry about Colin showing up here with a baseball bat?"

"Ha-ha. You're pretty funny when you set your mind to it." We all knew Colin showed little to no emotion, at least until tonight when he threw the brush at the wall. I shuddered at the memory. His clinical veneer had finally cracked.

"Seriously, what happened?"

My throat constricted, and I cast my gaze at the stainless steel sink. "He came right out and said he doesn't love me."

Tristan winced. "Ouch. That's a new one." He continued scrubbing for a moment, our shoulders grazing with the motion. "Did something happen that set him on edge?"

"Who knows anymore."

"And how did that make you feel?"

I slapped the towel against the sink. "Cut it out. Don't give me the psychology garbage. I need a friend."

He dropped the pan and pulled his soapy hands from the water and stared me down. "Fine. Then as a friend I have to ask, were you really surprised?"

The truth was attacking from all sides, and it hurt. I hurt. But I couldn't run from it, not with Tristan's probing gaze trying to unearth an answer. "No, I wasn't."

"What do you plan to do about it?"

"What *can* I do about it? I can't make him feel one way or the other. I have no control over Colin." I wound and unwound the towel around my hand, waiting for whatever was to come.

"Exactly." His tone, laced with sympathy and truth, delved into the bruised parts of my heart. "You only have control of you. What are *you* going to do about the situation?"

"I'm not getting a divorce, if that's what you're thinking." I rubbed my head to ward off the ache that was starting to form. "He already thinks Christians are hypocrites. Can you imagine what he'd think about that? I don't want to lead him in the wrong direction."

"Seems to me like he's leading himself in the wrong direction."

"But I don't need to make it worse. I don't want to be accountable to God for that."

Tristan set to work on the dishes again, seeming to consider my argument. " 'How do you know, wife, whether you will save your husband?' " The Bible verse he whipped out seemed a little too convenient.

"You're probably taking it out of context," I countered, though I wasn't really sure. It seemed I had some studying to do later, if I felt up to it. There were so many ways to use scripture that it boggled the mind, and frankly, I was too exhausted to parse words to find the truth. I wanted the truth handed to me and was fairly certain it wouldn't involve divorce.

"I'm just saying you have options. God doesn't want you to be a doormat either. I'm pretty sure there's a clause for adultery."

The word sounded so harsh coming from him. I wrinkled my nose and sprayed suds off the pan. "Well, thank you, Reverend Tristan."

He scoffed. "Fine—try to help a friend and look what happens."

I held up the pan. "Who's helping who?"

"Good point." He turned on the tap, tested the temperature, and added some more hot water and soap. "So any idea what set him off?"

I thought back to the fight and the way Colin had avoided me until I cornered him. The helpless look in his eye when we finally connected. A look I'd seen only one other time. Then it hit me, like a cold slap. "Oh no. No." I shook my head and closed my eyes, realizing how oblivious I'd been. How self-involved, when in fact his mood was probably not even about me, no matter how I'd twisted it.

"What?"

"I'll bet he didn't make tenure."

# CHAPTER 40

*Marissa*

Funny how it's the ugly, fetid parts of life that drive you to your knees and send you digging around in scripture until you find some morsel to keep you fed, if only for another hour until you can get another fix. Such was my life for the next several weeks that led into autumn. There were new lows that tore holes in my heart at every turn, and each time I emerged I would realize how much stronger I'd grown. Panic attacks dissipated, replaced by more exercise and a strict regimen of healthy foods, sleep, and daily pep talks in the mirror.

I'd even started to rethink my life—though I'd never admit as much to Tristan. It wasn't so much considering a life without Colin but how I could remake a life with him. How I could go on to try other things and quit obsessing about being childless. But just as I couldn't live without Colin, I couldn't quite imagine living without New Heights and all the goals and dreams and attachments that came with it. My life's purpose had been so singularly focused, there was little else I could see myself doing no matter how much I had to claw my way from despair to joy every single day.

On a crisp afternoon in early October, Colin and I finished one of our sporadic and highly polarizing counseling sessions. No one was more relieved than I was when the hour was over, except perhaps Dr. Graves.

I slid on my sunglasses to fend off the glaring light—a stark contrast to the muted, stoic office we'd just done battle in. "I'll see you at home?" These days I was never sure, and since we'd driven separately I might not see him anytime soon. Despite his not receiving tenure, Colin's work hours hadn't changed, if that's where he even was. For all I knew he was still seeing his mistress and preparing for his baby.

I'd never even asked how far along she was or how often they kept in touch because the details would only hurt worse. One thing I was sure of—they *were* keeping in touch. I knew it the same way I knew he was having an affair in the first place, the unexplained absences, the dodgy looks, the times he turned his back to send a text message. Only now I wasn't trying to catch him. There was no point.

"You tell me." He clicked his key fob and made his car chirp. "I never know your schedule."

"I'll be there." I narrowed my eyes and tried to gauge where his comment was going. Lately, I'd resisted the urge to snap out a snarky response to everything he said, which was a victory in my book. A small one, but I'd take what I could get.

Colin slung his elbow over the top of his car and rested his forehead in his hand, his hair spiking between his fingers. "That didn't go so well, did it?"

During the hour, he'd tried to bring up negotiations about what kind of relationship I'd allow him to have with the baby. What was I supposed to say? It would be unthinkable to tell him to abandon his child, but with the child came the mother. There was no separating the two. How could I ever compete with a real family? I fished around for my keys so I wouldn't have to look at him. "No, it didn't. I guess there's always next week. Or the week after that." I unlocked my door and started to climb inside, but his words halted me.

"Do you want to go somewhere and talk? I mean, by ourselves." He motioned to the gray office building. Dirt smudged the elbow of his dress shirt. "We don't need all this to have a conversation."

I begged to differ, but I wasn't going to say so. "What do you have in mind?"

He gestured with his head. "Climb in."

Would wonders never cease? Maybe my mother's prayers were being answered after all.

*Colin*

There was no more tiptoeing around the ugly stuff, as today's therapy session had proved. But there had to be a way to work with Marissa and get her to accept that he had new responsibilities. Kaitlyn still wasn't accepting much help with groceries or anything else, but once the baby came she'd take time off and he would need to step up and fill in the gaps—monetary and otherwise. Since he didn't get tenure and the pay raise that would've come with it, Marissa was going to have to be part of the budgeting decisions whether she wanted to or not.

Colin shuddered—and it wasn't from the cool breeze blowing inside the window.

The first thing Marissa did when she climbed into his car was change the radio station. He bit his tongue in favor of peace since he needed her on his side. Colin pulled onto the road and headed out of town toward the mountains. If anything would soften his wife up, this was it.

"Where are we going?" she asked over the lazy drone of the news.

"To check out the leaves." He shot a furtive glance at Marissa and noted the curve of her smile. A good start. Too bad he hadn't done more of this when their marriage started to crash—then they wouldn't have to duke it out in front of Dr. Graves and her smug scrutiny.

"Perfect day for it." Marissa gazed out the window, evidently content to stick to the weather. That was fine. At least they weren't fighting.

They left the houses and schools and office buildings behind and cruised on the open highway until they reached a dirt road that led up the mountain. Few people traveled out this way and instead favored the ski slope, but he and Marissa had discovered the little turnoff back in the days when they would spend weekends hiking and playing around outdoors, enjoying each other's company as newlyweds.

Colin pulled over and parked in front of a gate that blocked off a forest service road and climbed out of the car.

Marissa followed him, picking her way around a pile of rocks. "I'm not sure I have the right shoes for this." She wiggled a sandled foot at him.

"I'll help you." Colin scrounged up some courage before holding his hand out to his wife.

The sun shone just right between the trees to illuminate her eyes behind her sunglasses. She scrutinized him, as though she wasn't sure touching him was a good idea.

Slowly, she grasped his hand with cold fingers, stiff to his touch. It was a start, and more progress than they'd made since she found out about his baby. Little Nugget. The thought of his child—now seven months, according to Kaitlyn and her burgeoning belly—set a smile on his lips.

Marissa smiled back, pulling him from his thoughts. He had to focus and figure out how to fix his relationship with his wife in time. Colin pulled her close but not close enough to arouse suspicion as they set off down the path that wound between the towering aspens.

"What made you think of coming here?" Marissa's voice cut over the top of chirping birds.

"I remembered how we always used to hike around here this time of year." He let his gaze roam. Every fall hue colored the leaves—bright gold, brilliant orange, red, and everything in between. He stopped and slid the sunglasses off her eyes and onto her head.

She squinted. "It's bright."

"The view is better unhindered." He locked onto her gaze, the flecks in her eyes matching the fall colors that surrounded them, and beyond that was something he hadn't seen in a long time—hope. His breath caught unexpectedly.

"You're right," she said, breaking away, "the view really is better." The breeze kicked up, sweeping her hair off her shoulders. She wrapped her sweater more tightly around her and continued walking.

Colin's hand was cold without hers. He took long strides to catch up. "Maybe we don't need Dr. Graves. Do you think. . .maybe. . .we can talk without her? The way we used to?"

Marissa laughed politely. "We'd have to go a long ways back if you mean talking the way we used to before things went bad."

"And by 'things' you mean our marriage?" Colin wanted her to say it, to acknowledge they still had a marriage. He'd noticed lately that she'd stopped referring to them as a couple, stopped calling him her husband, stopped alluding to their future. While he would've been happy several months ago for that kind of change, he now found it unsettling.

"And other things." She sighed, a sad smile on her lips. "It doesn't matter. If you want to stop seeing Dr. Graves, I'm all for it."

Alarms sounded off inside him. She gave up awfully fast, even for her. Even though he'd been the one to suggest counseling as a last-ditch effort, her resignation didn't sit right.

Realization snuck up on him—he wanted her to fight for him.

"What's wrong?" Marissa stopped and looked back.

Colin winced. He hadn't even realized she'd walked on without him. "It's nothing." He swallowed, trying to gather his nebulous thoughts and come up with a cogent reason for him to feel that way. "I just didn't expect you to say that."

Marissa continued walking, the fallen leaves crunching under her sandals. "It's pretty clear that we either picked the wrong therapist or we haven't got a chance."

"I've never heard you say that before, that we haven't got a chance."

Her face remained placid. "There's probably a lot of things I haven't said. You've been pretty busy lately."

For all the times he'd worked late or occasionally checked up on Kaitlyn, it was Marissa who was gone from home more often than not. He caught up to her and tried to keep his tone casual. "You seem to have a busy schedule lately too. Where have you been?"

Her eyebrow tented. "Here and there. Trying new things."

Stupid Tristan. No doubt she was spending more time with him and didn't want to admit it. Colin flexed his fists. "With who?"

"Mostly myself, except the exercise class—it's a group thing. I've been spending more time with Mom and going to Bible study. Going to coffee with people from Bible study."

"And Tristan?" He couldn't help asking, and he was ticked at himself for doing it. "Are you spending more time with him?"

Marissa eyed him. "No more than usual."

Which was still more than enough. Sure, they never crossed the line, but he saw the way that man reacted to his wife. Not that he deserved to be jealous after having an affair, but the idea of another man looking at his wife that way provoked stronger emotions than he wanted to admit.

He shoved his hands inside his pockets before she noticed. "I wondered why you hadn't been home as much."

"I didn't think you noticed." She turned abruptly and held up her hand. "I'm not saying that in a bad way. I just know that you've been...occupied." Her eyes clouded before she turned away and resumed strolling.

"Maybe we should both try to stay home more." He kicked a rock off the path.

"Maybe." She frowned—not the reaction he was hoping for.

What was he hoping for? He had more freedom now than before, but he still wasn't happy. He inhaled the fresh mountain air. "Do you have any suggestions?"

Her eyes roamed the forest and the trail—everywhere but in his direction. "That depends. What are we trying to accomplish? If we both want peace, it seems we have more peace the less time we're under the same roof."

He craned his neck and tried to dig up answers. "I don't even know what peace is anymore."

They continued in silence. Marissa started to speak but seemed to swallow the words. Finally she stopped walking and placed her hand on his arm. "I know I've said this before, but there's only one way to find peace."

Colin's jaw tightened. His wife and his best friend were starting to sound an awful lot alike. That was fine in the early years. He'd become a champ at playing along. But once her mom got her more involved with church and the whole God thing, it seemed to take over their lives. Church wasn't going to help him now. Having his wife, his mother-in-law, and now his best friend gang up on him drove him further away. What he needed was practical advice for how to manage two separate families without anyone walking away. He was pretty sure sermons on that topic were in short supply.

"I know you think it's ridiculous—"

"It's fine for you; it's just not my thing."

"It could be." She smiled hopefully then turned away and continued down the dirt path. "God has seen me through a lot."

Was that why she was trotting around ignoring him lately?

"Prayer helps me sort out the future, to figure out what else I might want to do with my life. You know?"

He didn't, but he wasn't going to ruin the moment. "What else do you want to do? Are you thinking of. . ." No, he shook off the thought. Marissa wouldn't leave him. That wasn't her style. He tamped down the anxiety brewing in his gut.

"Leaving New Heights. . .maybe one day."

"Why? I thought you loved it. You've poured your heart into that place." Along with just about every spare dime they ever made. But he wasn't ready to think about the money yet, not when she was finally opening up.

Marissa rolled her bottom lip and her shoulders heaved. She sat on a rock and pulled her knees to her chest. "Working with mothers and babies and unborn babies. . .it's starting to take its toll on me."

"I thought you enjoyed that kind of thing." He sat next to her, arms pressed together. Thankfully she didn't inch away.

"I did—I mean, I do. Some parts. But knowing that I'll never have a child of my own. . ." She swallowed, her mouth puckering. "When there was hope, I could be happy for the women I worked with. Without hope, it's harder than I ever imagined."

The urge to take her into his arms was powerful, but he resisted. Their tentative truce was too new and he didn't want to scare her off. "I'm sorry. That sounds rough."

"I never told you, but I'd finally made an appointment."

"Appointment?" He cast a sideways glance.

"With the fertility specialist." She looked down and appeared to study the weeds sprouting at the base of the rock. "That was before you told me your news." She released a doleful sigh. "I went to the first appointment, but obviously I never went back."

Her words were like a sucker punch. He swiped his face with his hands. "I don't know what to say."

"You don't have to say anything." She gazed ahead and blinked several times. "I've made peace with it. What I haven't made peace with is working around it all day, every day."

"What else would you do?"

"Honestly? I have no idea. I never imagined myself doing anything else. Most likely try to find a job doing other kinds of ultrasounds."

"How soon do you plan to leave?" Colin forced himself not to think about the little bit of money her job brought in. That wasn't what mattered right now.

Marissa smiled in that way that used to light up his heart, the way that made him burn for her. Now he recognized that she was trying to cope with her feelings. "I have no firm plans, just thoughts. Trying to see what else God might have in store for me. But the more I think about pulling away, the more ideas I have to make New Heights even better." Her eyes sparkled.

"Like what?" His heart warmed at their conversation. Why couldn't it always be like this? Maybe she really had changed. The old Marissa would be morose and depressed, adding rocks to her proverbial pockets to make herself sink further.

"Like bringing in doulas and hosting more birthing and parenting classes to help prepare the mothers for labor and delivery. We're finally pulling in enough grant money and donations to make it happen." Her animated expression reminded him of the enthusiasm she used to have, about everything—life, love. Him.

"I have no clue what a doula is."

She grinned. "It's someone who helps mothers have a positive birth experience. I mean, I've always tried to connect moms with birthing classes and doulas and such, but most of them don't have the resources to follow through regularly, and until now neither did New Heights."

He rubbed his hands on his pants. "But now you have more grants?" He hoped she wasn't going to try to pay out-of-pocket, like she had so many other times over the years.

Her mouth crimped. "We sure do. I think it'd be a great way to help the moms, and I've already started making a few phone calls." She shook her head. "Anyway, those are the things I think about and want to accomplish, so I guess my work at New Heights isn't finished yet."

Colin turned to her, seeing the real Marissa. "I'm really impressed with what you're doing."

"It's all good for now, and I just hope. . . never mind. It's all good." She said it as if to convince herself. At least she was working in a positive direction, which was a lot more than she used to do. Frankly, he was surprised.

And a little unnerved.

"I meant what I said earlier." She nudged him playfully. "You're welcome to come to church with me anytime."

Colin scoffed before he could stop himself. He might be in a tough spot, but he wasn't that desperate, and didn't imagine he ever would be.

# CHAPTER 41

*Kaitlyn*

A knock on the door startled Kaitlyn from her mindless television marathon. She waddled over to the door and turned on the porch light.

She flung open the door and bear-hugged her friend. "Sydney, I wasn't expecting you this early."

"No, but you're definitely expecting." Sydney pulled back, eyes circling over Kaitlyn's stomach.

Just then, Little Nugget rolled, sending a rippling sensation through Kaitlyn's abdomen. "Here, feel this." She grabbed Sydney's hand and pressed. The baby responded with a firm kick.

"Wow, that's cool! How far along are you?"

"Almost eight months. The kicks get harder every day, and forget trying to sleep at night." She closed the door and ushered her friend inside. "I must be up three times to go to the bathroom, not that you probably want to know that."

"I guess if we're going to do this, I need to get used to TMI."

"I'm so glad you said yes. Thank you."

"You didn't think I was going to miss out on my chance to boss you around, did you?"

Sydney waggled her finger and bobbed her head.

"Being a birthing coach has nothing to do with bossing me around—I think." Though she'd read up on it since Marissa announced they'd be holding classes at New Heights, she still didn't know what, exactly, was supposed to happen. All she knew was that she couldn't ask Colin, no matter how many times he'd come over lately. He was so concerned over the people at the college finding out about his indiscretion that he was still keeping her pregnancy a secret.

"I guess we're about to find out how this whole thing is supposed to go down. You just need to make sure to have that pretty baby between my mom's and my grandma's doctor appointments."

Kaitlyn padded to the kitchen and poured her friend a glass of water. "How are they doing?"

"Same old, same old. They seem to need a lot more help than I thought they would. It's a good thing I moved home." She sighed, more than likely sad to put school on hold and live in a neighboring town. "Grandma can hardly get around and Mom can't drive. I'm running ragged between those two."

"I know you needed to do it, but I miss having you here. It's been way too quiet."

Sydney snickered. "Not for long."

It was nice to have someone here who laughed and talked and just told it like it was. Sydney never held back, even if it wasn't what Kaitlyn wanted to hear. She could use a little more of that in her life, rather than people skirting the obvious. Except Marissa, who was pretty honest but without the bluntness of Sydney. Kaitlyn could only imagine what Marissa might say if she knew the whole story.

"I've never even been around babies." Kaitlyn handed the glass of water to Sydney then eased herself into the recliner. "I have a lot to learn, and not just about the birth."

"I bet you'll be glad to stop wearing smocks." Sydney eyeballed the flouncy shirt Kaitlyn had picked up at New Heights.

"Very funny. I see you haven't lost your touch."

"That's why you picked me." Sydney took a sip. "Not only am I cool under pressure, but I can make you laugh at the same time."

"That's exactly why I picked you." Kaitlyn glanced at the clock. Thankfully they still had a little time to visit before the birthing class started.

Sydney slid a sideways glance at her. "So your picking me has nothing to do with Mr. Not-So-Wonderful not being"—she air-quoted—"available?"

"Well," Kaitlyn said as she lifted her chin, "he would still be my second choice."

They erupted with laughter just like old times. Sydney's expression turned stoic. "Seriously, though. Is he coming around?"

"He stops by when he can."

"And by 'when he can' you mean when it's convenient for him." Sydney's lips pursed.

Kaitlyn shrugged, unwilling to disparage a man she needed to get along with for the next eighteen years. As angry as she was, she knew from the stories at New Heights that it could be so much worse. "It's not ideal, but he wants to be involved. We've been talking about ideas for the nursery, and names." Their conversations hadn't gotten beyond the birth since he threw up a wall every time she tried, but she was done pushing. Frankly, she was too tired.

"One word of advice: give the baby *your* last name."

"Why?" Kaitlyn pressed her hand to her abdomen as Little Nugget did a somersault.

"I don't mean to be rude, but you just don't know. He's been a reluctant participant so far, and even if he's coming around, that doesn't mean he's going to stay around. Get my drift?"

All too well.

Kaitlyn nodded. "I suppose there's still time to think about that, but you're probably right. I wish I could say he'll be here for good, but I'd be lying."

Sydney's phone rang. "Ugh, what now?" She rolled her eyes as she answered. "What's up, Mom?" Loud, indecipherable words poured over the line as Sydney bolted out of her seat. "Slow down and say that again." She pressed her finger over her open ear and paced. "Can you call the neighbor? Not home. Okay, call the ambulance and I'll be home as soon as I can."

"What happened?" Kaitlyn hoisted herself out of the recliner.

"My grandma fell, and Mom can't get her off the floor. She doesn't think she's hurt too badly, but I could hear moaning in the background."

Kaitlyn covered her mouth. "Oh no. You'd better hurry, but be safe." She hustled her friend toward the door.

Sydney turned, disappointment in her eyes. "I'm so sorry about this. I really wanted to be there for you."

"Don't worry about it. Seriously, you have enough to handle right now."

"I know, but—"

"No buts. There will be a few more sessions before I go into labor." She opened the door and ushered Sydney onto the porch. "Go!"

"Love you, friend."

Kaitlyn said a silent prayer for Sydney, still unsure whether God was listening.

*Marissa*

The party was coming together nicely. I refused to think of it as a prenatal/birthing class, otherwise I never would have gone through with it. Instead I focused on the joy of friends getting together, with me playing the happy hostess.

"This doesn't look so healthy for pregnant women." Tristan picked up a lemon tart.

I slapped his hand. "Not so healthy for un-pregnant men either, if we're going to get picky about it." I continued arranging the tarts, cookies, cupcakes, and scones I'd picked up from the bakery around the corner. It wasn't in the New Heights budget, and it certainly wasn't in mine, but every party requires food. And with where we were at, Colin wouldn't have the nerve to confront me about spending. At some point he was going to be paying child support—legally or otherwise—so whatever money I chose to spend, I did so with a clear conscience.

"This is quite a spread you have going here." Grace White, the childbirth educator, peered over my shoulder. "You know we end the first session with a talk about nutrition during pregnancy, don't you?"

Honestly, I'd been trying not to think about it at all, but it was like telling yourself not to think of the pink elephant in the room. I dusted my hands and turned to her with a smile. "Then I'm happy to give them a good send-off before venturing into veggies and cardboard."

Grace offered a hearty laugh. "I think we have better options than cardboard. It might do you some good to sit in on this one."

My throat tightened. "As much as I'd love to, I'll be in my office catching up on some things."

Tristan threw me a pitying glance. "You can go home if you need to. I can stay until the end and clean up. I was planning on working in my office tonight too."

The offer tempted me, but this was my vision—if you could call something that killed me a little more every day a vision—and I needed to see it through. All our clients were so excited about attending, and I'd seen them through so many stages of their pregnancies already that it would be wrong for me to leave. But that didn't mean I wanted to sit through the class.

"I don't mind staying." I mustered up what I knew was a flimsy smile by the way Grace eyed me before she turned away to finish unpacking her supplies. "This was my idea, and I'm going to make sure everything runs smoothly."

Tristan's eyes narrowed but he let it go, thankfully.

More women than I'd anticipated began to trickle in with their partners. Tristan and I pulled additional chairs out of the kitchen and our offices to accommodate everyone. Thanks to me, we had plenty of snacks, but we needed more tea.

I headed to the kitchen and set the kettle on to boil water.

"Do you need some help?" Kaitlyn startled me from behind.

"I think Tristan and I have it under control. You should go relax and enjoy yourself. Maybe you could introduce your friend around." I opened the cupboards to scrounge for more tea bags.

"She couldn't make it." Kaitlyn's mouth turned down.

"Who couldn't make it?" Tristan strolled in and started opening and closing the drawers.

"My friend Sydney." Kaitlyn nibbled on a tart. "As soon as she got to my house, she had a family emergency." Her gaze swept the floor. She was not good at masking her disappointment, or perhaps disappointment had dogpiled her to the point that masking it was too hard. I remembered the feeling.

Tristan grabbed a stack of napkins and held them up like a prize. "I'd offer to be your partner, but Jenna already roped me into it." Poor

Tristan, Jenna had been trying to rope him into something for weeks, and he'd been totally oblivious. He didn't realize that by pairing up with her this evening, he was sending the wrong message. Since his breakup with what's-her-name, he'd been doing a lot of absentminded things that made me wonder if he missed her more than he let on.

"That's okay, I'll be fine." The faux lilt in Kaitlyn's voice reminded me so much of myself.

"I'll do it," I said too brightly.

Tristan's soft hand on my shoulder made me doubt myself. "Are you sure?"

"Why wouldn't I be?" Silly question—we all knew the answer.

"You don't need to." Concern coated Kaitlyn's voice, which only bolstered my determination to do the right thing.

"I want to." I sent up a silent SOS to God. "I made a promise to you, and I always keep my word."

The beginning of the session focused on everyone introducing themselves and their birthing partners, and telling how far along they were and any unusual symptoms they'd been experiencing. Though I obviously knew all seven women, I hadn't seen most of them since the early stages of pregnancy. Being with them now, so close to delivery, sent a shockwave of longing around inside me, ricocheting off every one of my hidden desires.

The sorrow was getting harder to bury.

I let my mind drift to safer shores as Grace pulled out her visuals and began instructing the excited pairs. It was good to see the mothers—most of them single, some of them abused, all of them broke—experiencing joy over their babies. I prayed for each one then continued trying to distract myself by running over my mental to-do list. That didn't help much since I'd forgotten to go grocery shopping, hadn't gone to the bank, and still hadn't picked up the coffeemaker Tristan had been imploring me to buy for months.

"Let's finish up with some simple techniques that will help you cope with stress now, as well as during labor." Grace clapped her hands as if grabbing the attention of five-year-olds. "Just a few exercises."

Exercise—that's what else I hadn't done. With all the recent planning I'd been doing for New Heights, I'd skipped a week of workouts and felt all the more jiggly for it. Who knew I'd actually become addicted to something healthy? I always felt more confident and assertive after a solid workout.

Kaitlyn and I situated ourselves, and she followed along with Grace's demonstration. She really didn't need me for this, but I was still glad to be with her. It felt right.

The whole thing felt right despite the fact it was another reminder of what I wasn't able to have. But these days, what wasn't? Besides, it wasn't about me—it was about these precious women who'd decided to have their babies despite imperfect circumstances, who'd chosen to believe that life was a precious gift, regardless. They needed all the support they could get, and ironically I was in a position to provide it.

But no matter how satisfying my work at New Heights was, I wasn't sure I could do it forever. Running New Heights and having children were the only two dreams I'd ever really had. Now that one of them had been bludgeoned, the other was becoming unbearable.

A half hour later the house was empty except for Tristan and me, and the ravaged pastry platters left behind by a herd of pregnant women. I grabbed the trash can from the kitchen and started the cleanup.

"That sucked for you, didn't it?" Tristan swept the crumbs off the table and into the can.

"Is that your professional opinion?"

"It's my opinion as your oldest friend." He stopped and forced me to meet his stare. "Why are you torturing yourself?"

"I'm not. I'm doing what's right for our clients. Don't you think tonight was a success?"

He pulled the trash can from my grip and set it aside. "You're sure you're okay with it? That it doesn't bother you to be part of the birthing classes?"

I wished I had never told him about my infertility, not if he could pull it out of the hat every time he worried. "I prayed about this."

Tristan tipped up my chin and searched my eyes. "Then why do you look so sad?"

I gulped in a breath of air and truth. "Because as much as I've wanted to build an organization like New Heights my whole life, I think I need to let it go."

# CHAPTER 42

*Marissa*

A gust of wind stripped more leaves off the tree outside Dr. Graves's window. The colorful foliage floated and swirled, stealing my attention away from the session that was quickly becoming more contentious than the last.

Colin's jaw flexed. "I don't know why we can't talk about it."

"We can talk about anything you'd like." Dr. Graves's mouth turned up a fraction. "The two of you need to decide what elements of your relationship you'd like to work on, and we can go from there."

"We can't have a relationship if we don't talk about how involved I can be in my baby's life." His knee bounced, sending an annoying tremor down the length of the couch. Grim lines appeared around his eyes and on his forehead, causing him to age in ways I hadn't noticed until now. "Everything is out in the open, so why can't we talk about this? It's not like I'm hiding anything now."

I lasered him with a glare. "Have you told your boss? I mean, why should they care what you do in your private life?" I already knew he hadn't said a word, but I wanted to needle him. And that was wrong. So wrong, but I couldn't stop myself.

*Forgive me, Lord. Have mercy on me too.*

Colin matched my glare head-on. "No. I don't need to. Like you said, they shouldn't care about my private life, and it's really none of their business, especially since I didn't get tenure."

Dr. Graves turned her attention to me. "Marissa, is there a reason you don't want to talk about Colin's relationship with his child?"

"A thousand reasons." I knew the answer wouldn't suffice but I tried to let it stand.

"You can't name one." Colin's tightly controlled voice unsettled me.

"How about the fact that I'm not ready?" I crossed my legs and leaned as far away from him as possible. "I'm not ready to hear more about your baby or your girlfriend—a nice little family you created while I was sitting home waiting for you with dinner on the table."

"I told you, we're no longer together."

"That's not the point!"

"That *is* the point. I'm not with her; I'm trying to be with you." He looked away and stared at the same falling leaves that had captured my attention.

I lowered my voice. "I'm sorry it takes so much effort to stay with me."

"At least you acknowledge that it does."

That stung. What I'd intended to be sarcasm unearthed what he saw as truth. I took a deep breath and tried to mask the hurt, to dial the conversation back to civility. "Then that's what we need to work on—how to put in the effort to stay together. If we put in the work now, we can eventually be happy, right?" I turned to Dr. Graves for confirmation.

"If you both do the work and you're both determined to create a good relationship, then it's possible." Her noncommittal tone didn't inspire much confidence.

Colin's face turned to stone. "Neither one of you gets it. I can't move ahead and try to be happy"—his air quote conveyed everything he didn't say aloud—"until I know how much I can be involved with my kid." He stood abruptly and lanced me with his pointed gaze. "I'm sorry you can't have kids, Marissa. I'm sorry I cheated. I'm sorry the world is against you. But maybe if you'd forgive me like Christians are supposed to, we could work this out. Maybe you could even be part of my baby's life—"

My mouth swung open. I sprang up and met him face-to-face. "Let's get something straight. I will *never* be part of your child's life. Don't act like you'd be doing me a favor to bring that kid to *my* home." I stabbed his chest with my finger. "And don't ever mention it again."

Silence stiffened the room as his gaze shot between me and Dr. Graves. Colin shook his head. "I'm done." He grabbed his jacket and whisked past me. The windows rattled when he slammed the door.

I dropped to the couch, limbs vibrating with adrenaline, and buried my face in my hands. It was time to compose myself. The session hadn't gone well—none of them really had—but there was still hope even when it looked bleak. With all the time spent on my knees and searching the scriptures, surely God had my back.

I released a tension-filled breath. "I'm guessing he won't be coming back."

"Today, or ever?"

"Ever. It's funny—he was the one who suggested this, but it's almost like he was doing it because it sounded like the right thing to do. All I really want from him is love and to know that he's truly sorry for hurting me."

"Is that why you're withholding your forgiveness?"

"Who says I am?"

"Aren't you?"

I looked away from her, not wanting to search my heart for the truth. "Please don't tell me that forgiveness is a gift we give ourselves. I really don't need the cliché."

Dr. Graves nodded. "I think you're trying—I think you both are. This is a situation where there aren't really any right or wrong answers, only answers that will be right for you."

"Can you be more specific? I need to know what to do. I'm ready to move forward and make progress in life. That's what I really want."

"What ways are you making progress for yourself, aside from your relationship with Colin?" She leaned back and crossed her legs, clearly more at ease now with Colin gone.

"I've been working out, going to church more, trying to get more involved with people and life." I rolled the hem of my shirt and took a shuddering breath. "I'm also considering a change in my work situation."

"What kind of change?"

"I think I'm ready to stop running New Heights and working with pregnant mothers. I'm a licensed sonographer, so I can do other kinds of ultrasound work. Maybe at the hospital."

"It sounds like you have a plan, but have you taken action? Or are you still taking time to consider?"

"Still just thinking. Should I be taking action? Applying for jobs?"

"I'm not here to tell you what to do, but to help you find clarity for yourself. Only you can decide when the right time is, but be aware that your judgment can be clouded at a time like this. You don't want to have regrets later for a decision made under duress."

Good point, and yet I felt ready for a change. I was ready to have a job where I could help people without the constant reminder of what I didn't have for myself. I wanted to be thankful and have joy over the life and relationships I *did* have.

I smiled with confidence. "No matter what happens, I'm going to make it through. God's got this."

"Your positive attitude will be an asset to you going forward." The expression on Dr. Graves's face turned from neutral to serious. She cleared her throat, and her mouth tightened. "Just be aware that 'God's got this' doesn't necessarily mean what you think it does."

*Colin*

Dribble, dribble, dribble, shoot.

Miss.

His rhythm was all off and he looked like a klutz. Colin wiped the sweat from his forehead before trying to block Adam, but Adam was swift and moved around him to take a shot.

"Nothing but net." Adam pumped his fist in the air then grabbed the ball and started dribbling again. "Ready for another round?"

"I'm done." Colin leaned over, hands on his knees, and sucked in a few deep breaths. "I've never seen you whup me like that before."

Adam cocked his head and waggled his eyebrows. "I've never seen you this distracted before. What gives?"

Colin vacated the court and sat on a picnic bench in the shade, relishing the autumn breeze. "Same old stuff."

"How's Marissa?" Adam parked himself on the table next to Colin, basketball between his ankles.

Colin grabbed his water bottle and took a long swig, stalling the inevitable. Long gone were the days when Adam wanted to get together just for the fun of it. Lately, all he'd done was lecture, but after today's session at Dr. Graves's office, a little b-ball sounded like a good idea.

"You could just tell me to butt out." Adam pointed his water bottle at Colin.

"Okay. . .butt out."

"I would, but that's not what friends are for."

"You just told me to say it."

"I didn't say I'd actually do it." Adam took a long pull from his bottle and wiped his mouth with the back of his hand. "If you don't talk to me about it, who will you talk to?"

"Not the counselor, that's for sure." Colin clenched his fists, remembering the way they'd fought and shouted. The way he lost control and stormed out. It wasn't like him to get flustered and show emotion on that level. He hated the guilt his behavior churned up inside him, especially since he had nothing to feel guilty about now that he was trying to do the right thing.

"Didn't go so well, eh?"

"That's putting it mildly. I'm done with it. It's a waste of money." Colin checked his watch. Time to get home, even though that was the last place he wanted to be. Facing Marissa after today would be brutal, and frankly, he wasn't up to it.

Adam cast a sideways glance. "Got any other ideas on how to save your marriage?"

"If you're going to tell me to get to church, forget it."

Adam's mouth puckered. "Dude, what's with the hostility? You didn't used to feel that way about going to church."

Colin didn't know which was worse—discussing his marriage or talking about God. Maybe he just stank at all relationships, and there was only one he really wanted anyway. He shook off the thought. "I can work out my own church thing." He sliced his hand through the air to emphasize just how done he was with the topic. There was no use beating a dead horse. "Besides, it doesn't have anything to do with my mess."

Adam caught him by the shoulder and forced him to meet his stare.

"It has everything to do with your life and what it could be."

"I screwed up; I own that. But now I'm ready to move past that. It's Marissa who won't move on and figure out how to get along." He stood and swiped his hand through his sweaty hair. "And to be honest, I'm about done trying."

Adam's eyes lit with fury. "You can't walk out on her after what you did. She deserves to have you put in one hundred percent effort. You owe it to her."

Colin's chest swelled and he turned to leave, until guilt swung him back around. He stood, dumbfounded. No one talked to him this way, and he didn't know how to respond. He glanced around to ensure the few people loitering nearby were out of earshot. "You have no idea what it's been like living with Marissa for the past several years. I did my best, and I was there for her every step of the way, but it sucked the life out of me. She drained me. So before you go around handing out unwanted advice, you might try to be a little more understanding."

Adam's jaw flexed, but his tone softened. "You're right—I don't understand exactly what you're going through, but every marriage, every relationship has issues. You're never going to find one that's perfect, so you might as well stay with the one you're already committed to."

Shame lapped over Colin, knowing that his friend was being generous by stating that he was committed to his marriage. Obviously he hadn't been or none of this would've happened. Colin looked heavenward at the clouds rolling in like a blanket over the evening sky. "I know you mean well."

"I do." Adam stood and palmed Colin's shoulder. "I want you and Marissa to have all that God has in store for you."

Colin's throat constricted. "I tried that road, man, and this is where it led."

"Did you? Did you give God your all?" Adam's eyes were filled with something Colin couldn't identify. Something that made him feel uneasy and small. "Only you know."

Colin flicked his hands in the air. "I'm trying to be a good guy now and it's backfiring. At least Kaitlyn's okay with me. She wants me to be part of my daughter's life."

"But you're not with her, are you?"

Colin focused on the last family in the park as they packed up to leave, stuffing their kids' arms inside jackets and grabbing their football and Frisbee. Could that be him one day? A family without secrecy? A happy family was all he'd ever wanted. He turned his attention back to Adam. "No, we're not together." He swallowed hard, but the truth bobbed back to the surface. "After all those soul-sucking years with Marissa, being with Kaitlyn was like having a whole new life, like I was someone she could love and admire. I really thought I loved her."

"But what about Marissa—do you still love your wife?"

Conflicting emotions agitated inside his gut. "I want to, but I don't feel that way about her anymore."

"Love is more than feelings."

Colin pointed at his friend. "Don't bumper-sticker me."

"I'm telling the truth. If it were all about feelings, no one would stay together." Adam threw his hands into the air. "Lani and I have had our share of troubles."

"Like I said, I want to love her, but I don't think that's ever coming back. But when I'm with Kaitlyn—"

"Don't go there," Adam said with an authority that rattled Colin to his core. "Whatever it is you think you have with this other woman, I guarantee it's not love."

# CHAPTER 43

*Marissa*

The smell of roasted turkey permeated the kitchen, peeling away the last of my defenses with the old-fashioned fragrance of home. I closed my eyes and inhaled, thankful for this one treasured moment. Despite Colin's absence and the holes in my heart, deep down I sensed God's presence and His assurance that all would be well, even if my future looked different than I'd planned.

"We just need to let the turkey rest a few minutes before we put it on the table." Mom toddled around the kitchen, apron tied around her thick middle and her white hair slicked back into a bun, just the way she liked it for cooking. "You'd better finish up with the potatoes."

Pulled out of my prayerful state, I resumed mashing, ready to add the cream cheese and sour cream to the buttery potatoes once all the lumps were vanquished. "Almost done with this, then I can finish setting out the other dishes."

"I can do that." She bustled over to the island at the center of the kitchen and grabbed the yams. "You'd better call Colin and tell him to hurry up. I don't want to start without him."

I winced. "Remember, Mom? We talked about this. He isn't coming."

Mom set the yams down with a clatter and scowled. "What are you talking about? Of course he's coming; it's Thanksgiving. Call him up."

"No, Mom, he's not." I tore open the tub of sour cream and dumped it in indiscriminately. Had she really forgotten about Colin, or had she chosen to ignore me when I told her? I started mashing again, this time with a vengeance.

"I wish you would have told me. Look at all this food!"

"I did tell you." Lately she and I had gone round and round over appointment schedules and cancellations and missing bills—the list was endless. But this time. . .had I actually forgotten to tell her? I didn't explicitly remember the conversation, just the impression of it. To be fair, it sounded like a conversation I would've avoided as long as possible. I opened the cream cheese and plopped it into the bowl, wondering what else I'd forgotten to tell her. "Did I mention that Tristan is coming instead?"

Mom stopped halfway between the kitchen and the dining area, bowl of gravy in hand. She scrutinized me the same way she had when I came home three hours late from prom. "No."

"Surprise." I injected lightness and folly into my voice and prayed she'd drop the subject.

Mom issued a lengthy groan. "That's not going to help matters."

Casually, I whipped the potatoes and hoped she would lighten up. Now that I'd stopped fretting as much, I wanted everyone around me to do the same. "What? Inviting my best friend to Thanksgiving? It's not going to hurt anything."

She fisted her hands on her hips. "Your marriage is a mess!"

Good ol' Mom. I could always count on her for truth, but I wasn't going to let that wreck my day. *My peace I give you*—the scripture I'd meditated on since Colin told me a few days ago that he wanted to be with his parents today instead of with me. My peace wasn't going to come through circumstances, so I had to rely on God, and truthfully I was getting good at it.

"Tristan has nothing to do with my marriage." I smiled at Mom as I wiped a splotch of gravy off her cheek. "So please be nice to him. He's a good guy."

"A little too good, if you ask me."

"I didn't."

"But what does he want from you? There's a reason he keeps coming around." She picked up the carving knife and held it aloft.

"Mom, listen to me." I stared her down. "Tristan and I are friends and business partners, nothing else. It's been that way for years. You know that." I couldn't count how many times he'd come to visit me when I was in college, living with Mom. There was no reason for her to get flustered about my relationship with Tristan now. "Trust me when I say he's my best friend and has been since before I ever met Colin. I don't think of him that way, so you can stop worrying."

"I'm just saying that having another man around isn't helpful when you're trying to fix your marriage."

"Mom, it's time to get realistic." I carried the mashed potatoes to the dining area. "My marriage might not be fixable."

"Don't tell me you're leaving him."

My shoulders went rigid. "I don't plan to." But that didn't mean he wouldn't leave me for his new family. Now that he'd stopped coming to counseling with me and we'd reverted back to the shallowness of polite conversation, I had no idea what he was thinking. And it scared me.

*My peace I give you.*

I drew a fortifying breath and focused on the scent of Thanksgiving, grounding myself in the here and now, not unlike what Grace taught in the recent birthing classes at New Heights. I'd made it through yesterday, I was still standing today, and tomorrow had enough troubles of its own. I didn't need to obsess over them prematurely. I would move forward with confidence in God and in the changes I was making for myself. Colin would join me if and when he chose to.

"Maybe you could just be happy for me as long as I'm happy, no matter what happens with Colin."

"But that's not what I'm praying."

"Well," I said as I stood taller, "maybe you're praying wrong."

The doorbell rang. Mom ambled to the door and swung it open, a grin dominating her face. "Come in." She extended her arms and pulled Tristan into a hug. Whether she wanted to admit it or not, she liked Tristan just as much as I did.

"I really appreciate you letting me come over, Mrs. M." Tristan handed over a bottle of sparkling cider.

Mom beamed as she ushered him inside. "You don't need to thank me. You're welcome here anytime." Funny thing was, I believed her despite her earlier rant. She was just trying to protect me and look out for my future, and I could appreciate that. Love for my mother swelled inside me.

"Let me take your coat," I said after Mom brushed past us to get back to her turkey.

"Thanks. Where's Kaitlyn?"

The buzz of the electric carving knife sounded from the kitchen, so I moved Tristan toward the dining area. "I invited her, but she said she'd be visiting with friends." My stomach clenched as I second-guessed myself for not insisting.

Tristan's forehead wrinkled. "Did she say who?"

"Not really, but I'm guessing Sydney, her birthing coach." I bit my lip, the peace I'd treasured moments ago leaking away. "Maybe we can check on her later. Sometimes I think she says things because she doesn't want to be a bother."

"I get that feeling too." Tristan swiped the back of his neck, concern etched on his face.

"The plans for her baby shower are coming along nicely." I smiled over the pain. "Sydney is helping me put it together and plan the games. It'll be fun. Too bad you can't go."

Tristan shook his head and grinned. "You couldn't pay me to be at a hen party like that."

"I don't know about that. You fit in pretty well at the birthing classes."

"I'm going to try to be flattered instead of offended." Tristan stepped aside as Mom entered the room carrying a platter nearly as big as she was. "Now that is one beautiful bird."

"Old family recipe." Mom waggled her eyebrows. Maybe *she* was the one with the hots for Tristan.

After prayer, the three of us dished up a meal made for dozens. How many of the struggling women at New Heights would this have fed? I resolved to take the leftovers to work, especially since it would be at least one step healthier than the pastries I'd been feeding the mothers.

Tristan spooned mashed potatoes onto his plate. "How's the job hunt coming?"

I stiffened, suddenly remembering the other thing I forgot to tell Mom.

"Job hunt?" Mom's turkey-loaded fork hovered between her plate and her gaping mouth. "What happened to New Heights?"

"Nothing." I dragged my fork through a puddle of gravy, my appetite stunted. "I've just been thinking about making some changes in my life, but New Heights will still be there."

"Sorry," Tristan mumbled. "I didn't realize you hadn't said anything."

"I wasn't telling anyone yet."

"I'm not just anyone." Mom spanked me with her glare.

"Well, now you both know, plus my therapist. That makes three." I forged a smile.

"You're in *therapy*?" Mom's fork clattered onto her plate.

"I guess we haven't talked as much as I thought." I took a bite of yams so I wouldn't have to continue justifying my lack of thoughtfulness.

Tristan grimaced. Poor man. Though he'd said all the right things since I'd told him I wanted a change, he was clearly unhappy whenever the subject came up. The way his shoulders hunched and the downward curve of his mouth said everything his words didn't. But he cheered me on and put my needs above those of New Heights. I loved him for that.

"Why are you doing this? What are you going to do?" Mom's eyebrows knit together.

I left her first question hanging and plowed into the second. "I applied to be an ultrasound tech at the hospital. They have a position coming open next month." I took a sip of sparkling cider and savored the tang. "I'm really excited. It'll be a good change for me." Even considering the prospect sparked a thrill inside me that I hadn't experienced since opening New Heights, when the possibilities appeared endless.

And yet, there were things at New Heights I still wanted to accomplish, people I didn't want to disappoint.

"You've always loved your job." Mom's wistful tone reverberated inside me.

"It's not a done deal." I resumed swirling my food around the overstuffed plate, reluctant to eat too much lest I undo all the work I'd done yesterday at the gym.

"Just make sure I get plenty of notice." Tristan didn't meet my eye. "You're going to be hard to replace."

I snorted. "Not too many people willing to work for almost free."

Tristan brightened. "If it's more money you need—"

"It's never been about the money." My painfully thin bank account testified to that. "But it'll be nice in case..." I shook my head, unwilling to go there. Unwilling to acknowledge my deepest fears. Unwilling to talk about what would happen to me if Colin left.

"So you needed therapy to make the decision?" Mom tilted her head and watched me, completely ignoring the meal.

"No, the therapy was originally—" I waved my hands back and forth. "Forget it, I don't want to talk about this. It's Thanksgiving. It's time for us to be thankful and happy. Can we focus on those things? Things we can be grateful for?"

Mom deflated, releasing a year's worth of sighs in one breath. "I know why you're leaving your job. It makes you sad, doesn't it?"

Finally she'd figured out my most painful secret without my having to say it.

Moisture pooled in my eyes until I blinked it away. There were no words to combat the obvious.

Mom leaned close and placed her hand over mine, her gentleness weakening my defenses. "I'm sad too, and what you're doing makes sense. You're right to take care of you."

"Like I said, it's not a done deal." I turned to Tristan and studied his face, searching for answers I knew he didn't have. "Plus, I still don't know about leaving New Heights in a bind."

"Don't think like that." Tristan covered Mom's hand with his and focused on me with an intensity and devotion I hadn't felt in years. "It's time for you to focus on yourself, and I'm here for you all the way."

Warmth, deep and comforting, spread through me and lifted my confidence. If two people as wonderful as my mother and Tristan supported me, then I would survive whatever came next. Maybe I would do better than survive; I could be an overcomer. With their support, maybe I could even forgive—truly forgive—Colin, and even the woman who had so little regard for me that she would have my husband's child.

## Colin

Colin gunned the accelerator and flew down the road. What was happening to him? He had always been cool and measured in his responses, getting neither excited nor flustered by circumstances. But lately he couldn't hold his tone or his manners to save his life.

He slowed the car and turned the corner, away from his parents' house. Deep breath. It went far worse than he'd anticipated, but that didn't mean Mom and Dad wouldn't come around eventually. They might stay mad at him, but they wouldn't let it keep them from their grandchild.

At least he'd told them, even if his timing was bad. One more item to cross off his list of things to get in order before the baby came. As long as Kaitlyn didn't reenroll in school, it really wouldn't matter if Dr. Crank and the rest of the staff found out, and even then it wasn't like he was up for tenure.

There was the question of his finances, though, and that was tougher to solve. If he and Marissa didn't pool their resources, he wasn't sure how he was going to support his daughter. They were still paying off their student loans, and they weren't going away anytime soon. They both could've used better judgment in the early years.

He rolled down the window and relished the stark breeze that whipped through the car. It was good for clearing his thoughts. All the advice coming to him from Adam plus his concern over Kaitlyn and the future really had him muddled and unsure of himself. That was a new feeling, and one he wanted to get rid of as soon as possible.

The only holdup was Marissa.

Some sort of understanding had to be formed. They were running out of time. With only a month to go, he needed answers, and his wife held the key to all of them. Of course, ditching her for Thanksgiving probably wasn't the best idea, but she also hadn't wanted to come to visit his family. Given that he'd started the latest round of issues, he should've given in and tried to make peace with her mother.

Reluctantly, Colin pointed his car toward his mother-in-law's home. Showing up unannounced was better than not showing up at all. Nothing would be resolved by all the time spent apart. More time together was what Adam had suggested a few days ago on the phone. Of course, that meant the strain of pretending.

But if pretending to love Marissa was what it took, then he'd man up and do it.

Ten minutes later he pulled into Alina's neighborhood and slowed to twenty-five. He took a fortifying breath as he rounded the corner.

Until he saw Tristan's car.

Adrenaline hammered through his veins. Colin stopped the car in the middle of the road and held the steering wheel with a death grip. What was *he* doing here? Looking for an opportunity to swoop in and take his place by Marissa's side?

So many times she'd assured him that there was nothing but friendship between her and Tristan. Right. No *friend* just showed up to a family holiday without the husband there.

Anger surged inside him. Marissa, playing the brokenhearted, wronged wife. What a joke. She'd probably been waiting for an opportunity just like this.

Colin pulled a sharp U-turn and sped up. "Sure didn't take you long to replace me."

# CHAPTER 44

*Kaitlyn*

K aitlyn didn't know whether to be surprised or weirded out when Colin showed up on her doorstep carrying a giant box with a picture of a crib on the front. But as they struggled to put the crib together, she decided it was okay to enjoy the moment. It felt something close to normal, and normal was what she craved.

"Who wrote these directions?" She turned the page over and tried to decipher the meaning of the words in conjunction with the picture.

Rails, bars, bolts, and assorted unidentifiable bits surrounded Colin. "Let me have a look. It can't be that hard." His fingers grazed her hand when he took the sheet, sending a small thrill through her. A thrill that she immediately snuffed out. She may have compromised her morals a few times, but she'd learned her lesson. No way did she want to be that person again.

"I really appreciate you buying this." She tried to hide her delight but failed, even to her own ears.

Colin met her eye and smiled. "You don't have to thank me. She's my Little Nugget too." His soulful expression was a reminder of the old Colin, from before. "I'll always be here for her, and for you."

Her breath snagged at his words, and though she tried not to fall headlong into his gaze, her heart remembered. Remembered all the hopes without promises that had filled her up before she knew who he was and what he'd done to his own family. She refocused her attention on the scant directions. "I have an idea. Let's see if there's a video. I'll just grab my phone."

With great effort, she attempted to push herself off the floor, her stomach leading the way.

"Let me help you." Colin popped up and reached for her hands. One gentle tug and she was standing, her hands still clasped inside his.

Quickly she pulled them away and hated that she had to do so. Why had she allowed herself to fall into such a mess? Correction—she hadn't fallen, which implied an accident. All along she'd known she was making bad choices, even if she hadn't known about his family at the time. Disappointment and shame burned inside her, and she wished just for a moment that she could still cling to the faith she'd had as a kid. The kind where God was merciful and forgiveness was a sure thing. She pulled in as large a breath as she could fit into her crowded lungs and massaged her stomach.

"I hadn't thought of looking for a video." Colin grabbed her phone off the small table by the door and handed it to her.

"That's because you're so much older than I am." She smiled though her joke fell like a stone, reminding them both of the obvious.

Colin's eyebrows flexed. "Well, now I'll have Little Nugget to keep me young."

Once she pulled up the video, Kaitlyn angled the phone toward Colin and let him watch while the baby vaulted off her rib cage. Another month of this would do her in, but at least it gave her time to get the baby's room ready and make final preparations.

"I think I can at least get this thing started now." Colin grabbed the headboard and a few brackets and got busy. "Have you thought about how long you're going to take off work?"

"That's practically all I think about." Kaitlyn rubbed her stomach as it tightened—a new sensation that made her belly feel rock hard. Vaguely, she remembered Grace mentioning something called Braxton Hicks at the last birthing class. Nothing to worry about, she hoped. "From everything my friends tell me, it's good to take at least six weeks off. Most people try to take more, but I can't—" She stopped short of admitting she couldn't afford it.

Though she knew it was only right for the father to pay child support, she still didn't like to admit how broke she was. It sounded so pitiful, which was the exact opposite of who she really was. Yet it was only a matter of time before they'd have to hash out monetary arrangements. Marissa had advised her to go through legal channels, but that kind of action seemed too extreme when Colin was already participating. Legal action would probably scare him off, and the last thing she wanted was a fatherless daughter.

Like she was right now.

At least that was how her dad's rejection felt. The closer she came to delivery, the more she wanted her parents there, involved and loving. But the longer they stayed away, the less likely it seemed they would ever give in. Thankfully she had whatever support Colin wanted to provide, and the help of Marissa and her friends at New Heights.

"Six weeks seems short." He tightened the screws and never looked up. "Is there any way you can stay off longer? I can help with the money, if that's what you're worried about."

Considering how depressed he'd been after not getting whatever promotion it was at the college that he'd been counting on, she doubted he had enough to cover all her bills. Anxiety hatched inside her at the thought of money—or rather, the lack of it.

Kaitlyn pulled a chair closer to Colin while he worked, slowly easing herself down. "Yes, I'm worried about it. At some point we're going to have to figure out how to pay for childcare."

"Do you have someone in mind to watch her?"

"A few ideas." Marissa and Christina had offered some suggestions last week, but Kaitlyn had yet to interview them. It was all becoming a little too real. She could no longer outrun decisions that needed to be made and issues that would change her life forever. The thought of her child was comforting and scary at the same time. "The cheapest sitter I've found is around four hundred and fifty dollars a month for full time. Then there are diapers and formula to consider. And health care." That one was a biggie. She was broke but not broke enough in the eyes of the system to qualify for help. An impossibility that was all too common, according to Marissa.

Colin paused and looked out the window, quiet for only a moment. "I don't think we should go for the cheapest unless it's also the best."

*We*—an interesting word choice that eased a bit of her anxiety. She tapped around on her phone. "I'm not sure we'll have a choice."

"I'll figure something out." Colin's voice, firm and steady, inspired confidence. "We'll also have to get whatever other furniture you need and all the baby gadgets."

"Baby gadgets?"

"You know, stuff. Whatever stuff babies need."

"Like pacifiers and diaper bags and bottles?"

"Yeah." He grinned and nodded knowingly. "Baby gadgets."

Kaitlyn laughed. "Thankfully my friends are holding a baby shower this weekend, and I put all the baby gadgets on the registry. After the shower, we'll see what we still need and I'll let you know."

"You must have really nice friends."

She smiled at the thought of Marissa, Sydney, and Christina murmuring and planning after the last birthing class. "They are the best."

*Colin*

After watching the video, Colin had the crib fully assembled in less than an hour. He cleaned up the boxes and supplies and hauled them out to his car, trying to plan where to dump everything. There was no way he could put it in the recycle at home without Marissa going ballistic. Honestly, he didn't blame her. Not anymore.

All the anger he'd felt toward her for depleting his mental energy over the last few years had finally dissipated. The scary part was, it had been replaced by apathy. He wanted to love her, but he just didn't care.

Adam thought he had all the answers, telling him to just do the right thing, as if it were that easy. Colin shook his head and closed the trunk with a thud that echoed off the paint-peeled houses that surrounded Kaitlyn's.

"Thanks for coming by," she called from the front door as a sharp gust of wind lifted the hair from her face. She waved and started to walk inside.

"Wait." He hustled up to the porch before she could close him out. All afternoon she'd been just short of standoffish. Warm and laughing one minute, cool the next, and it was driving him nuts. He wanted to spend at least a little time with her, talking and figuring out the future. He also wanted to feel the baby move again, but he hadn't had the nerve to ask, not with the way she held him at a distance. The last thing he needed was for her to freeze him out of his daughter's life.

Kaitlyn peeked out from behind the door. "Did you leave something?"

"No, I just. . .want to talk." He held up his hand as she started to protest. "There's a lot that needs to be worked out. I want to help you choose a sitter, I want to talk about how long you should consider staying home with her—I want to be part of it. All of it."

"You can't." Her eyes hardened.

Colin kept his foot wedged in the doorway. "Why not? I'm her father." He shivered against the cold wind and hoped it would inspire her to invite him back inside.

"You really don't get it." Kaitlyn's incredulous tone made him feel like a third-grade reject.

"No, I guess I don't." He shoved his hands deep inside his pockets for warmth.

"You're married!" Kaitlyn's eyes darted around as if she realized anyone could be listening. As if anyone else would care when he himself was tired of caring.

Colin ground his jaw and weighed the consequences of his words, whether they would draw her closer or frighten her away. After a deep breath, he forged ahead and spoke in a low tone, the same tone that had reeled her in when they were first together. "I know I'm married, but what if I wasn't?"

Kaitlyn's mouth formed an O, and she blinked furiously. "Did you just say what I think you said?"

"Just think about it—we could actually be together, just like parents should be. We could raise the baby, and you wouldn't have to worry about money and childcare." He leaned closer and attempted to hook into her gaze. "We could make this work."

Her lower lip trembled and her voice barely carried above the wind. "How stupid do you think I am?"

Colin's heart walloped him. That was not exactly the response he'd expected. "What do you mean? Think about what I'm offering you."

"You'll be lucky if I talk to you again after an offer like that." Kaitlyn's eyes blazed, searing his conscience the way nothing else had been able to. "After what you did to your wife, do you really think I'd be stupid enough to be with you?" Her mouth tightened and her chest and stomach heaved. "If you cheated on her, you'd cheat on me too. You are a man who cheats. No matter what you think of me, I'm not dumb enough to go there."

# CHAPTER 45

*Marissa*

With the food and the party favors in place early, I kicked back in Tristan's office while waiting for the guests to arrive. "What are you working on?" I tried to sneak a peek at his laptop screen before he deftly angled it the other way.

"The usual," he said without breaking the pattern of his typing.

"Is that code for working on your book?"

He closed the laptop and removed his readers. "I just came in to polish up a few things. I'm almost done with the proposal, if you must know."

"Just trying to be a caring, interested friend." Recently I'd noticed him hunched over the keyboard more than usual, which happened to coincide with his breakup with Sheryl.

"Believe it or not, I appreciate that." He rested his elbows on his chair and leaned back. "All ready for the baby shower?"

"I think so. Unfortunately Sydney is running late, but I think I have it covered. Are you going to stay? You know everyone who's coming—mostly clients, plus Sydney. I think she invited Kaitlyn's mom but never heard back." I picked at the hem of my shirt, trying not to show my disappointment. What kind of woman didn't show up for her daughter's big day?

Tristan scoffed. "Someone would take away my man card if I stayed for a baby shower."

"Would that be a no?"

"A resounding no. Plus I have some yardwork I need to get done this afternoon."

"It's December. What yardwork could you possibly have to do?"

"It's called winterizing."

"Ah." I picked up the stress ball he kept on his desk—whether for himself or his clients, I didn't know. I squeezed with one hand then the other, and it felt kind of good. "I got called in for an interview."

Tristan winced, and I didn't dare look up to meet his eye. "So this is really happening."

"It depends on the interview, I guess. You never know who else is in the lineup." Squeeze, release, squeeze, release. "Honestly, it scares me. I haven't had an interview since college."

"It's natural to feel some apprehension in a situation like this."

Finally, I looked at him straight on. "Don't talk like a shrink. I have my own, thank you very much."

"Fine. If you want honesty—it scares me too."

Silence buffered the room, and I held my breath at the realization that my life—our lives, our situation—would be changing. I squeezed the ball until my knuckles blanched. "I don't have to go."

Tristan reached across the desk and grabbed my hand to make me stop. "Yes, you do."

I issued a nervous chuckle. "Now you're trying to get rid of me?"

"Never. But you believe this is right for you—I know you do—and I back you up one hundred percent." His chocolatey eyes penetrated my defenses, inspiring both confidence and sorrow at what I was leaving behind. What I was *choosing* to leave behind.

Sure, I was leaving behind the pain of working with pregnant women, but I was also leaving behind support and friendship. Without those, I would have left a long time ago.

As if reading my mind, Tristan released my hand and spoke again. "Nothing has to change between us. I'll still be here for you." His promise was flimsy and we both knew it. It wasn't that he wouldn't be here for me, but that he couldn't—not if Colin and I stayed married. The only reason Tristan and I spent time together was because of New Heights—as it should be.

"We can certainly try." I set the ball back on his desk and gazed around the office, taking comfort from the familiar. With the diplomas on the wall and so few personal items, his office reminded me of my therapist's. I'd missed my regular appointment, partly because I'd been busy with Thanksgiving and getting together with Sydney to plan the baby shower, and partly because of Dr. Graves's disturbing words the last time I saw her.

"Maybe you can explain something to me."

Tristan offered a slight shrug. "I'll try, but with the kinds of things you come up with, I wouldn't hold your breath."

"Funny." I glossed over his comment, my mind focused on my last therapy session when Colin stormed out in a huff. "Dr. Graves said something that's really been bothering me. She said, ' "God's got this" might not mean what you think it does.' What do you think she meant by that?"

He tilted his head slightly, his eyes and mouth poised with a thought-ful expression. "What do *you* think it means?"

I ignored the fact he was turning psychologist on me and really considered Dr. Graves's words. "I don't like what I think it means."

"Then you're probably right." His eyebrows peaked as he rested his chin on his steepled fingertips. "I'm not a theologian, but if I had to haz-ard a guess, I think she's right. God has you and isn't going to let go, but that doesn't mean you won't face disappointment. It doesn't mean that your life will turn out the way you want it to with a happily ever after."

"Then what's the point?" I looked away from Tristan's probing gaze, not wanting to acknowledge the truths that already burned in my heart.

"Not just happiness, that's for sure. But in the end—" He sighed, long and heavy. "In the end all the troubles we face will make us more like Christ, if we let them."

"That's really not what I wanted to hear."

He shrugged as he powered down his laptop and shut the lid. "Take it or leave it."

I snarled in his general direction before heading out to greet Sydney and Kaitlyn, who'd just walked into New Heights. A gaggle of young women trailed behind them. Apparently they'd been congregating on the porch to watch the approaching storm, while crowding around Kait-lyn and taking turns feeling her baby kick. They were all still cooing over her beach-ball stomach.

"Let's get this party started." I hugged Kaitlyn and the others as I directed them toward the gift table set against the far wall.

"It's beautiful!" Kaitlyn awkwardly slid out of her coat as she gazed at the mint and yellow decorations that had transformed our workspace. It looked more like a home, the way it used to be.

"Sydney and I did most of it last night." I side-hugged my new friend. The young woman was a force to be reckoned with, and I was glad Kaitlyn had such a person on her side.

For the next two hours we played games and stuffed ourselves with fruit and pastries.

Diapers, formula, onesies, footed pajamas, baby mitts—the women of New Heights were generous to Kaitlyn, especially considering their own life circumstances. Marjorie, there with little Jacob, was no exception.

I was already desperately missing these precious women.

By the end of the evening, my stomach and heart were both full, and my face hurt from smiling. I grabbed some of the presents and headed for the door. "Let me help you get these into your car."

Kaitlyn stopped me with a gentle hand on my arm. "Thank you so much for a great shower." Her forehead wrinkled with concern. "I understand. . .that is, I know how hard—"

"You don't need to say anything more." I met her gaze, thinking how far she'd come in a short time despite less-than-ideal circumstances. She wasn't as bad off as many of the women we helped who were in abusive relationships or were homeless, sometimes both, but Kaitlyn was still largely on her own. The only thing I knew about the baby's father was that he was coming around every now and then to check up on her. My heart ached for Kaitlyn and her daughter—they had a long season ahead of them, and no one knew that more than me, a girl without a dad.

As soon as I loaded Kaitlyn up and she pulled away from the curb, Tristan's car cruised into the vacated spot. He rolled down the window and leaned over the seat. "Am I too late for cake?"

"I would give you some but they might take away your man card." I shivered as snowflakes began to fall from the almost-iridescent, bloated clouds. I walked over and leaned inside his car to catch a bit of warmth. "Seriously, what are you doing back here?"

"I came to see if you needed help cleaning up."

"No—really. Why are you here?"

He shifted into PARK and turned up the heat. "I'm dead serious. Just trying to be helpful."

"You are? That's so thoughtful." My voice cracked as I considered his gesture. Of all the people I knew, Tristan was the one who deserved true love and a great life. What was wrong with all the women who'd come and gone and not clung to him with everything they had? I beckoned him to follow me. "Sydney is inside—she's going to help me. But you can come in and keep us company."

"As long as you have help, I'll go on home."

"More yardwork?" I teased. "Why do I get the feeling you didn't really come by to help clean up?"

"Now who's playing the shrink?" His playful eyes engaged me.

"Don't avoid the question. Why are you really here?" I opened the car door and slid inside to get out of the snow.

Tristan rested his hand on the steering wheel and tapped lightly, as if weighing how much to tell me. "I wanted to see if you were okay after all this baby stuff." He swung his gaze to me, conveying a depth of feeling that went beyond his words. His kindness picked at my wounds, but I could hardly be upset with him for checking.

"I'm doing surprisingly well." I fiddled with the heater as our breath fogged the window. "I couldn't have done this for anyone else, but Kaitlyn is different. She's not just a coworker but a friend, almost like a little sister. Not that I would know what that's like, but I can imagine."

Tristan nodded. "I'm glad to hear it. You've come a long way, especially recently."

"I hope that's not a ploy to get me to keep working at New Heights."

"You know me better than that."

I almost wished he would beg me to stay. Apparently I hadn't come as far as he thought, but I wasn't about to tell him. Freezing, I angled the heater vent toward me. "I'm probably doing better because I know

I'll be moving on. That I won't always have to feel bad about my life and what I don't have."

"Does that include Colin?" His words hung in the air, taking on a frost of their own.

With a deep breath, I considered his implication. Even though Colin eventually came home every night, I didn't really have him. Was it only a matter of time until he made it official? My stomach curled at the thought, but only for a moment, because instead of feeling the old familiar ache, I focused on what was true here and now.

I had friends. I had my health. I had God.

"I'm going to be fine—better than fine." I met his concern with confidence. "I don't have control of him, and I don't have control of the future. But right now I'm choosing to forgive, because I can." Thankfulness welled in my heart, causing me to smile wholeheartedly. "No matter what, God's got this."

# CHAPTER 46

*Kaitlyn*

Colin's car was parked in front of Kaitlyn's house, and she wasn't quite sure whether it made her happy or upset. After their fight earlier in the week, she hadn't heard from him again. Not that his silence was unusual in itself, but for them to part in anger made her worry that they wouldn't have it resolved before Little Nugget made her appearance. They hadn't even settled on a name—mostly because she didn't want to bring it up after Sydney made her promise she'd give the baby her last name, not Colin's.

He stood like a sentinel in front of his vehicle, arms folded and ankles crossed, as though impervious to the wind and snow.

Kaitlyn hoisted herself out of the driver's seat and popped the trunk, weighed down with gifts. "As long as you're here, can you bring the gifts inside?" He might as well make himself useful, and whether she wanted to admit it or not, she really did need the help.

"I was starting to worry." He grabbed presents until his arms were full and then followed as she carefully made her way up the slick steps and unlocked the door.

"The baby shower was this afternoon." She flicked on the lights and ushered him inside, ignoring the wet spots from his shoes she'd have to sop up later, if she had the energy.

"Looks like you made out pretty well," Colin said before he ducked outside for the second load.

Kaitlyn left a crack in the door so he could easily push back inside, and then she eased herself onto the recliner. Little Nugget stretched and rolled before using Kaitlyn's bladder as a trampoline. Then her stomach tightened, causing her to wince. "What is going on down there?"

"Talking to the baby?" Cold air swept into the room when Colin came back inside, arms full.

"I do that a lot. I read that it's good for her, plus she keeps me company." She hoped Colin didn't take her comment as a condemnation of his infrequent visits. The last thing she needed was him coming around more often. Of course, she might change her mind once the baby came and she was up all night, knowing she had to be at The Bean before seven o'clock.

But she'd worry about that when it was time. There was no use adding to her troubles before they happened.

Colin issued a nervous smile before going back outside. The trunk of the car made a snow-muffled *clunk* before he came back with the last of the gifts. He closed the front door and kicked off his shoes, almost like he belonged here. "Do you want me to start unpacking?"

"Since we don't have the changing table put together yet, probably not. I really don't have anywhere to put it." Kaitlyn rubbed her stomach as it tightened again. The weight of her stomach was getting to be too much, especially since the baby seemed content to slide lower and lower over the last few days. She shifted to try to get comfortable, though that was impossible. As for sleep—she'd forgotten what a good night's sleep even was. "I can do it tomorrow."

"At least let me put the changing table together."

"Isn't it great? My bosses gave that to me. I think it'll look good by the window." She tried to get some air into her cramped lungs.

"What's happening?" Colin bent low to examine her.

She winced at the pressure against her bladder and hoped she didn't have an accident. "They're mini contractions."

"Isn't it a little soon for that? You still have four more weeks."

"Three and a half, but who's counting?" She forged a smile and wished Colin would go away. Having him watch her dealing with the discomfort made her uneasy. Her pain felt so private, and yet here he was invading her space. Too bad there wasn't a way to ask him to leave without sounding ungrateful.

"You look a little wiped out. Let me get you a glass of water." He headed for the kitchen. "Did you overdo it today?"

She was overdoing it every day, but telling him so would probably worry him.

They still needed to have the talk about finances and what to do about childcare when Little Nugget arrived. There were so many issues to deal with, but she was too uncomfortable to freak out about it now.

A deeper pain throbbed inside her then vanished. Kaitlyn sat straighter and tried to ease the discomfort.

Until suddenly warm liquid began to trickle.

Her eyes widened as she instinctively glanced down, though she couldn't see around her stomach. Had she actually not made it to the bathroom in time? Mortification enveloped her as she glanced at Colin in the kitchen.

"What?" He stopped filling the glass.

"Nothing." *I think. I hope.* How was she going to get him out of her house without him seeing her shame? What could she tell him to make him leave? She needed rest—that was a good excuse.

"Here, drink this." Colin crouched next to her and handed her the glass. "Are you sure you're feeling okay?"

"You're right. I probably overdid it at the shower, but I was having so much fun with the games and the food. It was a great time." She sighed, grateful for the good friends God—or someone—had put in her life. She'd bonded with these women so quickly, and yet it all seemed so natural. There was nothing like having a baby under dire circumstances to link women together.

"I really worry about you overdoing it."

"I probably need to rest." *And change my pants.*

Colin sat in the love seat across from her, clearly not getting the hint. He crossed his ankle over his knee, and his foot bobbed to an unseen rhythm until finally he spoke. "You don't look right."

"That's probably not what you really want to say to a pregnant woman. A little tact goes a long way." She sipped slowly.

"That's what M—" Colin looked away. "I've been told that. Sorry—I guess it's a scientist thing, sticking to the facts."

Kaitlyn cringed, knowing he was about to say "my wife." She'd have to get used to it eventually, but right now seemed like a bad time. For everything.

Another pain racked her body, this one deeper and more urgent than the last. "Oh no. This can't be happening." She shuddered as she caught her breath.

"What?" Colin bolted from the seat.

"I'm not sure." The thinness of her voice wasn't inspiring any confidence. She needed him to leave so she could figure out what was going on.

Was it possible she was going into labor? Was it her water that had broken instead of her bladder leaking?

It was entirely too soon for that to be plausible, and yet the wetness on her thighs and the aches in her stomach—at regular intervals, no less—said otherwise.

Colin had to go so she could think it through, or look it up on her phone, or—anything but go through labor with him there. They hadn't discussed it, but she'd decided against calling him during labor so she wouldn't have to worry about what he was thinking. Her labor plan called for Sydney to be there to coach her through, not Colin. Never Colin.

"Tell me what's happening." Colin knelt directly in front of her and forced eye contact.

"I think. . ." She drew a breath to quell her panic. "I think I'm going into labor."

*Colin*

Colin panicked.

He jumped up and felt his pockets for his phone that wasn't there. "We need to call someone." Car—it was in his car.

"No, wait." Concern lined her forehead as she gazed up at him and tugged his sleeve. "It might be false labor. That happens sometimes."

He scrutinized her face, a mixture of pain and worry. Whether or not she was going into labor, she wasn't in good shape, though he shouldn't have told her so earlier. That wasn't the way to win her over. "I still think we need to get you checked out. Let's go to the hospital and they'll let you know if it's a false alarm."

"I can't do that." Her eyes saucered with fear.

"Why not? Then we don't have to worry." He'd feel a lot better with a professional telling them there was nothing wrong, rather than Kaitlyn trying to convince him.

"I'll tell you why not—I can't afford the co-pay for more than one trip to the hospital." Her voice rose an octave. "I need to make sure it's the real thing before I go anywhere."

Despite the adrenaline rush, Colin shriveled inside. Why hadn't he ever asked her about how she was paying for the delivery? What else didn't he know? He reached for her hand, and she didn't pull away. "Look at me." He forced her to focus on his eyes. "Don't worry about the money. I can take care of that." He wasn't sure how, but that wasn't Kaitlyn's problem.

She hesitated. "I don't have my bag packed."

"I'll do it." He bolted toward her bedroom at the back of the house. "What do you need to take?" Never mind. It didn't matter. He rushed into her room and scanned for a suitcase or a carry-on, a duffel bag. Anything.

But there was nothing suitable.

She moaned in the living room, giving his heart a start. *False labor, my foot.*

Colin remembered the gifts he'd brought inside and darted into the baby's room. He grabbed a black and pink baby bag and hustled back to Kaitlyn's room. Quickly, he rummaged through her drawers. Underwear, pajamas, sweatpants, and a T-shirt. That would have to do.

"I'm ready," he called as he hurried down the hall.

As Kaitlyn pushed herself out of the recliner, he caught a glimpse of her wet backside. Definitely labor. Kaitlyn paused and squeezed her eyes shut as she clutched her stomach.

He hurried to her side and gripped her arm to offer support. "Another contraction?"

She nodded without speaking. After a moment, she took a deep breath. "I think this is it."

"Where's your coat?" He glanced around.

Kaitlyn pointed to the hook on the back of the door, right where it should be. Colin laughed at himself. All of a sudden he'd become the stereotypical worried father, panicking at the first signs of labor. He wheeled in a deep breath to compose himself. Now was not the time to fall apart. It was time to be strong and reliable. A real father.

"Do we need to call the doctor?" he asked as he slipped her coat over one arm then the other.

"I can do that while you drive."

Colin slung the bag over his shoulder then placed his arm around Kaitlyn to guide her down the front steps and over the slippery driveway to his car. Once she was safely buckled, he scampered around to the driver's side and started the engine. He didn't wait for it to warm up before he jerked away from the curb and headed for the hospital.

"This is Kaitlyn Farrows. Can you page Dr. Martin and tell him I'm on my way to the hospital?" She hung up and smiled. "I guess this is it."

"It seems too early." Colin's grip on the steering wheel tightened. Snow fell harder against the windshield, making it look like they were going at light speed.

"It is, but I guess that happens sometimes." She held up her phone. "I'd better call Sydney."

He switched off the radio while Kaitlyn called and left a message.

"She's not answering." Worry tinged her voice. "Maybe she has her ringer off. I'll text her."

"What happens if you can't get ahold of her?"

"She's probably helping her mom or her grandma, but she usually calls back within a few minutes." Kaitlyn set the phone on her lap. "We haven't even talked about a name yet."

"I figured you weren't ready to talk about it." There were too many things they hadn't gotten around to yet, thinking they had more time. Colin's breath hitched as the car slid on the icy road. He pumped the brakes and brought the car back into line. Probably a good idea to slow down.

"I wasn't, but it looks like we don't have a choice." There was a hard edge to her voice.

"What's bothering you?" He risked a sideways glance, embarrassed by his dumb question.

She sighed loudly—or maybe she was breathing through a contraction. "It's just that. . .the baby needs to have my last name."

Colin tensed. The thought had crossed his mind more than once. He'd tried to make peace with the idea of his daughter having a different last name before ever bringing up the subject, but he hadn't quite gotten there. A last name held people together; it was part of a legacy—something he'd tried to explain to Marissa when she'd insisted on keeping her own. And now for Kaitlyn to not want their child to have his last name implied she didn't think he'd stick around.

He remained silent for a few minutes, focusing on the road and avoiding the nut jobs who came out on a night like this when they didn't have to. A few more miles and Kaitlyn would be in good hands. Trying to keep his tone neutral, he spoke. "Maybe we should pick a first name. What do you like?"

"You're upset."

Colin wasn't sure whether to be flattered or dismayed that she knew him so well. Slowly, he reached across the seat and squeezed her hand. "I understand where you're coming from, but I do want to talk about it, later. Right now we have a baby to deliver."

She pulled her hand away in favor of her phone. "Sydney texted. She just got home from the shower and her grandmother fell again, so they're getting her settled in bed. She said she'll be here as soon as she can."

"Tell her to be careful. The roads are terrible." The car slid again, as if to prove his point.

"She lives thirty minutes away, and with all the snow it could take her a lot longer." Kaitlyn's eyes filled with worry. "What if she doesn't make it in time?"

"Don't first babies usually come pretty slowly?" Good thing he'd read up on labor and delivery.

"Supposedly, but now that the baby is coming early. . .I just don't know." Her voice went from concerned to worried.

"We're almost there. Everything's going to be fine." He kept his hand on the steering wheel instead of trying to give her a comforting squeeze.

With the hospital in sight, Colin slowed down, relieved.

Until he remembered Marissa. She was probably expecting him to come home soon, but there was no way he was dumping Kaitlyn off and leaving. His wife would understand, wouldn't she? Of course, they hadn't been on the same page at all lately. After he'd quit going to counseling with her, they'd almost completely stopped talking.

Yet she seemed more at peace, and that bugged him.

"Don't go to the emergency room entrance. We have to go in at Labor and Delivery, on the other side."

Colin rerouted and pulled the car to a stop at the front door just as Kaitlyn released a guttural moan. He leaned over and laid his hand on her shoulder. "Breathe," he said in his lowest, most soothing tone. For all the good it would do. From the sounds she emitted and the way her eyes pinched shut, she wasn't listening.

A moment later her moan subsided and her breathing slowed. The first thing she did was look at her phone and bite her lip. "Go inside and get me a wheelchair while I text my backup person."

# CHAPTER 47

*Marissa*

Playing hostess wore me out more than I'd wanted to admit. But it was emotional exhaustion, and I was slowly learning to deal with that in a healthy way. Tonight I considered flipping through mindless television healthy, at least compared to overeating, undereating, or crying my eyes out. I hadn't done that in a while, and I didn't plan on going back to such a dark place.

The clock struck nine and the television programming started to change. There was still no sign of Colin, and he hadn't told me he'd be coming home late—actually he hadn't bothered to fill me in at all.

Acid pooled in my stomach, and I hated that I cared that much. But like it or not, he was still my husband and I was bound to him. The ties between us weren't strong anymore, but maybe that was what had given me the space I needed to forgive him and let go of his mistakes. At least I was trying.

I turned off the TV and hunted for my phone to see if he'd called. It was silly of me not to have kept it by me, just in case.

But when I found it lying on the kitchen counter next to a pile of bills, I saw he hadn't called or left a message. I staved off the flash of disappointment and instead focused on the text message from Kaitlyn. She was at the hospital and going into labor and she wanted me there.

Panic lit through me as I calculated how far along she was in my head. It was early but not too early. Babies were born a month early all the time and turned out just fine.

I grabbed my coat and keys and rushed to the car.

Despite the slick roads, I drove faster than I should. Kaitlyn had texted almost a half hour before I'd seen it. Snow whipped against the windshield, obscuring the view. Had Kaitlyn driven herself in this awful weather? My heart broke for her. No woman in labor should be alone, not for the drive, not for the delivery, and certainly not afterward to raise the baby.

I skidded to a stop in the parking lot and hoped I landed in an actual parking space, though it was hard to tell under the blanket of ice and snow. Moisture leaked into my shoes as I picked my way through the slush. No wonder she'd contacted me. There was no way Sydney could get here from Mountainside in this weather.

*Lord, be there for Kaitlyn and the baby. Be her strength.*

Typically women labored with their first baby longer than subsequent children, and I prayed that was the case for Kaitlyn. A wrong prayer, to be sure, but I wanted to be there in time. I wanted for her not to be scared and alone during the most important event of her life.

A sign on the front door announced it was locked for the night. I could either press the buzzer and wait for assistance or drive to the other side of the hospital and enter through the Emergency Department. Considering the condition of my shoes, I opted for the buzzer.

I stood back and waited, heart pounding. My unkempt reflection in the glass door mocked me. Disheveled hair, baggy sweatpants, no makeup—I hadn't even thought to get a bra on. Thank goodness for thick sweatshirts.

Finally a woman appeared at the door and directed me to the second floor. Rather than wait for the elevator, I bounded up the stairs in record time, probably thanks to the workout classes Kaitlyn had gotten me hooked on.

My wet shoes squeaked across the tiled floor. "What room is Kaitlyn Farrows in?"

"What's your name? I just need to check the list." A nurse wearing rubber ducky scrubs slowly brought the computer to life.

"Marissa Moreau."

"Just a moment." The nurse perused the screen, muttering as she scrolled. "Ah, here you are. We just got Kaitlyn set up in room 205."

"So I'm not too late?" I grabbed my chest.

The nurse smiled and winked. "She's still got a little ways to go."

Relief swam through me for a brief moment until I remembered what I was there for. How hard it would be on me emotionally. I clutched the desk, unwilling to walk into her room just yet. Not until I composed myself and put Kaitlyn first.

*Lord, help me through these next moments.*

"You'll be okay. Just breathe." The nurse offered a knowing chuckle.

"You're right." I took a large gulp of air to ease my mounting anxiety. "God's got this." I laughed nervously at what had become my go-to phrase. Who cared what Dr. Graves had meant by it? God's strength would sustain me at all times.

It had to.

In spite of my efforts to remain calm, my heart rate skyrocketed. This was a big deal, but I could do this. I could be there for my friend, just like I'd promised.

I straightened my spine and willed myself down the hall. Muffled voices emanated from the room.

At least she wasn't alone.

Though the door was open, a privacy curtain separated her bed from view. I hated to interrupt.

But I wasn't interrupting. She had called me. She wanted me here.

Deep breath.

I entered the room and pulled the curtain aside. "I'm here—" My eyes landed on Kaitlyn then skipped to the man beside her.

The man beside her, holding her hand.

Colin.

Perplexed, my mouth opened. Closed. Opened.

No words—no coherent thoughts.

"Marissa." Colin's eyes, startled and uncertain, met mine. His jaw flexed. "Why are you here?"

Kaitlyn's face reddened, and her gaze volleyed between me. . .and my husband.

Her baby's father.

Angry words, punishing words, accusations—all jammed inside my throat, caught between shock and a sense of stupidity, as though I was being played the fool.

My legs froze, feet rooted to the ground. A familiar tingle began to prickle down my arms and my shallow breaths came faster. "I have to. . . have to. . ."

By sheer will, I found the strength to turn. To take one step then another, stumbling and catching myself against the doorway.

Faster, I had to move faster.

"Marissa!" Kaitlyn's voice echoed down the hallway, but it was too late.

My wobbly legs moved more quickly, down the stairs and through the lobby. "Let me out. Let me go," I called to the desk attendant as I moved past.

She jumped up and spoke words of concern that I couldn't decipher until finally the door opened and a cold gust of wind slapped my face as I ran into the night.

# CHAPTER 48

## *Kaitlyn*

This was what perfection looked like. Tiny round face, wispy eyelashes fanning delicate cheeks, and pink lips shaped like a bow. Her daughter was wrapped like a burrito, her little head covered by a thin knit cap. She had yet to wail, but instead she emitted a faint mewl.

"She's perfect," Colin said, echoing Kaitlyn's thoughts. He feathered the baby's chin with his finger, seemingly unbothered by what had happened.

Now that the baby was born, they needed to talk about it.

Unease pooled in Kaitlyn's stomach. The realization and surprise on Marissa's face. The betrayal in her eyes. The way she'd fled from the room without giving Kaitlyn a chance.

Had Marissa believed Kaitlyn already knew? Nothing could be further from the truth, not with the way Colin had kept her totally separate from his real life. But Marissa didn't know that. How could she?

A tear slid down Kaitlyn's cheek, and she tried to swipe it away without Colin noticing.

Somehow, he placed his arm between the pillows and her back and squeezed. "This is the most amazing moment of my life too."

Rather than answer, she nodded to avoid the conflict. That wasn't at all why she was crying. She was crying because what should have been the most amazing moment of her life was marred by what happened before, though Colin seemed unfazed.

What kind of man would completely blow off the fact that his wife and his former girlfriend had come face-to-face and actually knew one another? Not the kind of man she would ever want to be with, that's for sure.

Sydney parted the curtain and strode to her bedside, releasing a sense of calm inside Kaitlyn. Her friend had arrived about ten minutes after Marissa had fled, in plenty of time for the birth. Sydney had even firmly told Colin when it was time for him to leave the room and wouldn't take no for an answer.

Still, even with Colin gone her attention had been divided between laboring and wanting to get Marissa back and figure out exactly what was going on—until the contractions made her feel like her body was ripping in half. Pain like that had a way of sharpening one's focus.

"Sorry, I had to take that call." Sydney tucked her phone inside her back pocket and resumed her post at the bedside. "So have you guys decided on a name yet?" The way she narrowed her eyes at Colin showed she wasn't really looking for an answer from him.

"We haven't had a chance." Colin made it clear he intended for Sydney to feel like an intruder.

Kaitlyn nestled the baby closer, too tired to broker peace. "I have a few ideas. I've always thought Daphne was pretty."

Sydney tilted her head to get a better view. "She looks like she could be a Daphne. I've always liked Brielle. Remember that movie we saw with that character named Brielle? She was brilliant."

"My daughter will definitely be brilliant." Kaitlyn laughed, thinking back to their girls' movie night and all the popcorn they'd consumed.

Sydney cooed at the baby before speaking. "Do you have a favorite family member you'd like to name her after?"

"My grandmother, Violet. But it's pretty old-fashioned."

Colin cleared his throat. "I hear old-fashioned names are coming back in style."

Kaitlyn bristled at his nearness, but she was determined to be polite. She didn't need to pick a fight with her baby's father, a man who probably had some kind of right to speak up about naming their daughter. "Interesting." It was the only word she could think to say without getting snippy. Tangled emotions surged inside her, but she was too exhausted to sort through them. Too exhausted to say what she really wanted.

Too exhausted to completely tell Colin off and strike out on her own.

"I hope I'm not too late," a meek voice murmered before the curtain parted.

"Mom." Tears instantly blurred her sight as hope and astonishment mixed inside her. "How did you know?"

"I called her." Sydney stood. "And now it's time for me and Colin to step out."

"I, uh. . ." Colin eased away from the baby.

Sydney folded her arms. "I'm sure we can find something to do."

"Right, of course." His gaze swung between Sydney, Kaitlyn, the baby, and Kaitlyn's mother, whose pointed look seemed to prod him right out of the room.

Kaitlyn held her breath, unsure what had made her mother decide to come. "You're here."

"I'm here." Mom sat next to her and gazed at the baby, her eyes soft and misty.

"Would you like to hold her?" She angled toward her mother, offering her most precious treasure.

"I'd love to." Her mother's voice hitched as she held out her arms and received the baby. Granddaughter in hand, her forehead curled with emotion and her eyebrows peaked as though she were trying to widen her view to take it all in. "She's beautiful. So small."

"She's early, but she still weighed in at five and a half pounds." She recalled the most strenuous moments of the birth, the searing pain and the pushing. "I can't imagine what it would've been like if she'd waited until Christmas."

"She's perfect just as she is." Her mother glanced up and met Kaitlyn's eyes. "She reminds me of you."

Kaitlyn gave in to the swell of emotions. "I was so afraid you wouldn't come that I didn't call you myself. I'm sorry."

"No, I'm sorry." Mom shook her head, careful not to move too much and wake the sleeping baby. "I should've been here for you all along. It's just. . .the shock. . . But it was wrong for us to turn you away when you needed us the most. So wrong." Color filled her face. "Can you forgive me?"

Kaitlyn nodded, not trusting herself to speak.

"I want to be a family, and I want this little one to always know that she's loved no matter what." Concern tinged her eyes. "Just like you're loved. . .no matter what."

"What about Dad?" Kaitlyn shifted, afraid to hope.

Mom's eyes sagged at the corners. "He'll come around. This isn't one of his finer moments, but he's a decent man. We'll just have to give him time."

She wasn't quite as sure as Mom was, but it was a start. Maybe she could work on forgiving him before she saw him next, though the rawness of his rejection still burned. The hypocrisy, the lack of concern for her. . .

No, she couldn't go there or she'd be just as guilty. And wasn't that what she'd wanted all along, to become a better person?

"So." Mom punctuated the silence. "I assume that was him?"

Shame leaked through Kaitlyn, a culmination of realizing what she'd done combined with learning just tonight who else she'd hurt. She cast her gaze to the clinical hospital blanket that covered her. "Yes."

"Do you have plans?"

"No." She didn't know what else to say without ruining the tenuous bond with her mom. "He plans to be here for the baby, but we're not together. And I don't want to be."

Mom's lips tightened as though holding back all the things she really wanted to say about Colin. Things Kaitlyn completely agreed with, finally.

She checked her spirit, remorseful for what she'd done. "It's better this way."

"I'll take your word for it." Mom's flat tone said so much.

"I guess I realize what all your warnings were for when I was growing up. You were right. I should've made better choices." Her throat constricted. "Now I've hurt other people, and I feel so guilty."

"No, honey. No guilt." Tears slipped down Mom's face. "And for whatever part I played in making you feel that way, I apologize. We all sin; we all fall short of God's glory. Me most of all."

Mom, who had lived so perfectly? At least until rejecting Kaitlyn. She couldn't imagine what her mom sinning would even look like.

"The thing is," Mom began as she stroked the baby's cheek, "after you told us you were going to have a baby, it shook us up, badly."

"I'm sorry."

"Don't be. We needed it. I needed it." Her mother took a moment to compose herself. "It forced me to examine my own life, my own shortcomings. My own sins. I needed to get to that place and see what I really was."

Kaitlyn looked up. "And what's that?"

"A woman in need of God's grace."

"But you never did anything like me."

"We all have our own issues to deal with, or rather, to let God deal with." Mom's smile was full of hope. "All we have to do is ask."

*Colin*

It was after midnight when Colin left the hospital. Thankfully, the snow had subsided and the roads were clear of traffic.

Weariness saturated him as he slowly made his way across town. The drive was long. Too long. Enough time to stir up the stress of seeing Marissa.

The jolt of adrenaline that shot through him when she walked into the hospital room nearly gave him a heart attack. At first he'd thought she'd followed him, determined to wreck the moment. But to discover she knew Kaitlyn. . .nothing could've prepared him for the shock.

Had it really been that unrealistic, though? It had crossed his mind a time or two during Kaitlyn's pregnancy that they might know each other, but the odds were so low he'd convinced himself there was no way. Kaitlyn wasn't like the other women who needed New Heights, at least that's what he'd told himself.

Unreal.

He shook his head and turned off the heater. He was already sweating—and it had nothing to do with the temperature.

What would Marissa say? The last thing he wanted was to see her dissolve into tears, hiding away in her bedroom for days on end. Trying to coax her out of her dark places always took more energy than he had, and right now he wanted to focus his attention on his daughter. She was the one who mattered now.

To be fair, though, Marissa mattered too. She didn't ask for him to cheat and have a child with someone else—the one and only thing she herself had ever wanted. It probably hurt her in ways he could no longer understand now that he had a baby.

Joy surged inside him as he considered his daughter. So tiny and vulnerable. She'd felt like a feather in his arms when Kaitlyn had finally let him hold her. He'd wanted to spend the night in the hospital, but from the moment Kaitlyn's mother got there, that option was out the door. The way she'd scrutinized him really ticked him off, but she probably had her reasons. Plus, he needed to get home and smooth things over.

Which brought him back to Marissa.

One day she'd get over the hurt and mellow out. Maybe even come to accept his child, especially since she was already friends with Kaitlyn. It would take some getting used to, but it wasn't a situation that couldn't be worked out between reasonable people.

Colin rounded the corner and pulled into the empty driveway. Thankfully Marissa had parked in the garage, which would make shoveling a little easier in the morning. He turned off the ignition and paused to consider what to say, how best to smooth his wife's ruffled feathers.

If he were a praying man, he'd ask God for no tears and dramatics tonight.

Cool and rational. That would be the best approach.

He climbed out of the car, locked it, and cringed at the noise when it chirped. He stomped his feet on the mat outside the door before entering the house. Marissa hated a wet floor. The dim light was on in the foyer, but his wife wasn't waiting in the living room as he'd anticipated.

"I'm home," he called softly, kicking off his shoes and scanning for any sign of her in the kitchen. A light was on there too, but no Marissa.

Had she really given up and fallen asleep? That didn't seem like her.

He climbed the stairs and crept down the hall, unwilling to wake her if she'd actually fallen asleep. The door was ajar, and he risked peeking into the dim room. There was no form under the covers. He inched closer to be sure.

Nothing.

Shock pummeled him. Had she not made it home?

Colin switched on the light and scanned the room. His gaze landed on an open drawer.

An empty drawer.

"Marissa!" Where was she? He looked through her half-empty drawers then threw open the closet. Several hangers were empty and the suitcase was missing. "Marissa!" he shouted, desperate.

But to his utter shock, she was gone.

# CHAPTER 49

*Marissa*

"It's Kaitlyn." I stood in the doorway of Tristan's office, unconcerned that I was interrupting his phone call.

He made eye contact and held up his index finger. "Let me call you back." He hung up and watched me with narrow eyes. "Where were you this morning? I waited for you at The Bean, I texted, and then I gave up and came to work."

"I can't go there. I can't go anywhere associated with Kaitlyn." Tears brimmed in my eyes, but I refused to give in. I'd done enough of that yesterday at Mom's house while I waited for Colin or Kaitlyn to contact me.

Neither one did.

"Slow down and have a seat." Tristan gestured to the empty chair across from him. "Take a breath and then tell me what's going on. You had me worried."

I sat, lifted my chin, and forced myself not to slouch or look weak. Because I wasn't weak—I was angry and hurt. I folded my hands in my lap and moderated my tone. "The woman that Colin had a baby with is *Kaitlyn*."

Tristan's face paled and his mouth opened and closed but no words came out. It was the same reaction I'd had.

"I found out at the hospital."

"The hospital?"

"Kaitlyn went into labor early and texted me to come." Fury laced with betrayal burned in my veins. My foot tapped an angry rhythm. "I got there, and guess who was by her bedside? Colin." I punctuated his name with venom.

Tristan rubbed his face and groaned. "You have got to be kidding me."

"I wish." My voice hitched. I scanned the room to find something to ground me. The stress ball—I focused on the ball to hold back any emotion that hinted at sorrow, an emotion that would bully the rage aside and cause my mental health to circle the drain.

Tristan leaned forward and propped his elbow on the desk, covering his face with one hand. "I don't even know what to say."

"Neither did I. Of course, after I left I thought of a million things I wanted to tell them, things they deserved to hear." I grabbed the ball and squeezed it until my hand hurt. "It's just like me to think of all the right words after the fact."

Tristan glanced toward the outer office to assure our privacy. "What did they say?"

"Nothing—at least if they did I don't remember. I thought I was going to pass out, so I left."

"What did Colin say when he got home?"

I shrugged. "Who knows? I didn't wait around to find out."

"Where did you go?" His eyebrows peaked in the middle, as though questioning why I hadn't gone to him first.

I'd considered going to Tristan's house, of course, but I was too upset, too confused. Too vulnerable. I'd even started driving that way until I had a moment of clarity, realizing it was a bad idea. "I went to my mom's." I snorted. "There's no way he would come there to get me."

"Did you want him to come and get you?"

I paused and transferred the ball from one hand to the other. "At first I did, then I didn't." I stared at the diplomas on the wall until my vision turned fuzzy. "Then I didn't know what I wanted. The truth is, I wanted him to want me but only so I could turn him away." I sighed. "What's wrong with me?"

"Nothing. That actually sounds reasonable."

"But what does that say about me? About my marriage?" I looked at the ring on my finger—at least I hadn't lost mine, like Colin—and dug a little deeper. During the time at Mom's, had I actually missed Colin, the man? Or had I missed the idea of a faithful husband?

"It says you're going through a lot, and there's no one right way to feel." Tristan pinched the bridge of his nose. "But Kaitlyn? What was she doing with a married man?"

"No wonder she didn't want to talk about it, keeping everything so hush-hush." Shards of ice slid through my veins at the thought of her betrayal. "I tried so hard to be a good friend and help her out. I thought she cared about me too."

"Do you think she knew?" He leaned forward. "I mean, did *you* even have any idea?"

Events from the past several months had cycled through my tired brain multiple times since I'd fled the hospital. I'd dissected every memory for a clue, anything that should have tipped me off. "I didn't." I tossed the ball onto his desk. "Look at how many women have come in here since the beginning of summer. We deal with pregnant women in bad situations all the time, we have for years. The odds. . ." I shook my head. "The odds of my husband being the father of one of these babies. . .no, it didn't occur to me." I shot out of the chair. "Maybe I'm just stupid."

"Always trying to see the best in people isn't stupid. Not by a long shot."

"I feel so betrayed." More so by Kaitlyn than Colin, but I didn't want to reason it out.

"If you didn't know, it's possible she didn't either."

I braced the back of the chair. "But what if she did?"

"You know her better than that."

"I thought I did."

He twirled a pen then pointed it at me. "I'll bet she didn't know he was married until it was too late. Until after she was pregnant."

"That sounds like something Colin would do." Keeping both women in the dark. . .yeah, that was him. The fact that I was bound for life to such a man made me nauseous. For the first time in a while, the future looked long and bleak.

"Eventually you're going to have to talk to them."

I looked away, unable to face the truth. Not only was I going to have to talk to them, but I would have to forgive them. True forgiveness. The kind that loves unconditionally and keeps no record of wrongs.

But as long as they had the power to hurt me again, I didn't know if I could.

# CHAPTER 50

*Kaitlyn*

Mariah Joy.

The name rolled off her tongue and made Kaitlyn smile. Thankfully Colin had relented about their daughter's last name so it didn't have to get ugly.

There was already enough ugliness associated with the birth of her innocent baby.

By the time Kaitlyn and Mariah arrived home from the hospital, Colin had already put together the nursery, complete with freshly washed sheets in the bassinet. He'd even put together the changing table and stocked it with diapers, wipes, creams, and extra burp rags. Either he'd done a lot of reading or he had someone giving him advice.

And it certainly wasn't Marissa.

Kaitlyn winced as she coaxed the baby to nurse like the lactation consultant at the hospital had shown her. Not only was the latching on a bit painful, but her body was still distressed from the stitches and the bruising down under. More painful was her heart at the thought of what she'd done to her friend.

She teased Mariah's cheek to get her to open her mouth. Finally—success. Together they rocked in the recliner and enjoyed the afternoon sunshine streaking through the window before Colin—correction, Dad—came over.

Confusion had filled Kaitlyn's thoughts from the moment she saw Marissa part the curtain at the hospital. Marissa's reaction had stunned her, but it only took a few moments to piece together what was going on.

As if labor wasn't difficult enough.

Still, the whole situation baffled her. She'd always assumed Marissa was married to Tristan, from the inside jokes to the way they encouraged each other daily. And the morning coffee dates, though she'd never actually seen them show physical affection other than a hug every now and then.

To think that Marissa was Colin's wife blew Kaitlyn's mind. They were a mismatch in every way, especially now that she knew how deceitful Colin was. Marissa deserved better, much better. And so did she.

Hadn't Colin said he had a child, or at least implied it? Kaitlyn rummaged through her memories for their conversation. In some way he had indicated a child. What was that all about?

But the worst thing was knowing that she'd been part of wrecking her friend's life. It was bad enough when Colin's wife was a nameless, faceless woman, but now—Kaitlyn wasn't certain how she could live with herself.

Tears slid down her face, a mixture of joy and pain.

Somehow she'd have to face Marissa and make things right. Apologize and convince her friend that she had no idea, that she'd also been duped.

After she'd prayed with Mom, she'd finally realized God had forgiven her when she repented. But would Marissa?

The doorknob jiggled with a key in the lock. Kaitlyn rushed to cover herself before Colin entered and stomped his shoes on the mat. "How's Little Nug—Mariah?" His eyes zeroed in on the baby.

"She's been asleep most of the day after being up all night." Exhaustion leaked down into her bones. Though their first night alone together had been entirely too long, it would go down in her mind as a sweet memory.

Colin kicked off his shoes and shrugged off his coat. "I told you—I don't mind staying and helping."

"That's not a good idea."

"It's no problem."

"You need to think about Marissa." The baby squiggled under her sharp tone.

Colin recoiled. "I told you before, don't worry about it. That's my concern."

"Your wife happens to be my friend, and apparently I'm more concerned about her than you are."

Colin pointed but quickly retracted his finger. "You don't know anything about this or what she and I have been through."

"How could I? The little bit you told me was all lies."

"After I came clean, there were no lies."

He had a pretty loose definition of lying. Kaitlyn shook her head. "I don't want to argue in front of the baby." She shifted her little bundle and started rocking again. "You told me you had kids."

"That's not what I said." His eyes misted and his jaw ticked.

"It was implied."

"We had a miscarriage. But the baby was still mine, and it still mattered."

Kaitlyn's breath caught. Marissa hadn't told her about a miscarriage, only that she couldn't seem to get pregnant. So many blanks began to fill. She looked down. "I'm sorry."

"I'm just thankful *we* have a healthy baby. Can I hold her?" He leaned close and took hold of her. Mariah looked so tiny and delicate in his arms. He bent his head and kissed her cheek.

Kaitlyn shot up a silent prayer for courage. Knowing she was doing the right thing didn't make it easy. "You know you're welcome to see the baby anytime."

He silently acknowledged her with a smile that lit his eyes.

"But that's where it ends. I don't know what's happening with you and Marissa, but you need to know there will never be anything that happens between us." Her heart tapped out a staccato beat.

His lips formed a grim line. "I think you made that clear before."

"It felt like a good time to say it again." She pointed to the key on the table by the door. "You need to leave the key. I mean, I appreciate what you did, coming here and getting everything ready while we were still in the hospital, but that's where it ends."

Colin said nothing. He leaned against the love seat and gazed at their baby, his eyes unwavering.

A smidgen of relief eased through Kaitlyn. Everything in her life was overwhelming, but she was taking steps. Small steps. But at least they were steps in the right direction.

### Colin

Colin played it cool through the rest of the visit. There was no use getting Kaitlyn riled up. He'd read somewhere that new moms could be hormonal, and that's probably all it was. A few more nights without sleep and she might relent on letting him help more. He didn't want to be a part-time dad, only able to visit his child—his own child—at Kaitlyn's whim.

To be fair, things *had* gone badly.

The moment Marissa waltzed into the hospital room, he'd known there was no coming back to anything resembling normal. But he hadn't expected Marissa to pack up and leave. He'd given her a few days' space, and it was time for her to come home and work it out.

It was dark by the time he left Kaitlyn and Mariah. Uncertainty niggled him inside at the thought of an empty house. Maybe his wife had come to her senses. If not, he'd give her until tomorrow; then he would go to her mother's house and bring her home. Knowing her, that was probably what she wanted—to be pursued.

If he were a praying man, this would be the time. But no matter how hard he tried, he just couldn't go there. Because if God was real, things wouldn't be such a mess.

# CHAPTER 51

*Marissa*

The steaming mug of tea warmed my hands as I curled up on the couch in front of the fire. Mom's home was cozy like that, a place of memories and comfort, where I could always retreat and find my way. I released a contented sigh and closed my eyes as I slipped in and out of prayer.

When I chose to block out the swift turns life had taken and focus on the here and now, focus on what was right in my life instead of what was wrong, I experienced peace. Deep peace. I wanted to know that level of peace even when I faced the issues I needed to deal with, but I would think about those things later.

For now, God had me and this moment was good.

"Do you need more tea?" Mom hovered over me, pot in hand, spout pointed at my mug.

"Sure, thanks." I lifted it up and inhaled the scent of jasmine as she poured.

"Have you thought any more about talking to your husband?" Mom righted the pot and wiped a drip that slid down the side.

I wrinkled my nose. "I'm sure he's doing just fine." With his new family, a family that I wasn't part of.

*Peace, Prince of Peace, peace.*

"You can't avoid him forever. Or are you moving in with me?" She set the pot on a coaster and stared me down.

"You have plenty of room." I closed my eyes again and savored the tea.

Mom grunted. She was wrecking my moment, but it was so like her that it brought me comfort. "It's not that I don't want you here; it's that I want things to be worked out. You can't leave things up in the air." She waved her arms to prove the point.

I faced her, ready for answers. "How did you forgive my father for running out on you?"

Mom drew back and sputtered. "I. . . It didn't happen overnight, that's for sure. Forgiveness is sometimes an ongoing process. Some days you have to choose it over and over again."

"Hmm. I want it to be done now."

"Good luck with that." She harrumphed and folded her arms across her bosom. "You also have to realize your own imperfections."

"I know, we all sin."

"Not just that. I had to realize the part I played in what happened. Very few situations are the fault of just one person."

I sat taller, indignant. "It's not your fault my father ran out."

Her mouth flexed as she considered. "It may have been partially my fault he ran out, but it was his fault he chose to stay away from you. Everyone has a part to play."

What part had I played in my marriage? Time, distance, and prayer had a way of bringing clarity that didn't exist in the middle of the mess. If I were completely honest, I'd spent years brooding over my loss—our loss—rather than enjoying what I still had. For years I'd lived cycle to cycle, through mountains and valleys of hope and disappointment.

For years I'd probably bled Colin dry.

That didn't excuse what he did, but I could see the point Mom was making. But there were still so many questions. Could I forgive and carry on? Would Colin betray me again? Was there even any love left to build on? Of course, that would imply there was true love in the first place. Dubious, the more I thought about it.

Mom laid her hand on my leg, bringing me back to the present. "At some point you're going to have to talk to him."

My stomach soured. The idea of seeking him out and trying to piece our marriage back together made me sick. I didn't like always being the one to go to him, and I didn't like who I was with him. I no longer wanted to be that desperate for his attention—attention that would now be divided with his other family.

His other family that included my friend.

Sorrow leaked inside me as I thought of her. Originally I'd planned on being there for her after the birth, cooking at night and seeing that she got rest. Maybe Colin was filling that spot, or Sydney. The fact that I'd broken my promise to her stung, because the more I considered the circumstances, the more I realized she couldn't be at fault. At least not the part about deceiving me.

Though it chafed my broken heart, I knew I'd somehow have to keep my word and still find a way to have peace.

Once I made the decision to see Kaitlyn, I didn't waste time debating like the old me would have done.

I took the next afternoon off, both to check on my application at the hospital and to visit Kaitlyn and the baby. Anxiousness settled inside my chest, even though I'd made sure Colin was at work and not at Kaitlyn's, through a not-so-discreetly placed phone call to the university.

I stared at her little A-frame house, trying to collect the nerve to go inside. It was a big deal, but I could do this. It was more important to be a person of integrity than it was to keep my heart safe. It was too late for that anyway.

The sun shone through the window and warmed me. I closed my eyes and breathed a prayer before stepping out of the car and approaching the front door. I tapped softly in case the baby was asleep.

Moments later, a disheveled Kaitlyn opened the door and gasped. She threw her arms around me and pulled me into the warmth of her home.

"I didn't know, please believe me," she muttered against my neck. "I'm so, so sorry. I've been praying and thinking, and I've wanted to see you so badly."

Confusion pulsed inside me as I remembered everything, the good and the bad. But wasn't that what life was? I squeezed her back, determined to keep my promise going forward into a future I couldn't see. I pulled back and locked onto her gaze. "God forgives, and so do I."

# CHAPTER 52

*Marissa*

I ran out of clothes.

In my haste to get out of the house the night of Mariah's birth, I threw together a few shirts and sweatpants, none of which matched. The only thing I had plenty of was work clothes I'd grabbed off the hangers and my entire drawerful of underthings.

There was still time before Colin's official office hours ended, so after leaving Kaitlyn's I headed for home. The clock in the hallway kept a steady rhythm, as though nothing out of the ordinary had happened over the last few days. Everything in the house looked the same but felt so different in a hazy, out-of-touch way that I couldn't quite place.

My bedroom was just as I'd left it, the drawers still open and hangers on the floor. Had Colin even noticed I was gone? The thought jolted me. We'd stopped checking in with each other and spent so little time together, it was entirely plausible he didn't know I'd left.

The thought frustrated me, until I remembered my peace. God's peace. Peace that one moment flooded me and the next moment left me grappling.

This time I was more careful in my wardrobe selection, taking care to find matching outfits and workout clothes. I jammed them inside a carry-on bag. They could be fluffed in the dryer at Mom's.

"What are you doing?"

I startled, the hair on my neck rising. I whipped around. "Colin—I didn't expect to see you."

He entered the room cautiously. "I don't suppose you *would* see me with the way you've been hiding."

Without commenting, I continued to pack. There was no reason to offer an explanation for the obvious.

"Don't you think we need to talk?" He laid his hand on my arm, but I pulled away and stuffed another pair of yoga pants into my bag.

Forgiving Kaitlyn was easy, but Colin. . . The pain ran too deep. Silently I prayed for wisdom and release, for God's mercy. Like a gentle whisper, peace lapped over me and I could finally breathe. The problems were still here, but I wasn't walking through them alone.

Maybe I *was* ready to face Colin and to face life. To face the truth.

"I'm not sure what to say." My voice cracked.

"This is your home. There's no reason for you to leave." His eyes looked at me but without the warmth I'd once fought so hard to see.

"If I stay here then I have to be aware of all the times you're not." I lifted my shoulder and eased away from his touch. "If I'm not here, I'm not jealous and clingy—and I won't keep you away from your baby."

"We can work this out." His mouth tightened before he collapsed on the bed and buried his face in his palms. "I don't know what to do, what we should do."

I dropped the bag and sat next to him, risking everything to know the truth. "Do you love me?" In my heart, I pleaded for him to say yes, to give me one last spark of hope.

He angled away, his face hidden and his shoulders hunched. "I'm doing my best."

"It's a yes or no question." I swallowed. "Do you love me?"

"I'm trying." He breathed hard and fast and balled his hands into fists. "I don't know what else you want me to do. I don't know what *we* should do."

I stood, picked up my bag, and forced him to meet my gaze. "I don't know what you're going to do, and I'm sorry for that. I'm sorry for the part I played in what's happened. I know I share some of the blame." In that moment, clarity found me and gave me courage, wiping out the worry and indecision that had plagued me for months. "The thing is, it's time for you to reconsider your future, because I'm moving on."

I squeezed his shoulder and walked out the door, tears of relief clouding my vision.

The years of relentless pursuit, the years of clinging and begging for love, were finally, blessedly over.

# EPILOGUE

*Marissa*

Tristan's tires crunched the ice and snow as he pulled to a stop in front of the hospital. "You really need to get your car into the shop."

"After I get my first paycheck, that won't be a problem. Until then I'm sure you don't mind playing chauffeur." I forced myself to laugh despite the nerves tickling my stomach.

The first day of my new job had arrived, and I was as prepared as I could be. The imaging services department of the hospital would be my place now. I'd already met the people in the department and they seemed friendly, even if a lot less personal than I was used to.

I was grateful for the opportunity, though, especially since I hadn't worked on anything but moms and babies in years. It would feel strange to pull out my former training and work with actual patients again, but I looked forward to the challenge even if I was nervous. Success was not guaranteed—in anything—but I was slowly making peace with that.

Tristan shifted into PARK and hesitated before he spoke. "You know, you don't have to do this."

Until this moment, he'd been cheering me on, telling me I could do or be anything. I snickered, finally feeling the weight of the last few months lift. "That's not a very psychologist-like thing to say."

"That's because I'm speaking as a friend who's going to miss seeing you every day." The concern in his eyes nearly caused me to reconsider.

But I didn't, because I finally knew my own mind. "You'll survive."

Tristan groaned. "But all those women at New Heights—I'll be surrounded."

"You were surrounded when I was there." I loved giving him a hard time. Maybe he *had* thought of me as just one of the guys all along, and the realization actually made me happy.

"I know this is good for you." He attempted a smile but only made it halfway. "You're right. New Heights will survive. I have an interview lined up for your replacement, and if the funding comes through, then I might be able to pay them more than slave wages."

"You might want to work on your selling points." I offered him a playful nudge. "I'll miss you all too, but I have confidence you'll be okay. More than okay—you're still going to help a lot of people and do good things. I believe that."

"Then I guess it's time to let you go." He kept his eyes trained on the steering wheel in an unusual attempt to keep his distance.

"Who's the Chicken Little now? Don't sound so down," I said, adding extra pizzazz to my words. "If you're lucky I might find you a cute nurse."

His laughter filled the car as he shook his head, smiling. "From your mouth to God's ears. Now get out of here. I have places to be, a business to run."

Between Tristan, Kaitlyn, and Christina, New Heights would continue to fulfill its purpose. They were competent and invested, ready to help women and babies find their places in the world. Kaitlyn had even tried to come back to work early, bringing little Mariah with her to brighten our day.

At six weeks old, she was an adorable, pudgy little thing, with Kaitlyn's upturned nose and Colin's eyes. A perfect combination of both their best features. Some days it still hurt me to hold her, and some days I could love on her for who God made her to be. The day Kaitlyn asked me to watch her so that she could run down to the university and enroll in summer school, I promised Mariah I'd be there for her the same way I was for her mom because she was too precious to turn away from.

Colin and I hadn't talked much, but he'd relinquished the house to me and was bunking with Adam and Lani. Beyond that, I hadn't asked questions or pursued information that I didn't need. Forgiveness on both our parts would come eventually. I had faith.

I'd apologized for the part I played in the death spiral of our marriage—I knew I wasn't blameless. But his stony defenses were still high, like his last nerve was about to blow. Still, maybe my behavior now would influence Colin for the good. Or maybe it wouldn't. He had to work out his own journey to faith, if he ever chose to.

Mom continued to offer advice, reminding me how important it was to stay married. I reminded her that it was important for me to walk in love and live in peace as much as it depended on me. Honestly, it was easier for me to live in peace with Colin by not leaving my heart open for target practice.

As for my faith, it was different—stronger but different. The kind of faith that could weather a storm and come out intact, if bruised. Now when I prayed for bread, I understood the only Bread that mattered was the One I already had. What else did I really need?

"I guess I'd better get inside." My breath stuttered as I prayed for confidence. A refreshing wind blew over me when I opened the door and stepped onto the snowy curb.

"Hey," Tristan said, causing me to turn and meet his gaze. "God's got this."

Finally I was full of courage and full of faith. Most of all, full of hope. "Yes," I said, smiling as my heart lifted, "He does."

# DISCUSSION QUESTIONS

1. Have you ever been unable to have the one thing you wanted most in the way Marissa wanted to have a child? How did it affect your faith?

2. What part do you feel Marissa played in the demise of her marriage to Colin?

3. How much do you think being unequally yoked played a part in Marissa and Colin's marriage? How much do you think being unequally yoked plays a part in relationships in general?

4. Did you see any good qualities in Colin? What redeeming qualities might there be in the "bad guys" in your life?

5. Do you think Kaitlyn and Colin will be able to co-parent successfully?

6. What do you see for Kaitlyn and her daughter Mariah's future? Do you know any single parents you can encourage and support?

7. Do you believe married couples should have close friendships with members of the opposite sex like Marissa and Tristan?

8. Do you think Tristan had feelings for Marissa beyond friendship? What is a good way to handle close work relationships like that?

9. How do you feel about the role Kaitlyn played in the ending of Marissa and Colin's marriage?

10. What does "God's got this" mean to you?

# ABOUT THE AUTHOR

**Georgiana Daniels** resides in the beautiful mountains of Arizona with her super-generous husband and three talented daughters. She graduated from Northern Arizona University with a bachelor's degree in public relations and now has the privilege of homeschooling by day and wrestling with the keyboard by night. She enjoys sharing God's love through fiction and is exceedingly thankful for her own happily ever after.

# If You Liked This Book, You'll Also Like...

### *Home* by Ginny L. Yttrup

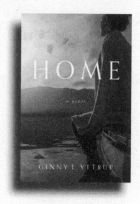

Novelist Melanie Vander runs away—from conflict, from pain, from reality. When Melanie finds herself faced with a looming deadline, she decides it's time for an escape to a novel-worthy locale. Call it research. Maybe a bit of distance will also inspire her husband to appreciate her again, she reasons. But once she's away, she further distances herself from reality as she becomes obsessed with the male character in the story she's writing. When hit with a dose of reality, Melanie must choose whether she'll check out completely, or allow her characters to lead her home.

Paperback / 978-1-63409-955-4 / $14.99

### *Stars in the Grass* by Ann Marie Stewart

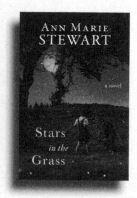

The idyllic world of nine-year-old Abby McAndrews is transformed when a tragedy tears her family apart. Before the accident, her dad, Reverend John McAndrews, had all the answers, but now his questions and guilt threaten to destroy his family. Abby's fifteen-year-old brother, Matt, begins an angry descent as he acts out in dangerous ways. Her mother tries to hold her grieving family together, but when Abby's dad refuses to move on, the family is at a crossroads.

Paperback / 978-1-63409-950-9 / $14.99